Flame and Fury

A Dream Walker Novel

MICHELLE MILES

ISBN: 9781393955344 (ebook)
ISBN: 9781734306866 (paperback)

For my husband. Always.

When you walk through the fire, you will not be burned; the flames will not set you ablaze.

Isaiah 43:2

The courage is in facing danger when you are afraid.

L. Frank Baum

CHAPTER 1

CHRISTMASTIME AT WALKER MANOR had never been as festive as it was with Ophelia Duffy in residence. She was like a Christmas elf with her decorating skills and insisted decking the halls from top to bottom, inside and out. She somehow convinced my stoic uncle to hire a crew to hang white outdoor lights around every inch of the manor giving it a festive luminosity I was sure could be seen from the International Space Station.

I met Ophelia in Istanbul when we killed demons together. Her shimmering sword was a high lord killer and so, she became a permanent member of my team. She moved into Walker Manor after returning from Istanbul with me. I had to admit I was impressed with her decoration skills. Perhaps she was meant to shower all us Scrooges in Walker Manor with good tidings and cheer.

When I lived in Walker Manor as a teen, I didn't recall a time there was anything more than a modest decorated tree in the parlor. Nothing like what Ophelia managed to accomplish in less than a week. Beribboned and lit garland wound down the banister. Mistletoe hung in the entryway to the library. I made a concerted effort to steer way clear of the abomination hanging in the doorway in light of recent events with Kincade.

Ah, Kincade. He and I had a strange relationship. Not friends—partners by necessity. I'd traded the Spear of Destiny to Azriel for his soul. That alone complicated everything. There had been a moment in the hallway when the distance between us collapsed and then snapped back into place. I didn't dwell on it. Dwelling was dangerous.

Christmas trees lit up the parlor and the library. The fireplace in the library was decked out in garland and lights and decorated with stocking hangers spelling out the words JOY and NOEL. She'd even managed to make red and white stockings with all our names on them and hung them. I was baffled as I peered at them wondering how she managed to pull that off. There was one for Edward, Ophelia, me, Kincade, Gideon, Gilli. Even Piers, the butler, had a stocking.

Three miniature trees adorned with gold ribbon and twinkle lights dominated the entryway. The plain white tablecloth on the dining table was replaced by a festive green and red plaid one. Gold placemats were positioned at every place setting. She'd even found a red and white sleigh and made it a centerpiece with a gorgeous winter-themed flower arrangement.

Christmas was everywhere.

I stood in the foyer at the foot of the stairs looking at all the trimmings wondering how she'd managed to sweet talk Edward into letting her decorate with reckless abandon when I spied the tiny bunch of mistletoe with a red bow hanging from the middle of the parlor doorway.

She was a sneaky one.

What was next? Carols, eggnog and gay apparel?

"Isn't it great?"

Ophelia bounded down the stairs and halted next to me to admire her handiwork. Her girl-next-door face beamed so bright with joy it was hard not to smile in return.

"It's nice."

"Nice?" She huffed. "That's all I get for my efforts? Nice?"

I peered at the Christmas tree in the parlor with its dancing twinkle lights. Blue and silver balls and tinsel adorned the branches. A blue velvet tree skirt completed the look.

"How did you manage to talk Edward into paying for it all?"

She blinked surprise. "Are you kidding? All the decorations were in the attic. I made the stockings." She beamed with pride.

Now I blinked surprise. "In the attic? Since when do you nose around the attic?"

"Since Gideon kicked my ass and I needed a break from training." She rolled her left shoulder. "I'm still sore."

I could relate. Gideon was the on-site trainer with his twin sister, Gilli. I steered clear of them since my return from Istanbul because I wasn't a glutton for punishment.

"I found all these decorations in tubs. Someone took great care organizing them and labeling everything. Someone who loved Christmas," she said.

"Huh."

That someone wasn't Edward. I'd never seen most of this stuff. I moved here from Dallas when I was thirteen and we had modest Christmas celebrations. Usually, it was just me and Uncle Edward. Sometimes a few other family members made an appearance, but never a houseful of people and Christmas morning was low key.

There was no Christmas magic. No leaving cookies and waiting up for Santa because I knew he didn't exist from the time I was young.

Maybe that's what I needed. What we needed. A little Christmas magic and belief in Santa.

"Well, it's lovely. You did a great job." I looked at her, smiled.

"You like it? Even the mistletoe?" She batted her long dark lashes and gave me a mischievous grin.

I narrowed my gaze. "What are you trying to pull here?"

She put on her best innocent look. "Oh, nothing. Just trying to move things along."

"What things?" My voice was laced with suspicion.

"You know. Things." She shrugged.

I didn't like what she was getting at. She saw me and Kincade together too often and drew conclusions that didn't exist. It was irritating.

Kincade and I were... something. Allies. Partners by necessity. Beyond that, there was nothing to define. I'd been distracted by him once—briefly—and that alone annoyed me. Distraction was dangerous. I didn't allow it space to linger.

Yes, Kincade was physically imposing. Tall. Broad-shouldered. Difficult to ignore when he chose to occupy a room. That didn't make him right for me. It made him another problem I didn't have time to deal with.

"I also understand someone has a birthday coming up."

My head snapped in her direction. "Who told you?"

"A little birdie."

I scowled. I imagined that little birdie was named Edward. "I am not interested in celebrating my birthday."

"Why not?" She looked hurt.

"Because it's four days before Christmas and it doesn't matter." I waved it away, trying to make sure she understood my birthday was nothing special.

"Anna, don't be that way. It's your special day."

I snorted. No one had ever made a fuss over me for my birthday since it was so close to Christmas. Oh, sure, Edward gave me the obligatory card, cake and present. I'd never had a party. I'd never gone to Chuck E Cheese. I never had a bounce castle in my back-yard. Or friends. Or party favors. Or party hats.

And I was okay with that. It wasn't a big deal. I was making a valiant effort to forget I was turning twenty-nine. The last year had been hell enough. I wasn't looking forward to what another year would bring me.

Likely more heartache and heartburn.

And hell.

"I don't need a special day." She wanted to say something else when I cut her off. "I'm going to work out. I think today is a good day for Gideon to give me a good ass-kicking."

"We're not done talking about this, Anna."

"Sure, we are." I flashed a grin as I walked away.

It infuriated her but I didn't want to talk about my birthday or Christmas. I left the main house and walked across the lawn in the chilly afternoon air. A cold soft rain started to fall, giving my exposed arms goosebumps and making me shiver.

I arrived at the workout room and came to an abrupt halt.

Kincade was lifting weights on the bench press.

I couldn't catch a break.

He dropped the weight and sat up. Our eyes met. We stared at each other in silence. I got a tingling sensation in the pit of my gut. For one stupid second, I forgot how to breathe.

"Where's Gideon?" I asked.

"Not here."

He pushed off the bench and stood, reaching for a towel and wiped his face. He wore a sweat-dampened gray shirt that clung to his torso, scars faint along his wrists—remnants of Azriel's prison. Our paths hadn't crossed much in the last few weeks while he convalesced. Mostly because I avoided him like he had a communicable disease.

"Oh, well, I'll come back later then." I started to leave.

"You can work out with me."

He didn't move closer. Didn't smile. Just waited—like he knew I'd either run or accept, and either answer told him something.

His deep inviting voice made me halt mid-reach for the door. I peered over my shoulder at him to see if he was kidding or not. His face was serious. His eyes hard and piercing. If I agreed, it would be the closest we'd been since that day in front of my mother's portrait.

"Oh, it's okay. I'll—"

"What are you afraid of, Miss Walker?"

That tingling sensation was back, prickling all the way up my spine to the nape of my neck. He hadn't called me Miss Walker in a while. Here I thought we were on a first name basis. "I'm not afraid of anything."

"You sure?" He tilted his head to the side in a challenge.

Kincade had this weird internal lie detector, so he probably sensed I lied to cover my feelings. He could have pointed out I was afraid of a lot of things, but he didn't. He could have told me he knew I didn't want to be that close to him. But he didn't. He could have told me I was a coward for wanting to put as much distance as possible between us.

But he didn't.

I thought when he was all the way healed, he would move on and go back to wherever he went. He stayed. He told my uncle once he could train me better than those "two idiots" Gideon and Gilli. I wondered how true that was and couldn't resist the invitation.

I matched his head tilt. "All right. You're on."

He tossed the towel to the floor then cracked his knuckles. "Let's see what you got."

We approached the workout mat on opposite sides, like I had before with Gideon. Kincade placed his feet shoulder-width apart and flexed his fingers. I hesitated, trying to decide my next move.

"Come at me." He waved his hands in invitation.

I hesitated so I stalled. "I don't want to hurt you."

He looked bored and annoyed. He cracked his knuckles once more and then charged. He moved so fast I didn't have time to brace myself or react. I landed flat on my back staring up at the florescent lighting.

"Sarcasm will not save you, Miss Walker." He stood next to me looking down.

Maybe not but it was the only armor I ever had. His six-foot-plus frame standing over me was intimidating. His thigh muscles were the size of my waist. He was a big guy that dwarfed my not-so-petite stature.

He held a hand down to help me up. I grasped it and he tugged, pulling me with ease to my feet.

Adrenaline punched through me. I dropped my head and charged, hitting him square in the chest and driving him back. He hadn't expected it and stumbled, losing his footing. As he started to fall, he wrapped his arms around me. I crashed against him as he thudded on the mat.

The impact knocked the air from my lungs. My body reacted before my mind could catch up—too aware of contact, of proximity, of the sudden loss of space.

He gave me that same sharp, assessing look he'd worn in front of my mother's portrait. Not hunger. Not softness. Something intent. Focused.

I shoved at his chest, but he didn't release me.

"What are you afraid of?" His deep voice was low, steady, vibrating through me.

"Nothing."

"You're trembling."

"I'm not."

"You are." His grip tightened, controlled, unyielding. "Is it because we're close? You don't want to be close to me?"

He'd know if I lied. I hated that.

"I don't."

"Why not?"

The question hit too close. My pulse hammered, loud enough that I was sure he could feel it. Heat crawled up my neck, sharp and unwelcome.

"I think you know why."

His hand slid to the nape of my neck, firm—not gentle—holding me in place. My vision narrowed, breath coming faster than I liked. The reaction infuriated me.

His other arm tightened around my waist. He shifted his weight and rolled, pinning me beneath him, half on, half off. Strategic. Controlled.

I sucked in a breath.

"Now try to get free," he said.

He wasn't breathing hard. That unsettled me more than the weight of him.

"What?"

"You heard me, Miss Walker."

"But you're bigger and stronger than me."

An eyebrow lifted. "And you're holding back. Afraid you're going to hurt my feelings?"

I laughed—and drove my knee up into his groin.

He grunted, his grip loosening just enough for me to twist free and scramble to my feet. I spun and kicked him in the side. He swiped at my leg and knocked me off balance. I hit the mat hard, landing on my left side. Pain jarred through my shoulder.

"That's better." His voice held approval, but his expression didn't.

"You are so twisted." I pushed up onto all fours and glared at him.

He sat on the mat with one knee raised, forearm resting casually against it, like we weren't in the middle of a fight.

"You like twisted," he said, like it was an observation, not a boast.

"Do I? I don't think so."

He surged to his feet and held a hand down to me. I stared at it, suspicious.

"Let me help you."

I took his hand. He yanked me up hard enough that I stumbled straight into him.

Definitely on purpose.

"Stop that."

"Stop what?"

Something flickered in his green-gold eyes—amusement edged with something sharper. It set my nerves on edge.

"You know exactly what you're doing."

"Do I?" His gaze lingered, assessing, searching. "Do you?"

I swallowed. I wasn't oblivious. I just didn't like where the conversation was drifting.

"What are you not telling me, Miss Walker?"

The shift was abrupt enough to knock me off balance. "What do you mean?"

"Don't play dumb."

There were a lot of things I hadn't told him. About my mother. About Lucifer. About Azriel. About how much worse things really were.

"There's nothing to talk about."

I turned for the door.

He caught my arm and spun me back. Fury hardened his features.

"Don't walk away from me."

I set my jaw. "You have secrets of your own, don't you? Secrets you haven't bothered to share with me."

He ground his back teeth. "It doesn't concern you."

"Bullshit. It does concern me." Gold sparks flared in his eyes. It was the first time I'd seen that, but I didn't back down. "You were kicked out of the Watchers."

"Who told you that?"

"It doesn't matter."

His fingers tightened on my arm, biting into muscle. "Edward should keep his mouth shut."

"I didn't say it was Edward."

"You didn't have to."

"Nor did I have to give up the Spear of Destiny."

For you went unspoken. I'd traded it to Azriel to save his soul, and I was still living with the fallout of that choice.

His grip stilled. For the first time since I'd walked in, something flickered across his face—shock, maybe. Or something close to it.

He pulled me in abruptly, rough enough that I stumbled. His other hand came up, holding me there—not gentle, not careful. Containment. Control.

"I told you to let me go." His voice dropped, dangerous and precise.

I flushed, heat crawling up my neck. "I... couldn't."

It was the truth. Simple and unadorned.

His eyes searched mine, looking for evasion. There was none. Azriel had nearly destroyed him—nearly taken everything—and I'd refused to let that stand.

His grip eased, fraction by fraction, though he didn't step back. His thumb brushed my arm once, absent, unintentional. Or maybe not.

Silence stretched. Heavy. Uncomfortable.

"Do you want to tell me what happened with Azriel?"

The question hit like a blade.

I wrenched free and stepped back, wrapping my arms around myself as revulsion crawled up my spine. I'd shoved those memories down deep. Buried them. Some things didn't improve when spoken aloud.

"No. I don't."

My voice left no room for argument.

Azriel hadn't just hurt me physically. He'd invaded my mind. Twisted memories. Dragged old wounds to the surface and tried to use them against me. Kincade had been there—had felt some of it—but that didn't make it easier to name.

He didn't press.

For that, at least, I was grateful.

If it hadn't been for Kincade dream walking when he did, I didn't want to think about how much worse it could have been. He'd pulled me back when I was losing myself.

"You gave him the spear for me," he said. "I think the least I can do is help you recover it."

I let out a breath, realizing he meant only that. The trade. The cost.

"Oh. Well. I'm not worried about that right now. I need the Staff of Moses next." I hesitated, then added, "Thanks for not kicking my ass too hard."

I headed for the door, putting space between us as quickly as I could.

"Anna, wait."

He crossed the mat in long strides, stopped halfway between us. Whatever he wanted to say, it didn't come easily.

"Yes?"

"I never thanked you for saving my life."

"You don't—"

"Yes, I do." His tone was firm. Final.

I pressed my lips together. "Then maybe we're even."

"For now." He nodded once.

I reached for the door.

He was suddenly there—fast, silent—reaching past me to slam it shut. The sound echoed in the room.

"Wait."

I froze. He didn't touch me. Didn't crowd closer. Just stood there, blocking my exit.

"That day in the hall—"

"I don't want to talk about that."

Silence stretched.

"Tell me what happened to your mother."

The question knocked the air out of me.

I braced a hand against the door. Memories surged, sharp and unwelcome. That portrait. The admission I'd never fully unpacked.

"Decker was there," I said. "Ask him."

"I don't want to ask Decker." His voice was low, close. "I don't know where he is."

No one did.

"I want to hear it from you."

I turned to face him, my back still against the door. His arm was braced above me—not touching, not forcing—but limiting my options all the same.

"It's a long story," I said. "Are you sure you want—"

"Yes."

One word. No hesitation.

Before I could answer, the handle rattled.

Then a knock.

"Hey! Anna? Are you in there?"

Ophelia's voice snapped the moment clean in half.

We moved apart instantly. Kincade crossed the room without a word as I pulled the door open and forced my breathing steady.

"Hey," I said, aiming for normal.

"The door wouldn't open." Ophelia glanced past me, then smirked like she thought she'd interrupted something else entirely.

She was wrong.

But explaining that felt impossible.

I shrugged. "I guess it was jammed or something."

I brushed by her and hurried away from the building through the rain, thankful I managed to dodge a bullet with Kincade. I wasn't going to be able to avoid him for much longer. I had to make sure I wasn't caught alone with him again.

I stalked across the wet lawn and into the house in a foul mood. I didn't have time to have for Kincade. Why was he so interested in me? It's not like I was anything special or did anything out of the ordinary for him.

Yeah, so I gave up the spear. I planned to use the Staff of Moses to help Darius, the warrior angel who'd managed to save me not once, but twice, in Hell. Because of me, he started to turn Fallen and I didn't need that on my conscience.

I stomped up the stairs to my room to take a shower. When I opened the door, Joachim stood in the center of the room waiting for me. The pesky messenger angel appeared at the most inopportune times. I scowled.

"What do you want?"

"Mind your attitude. I wish to speak with you about the relics."

"Get in line." I headed for the bathroom.

"I have a message from Michael—"

I spun around. "I know what Michael wants and what Azriel wants and what you want." And Kincade, but I stopped myself before finishing the thought. "The horn is secure for now. I'm sorry about the spear. Relay that to the archangel."

Joachim's expression tightened. "He—"

"It's the best I can do." I turned for the bathroom, already reaching for the door. A hot shower sounded like the only thing that might quiet my head.

"Anna." His voice shifted. Quieter. Measured. "I know what you did with the spear. And so does Michael. That isn't why I'm here."

I stopped.

Slowly, I turned back. "Then why are you here? To tell me I failed? To explain how handing a relic to Azriel was unforgivable?"

"No." He shook his head once. "It was a calculated decision. Michael understands why you did it."

That took a second to land.

"His request," Joachim continued, "is that you recover the spear from Azriel."

I stared at him. When I'd made the trade, I'd expected consequences. Judgment. Condemnation. Not...this.

"That was always my intention," I said finally.

"Michael was... not displeased," Joachim said. "By either of you."

"Either of us." I latched onto that. "What does that mean?"

"You gave up the relic," he said plainly. "Kincade relinquished his position within the Watchers. Those were conscious choices."

My grip tightened on the doorframe. "His position?"

"He was not insignificant," Joachim replied. "He held authority. Command. Stepping away from that was not a small thing."

The room felt suddenly smaller.

"He chose to help you," Joachim said. "Just as you chose to save him."

I drew in a slow breath. This wasn't validation. It was acknowledgment. And that somehow carried more weight.

"What does 'not insignificant' mean?" I asked.

Joachim regarded me steadily. "Anna, you are not naïve. You understand the implications."

He stepped back. "My message is delivered. Recover the staff. Retrieve the spear. Try not to die."

And then he was gone.

CHAPTER 2

I DIDN'T LIKE THE idea of Kincade giving up his position of importance for me. That's not what I was about. In fact, I didn't like he wanted to help me even when I specifically told him I didn't want his help.

The more I thought about it as the hot spray needled my skin, the angrier I got. How dare he insert himself into my mess and call it necessary. I hadn't asked. I hadn't agreed. And I didn't want the debt.

After my shower, I toweled off, dressed and stalked down the hall to his room with all the intent of having it out with him once and for all. I pounded on the door with my fist. It flew open a second later and a shirtless Kincade stood on the other side with a razor in one hand and shaving cream dotting his freshly shaved face. His hair was damp. Droplets of water still clung to his skin.

I blushed to the roots of my hair. The angry lines on his face morphed into amusement. His gaze dipped—just once—then snapped back to my eyes like it was a mistake.

"Something you need?"

"I'll come back later."

"No, you'll tell me why you were banging on my door." He swung it wider and waved me inside. "Please come in and share what crawled up your ass and died."

Anger flared bright and hot. I shoved past him and moved into the room as he slammed the door. "You don't have to be such a jerk, you know."

"I'm a jerk?"

He stalked to the bathroom and disappeared inside. I heard the clatter of his razor on the counter, the swish of a towel. He popped back into the doorway, wiping his face. Still shirtless. I was doing my best not to look at his naked torso with all the delicious muscle and that silvery scar running down the left side.

"You're the one pounding on my door."

I may as well get right to the point. I folded my arms over my chest. "When are you going to tell me you left the Watchers?"

"When are you going to tell me about the mysterious resurrection of your mother?"

Oh, I hated when he did that. I evaded and he countered. It was something Edward and I had perfected long ago. I didn't want to do that dance with Kincade, too, but I couldn't help myself.

"When are you going to tell me about the task force you led—about Ophelia?"

"When are you going to stop pretending you weren't terrified of what Azriel did to you?"

Crap. He was better at this than me. I huffed out a breath. "I don't want to talk about that."

"I don't want to talk about the Watchers."

He closed the gap between us. He stopped just short of touching me—close enough that I could feel heat, not contact. The clean scent of his aftershave drifted over me. That sandalwood smell I associated with him. It made my olfactory senses kinda happy. I didn't want to be happy about the way Kincade smelled.

"I'll answer your questions if you'll answer mine. Deal?" he said.

I searched his face for any sign of deceit or malicious intent. There wasn't any. Did I want to tell Kincade what memories had resurfaced when Azriel magicked me? Edward and I briefly discussed it and only because I confronted him.

"Deal," I heard myself say.

"You go first. Your mother."

I mentally kicked myself. I should have seen that coming. I dropped my arms, ran a hand through the length of my hair and paced.

"Station 211 in Antarctica is run by the Knights of the Holy Lance. We were searching for the spear there. I found out the leader was conducting experiments on women to make them like me."

"You mean a dream walker?"

I nodded. "They couldn't dream walk while the subject was conscious, like I can. I ran into one of them. It was my mother. She's a super dream walker. I found her blood sample in a vial in the lab. He used her as the prototype, I think. Edward doesn't think it's her, but it has to be. She looks just like the woman in the portrait in the hall. That and we have the same eye color."

Our violet eye color was unique. I'd never seen anyone else with that color of eyes. Except the woman who called herself Natasha.

"She tried to kill me." The memory still burned, bright and hot, deep inside me.

His jaw flexed once, hard. He didn't hide his shock. "How?"

"With her mind." I clutched my elbows, remembering the horrific way she punched into my mind. With her mind superpower, she made my internal organs hemorrhage to the point she blinded me. "I don't know how exactly but she has this...power...this control. It goes beyond dream walking. Schneider performed experiments on her brain to make her that way."

In Antarctica, I found his journal and all his notes on the serum he made from her blood. I still had the journal stashed in the bottom of my sock drawer for safekeeping. Not that Schneider would need it anymore since he was dead.

My stomach twisted like I was back under that fluorescent polar light.

"And you...*want* to find her?" he asked, careful, as though I might be out of my mind.

Maybe I was. Looking for a super dream walker who could kill me with her mind was one of those dangerous decisions. It wasn't the first one I had. Probably wouldn't be the last. There was something about the way she looked at me that last time with almost a hint of recognition. There had to be a way to bring her back from that dark place, to make her remember she was Annabelle Walker, my mother.

"She didn't know who I was. I think there may be a way to save her. Or to at least bring some of her back." I continued to pace, trying hard to ignore his shirtless muscled physique.

"You hope that." He padded over to the dresser and opened a drawer. Finally, he pulled on a shirt. Thank God. And also—damn it.

"Hope is all I have. Your turn."

I plopped down in the chair in the corner of the room while he prowled around looking for his boots. He was combat boots, Henleys and cargo pants much like what I liked to wear. He was stalling. He knew. I knew.

Finally, he paused and looked over at me with contemplation on his face.

"Do you know what the Watchers are?"

Ah, so that's how it was going to be. He wanted to see how much I knew. I nodded. The Watchers were a group of angels appointed by the Most High who were tasked with keeping humans safe from demons. They were also a clean-up crew when demons and Fallen ended up dead. I experienced them a couple of times.

"I was a general in the Watcher army assigned to hunt down the Fallen high lords killing guardian angels and stealing human souls. That's the task force Ophelia was part of." His face was devoid of all emotion as he said it, like it wasn't a big deal.

It was a big deal. And I hadn't agreed to be the reason.

Silence stretched between us—thick, charged.

He raked his hand through his hair. "This matters more."

I pressed my lips together in a thin line. "I highly doubt that. Protecting human souls and keeping high lords from killing angels seems way more important."

"Lucifer is building his army that way, yes. You're right that it was important. It is important. But if he gets his hands on those relics, then the world ends." He gave me a pointed look like I was supposed to agree with him. "Besides, there are others who can do that while I..."

His words trailed off. He took interest in putting on his boots and tying them.

"While you what?"

"I told you before. You can't do this alone. I'm not going to let you."

"I don't need a sidekick."

"No." His tone was sharp as he looked at me. "You need someone who has your back."

My throat tightened. Pathetic. I flushed. We looked at each other with all the unspoken things neither of us wanted to say. Edward told me he was my guardian but Kincade wasn't about to admit that. Nor did I want to admit how it made me feel safer knowing he was there.

When Azriel captured Kincade, I was driven by an inherent need to get him back. I had to make sure he wasn't a casualty in this war on humanity. Like Ben was. Azriel took him from me, I wasn't about to let him take Kincade, too.

"Get it now?" he asked.

I nodded. "I get it."

No one had ever had my back. I was afraid I was going to get all touchy-feely about it because the idea unsettled me more than I expected. I didn't want to go there. I preferred to be an unemotional android sometimes because it was easier than having to deal with feelings. I pushed out of the chair. I wanted to run for the door as quickly as possible.

"I think I better go see what Edward is up to."

"We're not finished here."

"Sure, we are," I said.

"You were supposed to tell me about Azriel."

Telling him about Azriel was the absolute last thing I wanted to do. "You were there. You saw what he did to me."

"I don't know the whole story."

"You don't need to know the whole story."

The image of Kincade shoving Azriel against a wall in that dream-memory was unforgettable. The way his hands curled into fists that day in the Hong Kong hospital when he told me he'd kill the fallen angel if he touched me again was also a memory burned into my mind. Kincade had a fierce protection of me. While I liked the thought of it, it also scared me.

His eyes narrowed. "Fine. You don't have to tell me. Today."

The word tasted like restraint.

I knew what that meant. We'd revisit this subject again but at the moment I was free to go. As I headed for the door, I paused next to him, looking him in the eye.

"I'll tell you someday. I'm not ready yet."

Understanding and compassion flickered in his green-gold eyes. He nodded. "Fair enough."

I left his room without looking back and hurried down the hall back to my room. Once inside my sanctuary, I closed the door and leaned against it, blowing out a breath.

How could I tell Kincade who Azriel had been to me in my past? The fallen angel masqueraded as a human, pretended to love me and tried to take my innocence. He tattooed his demon magic into the butterfly on my left shoulder to track me. At the time, I had no idea who or what he truly was and, looking back, I was nothing but a stupid lovesick girl. If I knew then what I knew now, I would have realized he was a fallen angel in disguise.

You know what they say. Hindsight was always 20/20.

I wanted to go back and change it, but I couldn't.

I couldn't erase my past any more than I could control my future. My life was not my own. It belonged to everyone else. And I resented that sometimes.

Most times I ignored the prophecy that said I was the one to save all mankind. When I was searching for the relics, trying to save Kincade, or merely going about my business it didn't cross my mind.

But there were times when I thought about it, truly thought about it, and worried I wasn't brave enough or strong enough or smart enough. I'd been beat up, stabbed, blinded, left for dead. And yet I still managed to come out alive.

Perhaps I was like a cat with nine lives. Or just damn lucky.

A knock sounded on the door. Since I still leaned on it, it pounded through my head. I hadn't seen Edward today, so I figured he was on the other side. I pulled open the door expecting to see my well-dressed uncle, but it wasn't.

It was a stranger. A man. Leaning casually against the jamb right in the doorway with a Cheshire Cat grin on his thin face and black eyes piercing the very depths of my soul. A familiar tingling sensation went through me as I looked at him and inhaled, smelling nothing out of the ordinary.

"Hello, Anna." He continued to smile.

"Who are you? Did Piers let you in? Where's my uncle?"

I tried to look past him but saw nothing but darkness. Like literal darkness. As though I stepped into another dimension. He steepled his long slender fingers. His nails came to a sharp point. His skin was paper thin, pale with a roadmap of blue veins crisscrossing.

"Oh, my dear, how quickly you forget me."

He pushed past me and entered my room. I squinted, trying to see into the hall. There was nothing but a void.

"Shut the door and let's chat."

I hesitated.

"You have no choice. Even if you scream, no one can hear you."

Demon magic was at work.

I closed the door with a shaking hand and turned to him as he stood at the balcony door and peered out over the gardens. He clasped his hands behind his back. I spied the pinky ring on his left hand. Silver with an onyx stone and a pentagram etched in red. It was hard to ignore the knotted fear in the pit of my stomach. Whoever he was, he wasn't friendly.

"Quite a view you have." He turned to face me. "It's been a while since we've seen each other."

I narrowed my eyes, trying to figure out who he was. "And you are?"

He chuckled. "You don't recognize me with my human glamour, do you?"

He transformed from the tall, thin man before me to the demon I recognized from the First Circle where I retrieved the Horn of Gabriel. Dark shimmery wings threaded with gold appeared behind him. His skin was paper thin. His mouth was full of sharp pointy teeth, black lips, black tongue, black eyes, black hair slicked back from his high forehead, sharp cheekbones protruding through his skin. His pale hands hosted black pointy fingernails.

It was the Prince of Greed. The one to whom I owed a favor.

Icy fright balled in the pit of my stomach. It disturbed me greatly he managed to breach my uncle's walls and appear in my bedroom. It was a violation of my sacred place. How the hell did he get through the wards?

"Mammon," I said.

"Ah, there, you do remember. I'm so glad. We have much to discuss."

"We have nothing to discuss." My tone was full of haughty derision.

"Oh, but we do. As I recall, you owe me a favor. One of my choosing at a time of my choosing."

When I made the promise to him, I did it to get the Horn of Gabriel. Edward was vehemently opposed to me agreeing to him but for me, it was a means to an end. I got what I wanted. And now it was biting me in the ass.

"I suppose that time is now."

"You are as smart as they say." He gave me that thin lipped smile as he replaced the human glamour.

I didn't know who "they" were though I ventured a guess it had something to do with the dark angels of Hell I'd interacted with. Was there a gossip network between demon lords, Fallen and dark princes?

"Whatever it is you want me to do I won't do it." I didn't know how I was going to get out of it but if there was a will, there was a way.

"I'm afraid you don't have a choice, my dear. You gave me your word. If you choose not to follow through, then you will give me your soul."

"My soul is not mine to give. It belongs to God and only God and only He can decide what to do with it." I lifted my chin in defiance. I wasn't sure where that came from, but I managed to pull it from the depths of my brain.

He didn't like that answer. Not one bit. His eyes narrowed and red sparked in them. "But I can take it, whether you give it willingly or not. And I will if you defy me."

I thought of how Azriel took pieces of Kincade's soul, bit by bit. And how painful it looked when he did it. I was kind of wimp. I couldn't handle the pain like he had. I played along.

"What do you want me to do?"

His glower removed and his expression turned almost pleasant. "You will kill Edward Walker and bring me proof of death."

I stared at him, dumbfounded, as nausea twisted my gut. "You want me to do what?"

"Edward Walker must die. I want him dead and you're going to kill him for me."

My denial rose to my lips, but flat out refusing the Prince of Greed was a death sentence. I had visions of him taking my soul like Azriel had taken so many others.

"Can you do that for me?" He glanced over his sharp pointy nails as though we merely discussed the latest news report.

"It won't be easy for me. You have to know that." I stalled, trying to come up with another response to get him out of here and off my back. Even if it was temporary.

"Your uncle is your family. I know. I don't care. Kill him, my sweet, and I will allow you to live."

And with that, he was gone.

CHAPTER 3

As soon as Mammon disappeared, I ran to my door and yanked it open with a fierce force. The hallway had returned, and everything had righted back to the way it was. I had to talk to Edward. He was the only one who could explain to me why the Prince of Greed was able to pierce his wards and get inside the manor.

I hurried down the hallway to the library, where he often took tea in the early afternoon, knocked and then opened the door. The scent of bergamot and lemon filled the room.

"Uncle, I need to...Oh, I didn't realize you were busy."

Kincade was there, his elbows on his knees as he leaned forward listening intently to something my uncle said. They both jolted to their feet.

"We're finished here. Do come in." Edward waved me inside.

Kincade moved from his chair toward me and suddenly my heart was in my throat, pounding a wicked tattoo as our eyes met. I stopped short, like my body had decided for me. There was something about the way he looked at me, something that changed since our last discussion in this room, that made me realize he and Edward were talking about me.

I didn't like it. Not one bit.

Heat flickered over me as Kincade brushed by, his shirt sleeve whispering against mine, the contact so brief it shouldn't have mattered. It did. I swallowed the sudden lump in my throat as he paused under the mistletoe and hoped like hell he'd move on. He lingered there for precious seconds while I held my breath. Our eyes met. His searching mine, leaving me with a feeling he wanted to say something, but he didn't know what or how. Or maybe he wanted to take me in his arms and kiss me senseless. His jaw tightened, like he was bracing himself against something.

Finally, he left, closing the door behind him.

Still, it gave me hives to think he might have kissed me. Okay, maybe not hives exactly. More of a heaving bosom. Which was deeply inconvenient. But I was so not the heaving bosom type. Or the swooning type.

I had to stop thinking that way about Kincade.

Once he was out the door, I placed my hands on my hips and glared at Edward.

"What did you tell him?" I demanded.

"Would you like some tea?" He picked up a cup already poured and stretched it to me. "We have lemon cakes."

He avoided the question. It annoyed the crap out of me. But I wasn't one to refuse a cup of Earl Gray and a lemon cake. I moved to him, taking the cup. I added cream and stirred.

"Don't think you're getting out of answering my question. I know you were talking about me so spill your guts." I sat in the chair Kincade had previously occupied and sipped.

"Nothing of the sort. Kincade and I were merely catching up."

I gave him the stink eye. It wasn't like they were old friends and had anything to catch up about. Evasion was one of his favorite tactics. "Sure, you were."

"What can I do for you, Anna?" He deftly changed the subject.

I dropped it for now because I had more important fish to fry. "You can tell me why the Prince of Greed was able to pop into my bedroom."

His delicate teacup clattered against his saucer. He looked at me, eyes wide. His face paled. It wasn't often I saw my uncle react with utter and complete surprise. That got his attention at least. I shoved the lemon cake in my mouth. I was a stress eater and the sugar rush gave me comfort.

"What do you mean he was in your bedroom?"

"I didn't stutter," I said around a mouthful of cake. "I thought you had wards around the manor to keep those unsavory types out."

"I do. Or did." He reached for a lemon cake, held it in his palm as he considered. "Something must have happened to weaken them."

"Or maybe Mammon is stronger than your wards," I suggested.

He frowned. He didn't like that idea. Neither did I for that matter. "Either way, it's not good. When we're finished here, I'll do a perimeter check. I don't want you leaving the house until I've checked every door and window."

Now I frowned. I had stuff to do. I didn't have time to sit and do nothing. "You're keeping me under house arrest?" Trapped in the same house with Kincade and Ophelia who was determined to get us under the mistletoe one way or another.

"For the time being. Please cooperate with me on this, Anna. I cannot worry about your well-being. At least, not any more than I already do."

I was touched. It was nice to know he worried about me. I almost wanted to hug him. "All right."

"He's come to call in his favor, hasn't he?" He knew. I wasn't fooling Edward. I didn't have to tell him.

"Yes." I swallowed hard, crumbs of lemon cake sticking in the back of my throat.

"Well? What does he want?"

I took a sip of tea to wash down the remaining cake, my hand suddenly shaking. "He wants me to kill you and bring him proof."

There was a long silence as we looked at each other. Edward didn't look the least bit surprised and that surprised me. In fact, he seemed to have taken the news rather calmly.

"Proof on a silver platter, no doubt."

"How can you be so casual about this?" I put the cup aside and leaned forward. "Do you understand he wants me to kill you?"

"Of course, I understand. I'm no wanker. But I know you better sometimes than you know yourself. You won't do it. You've already made up your mind about that."

I sat back in the chair and blew out a breath. Sometimes it was completely annoying he read me. He probably already knew I'd come to him, terrified and unsure about what to do. I waited for him to give me the answer—how to get out of doing the favor for Prince Mammon.

"I'm afraid, though, there's no way around doing what the Prince of Greed wants."

See? I knew he'd be able to read my mind. Someone told me once my thoughts were always on my face. I wasn't good at hiding them. I never had been. And I didn't want to be. I believed in face value. What you see is what you get. No sugarcoating.

"Well, that's not good news. I thought you'd have a better answer."

"As you'll recall, Anna, I told you then not to agree to his terms. You didn't listen. And now you're faced with an impossible decision."

"Thanks for the I told you so. Am I supposed to kill you?" I threw my hands up in aggravation. He and I both knew the answer to that. I wasn't going to do it anymore than I would kick a puppy.

He chuckled. Actually had the nerve to laugh at my impossible dilemma. "You won't. You can't. Don't worry, Anna, we'll think of something."

"I can't believe you're making light of this."

He turned serious then. "Far from it. Mammon is a dangerous demon. Almost as dangerous as Lucifer himself. I have to find out how he breached the wards and made it into your room."

"Oh, he used some sort of demon magic. I tried to leave but he had somehow managed to block us off from the rest of the house."

Edward gave me his classic straight face. "You might have mentioned that sooner."

"Sorry."

"It's important I have all the details. Anything else?"

"He liked the view from my balcony." I said it mostly to annoy him.

He scowled. "That's not what I meant."

I thought back to everything Mammon said to me. "He said if I didn't do it, he wanted my soul."

Edward stared at me, not blinking, his expression blank and unreadable. Unlike me, Edward was a world class champ at hiding his emotions. I never knew what he was thinking or feeling. He kept it all close to him much like he kept information he thought I needed to know, parceling it out when it was pertinent.

"Well?" I prompted. "How am I going to get out of this?"

He shook his head slowly. "I'm not sure you can."

"That's not very comforting."

"I'm sorry, Anna, but I did warn you about making a deal with him."

"So that's it? My fate is sealed?"

Edward took a bite of the lemon cake as he contemplated. "Give me time to think. Perhaps I can come up with something."

That gave me some comfort. Edward was a magician. He could pull a rabbit out of his hat from anywhere. He'd proven that time and time again.

"I'm sure you can figure something out. You're good like that," I said.

"It does not bode well, though, Anna. Someone wants me out of the way."

I nearly snorted. "I think we know who that someone is." When he lifted an eyebrow in question, I said, "Lucifer. Duh."

"Indeed, you may be right."

I thought of the vision I had of Azriel taking the spear to Lucifer. Tracking the relics after touching them was one of my dream walking abilities. After I handed the spear to Azriel in exchange for Kincade's life, I tapped into that and found Azriel trying to hand it to Lucifer. What I learned that day haunted me as much as knowing my mother was still alive out there, somewhere. Alone. Powerful. More powerful than me. A frosty shudder went through me and I shivered.

"Is there something else you need to tell me?" He ate the lemon cake in one bite, then reached for his tea.

"I don't know. Is there?"

"Come now, Anna. When you have information you wish to share, you chew your lower lip. Out with it now. What is it?"

I realized he was right and immediately stopped chewing my lower lip.

I debated whether to tell him. I hadn't breathed a word of it to anyone. Not even Kincade. The one person I trusted one hundred percent was Edward. But even then, it was still terrifying to voice what I saw and heard.

"There is but...I'm scared."

He placed the cup back on the nearby table, then grasped the teapot and refilled it. "Is it all that bad?"

"When I handed Azriel the Spear of Destiny, I had to know what he intended to do with it. I tracked it." I paused. Bit my lip again. Stopped. Damn it.

"You didn't like what you found, I gather."

I didn't have to explain. He knew what I meant by tracking it.

"He took it to Lucifer. He told Azriel he would give him one more chance to break through the protection surrounding me. He wasn't interested in the spear alone. He wants all five relics." I paused for dramatic effect. "And me."

Edward stiffened. "What were Lucifer's exact words? Do you recall?"

How could I forget? "He said the relics were useless to him until he had all five and the woman. He said he couldn't use them without me." I omitted the part about him handing me over to Azriel once they had what they wanted. That was a fate worse than death and something I wasn't prepared to deal with. At least not yet. "What does that mean? Do you know?"

"No. The prophecy says if evil overcomes you, you will falter. If you chose Darkness, the world will suffer. The world will change forever and the evil cannot be undone. It says nothing about how the relics are to be used to fight for mankind."

That wasn't helpful at all. I recalled the line about the Keeper—me—being tempted beyond all temptations. Maybe Azriel coming after me the way he did was part of that. He was desperate to seduce me, to make me accept working for him.

"There has to be more in the book than that." I glanced toward the bookshelf where he sometimes kept the family history book. I didn't see it. He must have it locked away.

"I'll research it. See what I can find out. Try not to worry about it, Anna." He took one last sip of his tea, then stood. "I'm going to check the perimeter."

"You'll let me know what you find out?"

"Of course."

"I guess I'll go back to my room since there's nothing else to do." I felt like I was under house arrest but deep down, I knew Edward was right. If Mammon breached the wards, then we had bigger problems.

"Fear not, Anna. You'll be back to your relic hunting in no time. By the way, have you received any more postcards?"

I hadn't told him about the latest one I received. He suspected, as I did, they were clues to the location of the Holy Relics. Clues that led me right to them. Neither one of us knew who was sending them. They merely appeared out of nowhere.

So far, I'd managed to collect one of the five relics—the Horn of Gabriel was safely hidden away in the vault in the library.

"I did. It was Acre, Israel."

"Have you alerted Kincade?"

I shook my head. "Not yet."

"You best do that and start packing. I'll call Harry and make necessary arrangements."

I cocked my head to the side. Edward never mentioned his contacts. "Harry?"

"Harry Humphrey. He's the pilot." He said it as though it was something I should know already.

I nodded. He was right. I'd delayed long enough. It was time for me to search for the Staff of Moses.

CHAPTER 4

I TRUSTED EDWARD TO look into it, but not to tell me everything if he didn't like what he found. He had a long history of deciding what truths I could and couldn't handle. I wanted to remind him I'd been to Hell and back—literally—and didn't need him or Kincade shielding me from reality.

Speaking of Kincade—

He was outside the parlor when I exited. Not lurking. Not listening in. Just there, like he'd positioned himself deliberately and waited.

I scowled.

"Hovering?" I asked.

"No. Just waiting for you."

"That means you're hovering." My eyes narrowed with suspicion. "Why?"

He cut right to the chase. "Do you have information about where to search for the staff?"

I relaxed a little. My uncle did suggest I talk to Kincade about it since we'd be traveling together. At least, that was my assumption since he insisted on going with me. I wasn't going to get out of it no matter how hard I tried.

"I have a lead."

When I didn't elaborate, he asked, "And that is?"

"I have to research it first. I don't know how legit it is." It wasn't far from the truth. The postcards I received hadn't led me astray yet.

"Lie. What's the real story?"

"I think it's in Israel." I hated he could do that. There was no sense in hiding it.

"What makes you think that?"

"Woman's intuition." I smiled, deliberately unhelpful.

He did not smile back. "Try again."

"I have a source, okay?"

"And that is?"

Sometimes I considered throwing myself on the floor and having a tantrum. It wouldn't work. Between Edward and Kincade, secrets had a very short shelf life.

I pressed my lips together, considering how to answer. No matter what I said, he would somehow ferret the truth out of me. Maybe it was better to tell him and get it over with.

"It is better to tell me. What's your source?"

"I hate when you do that."

"I hate when you're not straight up with me."

We had another silent standoff. We did this a lot and were getting good at staring each other down. Sometimes, I heard him in my head. Most of the time, he annoyed me by reading my thoughts. He was infuriating either way.

"All right, I'll tell you. Remember when you took me back to my Dallas apartment after Ben was killed? There was an envelope on the floor with a postcard of Hong Kong in it."

He nodded. "I remember."

"It was a clue. It led me to the Horn of Gabriel. Likewise, I got a postcard of Istanbul that led me to the Spear of Destiny. I also got a note about Station 211 in Antarctica that led me to my mother."

"And you got one for the Staff of Moses, I presume?"

I nodded. "Acre, Israel."

For a brief moment, something crossed his face—surprise, recognition, maybe concern—before it disappeared behind his usual control.

"Who's sending these postcards?"

I shrugged. "I have no idea."

He peered at me a long moment. "That, at least, was the truth. Very good, Miss Walker."

"Back to calling me Miss Walker, huh? Should I call you Mr. Harrison?"

He scowled. "When do we leave?"

"Edward is making arrangements for us. If I know him, probably tomorrow. I still have to research the city."

"I can help." His offhanded suggestion caught me off guard. Kincade wasn't a research kind of guy. He was an action kind of guy. That's what I liked best about him.

"No, thanks. I got it. I'm going to pack."

I trudged back to my room, leaving him at the bottom of the stairs. The thought of getting on a plane made me tired and I hadn't even packed yet. There were so many things I wanted to accomplish. Find my mother. Find the Staff of Moses to heal Darius. Get back the Spear of Destiny.

I had a lengthy to-do list and enough energy to fill my pinky.

I pulled out my travel duffel and flung it on the bed. I traveled light these days since I tended to end up with demon guts on me at one point or another, forcing me to buy new clothes. I had a small arsenal of daggers and knives I liked to travel with, but my favorite was the jade-handled dagger, the one with the symbols of alpha and omega carved into the handle. I tucked it into the sheath at my waist.

I never knew how long these trips lasted, so it was impossible to pack. I threw a stack of socks and underwear in the bottom. As they landed in the bag, my bedroom door flung open and Ophelia dashed inside. Panic was all over face.

"Look outside." She pointed to the balcony.

I hurried over and flung open the door. It was so dark, it appeared to be nighttime which wasn't right because Edward and I had mid-afternoon tea. Big black storm clouds filled the sky. It looked like a black cloud on the nearby horizon moving at a quick clip toward the manor. I squinted, trying to make it out when I realized it was a line of demons.

My heart instantly went into my throat. We were about to be under attack. I whirled to Ophelia.

"We have to tell Edward."

As soon as the words were out of my mouth, Kincade burst through the door, gun in hand. He slammed the balcony door, locked it.

"Is it what I think it is?" My voice shook when I spoke.

"Demon attack," he said. "They're coming from every direction."

"What the hell is going on? Why?" Ophelia asked.

"If I had to guess, I'd say they're after you." Kincade gave me a pointed look.

"I need to grab my sword." She wasn't one to shy away from a fight. She dashed out to retrieve it.

To Kincade, I said, "Where's Edward? He said he was going outside to check the wards along the perimeter."

"I haven't seen him."

"We have to find him." I headed for the door.

"Why is he checking the perimeter?" Kincade was hot on my heels. "Why didn't he ask for help?"

To answer that, I was going to have to tell him about Mammon and I wasn't ready to spill my guts about that yet. "He thinks the wards may have been breached."

We pounded down the stairs to the first floor. Piers stood at the front door. I wondered if he was there to keep me in or them out. Edward was outside. I had to go after him. I brushed by him and reached for the door.

Kincade was behind me a second later. "Where do you think you're going?"

Piers moved between me and the door. "His lordship asked that no one leave, especially you, Miss Walker."

"In a few seconds, we're going to be overrun with demons."

I wasn't sure if the butler understood who and what we were. Edward wasn't too keen on making that public knowledge. But Piers took it all in stride even though he glanced at Kincade for confirmation. I almost snorted. As if I'd make up something like that. Concern mixed with question flickered over the old butler's pinched face. Kincade nodded.

"I'll find him," he said and turned to me. "You stay."

"But—"

"I mean it, Anna. Stay here."

As he left, I pouted. They wanted me safe inside, but it still pissed me off. As Edward worried about me, I worried about him. I didn't want anything to happen to him. A few minutes later, Kincade returned with Edward. I breathed a sigh of relief. He closed and barred the door.

"I was on my way around the north end when I saw them," Edward said. "I headed back straightaway."

"What are we going to do?" I asked.

Ophelia arrived, sword in hand ready to do battle.

"Stay calm for starters. Then we'll—"

Edward was interrupted by the sound of glass breaking. Something shattered the parlor window and landed with a thunk on the floor. We hurried to the doorway in time to see the Christmas tree fall over, glass balls shattering. Ophelia sucked in a breath as all her hard work was destroyed.

Demons poured inside. Kincade didn't waste any time as he fired off shot after shot, killing several before they could make it through the parlor. Ophelia, Kincade and I were faced with a horde of demons invading the house.

My house.

I went into action, charging them. I wasn't afraid of them. They weren't afraid of me. Ophelia shrieked a battle cry and started for them, too. Kincade kept shooting every one of them until he was out of ammo.

"I'm out," he said and flung aside the useless gun.

"Here." Edward handed Kincade another gun that looked like an assault weapon but wasn't. Instead of a trigger, there were two buttons. One blue. One red. "Charge here. Fire here."

"Blue, charge. Red, fire. Got it." Kincade took to the gun as though he'd used it all his life and took out demons as fast as they poured inside.

Edward tried to hand Ophelia a gun, too, but she waved him off, preferring her sword. Behind me, Edward took out more invading from the other side of the house.

"We can't keep this up much longer before we're overrun," Kincade pointed out.

Quite the optimist.

"They've breached the wards," Edward said. "There's not much I can do."

"Can't you call in reinforcements?" I asked. "You know everyone. Don't you have a magical rolodex or something?"

There was a high-pitched sound that exploded somewhere in the distance. All the demons jumped as though they'd been scared out of their wits. They turned, looked in the distance at some unseen force and then scattered like cockroaches, retreating as though they were on fire.

"That was weird," Ophelia said, still holding her sword.

"Where'd they go?" It was a rhetorical question, but I asked it anyway.

Before anyone replied, the front door blew open destroying more of Ophelia's Christmas decorations. It landed on the floor with a resounding crack and shattered, which took some doing since it was a heavy oak door on wrought iron hinges.

Edward, Kincade and I exchanged glances ready to fight whatever was next to step through the door.

"I don't like this," Kincade muttered.

I didn't either, truth be told. Nothing good could come of whatever blew off the door. Especially because the demons left in a hurry. I clutched my dagger in my sweaty palm and stared at the opening as cold air poured inside. A gust of wind sliced through me and cut me to the bone as silence descended upon the manor.

A cold, eerie silence.

A man stepped through the threshold. Tall, lanky, dressed in all black with his black hair slicked back from his high forehead. He had a thin nose and lips, wide eyes and high protruding cheekbones. He pinpointed me with his glittering gaze, smiled as though he recognized me and lifted his hands, pointing long slender fingers at me.

I braced myself but a second too late as the stream of light smacked into my chest. I flew backward, landing on the floor of the parlor near the broken Christmas balls. I dropped the dagger. It clattered somewhere on the ground. Pain exploded through me, a burning sensation radiated outward from the center of my chest to my arms, hands, legs and feet. My nerve-endings were on fire as a scorching prickling sensation went through me. As though someone placed a red-hot poker under my skin and twisted.

Kincade shouted something, then Edward. Then a crash. All I was aware of was the Persian rug under me as pain shot through every part of me.

Stars sparked my vision as I shook my head, trying to clear it. It hurt to turn my head, but I did, and, through the haze, I made out a hulking form on the ground that looked suspiciously like Kincade. Only something powerful could do that to him.

And that's when I got scared.

The tall man stepped over him as though he were nothing but a speedbump and approached me. He did the thing with his hands again and the bolt hit me. Burning. So much pain. I cried out, coughed. Tried to fist the rug. Couldn't. My nails scraped across the fibers leaving an indentation. I thought I smelled burning hair and wondered if it was mine.

He took a knee and leaned down close, so we were eye to eye. He smelled like a demon. Death and rot and decay and general disgustingness.

"The pain is all-consuming, isn't it? How does it truly feel?"

His voice sounded like a thousand blades scraping together. It grated on my nerves, made a terrible tremor skitter across my skin and inflamed the burning sensation inside me even more. My ears started to ring from the horrible sound.

"Tell me, my dearest one."

I cried out with the sound of his voice again but couldn't find the words to speak. He chuckled, low and deep under his breath. He did the thing with his hands again. The bolt of white light hit me again. I curled into the fetal position, drawing my knees under my chin, trying to make myself as small and insignificant as possible. It didn't work. He still hit me with everything he had.

The only movement I was able to do now was blink and even that was painful.

He reached for me, scooped up my paralyzed body into his arms and turned toward the open door.

He stepped over Kincade, walked past my uncle who was also paralyzed on the floor, past an unconscious Ophelia. A deep panic arose inside me, bubbling up through me. All I could do was blink. What the hell had he done to me?

I whimpered, a small sound coming from deep within that struggled to get out.

"He's taking her," my uncle's fear-laced voice ricocheted off the walls around us, reverberating in my head. "Kincade—"

"I can't bloody move." He practically growled the words.

"Do you hear that, love? Their fear? They know they are losing you. And once I walk out that door, they will never find you. I promise to take good care of you." His screeching voice rumbled through his chest into me. Like fingernails on a chalkboard. He punctuated his words with another chuckle.

There was a sudden splintering of ceiling and then a crash. I wanted to turn my head but couldn't. Whatever it was, caused the stranger stop mid-step.

"Step aside, angel."

Angel? Who?

There was no verbal response. The stranger grunted and the next thing I knew, I was on the floor. He dropped me like a hot potato. All I saw was a bright white light as it moved between me and the menace that had me, as though it was a protective shield. I barely made out the wingspan of an angel but still couldn't discern who it was. I had no idea what happened nor did I care when my head hit the floor seconds before I blacked out.

◆————◆

WHEN I CAME TO, I was on a bed. Mine? I had a raging headache and a burning sensation still prickling through me from head to toe. Someone sat beside me, holding my hand. It was a delicate but strong hand with soft skin. It had to be Ophelia. My eyes were glued shut, but I heard hushed voices around me.

"She's resting now," a familiar male voice said. My brain couldn't figure it out. Kincade, maybe.

"What the bloody hell was that, Darius?" Edward asked.

Darius? What was he doing back here? Was he the one who saved me from whatever that thing was? And, more importantly, my uncle didn't know what it was that attacked. That struck fear into me because Edward knew everything.

"A destroyer angel," Darius said.

What the hell was a destroyer angel?

"Why would a destroyer angel come after Anna?" That was Kincade.

"I think the answer is rather obvious," Edward said in his sour tone that said everyone should know the answer already. "He was sent here to take her away."

"Yes," Darius agreed, and I pictured him nodding in agreement. "To Lucifer."

A whimper escaped.

"She's coming around." Ophelia patted my hand. "Anna?"

My eyes felt like they were sealed with cement, but I managed to pry them open, blinking to clear my vision. I recognized my room as the three men gathered around the bed, concern etched on all their faces. Kincade was to my left. Darius stood at the foot of the bed.

Edward nudged Ophelia out of the way and pressed a hand against my forehead as if checking for a fever. "You're still burning hot. How do you feel?"

"Like hell." My voice was raspy, like I was up all night smoking cigarettes and drinking gin which was way more fun than what happened.

"Don't try to talk right now." He patted my shoulder. "Rest. I'll ring for tea. Come with me, Ophelia."

God love the British. They solved any of life's traumas by ringing for tea. But I didn't want tea or anything. The two of them left the room. Darius and Kincade stayed behind.

My leaden limbs wouldn't move even if I wanted them to. I was curled into a tight ball, my knees on my chest. I closed my eyes again and groaned, then regulated my breathing with long, slow breaths trying hard to make the pain go away. Wishing it would go away.

"She's sleeping again. Good. She needs the rest," Darius said.

Joke was on them. I wasn't sleeping. But I pretended to be just to hear the two of them interact.

"Will she recover?" Kincade kept his voice low, as though not to disturb me.

"Hard to say," Darius said. "He used the darkness inside her to paralyze her. He would also use it to turn her against the Light. I don't know what damage it did to her."

The tattoo on my shoulder tingled. Azriel's dark magic.

I cringed, waiting, but Kincade didn't ask about the dark magic. That didn't mean he wouldn't at some point.

Silence. I sensed no movement. They both stood like sentries on either side of the bed. There was some comfort knowing they were there, watching over me and keeping me safe. Though Kincade had been there and so had my uncle when the destroyer angel attacked taking us by surprise, they were both rendered powerless against the demon.

"Why did you come back?" Kincade's question surprised me. If I didn't know better, he was jealous. I continued to feign sleep to see where this conversation headed.

"You know why." Darius's tone held a defensive edge.

"Are you watching her?" Again, Kincade sounded suspicious. Like he didn't trust Darius.

But this was Darius. He couldn't hurt me. He wouldn't. If he was watching me, then it was for the same reasons Kincade was—to make sure nothing bad happened to me. He may be turning Fallen, but that didn't mean he was evil. He was still the fearless warrior angel. The one who risked his life to save others. To save me.

"I have no ill intentions for her, if that's what you mean."

"I know why you're here. Do you think she can help you with the Staff of Moses? Your feathers are mostly black."

"You don't have to remind me." Darius sounded terse, on edge.

A pause. Then, "It was demon poison, wasn't it?"

Demon poison? Since when did Darius—

"Yes." He sounded grim. "I could not let Edward Walker die. Anna needs him more than she knows."

Oh, God. I suspected he helped Edward again after we were attacked in Rio by my mother and the demons. I remembered the bandage on my uncle's arm, his head. But Edward downplayed the situation. Like way downplayed as though his injuries were no big deal and he was fine.

Of course, he was fine. Darius had healed him again. He already removed demon poison from me and Edward after our stint in the First Circle. How much poison was in his system now? And how many of his feathers were black? I hadn't noticed when my eyes were open.

"I know my fate," Darius said. "I am prepared to become a Fallen."

Kincade gave a small laugh. "That's what you think? That you're turning Fallen?" he asked, as though the thought was ridiculous in and of itself.

"Isn't it?" There was a hesitation in his voice.

"No."

Kincade paused and then, in a softer voice said, "Turning Fallen is not your fate, my friend. Demon poison killing you is. That's why your feathers are turning black." He sounded like a know-it-all.

"But I went into the First and Second Circle..." Darius's voice trailed off.

"You did. To help Anna and Edward. That doesn't mean you're turning Fallen. The way to become a Fallen is if you choose to become a Fallen."

"Why would I?"

"For dark power," Kincade said, his voice distant as though he had a memory.

"You sound like you know something about that, Watcher."

"Perhaps I do," was his response.

I imagined them staring each other down as Darius digested this new information. I was trying to understand, too. My uncle and I both thought Darius would be punished for entering the First and Second Circles and that's why his feathers were turning black. Now that I thought about it, though, it didn't make sense. To become a fallen angel, he would have to be banished from the heavens and, as far as I knew, he hadn't been. Or, as Kincade said, choose that path. He was still inherently good which meant there was hope for him if I found a way to remove the poison.

"And you know this for certain?" Darius asked.

"I'm a Watcher. I know lots of things. It's the demon poison that's killing you." He paused. "I can get you to one of our healers to see if he can help."

Wait. Wait. Wait.

Surprise rolled through me. Darius was dying? Kincade was offering to help Darius? This conversation was getting more and more interesting. My goofy imagination had me thinking of the two of them as buddies. It was an image I had a hard time getting out of my head and one that almost made me giggle.

It hurt too much to giggle.

"I appreciate your offer, Watcher, but I understand nothing can remove demon poison."

Except for the Staff of Moses. I hoped.

"So, you're going to let it kill you?" Kincade asked, his voice sullen.

I heard footsteps away from the bed and guessed Darius headed for the exit. "If that is my fate, then I must accept it."

A sharp pain of sadness went through me. So sharp I winced. I wasn't going to accept that death as Darius' fate. I had to help him. I had to get my hands on that staff.

"Darius, if you change your mind, let me know."

"I will." He paused then, "Thank you, Watcher."

His footsteps faded, leaving me and Kincade alone. Guilt pressed into me for having overheard their conversation, but I was glad I had. It was important information. I doubted Kincade would share. I still had a lot of questions. Like how Kincade knew what my plan was with the staff. And what did this destroyer angel calling to the darkness inside me mean? And, further, what did Kincade mean when he asked Darius why he came back? Did Kincade know he was here before? It seemed likely. He knew everything else.

Darius had been with me the night the car exploded in Hong Kong sending Kincade to the hospital. They'd eyed each other then. Their conversation here seemed terse.

The mattress sighed with Kincade's weight as he sat next to me on the bed. My heart fluttered. Which was stupid because I was so not a heart fluttering type. I didn't know what he was doing next to me. A sigh escaped as I stretched my legs and rolled to my other side.

And there he was sitting on the side of my bed in my teenage bedroom looking at me with those green-gold eyes full of worry and concern. That did something to me. A lot of somethings I didn't want to acknowledge.

"You all right?"

"I don't know." That was the truth. And my voice still sounded funny. "I guess I will be."

"You sound like a bar ho."

"You have experience with those?" I enjoyed needling him.

He didn't answer. He reached for me, his hand brushing hair back from the side of my face. I remained still and tried to calm my suddenly erratic breathing. If Kincade was feeling generous with information, maybe he'd answer some of my burning questions.

"What's a destroyer angel?" I asked, mostly to distract myself from the way his hand felt on my hair which was far too gentle for a big, strong guy like Kincade.

"You weren't unconscious for that?"

"No."

"Cheeky girl. What else did you hear?"

Crap. If I lied, he'd know, so I deflected. "What is it, Kincade?"

His jaw flexed as he clenched it, the muscles working there. "Something that will never stop hunting you."

I didn't like that sound of that. "What is he? A demon?"

"Not exactly. He and his minions are typically sent to torture humans. Also called an angel of the abyss," he said. "His name is Abaddon."

Nope, I didn't like the sound of that at all.

"Abaddon was sent to—"

"I know." I cut him off.

I didn't need details and he didn't ask me to elaborate. I already knew what he wanted. I saw it in my vision with Azriel and Lucifer. It went beyond me working with them to find the Holy Relics. It had something to do with me being part of the Holy Relics. But I hadn't shared that information with Kincade, nor did I particularly want to.

Something else bothered me, though. I wanted to ask what Darius meant by the darkness inside me used to turn me against the Light. Did Azriel's butterfly tattoo have something to do with that? Was that how this destroyer angel found me in the first place? It was clear he was sent to capture me and take me away from here.

Probably to Lucifer. Two of the relics were already recovered. If Lucifer had me, then he'd use me to find the remaining three.

"When were you going to tell me?" he asked, breaking into my thoughts.

"About what?" Confusion flickered through me at the sudden shift in topic.

"About him."

"Who him?" I was genuinely puzzled.

"The warrior angel."

Oh, so maybe he was jealous? That was interesting. "There's nothing to tell. How did you know what my plan was with the staff?"

"You have to get better at hiding your thoughts and feelings."

I flushed. Was I that transparent?

"Yes, you are."

I glared at him. "Stop doing that."

"Stop thinking so loud."

Yeah, like I had control over that.

"There's no guarantee it will work, you know," he said.

"I have to try."

"I figured." He said it on a sigh and sounded resigned to it, like he understood he couldn't stop me. "Darius is the least of your worries right now, though."

"What do you mean?"

"Abaddon didn't take you because Darius intervened." He looked away into the distance as he remembered the incident. "Edward and I had no power to stop him. The magic he used on us paralyzed us like it did you. We couldn't get to you even if we wanted."

It bothered him. A lot. Maybe he thought he failed me. He was powerless to stop this angel of the abyss from doing whatever he did to me. Only Darius managed with his warrior angel magic.

"Anna…" He met my gaze, his face a map of serious lines. I never saw him look like that before and it scared me. "Abaddon has unspeakable power."

I was aware. Kincade sounded…afraid. Which fucked me all the way up. My mouth went dry. My throat constricted as I swallowed hard. He confirmed my thoughts. I was screwed.

"There's…something I should tell you." I swallowed again and cleared my throat. I had to confess all to Kincade before something dreadful happened. "Once I touch the relic, I'm able to track it through my dream walking skills. When I gave Azriel the spear, I wanted to find out what he did with it. I saw it in Hell when he tried to give it to Lucifer."

His brows knit. "Go on."

"Lucifer didn't want it. He told Azriel to take it away because it was useless to him until he had all five of them and me. He said he had no use for them without me."

Kincade took a deep breath and swallowed, hard. For a moment, I swore his face paled, but he quickly recovered by swiping a hand down it, leaving a bloodless trail.

"You know what it means, don't you?" I asked.

He gave a slow nod. "I think so."

When he didn't elaborate, I said, "Well?"

"It sounds to me like you're one of the relics."

CHAPTER 5

I DIDN'T LIKE THE sound of that but in the grand scheme of things, it made sense. I was the one with the ability to retrieve the relics, but I had to wonder why someone hadn't shared that information with me before. If Edward knew, it was one more thing he hadn't told me.

Speaking of Edward, he re-entered the room with a tea tray. I smelled the heavy scent of bergamot tea and spotted lemon bars. My stomach rumbled.

Well, that was a good sign, at least. My appetite was back.

He placed the tray on the nearby bureau and poured a cup of tea. Kincade rose from the bed.

"I think you two should talk," he said as he made his way to the door. He gave Edward a pointed look as some silent communication passed between them.

Edward nodded. "Quite right."

As Kincade departed, I pushed up on the pillows finally able to move without feeling sick. I took the offered cup of tea and sipped, happy for the soothing effect. Edward offered me a lemon bar on a small dessert plate, then poured his own cup of tea.

"Kincade is right. We should talk. There are things I need to tell you, Anna."

I didn't like where this was going. "That sounds ominous."

"It's not easy for me to tell you this." He sipped his tea and perched on the end of the bed.

Yeah, I didn't like where this was going at all. I wasn't sure how much more bad news I could take. I shoved the lemon bar in my mouth and chewed before whatever he said ruined my day and appetite.

"But you should hear it from me and no one else."

"Uncle, whatever it is, just tell me. I'm not a child. I can take it."

He peered at me over the rim of his cup. The worry was clearly etched on his face. "A destroyer angel has been dispatched to take you back to Lucifer."

"I gathered that," I said with a nod. "Now what?"

"He will never stop until he has you and delivers you. If that happens..." His voice trailed off.

"It's not going to happen. There must be something we can do. Some way we can keep him from tracking me."

Again, that butterfly tattoo tingled on the back of my shoulder.

Edward placed the cup gently in the saucer and looked at me. For the first time, I saw fear in his eyes. Fear and sorrow. It sent a pang of worry through me.

Before he spoke, though, I asked, "Are you aware of the tattoo?"

His face was impassive, then his brows creased in confusion. "What tattoo?"

Great. So, he had no clue.

Our last discussion over whiskey regarding Azriel revealed long-buried information deep inside my head. Azriel used his demon magic to help me remember he was disguised as the man I thought I loved in my youth. My uncle and the angel, Sariel, used their own magic to shroud my memories and make me forget him. I recently recalled the whole sordid incident.

Edward told me then Azriel marked me. At the time, I figured the butterfly tattoo on my shoulder was common knowledge. Perhaps it wasn't.

"You have a tattoo?" he asked.

I sighed. "Unfortunately, yes."

Edward's expression didn't change as he calmly sipped his tea. "Am I to infer said tattoo was put there by Azriel?"

"I assumed you knew he did since you told me he marked me."

Edward's eyes cut to mine with an expression glittering there that said he was both pissed and caught off guard. "When I said that, I assumed he marked you in another way. When did this happen?"

"What other way?" I asked ignoring his question and stalling.

"There are many other ways. When did it happen, Anna?"

Ugh. I didn't want to tell him, but I wasn't getting out of this one. We already started down the rabbit hole. May as well continue. "One of those nights in the stables. Before you discovered he was Marcus and Sariel killed my memories."

With a calm hand, he placed his teacup back on the saucer. "And this tattoo...what does it look like?"

"A dark blue butterfly outlined in black."

His lips thinned. "You never told me."

"I never thought it was pertinent. Until, you know, now."

"He used his demon magic to ink the marker on your skin, Anna. That demon magic is now inside you."

"Yes." I hissed the word. "I am all too aware that's how he's tracking me."

"And now it's nothing more than a homing beacon for Abaddon and any other dark demon Lucifer decides to send after you." He paused, met my gaze. "Including the Prince of Greed."

For fuck's sake.

I may as well have a target painted on my back.

"So, what do I do about it?"

"It cannot be removed," he said. "That much I know. Not with the dark magic infused with the ink."

I set aside the tea on the nearby nightstand and laced my fingers, placing them in my lap, trying to remain calm. Deep inside, I wanted to scream. What else would Azriel do to me, take from me, before this was all over?

How much more indignity would I endure from him? How much longer would he stalk me and send demons after me? The anger seared through me. More than an emotional reaction. The anger pulsed there like a black oozing pool ready to boil.

I leaned my head back into the pillows and looked up at the canopy overhead. My hatred for Azriel increased tenfold. I wanted him dead now more than ever.

"And this darkness inside me. It's permanent?" I used a carefully controlled tone.

"I cannot say."

It didn't escape me the way his answer was phrased could be interpreted in a couple of ways. Either he didn't know, or he didn't want me to know.

"Why didn't you tell me sooner?" he demanded.

"I didn't think of it sooner," I said.

"The relics are important—"

"The relics," I scoffed. "Always the relics. Never about how I feel. How I have to deal with all this and more." I tasted bitterness in the back of my throat.

My life truly was not my own. It was hard not to resent that.

"Anna—"

"I'd like to be alone now, uncle."

He hesitated but finally nodded and rose from the bed. "I was going to say the relics are important, but your life is more important. If there's a way to remove the dark magic, I'll find it."

A moment of guilt slashed through me for jumping to assumptions. I was touched by his sentiment. "Thanks."

He took a deep breath, exhaled. "I worry for you. You're right. It is a lot to contend with."

"No need to worry, uncle. I'll do what I always do. Persevere." I leaned my head back and closed my eyes, dismissing him.

He left without another word.

But I was pissed. And I wanted blood.

AFTER MY UNCLE LEFT, I flung off the blankets and swung my legs over the side of the bed. I tried to stand, but I was still too weak. It took everything I had to walk across the room to the bathroom. By the time I got there, I was exhausted and sagged against the door, holding on for dear life.

That's how Ophelia found me when she entered my room.

"Let me help you." She hurried to my side, wrapped an arm around my waist and helped me walk into the bathroom.

I got a glimpse of myself in the mirror and scowled. They'd put me in bed in dirty, demon-blood splattered clothes. I smelled. I felt like crap and I needed a shower. But I didn't have the energy for any of that. I shrugged her off and leaned against the vanity, peering at the dark circles under my normally vibrant violet-colored eyes.

I looked like hell. Felt like it, too.

"Do you want me to stay and help you?" she asked.

"I don't know. Maybe." I didn't like being helpless. I liked even less feeling like I was nothing more than a weak kitten.

"Should I get your uncle?"

"No."

"Kincade?" There was a slight humorous edge in her voice.

"For sure, no."

She giggled. "Then let me help you. Let's at least get you out of those smelly clothes."

She disappeared into my room and came back a minute later with a clean pair of pajamas I hadn't seen in ages—a gray shirt and gray lounge pants in the softest material.

"Where did you dig those up?"

"Bottom drawer of your chest. Can you undress?"

I nodded and stripped off the soiled shirt, then pushed down the pants. But I still smelled the demon gunk on me.

"I need a shower," I said.

Nodding, she turned on the water and got it to temperature, then helped me inside. As though she didn't mind one bit. I, however, was mortified at having to ask for help. It was so not my style.

After getting cleaned up, toweled off and re-dressed, she helped me back to bed. She parked in the nearby chair, as though taking first watch.

"What are you doing?" I asked.

"Keeping an eye on you." She smiled at me.

I scowled. "I don't need a babysitter."

"Anna, just go with it, okay?" She huffed out a breath, then got up and took an interest in the bookshelf. She slipped one of the older tomes off the shelf. "Alice's Adventures in Wonderland. I've never read it."

"You should enjoy it, then."

She plopped back down in the chair and cracked open the book. *"Alice was getting very tired of sitting by her sister on the bank, and of having nothing to do."* She paused, looked up at me. "Sounds boring."

"Keep reading," I said over a yawn.

She laughed. "Are you sure? You yawned."

"Just keep reading," I urged.

And so, she did. Aloud. Until I fell asleep.

CHAPTER 6

WHILE OPHELIA READ ALICE'S adventures, I fantasized a hundred ways to kill Azriel as I drifted off to sleep and dream walked him. He was clearly top of mind when I found him smiling, looking very well pleased with himself.

"Ah, *chérie*. It's lovely to see you. Have you come to allow me to fill in the gaps of your memory?"

"I already know everything, you bastard."

I clenched my fists, wanting to do battle but trying to keep myself in check. A wave of his demon magic hit me as he tried to hold me in place, to control me. Demon magic I resisted with everything I had inside me. Including his own demon magic. If there was a way to fight fire with fire, I found it. He understood I deflected his attempted hold on me. I loved the look of shear surprise on his face.

"Impressive. You have learned how to control it. Perhaps you understand now how important you are to me. To us. To our cause."

Hours of practice with Edward forced me to learn to control it.

"Fuck your cause and you. I want nothing to do with either. I told you that from the start."

He continued to smile, but it was forced. Stretching his face thin over his razor-sharp bones giving him a terrifying mask. "Then why are you here?"

I uncurled my fingers. Inhaled, exhaled. It wouldn't do to lose my temper here. I looked over my cuticles trying to be casual. "Let's just say the hunter will become the hunted."

He snickered. "You are a funny girl, Anna, if you think you can threaten me. You cannot defeat me."

"I can and I will."

"I am more powerful than you know. More powerful than your Watcher lover. More powerful than even your beloved uncle. You cannot hunt me. You cannot even come close to me."

It irked me he referred to Kincade as my lover, but I never bothered to correct him. What was the point? It'd add fuel to the fire. Despite my annoyance, I grinned.

"Is that a challenge, Azriel?"

He stiffened. "No. Mere fact."

"I heard it as a challenge, and I accept." I blew him a kiss, like he had to me once. "See you around, asshole."

I woke up with a pounding headache and a nagging idea that would not leave me alone. The solution to what I needed to do about Azriel came to me as I woke. I tried to clear the fog from my muddled brain still plagued by memories of the destroyer angel.

But the idea nagged me and wouldn't go away. I needed to send Azriel a message. Sneaking out of the manor without my uncle knowing was going to be a feat.

Or Kincade knowing. The man was like a bloodhound.

As I blinked and tried to make the pain in my head subside, I turned my head on the pillow and saw Ophelia dozing in the nearby chair, the book open and face down on her lap. She snored softly, her chin on her chest and her breathing heavy. Her blonde hair fell over her shoulders in long messy waves giving me a twinge of envy. My black hair was straight and boring. Well, except for the streaks of white I had going on at each temple.

I shoved back the blankets and swung my feet to the cold floor. A shiver crawled up my spine from the contact, making me cringe. I hated to be cold.

I hated being incapacitated even more and right now I was useless lying in bed. I pushed to a stand. My muscles wobbled, my legs clearly still weak from the ordeal. I scowled, unhappy with the state of my body. But I was determined and forced a step. A quiet one so as not to wake sleeping beauty. Another step and I was a few inches from the bed.

Progress.

It took long agonizing minutes to dress myself without making a sound, but I finally managed it. The more I moved, the stronger I felt. I didn't think I'd be running any marathons anytime soon, but at least I could walk of my own accord. I stuck my dagger in the sheath at my waist. Someone returned it to my room after the Abaddon attack.

My plan to send Azriel a message was simple—get back to Greenwood Cemetery in Dallas to the underground crypt where his demon nightclub was and blow it up.

How I was going to accomplish that was another matter altogether. I hadn't a clue, especially since I still felt like I'd been hit by a Mack truck.

I pulled open the door to my room and peered out into the shadowy hallway. The manor was quiet, like everyone had gone to sleep. I tiptoed out the door and pulled it closed with a soft snick behind me. I stood there trying to muster up the energy to make it down the hallway to the library that also doubled as Edward's office.

My thought was to rifle through his desk until I was inspired by some piece of information that would help me achieve my goal of seeing Azriel's crypt go up in flames. I glanced down at Kincade's closed door and prayed it would stay that way. I didn't need him interfering.

Edward's suite was at the far end of the hallway. I hoped he was in his bed snoring and not out wandering the rooms of the manor. There was one way to find out.

With slow, labored steps, I made it down the hall to the library doors and paused, gripping the doorframe and taking deep breaths. Just those few steps managed to wind me. How in the world did I think I was going to make it all the way to Dallas?

I shook off the negative thoughts. I was determined to do this.

I stepped into the library and made it to the desk where I halted once again, gripping the edge and gazing at the tidy desktop. Edward was orderly and organized. He didn't like to have one paper or pen out of place. The desk pad was in the center, a cup of his favorite pens to the left of it. He was old-fashioned in that he preferred to pen his letters instead of email them, so a stack of personal stationery was on the right. I glanced at it and saw the Walker crest embossed in the top center of the paper.

I moved around the end of the desk and lowered into the leather executive chair, looking at all the drawers. Three on the right, two on the left, one in the center. The drawer that wasn't locked was the center one.

Figures.

I pulled it open and peered down at the contents with a curious eye. More pens. A scatter of paper clips. A small stack of yellow post-it notes. Nothing of note. I stuck my hand in the drawer and reached toward the back and stopped on what felt like a small notebook. I pulled it out and stared at the plain cover with one word embossed in gold. CONTACTS.

Bingo.

So, he didn't have a magic Rolodex, but he did have magical contacts.

I flipped open the cover of the contacts and stared at the first entry. It was a man named Harry Humphreys who was a pilot. His address at a London hangar and phone number followed his name. I recalled Edward mentioning Harry the pilot before the destroyer angel showed up.

I got warm tingles as I peered at his name. This could come in handy.

I flipped the page. Ioan Drăgoi was next. He was an art dealer at a gallery in Bucharest. He was internationally known for his personal collection of artwork and sculptures according to Edward's notes. There were a few money amounts noted next to his name. I had no idea what it meant.

The next page showed me his contact in Marrakesh, Rafiq Al-Ashab, a merchant in the square, Jemaa el-Fna. We'd met him earlier this year before heading to Antarctica. He'd given up valuable information about Station 211.

The rest of the book had more names and numbers, but I had all the information I needed.

I flipped back to the page with the art dealer's name and number, my quest for revenge finally taking shape. I snatched a pen, grabbed a sheet off the post-its and scribbled down the man's name and number. Then added the name and number of the pilot. I closed the book, slid it back into the drawer and stood.

I folded the note in half and stuck it in my front pants pocket then turned to the secret vault door and opened it. Once inside, I stood there looking around for something worth a lot of money that perhaps my uncle wouldn't miss so much. Definitely not the Horn of Gabriel that resided on the shelf in a box with the velvet lining. Next to it was an empty space where the Spear of Destiny had been. The last time I was in this room, I swiped the spear.

I spotted the painting of the ship in the storm in the ornate gold frame on the other side of the room. It was propped up on the floor leaning back against the wall. I noticed it the first time I was in this room. I picked it up, turned it over. A label indicated it was named *The Storm on the Sea of Galilee*.

That would do nicely.

I had no idea what the painting was worth. It didn't matter much except I needed cash and fast. I needed it wired to an account I could easily get my hands on. I wasn't one to carry a smartphone around, so I'd have to use the landline. I picked up the receiver and dialed Ioan Drăgoi. Time to make a deal.

◆――――◆

NEGOTIATION WASN'T ONE OF my best qualities. I kind of sucked at it. But I got the money I wanted for the painting. My second phone call was to Harry the pilot. I sweet-talked him into flying me to Bucharest on my uncle's dime to hand-deliver the painting and collect the cash. I removed the painting from the frame and rolled it up, placing it in a white tube. I wasn't sure I could trust this Ioan person, but I had no choice. I needed the money to launch my plan of revenge and he was willing to give it to me.

I made my way out of the vault, closing the secret door behind me. When I turned, the sight of Kincade blocking the exit to the room with his arms crossed startled me. I sucked in a sharp breath. We eyed each other. He glanced at the tube in my left hand, then back at me. Suspicion was written all over his face.

"Miss Walker." He gave me a hello nod.

"I don't have time for this." I huffed out a breath and started to stomp by him with as much energy as I managed to muster.

He gripped my arm, hard, stopping me. His eyes narrowed. "What are you up to?"

"Nothing."

"Lie."

Adrenaline shot through my weakened body giving me a power surge. I jerked my arm away and landed a punch on his jaw that nearly shattered my hand. He was so taken aback he took a step backward. I made a dash for the door, but he tackled me from behind. We tumbled, crashed against the carpet. The tube bounced from my hand and the top popped off. It rolled several feet away.

"I can't let you do whatever it is you're doing." His breath was hot on the back of my neck.

He meant it, too. How did he know I was here? Was he watching my room? "I can't let you stop me."

I jabbed my elbow backward into his rib cage. He grunted but didn't release me. In fact, he tightened his grip.

"What's in the tube, Anna?"

"Nothing that concerns you."

"That, at least, was the truth."

I didn't move, hoping he would give me enough slack to attack him again. He shifted his weight off me. It was all I needed. I sprang to my feet. He was as fast as me and was already on his feet as I spun to face him. I high kicked him in the chest, my foot landing in the center of his breastbone. It jarred me all the way to my back teeth. It was seriously like kicking a brick wall. He lost his footing and stumbled backward. It gave me enough time to snatch up the tube and run out of the library. Kincade didn't follow right away which sounded alarm bells in my head. I didn't have time to consider the implications, though.

With my heart pumping hard, I pounded down the stairs and to the foyer. The front door had been patched but that was all I noticed as I made my way through the dining and then the kitchen, out the door and into the cold night.

Kincade hadn't followed me but I was not so naïve to think he wouldn't, or he wasn't getting my uncle involved. I ran across the lawn to the garage and burst through the door, closing and locking it behind me. I sagged against the door, trying to catch my breath, still clutching the tube in my sweaty palm.

My uncle liked to collect classic cars. He had twenty or so in the oversized garage behind the manor. Some were in various states of restoration. Others were show cars. I flipped on the overhead fluorescent light. It illuminated the metal beasts in a garish yellow glow.

I moved through the garage, looking for something to drive. The problem was I didn't have keys to any of them and I didn't know how to hot wire. How was I going to make my escape if I couldn't even get off my uncle's estate?

Kincade pounded on the door. I jumped and glared at it, willing him to go away.

"Anna, let me in," he called.

I kept walking, ignoring him.

But when the lock clicked, I knew my uncle had arrived with keys. As the door swung open, I flattened myself against the cold concrete and peered under the cars, watching their feet as they entered.

"Anna, don't be stupid. I know you stole the painting," my uncle said.

Damn, that didn't take long for him to figure out.

"Whatever you're planning to do with it..." He paused, then, "don't do it. I know this is about Azriel."

Then he must realize I wasn't going to back down. I refused to answer him. They spread out and started weaving through the parked cars. I inched down the line on my stomach, heading for the back wall. I needed a way out, but I had no idea what that way out was.

"Anna, let me help you," Kincade said.

Help me? How? He couldn't help me. All he'd do was try to talk me out of it. I didn't want to be talked out of it. I was furious. The anger was all-consuming.

"I know how to track him," he said.

Oh, sure. Dangle that carrot in front of me. I wasn't going to take the bait. He was saying that to get me to give up my location. That was so not going to happen.

I paused and stared at his boots ten feet away. He was close. Too close. And I didn't like it. I didn't want his help. I wanted to do this myself. I needed to do this myself. I clutched the tube and scanned the area for something—anything—to use as a weapon, a means of escape.

I noticed the manhole cover and wondered what the hell it was doing here in the floor of the garage. I belly-crawled to it, trying to maintain stealth mode.

"Anna, please," Edward called. He was to my right. I saw his highly polished Ferragamo shoes three rows over behind the Austin-Healey and the Bentley.

The manhole had a handle. I put the tube aside and got on all fours for better leverage. I yanked it open. Hidden hinges made a gawd-awful screech when I opened it.

Great.

"Anna, stop!"

Edward's urgent voice and running footsteps spurred me into action. I snatched the tube and jumped down into the hole, slamming the cover over my head in one fluid motion.

And I was immediately plunged into total and utter darkness.

Fantastic.

CHAPTER 7

MY WHIMPER ECHOED AROUND me. As I stood there letting my eyes adjust to the darkness, my heart rammed hard against my chest. Above me were the muffled voices of Kincade and my uncle. It was enough to spur me into action. I did not want them following me.

But at least one of them would. I clutched the tube in one hand and reached out with the other. Nothing in front of me. I swung my arm to the side and connected with a cool concrete wall. Okay, that was progress. Taking a tentative step, I moved forward sliding my hand down the wall.

Far in the distance was a tiny pinprick of light. I decided my best way out of here was that light. Behind me, the scrape of metal against metal. They opened the cover. Light spilled inside, illuminating the passageway. My heart skipped as Kincade dropped down behind me. I glanced around quickly to get my bearings and saw it was a long tunnel with overhead lighting. I didn't linger to find the switch. I took off down the corridor, my feet pounding against the stone.

A click and suddenly fluorescent lighting flooded the passage-way. A quick glance over my shoulder and there was Kincade chasing me.

He was faster than me, so I had to push my tired body to the limits to make it to that pinprick of light in the distance.

Fuck.

I ran harder. My entire body broke into a sweat. My leg muscles screamed in pain. There was no way out of this. No way I was going outrun Kincade.

But I had to try.

The stale air in the passageway shifted suddenly. A black rancid breeze fluttered through me and I froze, sucking in a sharp breath.

Abaddon, the destroyer angel appeared with a terrifying grin on his horrible face. How the bloody hell did he end up down here? I thought my uncle had warded the entire manor. But maybe because I was underground, the wards didn't work. I didn't have a clue as to how it all worked.

Kincade was at my side a second later, wielding his gun and firing shot after shot at Abaddon. It didn't even faze him. He dodged each bullet, then used his dark angel magic to paralyze me and Kincade. My knees buckled and gave out. I crumbled to the floor in a second. Kincade was frozen, too.

"Fuck all, Anna."

He said it as Abaddon scooped me into his arms, cradling my lifeless body against his chest. He turned from Kincade and started down the passageway, away from him and toward that pinprick of light.

"How fortunate I found you down here," he said. "Lucifer will be happy to have you as his prize and I will be rewarded."

I wanted to say a thousand things, but my voice was as frozen as my body.

The punch of pure air went through both of us and he stopped walking. He stiffened and suddenly, I sensed someone else in the corridor with us. Tingling sensations returned to my limbs, but I was still rendered immobile.

"Release her."

Darius. He'd returned. I wanted to shout for joy.

"Step aside, warrior angel. This does not concern you."

Darius's response was to wield his sword. I heard the shing as he unsheathed it.

The angel of the abyss chuckled. "Your sword does not frighten me, angel."

"Then perhaps mine will." Edward's voice rang out inside the narrow passageway.

Abaddon turned allowing me to see Edward holding his flaming sword standing next to Kincade who pointed his gun at both of us. Perhaps the punch of pure air that went through me released the paralysis in Kincade.

"You have powerful friends, my lovely. But I will not be defeated."

"Put her down," Kincade said, a warning tone in his voice.

My heart pounded harder as Abaddon clutched me tighter. There was no way he was going to let me go. Feeling was starting to come back in my hands and feet.

Do not move. It was Kincade's voice in my head.

He was about to do something crazy and stupid. I braced myself, tensing every muscle for what was to come next.

Kincade fired his gun, landing a shot right between Abaddon's eyes. Abaddon took the bullet in his head as though he'd been bitten by a mosquito. It didn't do anything to deter him or release me. Edward charged with his flaming sword and again I stiffened, tensing every muscle.

Abaddon laughed as he took a step backward away from Edward.

He didn't attack Edward and Kincade as he had before because he held me. Last time, he used his hands to create the spell and now he couldn't. So maybe that was the silver lining. Seeing Edward charge with his flaming sword was a sight to behold. His face was a mask of rage as he held aloft the sword. Kincade backed him up still wielding his gun.

Abaddon forgot Darius was there because suddenly, there was a light surrounding us both. He released me as though I were on fire. I dropped to the floor, crying out as I landed with a thud against the cold stone. I glanced up in time to see Abaddon disappear in a puff of black smoke.

Darius' sword had black blood on it. He had stabbed him. He put it away and knelt next to me, pulling me closer to him. Though feeling returned, paralysis still gripped me.

"Keeper, are you well?"

I was unable to answer. The best I could do was shake my head slowly back and forth once.

"Darius, bring her to her room so I can tend her," Edward said.

As the warrior angel picked me up, Kincade was next to us with annoyance and anger pinched on his face.

"I will take her," he said.

If I didn't know any better, I'd swear he was jealous.

"Her nerves may be damaged from the attack," Darius said.

Wait. What? What did that mean? The destroyer angel magic did something to my nerves?

"All the more reason to get her upstairs and make haste," Edward said, his voice raw and urgent.

"Time is of the essence," Darius said, his voice calm and controlled.

I lifted my eyes as Darius looked down at me and suddenly, I understood what he meant to do. I gave him a nod he would see and then we were gone in a blink. My stomach bottomed out as he sifted us from the narrow passageway under my uncle's manor and into the clouds.

And then I mercifully passed out.

I AWOKE SOMETIME LATER in the bed I'd occupied after my journey to the First Circle to retrieve the Horn of Gabriel. I was in Darius's cloud. I had to admit, I felt a thousand times better than when I woke up after the first Abaddon attack. It seemed as if everything had returned to normal.

"You are awake. Good. How do you feel, Keeper?"

Darius moved into my line of vision as I pushed up on the pillows. I yawned and stretched thankful I was in one piece.

"I feel great. But I bet my uncle and Kincade are pissed you brought me here." I chuckled.

"I will return you soon enough." He pressed a hand against my forehead as if feeling for fever. "Your body temperature has returned to normal. I am pleased."

"I didn't think I'd see you again," I said. "You told me when you handed me the Horn it would be the last time."

He looked away, his cheeks coloring with a blush he managed to control. He took a deep breath, expelled it.

"You have an uncanny ability to continue to find trouble." He met my gaze, his eyes glittering with mirth.

I grinned. "I think trouble finds me. I seem to thank you a lot for coming to my rescue and healing me."

"Not me this time, Keeper." He shook his head and then moved to the door, opened it.

Sariel stepped into the room, his broad-shouldered tall frame filling up the entire doorway. He didn't bother to hide his enormous snowy wings threaded with gold. Every time I saw him, I was always struck by his deep green eyes and the way they sparkled with life.

I sat a little straighter. I hadn't seen him since Rio and was surprised he was here. He smiled as he walked toward the bed.

Darius slipped out, closing the door behind him. Sariel perched on the edge.

"I'm glad to see you're better."

"Thanks to you."

He nodded. "To me."

"What did that angel of the abyss do to me?" I asked.

"He used his powerful dark demon magic to render your body lifeless. If Darius hadn't contacted me, I don't think you would have regained the use of your arms and legs."

"You mean, I would have been paralyzed forever?"

He nodded as concern creased the archangel's forehead. "Anna, Abaddon is one agent of evil sent by Lucifer. The Dark One will never stop trying to turn you to his cause."

"That will never happen." I said it with such vehemence, I almost didn't recognize my own voice.

"I do hope so, Anna."

He shifted on the bed. He had something else he wanted to say.

"There's something else. What is it?"

"Lucifer will continue to send dark angels and demons to trap you, to seduce you, to capture you. He tried with Azriel and failed. Now he sends the destroyer angel. It is a matter of time before he comes after you himself."

My turn to shift uncomfortably in the bed. I didn't like the sound of that. "You think he will?"

"I think he will do whatever necessary to take you."

I crossed my arms, defiance flickering through me. There was no way I was going to let Lucifer win this fight. I'd fight until my death if that's what it took.

Sariel scooted closer on the bed, dropping his voice to a near whisper. "Anna, there is something your uncle doesn't know. Something you need to know."

I didn't like the sound of this at all. "What is it?"

"When the Most High hid the relics around the world, he did it to protect them. To keep them out of the hands of the one dream walker who used their power for his own gain. Now that we are faced with this fight once again for mankind and you are the new appointed Keeper...well, you are more than merely a Keeper of the Holy Relics."

A cold tingling sensation began at the base of my neck. I suspected what he was going to say next.

"And what am I?"

"You are a relic."

I expelled a great breath, reminding me of words I'd heard in the underworld when I followed Azriel and the Spear of Destiny there.

It's useless to me until I have all five and the woman. I cannot use them without her, Lucifer had said.

That's why he wanted me so bad. I sat back in the pillows, not looking at Sariel or anything. I didn't understand what it all meant, nor did I understand why the archangel had that information and Edward didn't.

"How is it even possible?" I asked at last.

"Because of your lineage. Because..." He snapped his mouth shut as though he was about to reveal something he shouldn't.

I narrowed my eyes, suspicious. "Because?"

He forced a smile. "Because you are so powerful. Because you can see the relic's location after you've touched it. Because you know how to wield them."

Lame. That was the first thing that came to mind. Deep down, I suspected there was something else but Sariel didn't want to spill. Fine. I played along like a good girl.

The truth was I didn't know how to wield them. I accidentally figured out the Horn of Gabriel. The Spear of Destiny tried to make me change who and what I was when I held it. Like I had no control over it or myself. I didn't know about the others because I hadn't located them yet.

"With that knowledge, you will be able to defeat Lucifer and his dark army," Sariel said.

I didn't understand how that would be possible either. I opened my mouth to object when he interrupted by placing his hand on my knee.

"Anna, trust in yourself, in your faith. There will come a day when you will be faced with impossible odds."

"You make it sound like I'll face Lucifer and his dark army myself, Sariel." I said it mostly as a joke but the grave look on his face told me I'd hit on something.

"I hope, for your sake, you do not. But if you do, know that I will be there to stand with you." He squeezed my knee and then stood. "I must take my leave."

He left through the door instead of disappearing. I was alone once more.

There were things I didn't understand and perhaps never would. I decided that was just going to have to be okay.

I leaned back in the pillows, my mind racing with thoughts of what to do next. I lost the painting in the underground garage, so my initial Destroy Azriel plot had gone awry. It was probably a bad idea but something deep inside drove me. Something dark and dangerous and stupid. My mind was clouded with thoughts of revenge. I was unable to remove those thoughts from my mind, no matter how hard I tried.

And anyway, I wasn't getting out of this place without Darius' assistance.

I pushed off the bed and stood. Darius hadn't bothered to change my clothes or tuck me in the bed this time. One item missing was my jade handled dagger. A cursory glance of the room indicated it was nowhere to be found.

I left the room and stepped into the hall. Darius' home was in the clouds, a stark white residence with nothing on the walls. The floors, however, shimmered in the overhead glow—they weren't exactly lights since nothing mechanical or man-made seemed to be here. In this light, the floor looked like it had stardust scattered over it which delighted every bit of my female senses.

I squashed that in a hurry. I didn't need to get all mushy about Darius' sparkly floor. I headed down the hall and found him in the room where my uncle and I made plans to retrieve the Horn of Gabriel. Darius stood at the mantle of the white marble fireplace, turning when he heard me enter.

I halted in place and looked him over. Almost all his feathers had turned black. For the first time, I noticed his skin had a sickly pallor. Dark circles had formed under his eyes. I thought of what Kincade said—that it was demon poison coursing through him instead of him turning into a Fallen. I hated both fates but was glad it wasn't the latter.

"Do you have my dagger?"

He held the sheath out in the palm of his hand. Grateful to have it back in my possession, I strapped it to my waist once again.

"You are ready to return to your uncle's, no doubt."

I started to respond but snapped my mouth shut. I gave a sharp shake of my head. "No."

His brows knit in confusion. "No?"

"When you took me out of the underground passageway, I was trying to escape."

He tilted his head to the side as though he didn't understand. "Why?"

I clenched my fists. One word came to mind: Revenge. I wanted revenge and death and destruction on Azriel. I wanted to destroy something dear to him. And I wanted him to know it was me.

"Ah, you do not wish to tell me. Do you, Keeper?"

I wanted to but I wasn't sure if he would understand why I was so driven. Azriel got away with doing many horrible things to me. I wanted him to pay.

"I don't think you'll understand."

One corner of his mouth ticked in a smile before he contained it. "Perhaps I will."

I swallowed hard. "I want to destroy Azriel's underground nightclub."

"Azriel has an underground nightclub?"

"Yes, in Dallas. Below a crypt in a cemetery."

He didn't speak for a long moment, then asked, "Why do you wish to do this?"

"Because of all the horrific things he did to me."

"Eye for an eye?"

"And a tooth for a tooth," I replied.

"Resist not evil, Keeper."

I rolled my eyes. "Spare me the scripture, Darius."

Annoyance flashed across his handsome face before he got it under control. "Are you asking me for help in this endeavor?"

"I am. I want you to take me to Dallas."

His face hardened as disappointment flashed through his eyes. "I will take you there but that is all."

And leave me. Got it. The rest was up to me. I didn't need his help anyway. I'd find a way to destroy that crypt no matter what.

"Fine. Let's go."

⸺✦⸺

TRUE TO HIS WORD, Darius flashed me all the way to Dallas and dropped me off at the corner of Glory and Peace Avenue in Greenwood Cemetery.

And left me there in the dark.

It took several agonizing moments before I got my roiling stomach under control. No matter how hard I prepared for the flashing, it always left me woozy. I bent over, hands on my knees, deep breathing in the chilly night air. Thankful for it burning my lungs and clearing away the illness.

Standing straight, I glanced around the desolate cemetery. I had no idea what time it was but judging by the evening sounds, I guessed it was around midnight.

Good. Things would be in full swing in the nightclub under the crypt. I decided to make a quick club run to scope things out. My hope was a plan would come to me while I was there.

I headed down the street and into the cemetery trying to ignore the nerves pounding through me. I had a sinking sensation in the pit of my stomach telling me I was about to make another bad decision. Determination overwhelmed good sense and I pressed onward.

Oh well. Just another one in a long line of bad decisions.

The crypt was easy to find. Four columns dominated the front steps leading up to a medieval-looking door with heavy iron hinges. The same two leather-clad guys—demons—flanked the door. Overhead, *Luciferus* was in large stone letters across the top.

Yep, I was in the right place.

I headed up the concrete steps and paused. The two demons looked at me with curious red eyes. I straightened my spine and steeled my nerves.

"I'm here to see Azriel," I said.

They both exchanged a glance. The one on the left said, "Who you?"

"Anna. He knows me."

Before either of them responded, Azriel's voice boomed out from overhead. "We are well acquainted. Let her in."

I glanced up and noticed for the first time the camera perched in the top corner of the crypt. How funny Azriel had a security system. Was he worried about trespassers? It made my plans for blowing it up a little more difficult.

The two demons reached for the doors and opened them at the same time, the iron hinges groaning. I stepped inside and paused. Behind me the doors slammed shut, sealing me in shadowy darkness. One lone torch lit up the interior, the yellow-orange light flickering over the silent tomb in the center.

That same horror-chill I experienced that first day I came here rushed through me. Gooseflesh exploded across my bare arms. The last time I was here, I recalled one of the demons, whom I called Tank, pressed a hidden button on the tomb to open it. I ran my fingers along the top edge of the tomb and then heard a click. The trapdoor opened in the floor, the damp earth smell wafting up to me as I peered down at the exposed stairs.

Good times.

I headed down the stairs. The closer I got to the bottom, the louder the music thumped through the walls. At the bottom of the stairs, another door. I pulled it open and stepped inside.

I didn't think I would ever end up here again. I never wanted to end up here again, that was for sure. But I wanted Azriel to pay and I wanted to send him a message loud and clear.

Inside was the yawning abyss of dark, death metal and supernaturals beckoning me to enter. Fluorescent paint splattered across every surface, illuminating the place in strange colors. The crowd was full of vampires, fallen angels and demons. That demon smell pierced through the putrid scent of sweat and sex and booze.

I weaved my way through the shoulder-to-shoulder crowd to the bar. I didn't need a drink. I didn't even want a drink. Hell, I didn't even know what my next move was going to be.

I took a seat at the end and glanced down the length of the bar. The crowd was a mix of vampires, and angels. A few gave me cursory glances. Others looked at me like they thought I didn't belong there.

They were right. I didn't.

The bartender spotted me and came down to take my order. "What can I get you?"

I met her gaze. Her long black hair was plaited, hanging over one shoulder. She had piercing blue eyes, a square jaw with a dimple in the chin, small pert nose, sharp-angled cheekbones and wings.

"Nothing, thanks," I said, finally finding my voice.

A dark brow lifted. "Nothing?"

"She'll have a whiskey." Azriel appeared beside me, deciding my order for me. Unlike most of the times we met, he didn't bother to hide his wings. They stretched out behind him like a giant bird, the black feathers almost sparkling in the wicked half-light.

"Will she, brother? She said nothing."

Brother? I glanced from her to Azriel and back again.

"Whiskey. Two fingers neat," Azriel said. Then turned to me, "That is how you like it, isn't it, *chérie*?"

How did he know that?

Who was I kidding? Azriel knew all kinds of things about me.

"Coming up," the girl said. She pulled out a highball glass and poured the whiskey. Then slid the glass over to me. She paused a moment, looking between the two of us. Waiting.

"That will be all, Astrid," he said, dismissing her.

Astrid shot him a glare full of daggers before strolling down to the other end of the bar.

"She called you brother." I gripped the glass but didn't drink. My stomach was in such knots, I wasn't sure the whiskey would do me any good.

"She did." He nodded agreement but that was clearly all he was willing to share. "What brings you here, *chérie*?"

"Just visiting the old neighborhood."

His expression told me he was far from believing my story. "A stroll down memory lane does not suit you."

He was right. It didn't. I was never one to revisit the old 'hood for good times sake. I wasn't the sentimental type.

"Let's say I have some unfinished business." I cut him a sideways glance.

A smile quirked his mouth. "Is this what you alluded to before? The hunter becomes the hunted?"

May as well play along. "I found you, didn't I?"

"Indeed." He turned, learning his back against the bar and propping his elbows up on either side. "I would ask if you've finally come to your senses and decided to help me, but I know better."

I nodded. "You do."

I sensed Astrid hovering close by, likely trying to eavesdrop on our conversation. I kept my attention focused on Azriel. Something about him was different. He wasn't his usual cheeky or perverted self.

"So, what are you doing here?" He genuinely looked perplexed.

"I came to kill you."

I don't know what made me say it. The second the words left my mouth, I heard Astrid inhale with surprise. Azriel's head snapped in her direction, his eyes narrowed in a heated glare. She skittered down to the end of the bar finally out of earshot. When she turned her back, I got a good look at her wings. In the dim light, they were much smaller than Azriel's. When the light caught them just right, silvery threads sparkled through the grayish feathers.

I looked back at Azriel wondering who she was to him. She called him brother but that didn't mean he was. Maybe it was a pet name for him. If so, weird.

He gave me his full attention once again and plastered on his familiar wolfish smile. "Do you think you can pull that off?" He reached for me, twining a loose strand of hair around his forefinger.

At least he was back to his old self. I was most familiar with this Azriel. That, oddly, gave me comfort.

I slapped his hand away. "Don't touch me, you sleazeball."

He held his hands up in surrender. "You are welcome to try all you want, *chérie*. In the meantime, tell Astrid to give you whatever you want on the house."

He pushed off the bar and sauntered away, disappearing through the crowd. I blew out a breath, annoyed. Why did I let him engage me in conversation? I gripped the glass of whiskey so hard my fingers ached.

Astrid sidled down the length of the bar and stopped in front of me. She made a show of wiping down the lacquered top while keeping a keen eye on the gyrating crowd on the dance floor.

"Who are you?" she asked, her gaze never meeting mine.

"It doesn't matter." Because in the grand scheme of things, it didn't. She wouldn't care I was the Keeper of the Holy Relics any more than the vampire at the other end of the bar.

"It matters to Azriel. Therefore, it matters to me."

I lifted my gaze and met hers. Those eyes were sparkling and brilliant and took me aback. I had never seen eyes that blue before.

"You called him brother."

She nodded. "I did."

"Is he?"

"He is. We have different fathers."

That explained a lot. She stopped wiping and leaned closer to me, dropping her voice. "Who are you?"

"My name is Anna."

Her face went completely still as she peered at me. "Anna Walker?"

I blinked surprise. "Yeah."

She straightened, her gaze focused once again on the crowd. "I want in."

I frowned. "Want in what?"

Her sharp glare made me shift on the barstool. "Don't make me say it out loud here."

I continued to frown. "I have no idea what you're talking about."

She huffed and tossed the rag under the bar. "Meet me at the Bradford grave in one hour."

"How will I find it in the dark?"

She rolled her eyes. "It's the one with the angel statue missing a hand."

With that, she headed to the other end of the bar and ignored me as if I didn't exist.

Just what I wanted to do. Hang out in a cemetery in the middle of the night. But then, what else did I have to do?

CHAPTER 8

I LEFT THE UNDERGROUND club after downing the whiskey in one gulp. It burned all the way down to my toes.

I stepped into the night, my ears ringing from the loud music I left behind. I took a deep breath, inhaling the crisp night air, and shivered a little. I blew out my breath, watching it crystallize. December in Texas wasn't like December in England. While it was warmer here, there was still a cold bite to the wind which made me wish I had a coat. At least the whiskey warmed me from the inside. I clutched my elbows and headed through the graves to find this Bradford grave Astrid mentioned.

I thought about her as I walked along the pathway, trying to make out the carved names on headstones in the pale moonlight. The statues stood like silent sentries over the dead, guarding them as if waiting for Judgment Day.

I spotted the angel with the missing hand and headed that direction. Astrid was already there waiting for me. Her hands were shoved deep into the pockets of her oversized coat. I envied how warm she looked standing there in the darkness, the moonlight shining down on her like a halo.

"I don't have much time, so I'll get right to the point," she said when I arrived. "You intend to kill Azriel. I intend to help you."

"You want to help me?" I repeated, sounding dumbfounded.

"Are you dense? Yes."

"Why?"

"I have my reasons."

I didn't understand. No one wanted to help me take out Azriel. Not Darius. Not even Kincade, who, despite his claims of hunting him for ages, seemed completely uninterested in the idea. Not that I ever asked him. We'd never discussed the subject.

My mind worked quickly to come up with an excuse. Azriel was my kill. I wanted his blood on my hands as payment for all the hell he'd put me through.

"You can't."

"I realize you may not want my help, but you'd be foolish not to take it. I have certain...abilities."

I lifted an eyebrow. "Like what?"

"I can't tell you. I can't even show you." She glanced back toward the crypt where the underground club resided and shifted from one foot to the other, nervous. "What is your plan?"

"My plan was to blow up the damn crypt but seeing as how I don't have any type of explosives..." I paused for dramatic effect, letting my words trail off.

Her head snapped back in my direction. "Give me two hours. You'll have what you need."

She stripped off her coat and tossed it to me. I caught it midair.

"You'll need that," she said and then took off at a dead run back toward the crypt without waiting for a reply.

Was I supposed to hang out here for two hours? How did she know what I needed? Where was she going? At least she left me her coat which was still warm from her body heat.

I heaved a sigh and glanced around. There was a concrete bench at the next grave. I perched on the edge, the cold seeping into my bones, and waited.

***

WAITING WAS NOT MY favorite thing. I was an impatient sort, so having to sit in the cold dark waiting for Astrid to make an appearance started to get on my last nerve. I gave up sitting and paced the length of the walkway in the cemetery, wondering why I didn't just leave and find another way to blow up the crypt.

But for some reason I stayed and paced, my blood pressure rising with every step. Where the hell was she?

Being alone in that cemetery gave me a lot of time to think about her. When I got close to her, I didn't sense anything supernatural about her. With Azriel, I smelled cinnamon. With demons, I smelled death, decay, and rot. With her, nothing.

Come to think of it, I didn't smell anything with Sariel either.

Why was that? Because he was of a higher order?

One thing was for sure. Nothing was consistent with these angels, fallen or otherwise.

I was ready to give up on her when I saw a form heading my direction. It wasn't Astrid, though. It was a man judging by the shadowy shape. His face came into view as he neared.

His height was that of Kincade's—tall enough to stand a head over my non-petite frame. His face was all hard angles with a five o'clock shadow. He was dressed all in black, complete with hoodie covering his head, so it was hard to make out much else about his appearance. I inhaled the air around him, trying to get a read but came up with nothing. He wasn't angel or demon. Perhaps something else? He halted near me.

All I saw under that hood were his eyes. They were nothing short of spectacular. They held an iridescent otherworldly glow with a kaleidoscope of colors. Blue, green, purple. Mesmerizing.

"You Anna?"

"Yeah," I replied, wary.

"Astrid sent me." He waved for me to follow him and headed back up the walkway.

"Who are you?"

"Someone you can trust," was all he said.

But I didn't even know if I trusted Astrid.

"You got a name?" I asked. "You know mine. Seems fair to know yours."

"Killian." He threw the name over his shoulder as if it were an afterthought.

As soon as I heard his name, images of a shimmering sword-wielding king complete with golden crown burst into my mind. Where had I heard that name before? Or was this another one of those mind tricks? Like when I was certain I met Azriel before and recently realized the horror of learning the truth about him—he was the boy I once loved in disguise.

"Nice to meet you, Killian. Where are we going?"

"To Astrid."

Okay. That didn't explain anything to me. But fine. I'd go with it. I shoved my hands deep into the pockets of her coat and continued to follow him. We ended up back at the crypt. He didn't bother to acknowledge the two demons standing guard. They, in turn, seemed uninterested in him. He pulled open the heavy door as though it weighed nothing.

Noted. The guy was like super strong or something.

Instead of entering the underground club through the tomb, he continued through the crypt. Shadowy darkness pressed all around us making it hard to see anything at all. Killian, though, walked through the place with no problems at all.

Almost as though he could see. Like a cat sees in the dark.

Cat eyes! Yes, that's what those eyes reminded me of. They glowed in the darkness with a wondrous strangeness.

He halted at the back wall of the crypt and turned to face me. All I saw were those eyes of his and his chin beneath his hood.

"We wait here."

"Okay," I replied.

Though I didn't know who or what we were waiting for. I didn't complain. At least we were out of the cold night air. The scrape of concrete against concrete sounded nearby. The tomb opened and Astrid ascended the stairs to join us. I slipped off the coat and handed it back to her. In the flickering darkness, I noticed her face seemed paler than it had before. Sweat beaded her forehead. She was out of breath, as though the short flight of stairs winded her. And, I noted, she had dark circles under eyes that weren't there before.

Huh.

"Thanks," she said, then eyed Killian. "Any problems?"

"None."

"Good." She turned to me then. "Here's how this is going to work. You'll follow me back to the bar. Azriel is in his apartment doing some private entertainment." She shuddered with revulsion. I imaged what sort of private entertainment that was. "I have everything you need behind the bar ready for pick up."

"Everything like what?" I asked.

She leaned closer and dropped her voice. "C4. Blasting caps. Etcetera."

Her response took me aback. What the hell was etcetera? "How did you get that?"

She cut a glance to Killian who gave her a quick shake of his head. I saw his chin and nothing more. His hoodie continued to shroud his expression.

"I'll explain later. Do you still want to do this?"

"Yes." The emphatic word was out of my mouth before I had time to change my mind.

"Then let's go."

Despite my best judgment, I followed her down the steps of the tomb back into the club. Killian fell in step behind me. I stayed right behind Astrid as if nothing was amiss. As soon as we were inside, she headed for the bar. I kept pace with her while Killian broke off and disappeared through the crowd.

Behind the bar, Astrid reached down and picked up a black duffel. Without a word, she shoved the bag into my hands, gave me a nod and then turned on her heel. I watched her make her way down the length of the bar, exit from behind it and then meld into the crowd.

I was left standing there holding the duffel and wondering why the hell I agreed to this. I glanced out at the dance floor, the loud punk rock music vibrating through me. Waiters, waitresses, demons, vampires, fallen angels. What had happened to the world? This wasn't how things were supposed to turn out. The world wasn't supposed to be inhabited by these underworld supernatural creatures.

There were a few humans in the mix. I wondered about that. I hadn't seen any the last time I was here. How did they figure into this sordid underground world?

I didn't know.

Maybe I didn't care.

I made my way through the club, ignoring the sights of debauchery by the supernaturals who crawled along the seedy underbelly of humanity. One thing I learned was very few of us saw them. The normal human could not see the darkness slithering through mankind, nor were they aware of Fallen high lords killing guardian angels and stealing human souls so Lucifer could build his army.

I wound my way through the crowd, garnering a few glances here and there, but for the most part they ignored me. I headed for the door marked Office and walked through it like I owned the place. No one stopped me. Inside, silence descended. I found myself standing in the middle of the room where I met Azriel for the first time.

I was alone.

The décor hadn't changed. There was still the plush red carpet covering the floor, a settee and several chairs in front of the gas fireplace that hosted a cheerful, flickering fire. The oak bar loaded with decanters, bottles and glasses. The door to the private apartment was closed. I went to it, pressed my ear against it but heard nothing. I wrapped my fingers around the knob and tried it, slowly. It was locked.

But Astrid said Azriel was in there entertaining.

I dropped the duffel, knelt and unzipped it.

Astrid wasn't kidding. Inside was C4, blasting caps, a detonator.

And a note with instructions on how to make it all work.

I blinked, staring at the hurried script handwriting. It was simply signed "A."

"Astrid. Who the bloody hell are you?" I muttered.

I went to work, placing the C4 around the room. I wanted to make sure the place was gutted by the time I hit the detonator. I wanted to watch it cave in on itself. An eerie sense of doom came over me like a sudden wave of nausea. The hair on the back of my neck stood at attention. I put a shaking hand to my head.

Had to be nerves. I shoved it aside and continued.

As I placed the last charge, the apartment door lock clicked and suddenly it swung open. My heart clawed its way to my throat as I snatched up the bag with the detonator and started to back toward the exit, keeping my eyes on the door.

I slammed into something smelling a lot like a demon. The terrifying thing was I never heard him enter.

That must have been that wave of nausea I ignored.

Crap.

The fallen angel who came through the private apartment door was not Azriel. It was some other high lord with which I managed to come face to face. How did I know he was a high lord? While Azriel smelled like cinnamon, this one reminded me of peach cobbler. His black wings spanned nearly twenty feet—bigger than Azriel's. His hair was white blond, flowing down over his shoulders. He had a chiseled face that looked as though it had been carved from alabaster. His pale white skin shimmered, as though kissed by starlight. His eyes? Crimson.

He was an albino with black wings the color of coal which was strange. Quite the dichotomy.

I never figured out why these Fallen high lords smelled so decadent.

He halted in his tracks as the demon behind me put a hand on my shoulder to keep me in place. We stared at each other a long, hard, silent moment. His gaze roamed over me, paused at the bag in my hand and then went back to my face. He gave a glimmer of a smile.

"A human without a guardian. How did you find your way in here, love?"

I thought of Kincade, my supposed guardian, and wondered where he was. Wondered if he was coming after me. I shifted from one foot to the other, aware of my dangerous predicament.

I sucked it up. I didn't need Kincade. I was smart and savvy. I could get out of this without him.

Plus, I had the detonator. Not that I wanted to use it while I was still inside the place. Dying was not an option today.

"Azriel invited me. Is he here?" I put on my best sexy voice, hoping it would convince him I was here to see the fallen angel. I had no interest in Azriel other than to see his blood splattered all over the walls and floor.

"Sorry, no. I suppose you're the new bitch since the one he had died." He had a curious glint in his eyes as he looked me over.

My ears perked at that. "She did?"

"Stupid whore did nothing but waste his time, though I suppose he wasn't interested in her for anything other than what he got."

I imagined what that was. I wondered if the albino referred to my cousin, Lexi. I hadn't seen her in person since she betrayed me on the rooftop of that Hong Kong high rise. I dream walked her once while she was in Hell to find out the location of the Horn of Gabriel. She told me to get lost. I wanted to go back for her, to get her away from Azriel, but I'd been a little busy and hadn't gotten around to it.

"What's your name, love?"

I considered giving him a false name, but what was the point? He was about to be dust anyway. "Anna."

He made a dismissal hand motion to the demon guard behind me. The demon removed his hand from my shoulder. A blast of acid rock filtered in as he opened the door, then closed it with a soft snick.

"Looks like it's just the two of us now, love. Take off your clothes."

Yeah, right. Like that was going to happen. "Kind of forward, aren't you?"

"Azriel's bitch is my bitch. Take off your clothes and spread your legs. Just like that Lexi cunt."

It had been Lexi and now she was dead. A wave of guilt washed over me. Not that she wanted to be saved. I doubted she had any regret for betraying me and letting demons, minions, Azriel and others use her like a dirty whore. The last time I saw her, she was in a pitiful state. Maybe she found peace in death.

He unbuttoned his jeans, unzipped them and opened the fly to show me he was commando. His skin below the waist was also star-kissed and shimmered. Not that I expected it to be any different from the rest of him. I don't know why I was surprised.

"I'm not sure who you think I am, but I'm not that kind of girl."

"Any girl Azriel invites here is that kind of girl. Are you going to strip, or am I going to do it for you?"

This was not going the way I planned. I swung around to the door, intending to flee when I heard the lock click. I tried the knob, but it didn't budge. He used his demon magic to lock me inside. I spun around to face him, trying to decide my next move. His smile was not a pleasant one. In fact, it reminded me a lot of Azriel's wolf smile I hated so much. He stuck his hand down his pants and pulled out his albino cock, pumping his hand up and down.

For fuck's sake.

I sighed.

"Dude...If you're trying to arouse me, that ain't doing it."

He moved toward me in a flash of light, shoving me against the closed door with such violence, it jarred the duffel from my hand and rattled my bones. He pressed his brick-hard body against me, shoving his hard length against my abdomen. One hand wrapped around my throat, his fingers pressing into my flesh, while his other hand groped me.

I ignored the fear trickling through my veins. Sure, I was in a bad spot, but I wasn't going to lose my cool. Not yet. The butterfly tattoo on my left shoulder began to burn, the heat coursing through me. A darkness I had never sensed before whispered through me.

Use the demon magic.

The demon magic churned inside me, threatening to boil over. I tasted it in the back of my throat.

"Let me go." My voice didn't even waver. Not even a little. I was kinda proud of that.

"I'm going to turn you around and then I'm going to fuck you in the ass. How about that, love?"

This guy was starting to piss me off.

"How about you take your filthy hands off me before I kick your ass?"

He laughed. Like it was the best joke ever.

The demon magic bubbled through me, pounding into my skull. My eyes narrowed as I dropped my head and imagined the way he'd look flat on his back. A pop, a blast and then suddenly he *was* flat on his back. He grunted as he snapped in his wings and rolled to his side, his crimson eyes wide with shock. It told me everything I needed to know about him in that one second.

He wasn't so tough even though he thought he was.

Albino climbed to his feet and came at me again. This time I was ready for him and so was the demon magic boiling inside me. I imagined it striking him. I tried not to act shocked when it did, hitting him square in the chest. He growled, baring his white teeth and charged once more.

This guy was a glutton for punishment. I suddenly remembered the dagger at my waist. Thankfully, he hadn't bothered to search me to see if I had a weapon. He didn't know I had the jade-handled dagger. I slipped it from the sheath at my waist and stabbed him in the ribs as he barreled into me. He stumbled backward, putting his hand against his side. The dagger came out covered in blood.

"You bitch."

"Call me what you will. I don't have time to play games with you. Now put your cock up, unlock this door and let me the fuck out of here." I waved the bloody knife at him to press my point.

He used his demon magic to unlock the door. I heard the click behind me. With his erection gone, the head of his flaccid penis barely peeked out of his jeans. My own demon magic swirled inside me, but I hadn't a clue how to use it to lock and unlock doors.

"When you go back to where you came from, give Azriel a message for me, will ya?"

He backed toward the apartment door across from me still holding his side. Blood seeped between his fingers. "And what is that?"

"Tell him Anna said hi." I flashed a smile.

He disappeared through the door to the apartment. It closed and locked behind him. I chuckled, wondering if he locked it to keep me out. I wiped the blood off the dagger on the thigh of my black cargo pants, then sheathed it. Then I snatched up the duffel and hauled ass out of there.

I ran through the club, back to the door, up the concrete steps and out of the crypt. I barreled down the steps and halted on the gravel road in front of the place, dropping the duffel at my feet. I kneeled, unzipped the bag and pulled out the detonator.

My thumb hovered over the button as I took a deep breath and gave the crypt one last look. After this, there was no turning back.

"Press it, Anna," Astrid said from behind me.

When I barreled out of the crypt, I hadn't noticed she was there. Glancing up, I saw her standing several feet away. Killian was next to her. The two demons that guarded the door were dead.

"Do it," she urged.

I pressed it.

It started as a loud rumble beneath the earth followed by a muffled boom as every charge went off simultaneously. It was like watching an earthquake as the ground split and then caved. The crypt in front of me shook, the pillars cracking and then falling in on the roof.

I snatched up the bag and ran away from the explosion as the stone mausoleum came crashing down and fire belched from the ground where the club had been. Astrid and Killian started running the second I hit the detonator and were several feet ahead of me.

I halted to watch it burn, satisfaction oozing from my pores at the deed. I sent Azriel a strong message he couldn't fuck with me anymore.

Idly, I wondered if the albino had flashed away before the place was destroyed. I imagined the screams of all those demons, fallen angels, vampires and humans as the roof caved in through the underground club. Maybe I should have remorse for killing them all, but I didn't.

Suddenly, Astrid dropped to the ground as though she was tackled by an invisible linebacker. Killian fell to his knees next to her, gathering her up and pulled her into his arms. As he did so, his hoodie fell backward off his head. I was finally able to see him clearly.

I stifled the gasp that wanted to erupt. His hair was the color of spun gold. I wasn't sure if it was the firelight flicking over his hair giving it that illumination or not. But that wasn't even the thing that startled me the most.

He had pointed ears.

Was he Fae or elf?

"Astrid, can you hear me? Are you all right?"

I moved closer to see her convulsing in his arms. He held tight, trying to keep her small vibrating body contained.

"I'm here. I'm here," he crooned.

He clutched her tight, pressing her face into his chest and stroking her hair. I was in dumbfounded silence, trying to figure out what was happening to her. When her body finally stopped trembling, she went limp. He pulled her face away, cradling her head in his arms as though she were a delicate creature. She was unconscious.

"Is she...okay?"

"She will be." Killian lifted his face, that otherworldly gaze meeting mine. "Thank you."

"For what?"

"You helped her."

I didn't understand. "How?"

"She wants to explain it to you herself. And she will when she wakes," he said.

This was getting weirder and weirder. As I watched him hold her, that image of him wielding a sword and wearing a crown came flooding back into my mind. With a tentative touch, I reached out with my mind to his. He was aware of what I was trying to do, though, and shoved me back with a mere thought. His gaze never left mine.

But I sensed much in that brief second of connection. He was not human, that much I knew. There was something ancient and ethereal about him.

"Are you Fae?" I asked.

"Are you?" he countered.

"No."

"You are no mere human."

My brows drew together. Had he sensed my dream walking abilities? "Perhaps not," I agreed. "I can see into the minds and dreams of others."

He was silent a long moment. "I am Fae."

Sure, why not? There were already vampires and angels walking around under the noses of humans. Why not Fae, too?

I kept my mouth shut, though, and nodded understanding. I had more questions but didn't get a chance to ask them.

"Well done, my dear. Well done, indeed."

I recognized that voice. A voice I hoped to never hear again.

My head snapped up. There, walking out of the flames, was Abaddon, a broad smile on his narrow face. I snatched my dagger out of the sheath and pointed it at him. It didn't even faze him.

"I must say, I'm impressed."

My brow furrowed. "Stay back."

"You and I would make a formidable pair, don't you think? Come with me." He ignored my command and stretched a hand to me.

Killian scooped up Astrid and took off without so much as a by-your-leave. Couldn't blame him one bit. Shit just got real.

Before I answered, someone shouted my name. Kincade ran toward me out of the shadows. He halted a few feet from me. Our gazes met. How the hell did he find me?

There were things he wanted to say but didn't. Maybe he wanted to chastise me for leaving him behind. Maybe he wanted to tell me what a huge mistake I made blowing up the crypt. Maybe I didn't care. He eyed the destruction, the firelight flickering on his face giving it a strange glow. Almost as though he shimmered.

"What did you do?" He turned back to me and our eyes met again.

My gut clenched at how disappointed he sounded. "What I had to do."

"And a fine job she did, too."

"What's he doing here?" Kincade nodded toward Abaddon, never taking his eyes off me.

I shrugged. "No idea. He just showed up."

"I came because the demon magic inside you calls to me, Anna. It came alive while you were inside with the albino. When he threatened to rape you. Put down the dagger, my dear."

I kept my hand steady as I looked at him, aware Kincade inched toward me. "Stay away from me, Kincade."

He halted. "Anna—"

"I'm not going back with you." I shook my head.

"That's right. She's coming with me." Abaddon nodded as though this was common knowledge.

"You stay out of this." I waved my dagger at him, then addressed Kincade again. "I have more to do. Azriel wasn't here."

His mouth drew down in a grimace. "If you start down this path, I can't protect you."

"What path?" My brows knit. I didn't understand what he was talking about as the darkness continued to consume me. "I have one purpose. Find Azriel. Kill him."

"The path of vengeance," Kincade clarified. "The path of darkness. You killed innocent people. You're letting your anger and hate consume you."

"I killed demons and fallen angels and vampires," I insisted.

"And humans," he clarified.

A pang of guilt pierced me for a moment before dissipating into a dark cloud. "It's what had to be done. I'm tired of him hunting me. I have to do something about it."

Abaddon moved closer. "Then come with me, my dear. I will help you find him. Together, we will destroy him."

"This isn't the way to do that, Anna," Kincade said.

My head swiveled in Abaddon's direction, ignoring Kincade. Fury raged within me, burning the demon magic through me, pushing me toward the destroyer angel. Urging me. He waved the fingers of his outstretched hand, motioning me to take his hand. To accept his help.

Irresistible temptation pulled me.

"Anna, no. Don't do it."

"Anna, Kincade is right. If you embrace the darkness, we can no longer help you."

Another familiar voice.

My heart skipped as Decker stepped out of the shadows and stood next to his brother. I wondered how Kincade managed to find him and convince him to help track me down. Aside from that, I wondered how they managed to get to me so fast. I had a pretty good head start with Darius's help.

My gaze narrowed on Decker. Had he managed to get his powers of teleportation back? Could he turn invisible once again? Darkness boiled again deep inside me, weakening me. Pushing me closer and closer to the edge.

An edge I no longer resisted. I had to do this.

"Tell my uncle I'm sorry."

I reached for Abaddon's outstretched hand.

CHAPTER 9

MY FINGERTIPS WERE CENTIMETERS away from Abaddon's. Absolute delight on his wicked face should have clued me into my bad decision, but no. I kept reaching for him. Somehow, deep in the dark recesses of my mind, I was doing the right thing.

Kincade's big body slammed into me, tackling me and shoving me to the ground, making every bone rattle all the way to my back teeth. The jade-handled dagger fell from my hand. His hefty weight crushed me underneath him against the cold concrete.

"I'm not letting you do this." His hot breath trickled over my ear.

Something inside me snapped. "Get off me, you overgrown muscled goon."

The high-pitched squeal of the demon gun preceded two consecutive blasts followed by Decker's vile cursing.

"He's gone," Decker said.

I wiggled beneath Kincade, trying to free myself.

"Stop struggling, dammit, Anna."

The dark magic coiled, tightened like a snake ready to attack. I growled, deep and low in my throat, and allowed it to consume me. Bright light exploded all around us and suddenly Kincade's weight was gone. I rolled to my feet, my breath see-sawing in and out and admired my handiwork. He was on the ground, shaking his head trying to clear his senses. Decker charged me.

I threw out a hand and that dark magic burst from me, hitting him square in the chest. He flew backward and landed so hard, there was a shower of gravel. He skidded to a halt.

A demonic laugh bubbled up and out.

What the fuck is wrong with you?

Kincade's angry voice burst inside my head. I winced, a glimmer of my normal self returning. I stumbled back a step, my hand pressing the side of my head. My mind was muddled. I couldn't think.

The momentary distraction gave Kincade enough time to wrap his steely arms around me, crushing me in his embrace. I struggled again, trying to get free.

Stop it, Anna. NOW.

But that dark magic was there once again, twisting into a tight knot ready to strike.

Something blunt and hard smacked me in the side of the head. Pain exploded and then there was darkness.

WHEN I AWOKE, I was on top of a bed still in my clothes. Everything that could hurt did hurt. I stared up at the unfamiliar ceiling trying to figure out where I was. I wanted to bolt to a sitting position. Instead, I groaned.

"Good morning, sunshine," Kincade said. Sarcasm and annoyance laced his tone.

That didn't bode well.

I didn't move but by the location of his voice, he was off to my left. And pissed.

"What happened?" I croaked. My throat was scratchy and dry.

"Oh, you don't remember?"

I was too tired and hurt too bad to fly an acid retort. "No."

"It's because she's more than marked," Decker said, sounding bored.

Decker. The vision of him flying backward and smacking the gravel road flickered through my mind. Did I do that?

"You almost turned yourself over to Abaddon. Remember that?"

Okay, yeah, he was super pissed at me. I squeezed my eyes shut and tried to remember but the images were fuzzy. Like I was looking through foggy glass.

"Not really."

"She doesn't remember because the black magic in her veins clouds her vision," Decker said. "Abaddon said it himself."

"You blew up the crypt," Kincade said, ignoring his brother entirely. His voice was tight. Controlled. "I don't know how. I do know I stopped you from joining the destroyer angel."

That landed.

The memory surfaced then—Kincade slamming into me. Hard. That explained the pain radiating through my body.

"You called me an overgrown, muscled goon," he added. "For the record, I am not a goon."

I huffed weakly. Of all the things—

"Abaddon didn't use his magic on any of us," he continued. "Why do you think that is, Miss Walker?"

How the bloody hell should I know?

"I'll tell you why," he went on, not waiting for a verbal reply. "Because he sensed you were close to turning away from the Light."

"You magicked us both," Decker added. "Sorry about your head but I had to."

I reached up to touch the side of my head with gentle fingertips. A huge knot formed there. I vaguely recalled hearing the whine of his demon gun. He must have used the butt of it to smack me in the side of the head to knock me out.

Likely how to get me under control.

The demon magic inside you calls to me.

Abaddon's words whispered through my mind. He was right. The demon magic inside me did more than call to him. I somehow used it to defend myself from the albino and Kincade and Decker.

"I knew you were marked," Kincade said. "I did *not* know how deeply." His gaze pinned me in place. "Tell me exactly what he did."

Crap. I didn't want to have this conversation right now. Or ever. I didn't want to tell Kincade anything.

But seeing as how he saved my ass from the clutches of Abaddon, I probably needed to tell him the whole story.

"How did Azriel mark you?" he demanded.

Wait a second. I never told Kincade that. "How did you know about that?"

I wanted to push to a sitting position and glare at him, but it hurt too much to move. I remained where I was, trying to sound angry and accusatory from the fetal position.

Silence descended in the room.

"I think I'll wait in the other room," Decker said. The door opened and closed as he made his getaway.

Lucky bastard. He was no fool. He sensed the coming storm between the two of us.

"How, Kincade?" I wasn't letting this go.

A beat. Then, "Edward told me."

Anger detonated. I shoved myself upright, realizing for the first time we were in his high-rise apartment. I staggered off the bed. Kincade crossed the room to steady me. I shoved his hands away.

"He had no right to tell you."

If I had a cell phone, I'd call my uncle right now and give him a piece of my mind. Emotion clotted in the back of my throat as my breath hitched. I was seconds away from bursting into tears and that was the absolute last thing I wanted to do in front of Kincade.

"I pressed him," Kincade said. "So be angry with me."

"I am," I snapped. "You don't get to go digging in my blood like it's a file."

I clamped my mouth shut, the blood beating hard in my head. The headache I nursed while lying on the bed throbbed harder than ever before.

"Well, it's my fucking business now. So, tell me the whole story, Anna. I can't help you if you don't."

"I don't want your help! I thought that was clear since the first day we met."

His face flushed red hot as he pursed his lips, trying to keep his own temper in check. His superpower was sensing when I lied and likely he realized I wasn't lying even a little. I rushed on.

"Besides, didn't my uncle share with you the whole sordid tale? I'm sure you enjoyed the story over tea and fucking biscuits."

"Am I supposed to sit by and watch you destroy yourself after everything you did for me?"

The words landed harder than I expected.

He meant the spear. The trade. The decision neither of us had named out loud.

I was completely caught off guard by that. Again, my breath hitched. "What's that supposed to mean?"

He raked his hand through his hair and turned away. "Nothing."

But it wasn't nothing. There was a glimmer of something in those words I was too damn stubborn to acknowledge. My heart kicked into high gear, pounding against my breastbone as I stood there, staring at him. The blood whooshed from my head in a matter of seconds, leaving tiny black pinpricks in my vision.

Kincade blew out a breath, hands braced on his hips. For a moment, I saw the version of him I'd first encountered outside All Saints Hospital—controlled, unreadable, already assessing how bad things were going to get.

He stood there in battered clothes, scraped and bruised from the fight. His black cargo pants still had dirt and gravel dust on them. His boots were scuffed. He looked exactly like someone who'd arrived too late and hated himself for it.

Those green-gold eyes of his met mine, making my innards jangle with an emotion I did not want to accept.

"Abaddon is a destroyer angel. He's not going to take you for frozen yogurt."

Memories of our second encounter flashed through my mind. That day was the day I discovered demons walked among the humans. I was mesmerized by the veil separating the demon world from the human world. He'd clamped a hand around my arm and dragged me into the frozen yogurt shop where he grilled me about who I was. I made him buy me yogurt. At the time, even I didn't know who I was.

Why was he bringing this up now?

"I know what he is," I said, quietly.

Damn Edward for telling Kincade. Why did he have to do that? Further, why did Kincade have to follow me? Which reminded me.

"How did you find me?" I asked.

"Darius paid your uncle a visit."

I clenched my aching jaw which made it ache more. "He ratted me out."

"He came to Edward because he was concerned you'd do something..." His words drifted away.

"Stupid," I finished.

"I'm sorry I didn't get there in time."

To stop me. That's what he meant.

I thought about the crypt, the explosion, killing those people who didn't have a snowball's chance in hell of escaping. I killed them. Guilt and remorse overwhelmed me. I slid down the wall and sat on the low-pile carpet, drawing up my knees and hugging them. That was a decision I was going to have to live with for the rest of my life.

Hot tears prickled the backs of my eyes, but I blinked them away. Took another breath. Exhaled it.

"How did you blow up the crypt?" He folded his arms over his massive chest, staring me down with those eyes I desperately wanted to avoid.

If I lied, he'd know. May as well spill my guts. "I had help."

"From who?" Impatience laced his tone.

"A woman named Astrid."

His eyes went wide with surprise. "Astrid? Are you sure her name was Astrid?"

My mouth thinned in annoyance. "I'm not an idiot, Kincade. She said she was Azriel's half-sister. She volunteered to help me."

"Why?"

"How should I know? Probably because she hates him for some reason or another."

He stared at me in stark silence for a long moment. "You do know what she is, don't you?"

Uh oh. Uncertainty cascaded through me. "No."

"She's a time warper."

My brows drew together. "A what?"

"She can do things like bend reality, time, anything. They're rare and she's the most powerful I've seen. She can create something out of nothing with her mind."

Understanding dawned. "That must have been how she got the C4."

"Good god, woman. Do you know what you've done?"

"Yes, Kincade. I'm very clear on that. I conspired with Azriel's half-sister. I blew up the crypt. I killed innocent people. I'm a terrible person. Is that what you wanted to hear?"

What did he want from me? Remorse? Guilt? A confession of all my sins? If there was a way for me to get away from his scrutinizing gaze, I'd be out of there so fast his head would spin. But as it was, my body was in too much pain to make a run for it.

Besides, he'd tackle me again anyway.

He didn't say anything. Just took two steps and reached his hand down. I hesitated, thinking back to Abaddon's outstretched hand. Those menacing long fingernails and his wicked grin of pleasure. But Kincade was not Abaddon.

"It's not a trick."

I reached for him, took his hand and got to my feet. He held it longer than necessary before releasing it. His grip was steady. Practical. He released me as soon as I was upright.

"You should rest."

And that was that. He turned on his boot heel and left.

CHAPTER 10

I WAITED FOR THE door to click closed before I flung myself on the bed. This was the same room I had been in when Kincade brought me here after Ben was killed. I understood why he brought me here now. It was close to the cemetery. I suspected he, like my uncle, had the place warded to keep demons and other unsavory things out.

Exhaustion pressed into every pore as I lay there staring up at the ceiling questioning my life choices. I thought of the prophecy in the family history book. The part about me being tempted to turn away from the Light and to the dark was top of my mind.

"She will be tempted beyond all temptations," I whispered to the ceiling.

I pressed cool fingers against my eyes.

Abaddon was that temptation. He somehow tapped into the dark magic floating through my veins to find me, to weaken me, to make me want to do things I shouldn't. To bring me down. To defeat Good and make me follow Darkness. To change the world forever.

If I wasn't so angry with my uncle, I might dream walk him and ask him if he managed to find a way to reverse this darkness inside me.

I was exhausted and too emotionally drained for that.

I allowed myself to fall asleep. When Azriel stepped into my dreams and took control, I realized I forgot to put up my mental walls. A stupid, careless mistake.

We were in a room with dark walls. Both of us stood under a bright light. He did not look pleased at all. The wolf grin I was so accustomed to seeing was gone from his face. There was an evil glint in his dark eyes.

"You dare to launch an attack on me."

"I'm sorry you weren't there," I spat, sounding brave.

Fury creased his face. "You will pay."

"If that's supposed to scare me, it doesn't." But deep down, I was terrified. Launching an attack against Azriel was like holding a box of lit matches.

He stepped close to me, his face inches from mine.

"You think this is a game, *chérie*?"

"Not really," I said, flippantly.

His hand clamped around my throat, his fingers digging into my skin as he pulled my face closer to his. I was forced to look deep into his eyes since I didn't have the power to move of my own accord. It was almost as though I saw right into the depths of his soul. I noticed a tiny gold fleck in the black iris near the pupil. One in each eye.

As he stared into my eyes, my body jerked in one violent shudder. Memories flipped through my mind as though he were flipping through a photo album. I realized then what he was doing—he was searching my memories. Scanning for a weakness to use against me.

Panic welled inside me. I couldn't stop him even if I wanted. I stood there, limp, while he rifled through everything from my teenage years with Edward to my childhood.

Oh, God. My childhood.

Mama.

As soon as her image floated through my mind and he got a good look at her, he released me. He shoved me backward. That wolf smile returned.

"I have what I need. Adieu, *chérie*."

"NO!"

I shouted myself awake, sitting bolt upright in the bed. My heart hammered a wild beat. Sweat slipped down the sides of my face. The back of my neck was damp with it.

Kincade burst into my room, the light from the hallway flooding into the doorway making him nothing more than a silhouette ready to do battle. He flipped on the light which nearly burned my eyes out of their sockets. I squinted and blinked at a furious pace to get used to the sudden brightness.

"There's no one here." His wild eyes scanned the room.

Seconds later, Decker appeared behind him, gun drawn.

"I-I had a nightmare."

Decker holstered his gun. Kincade relaxed his on-guard stance. It was as close to the truth as I was willing to say. If I even uttered Azriel's name, Kincade would be all over me for more details and I wasn't ready to share.

"Are you all right?" he asked.

"I'm fine."

Kincade's eyes narrowed, as if he tried to decide if I told the truth or not.

"Sometimes I have these nightmares. It's rare, but it does happen. It's because I'm tired."

Decker, no longer interested in my nightmare, stalked away. Perhaps he was disappointed he wasn't able to kill demons. Kincade paused a moment longer in the doorway before giving me a nod, which was mostly one jerk of his head.

"All right."

He snapped off the light and shut the door, leaving me alone again.

I laid back on the bed, staring up at the ceiling once again. But I knew exactly what my next move was going to be. And neither Decker nor Kincade were invited to attend.

I FORCED MYSELF TO stay there for as long as possible, regulating my breathing and steadying my erratic heartbeat. I glanced at the bedside clock to see it was a little past four in the morning.

Time to go.

I swung my legs over the side of the bed. Still dressed, my shoes still on because I never took them off, I crept toward the door. I placed both hands on the wood and pressed my ear against it, listening for sounds of movement or anything on the other side.

Nothing.

Taking a deep breath, I wrapped my hand around the knob and slowly turned it. Then cracked open the door and peered into the hallway.

It was deserted.

I pushed the door open wider and took a tentative step into the hall and stopped. No Kincade. No Decker.

I took a few more tentative steps down the hallway, passed two closed doors which I assumed were bedrooms containing, I hoped, two snoring Watchers. As soon as I was down the hall and in the living room, I halted. The shades were open on the floor-to-ceiling windows giving a spectacular view of downtown Dallas lit up against the pre-dawn skyline. Beyond that, a few cars zipped along the freeway.

This was the city I was born in, grew up in.

The city my adopted mother raised me in until I was thirteen.

I had to find her before Azriel did.

As I turned toward the front door, I spied the car keys next to my jade-handled dagger on the glass coffee table. I snatched them both, sheathing the dagger and clutching the keys as I headed for the front door. There was no time to waste.

I DROVE LIKE A madwoman out of the parking garage and to the north part of Dallas. It was still in the pre-dawn hours, but even so traffic was already starting to pick up in the city. When I arrived at my early childhood home, I parked outside the red brick house with white shutters. I never thought I would be back here.

Truthfully, I thought of my adopted mother a lot these last few months. She'd been in the back of my mind and now that I was back in Texas, and Azriel had threatened her, I had a real reason to find her.

While the house looked the same on the outside, there were subtle differences indicating she no longer lived there. All her prized rose bushes had been replaced by holly bushes, which cut me to the core. She loved those roses. She cultivated them, cross-bred them to make gorgeous, sweet-smelling hybrids that bloomed every spring and fall. The new owner ripped them out for those horrible green abominations.

All the flower beds she spent hours on were gone, too. The lush green grass was overrun with weeds. Even the house looked as though it hadn't been taken care of as well as she had.

I stayed in the car and waited until the sun came up to ring the doorbell. A disheveled-looking woman wearing a fuzzy pink bathrobe opened the door a crack. The sliver of face I saw through the small opening was a roadmap of wrinkles. She gave me a suspicious glare.

"Who are you?"

"I'm looking for the previous owner," I began.

"Keep looking."

She slammed the door. The lock clicked. Infuriated, I rang the doorbell again and again until the door flew open again. This time, she was clearly angry.

"How long have you lived here?" I asked, preempting her.

"Ten years. Now get off my porch before I call the police."

Again, the door slammed.

I backed down off the porch, pausing a moment before going back to the car. Ten years. Edward plucked me from Texas fifteen years ago and took me to England. I tried to recall the last letter I received from her, but the memory was fuzzy. How was I going to find her?

"Oh, my dear, how wonderful to see you here."

Shit.

Abaddon stood in the middle of the street, appearing out of nowhere.

I was an idiot for leaving Kincade's apartment, but I was driven by a deep-seated need to protect the woman who raised me for half my life. I took a deep breath, trying to decide my next move. As we stared at each other with the expanse of yard between us, the twinge of darkness inside heated.

He held out a hand to me. "Come with me."

The dark magic stirred in a flurry of activity. It was hard to resist as it pulled me towards him. I took a step, two. Ready to turn myself over to him, to the dark. Ready to give into all those carnal thoughts. Ready to allow him to lead me down that dark path.

"That's right. Joining with me is what you want, isn't it?"

The darkness swirled, pushing me to answer yes. I clenched my jaw, pressing my lips closed and yet my feet disobeyed and continued to walk toward him.

I halted at the edge of the sidewalk. The car was between the two of us now. He smiled an oily smile.

"Together, we will be invincible. Together, we will do unbelievable things."

As I started to answer, a car skidded around the corner, tires screeching. On the driver's side, an arm stuck out the window pointing a gun at Abaddon. The driver fired off several shots that went right through Abaddon as though he were invisible.

The car screeched to a halt inches from him. He looked unconcerned. I was frozen in place as I watched the passenger lift something that looked like a rocket gun, point it through the windshield and fire.

Abaddon shot up into the air as the windshield shattered into a thousand shards of glass. The missile found its target in a parked car down the street. It exploded in a bright fireball that rocked the entire neighborhood and set off car alarms. Debris flew into nearby houses.

Behind me, the door to my childhood home flung open.

"Anna, get down!"

Kincade. It was Kincade in the passenger side shouting at me. I glanced over my shoulder in time to see the haggard woman with a rifle, cocked. She fired. I dropped to the hard ground, breaking my fall by flinging out my arms. My wrists and palms objected to the jarring.

The next thing I knew, Kincade was at my side, manhandling me. He grabbed me by the arms and dragged me to my feet. He wrapped his massive arms around me and picked me up like I weighed nothing.

Meanwhile, Decker, the driver, continued to fire round after round with this demon gun at Abaddon. I realized then he was keeping him busy while Kincade snatched me up. He shoved me into the back of the car and followed, slamming the door behind him.

"Go!"

Decker threw the car in reverse and floored it. Tires squealed as he backed up to the corner where they turned. He spun the wheel, turning the car to face the street they'd entered from and again floored it. We fled the scene as the sun rose higher in the sky.

But I was furious. Dark magic swirled inside me like venom. I gulped in air, forcing it to abate. I didn't want to hurt Kincade, but I also didn't want to sit next to him. I shoved away from him trying to get as far from him as possible. The small seat yielded about six inches between us.

"What are you doing here? Do you have a fucking GPS on me or what?" I demanded.

"I expected you were going to do something stupid," he said. "I put a tracker on the car."

And left the keys where I easily found them.

"You son of a bitch—"

Darkness pulsed as I swung my fist. He caught my wrist in his hand, clamping his fingers around it so hard it hurt. The moment we touched, the throb of dark magic waned.

"Listen, sweetheart, from now on you're going to do exactly as I tell you."

"No, I'm not. I'm—"

"You are," he said, cutting me off with a firm voice. His green-gold eyes blazed fury. "Because this is the third time I've tried to keep you from handing yourself over to the destroyer angel."

"Actually, Darius intervened one of those times," I pointed out to needle him and smirked.

He growled low and deep in his throat. He didn't like when I mentioned Darius. "Do you even realize what that would mean for you if you did that?"

"I have—"

"If you go with him, he will use you until he can't anymore and then he'll turn you over to Lucifer to finish you off. Is that what you want?"

I pressed my lips together and stared at him. No, it wasn't what I wanted but he didn't understand why I was so compelled to answer Abaddon's call. And I wasn't in a sharing mood.

"We're going to Acre. Or have you forgotten your true purpose." It wasn't a question.

"Acre can wait. Azriel is going after the woman who raised me. I have to find her before he does."

Slowly, his fingers uncurled from my wrist. He released me. I dropped my hand in my lap. My skin throbbed in the wake of his touch. The ache of dark magic had vanished.

"That's why you were here?" His voice was calm when he asked.

"Yes. I lived in that house until I was thirteen. Until Edward found me. But she doesn't live there anymore."

I clamped my mouth shut. It was the closest I came to asking him for help. I wanted to ask but didn't. He sat back in the seat, the leather squeaking.

"I think it's time you and I had an in-depth discussion, Miss Walker."

Aw, hell.

CHAPTER 11

WE ARRIVED BACK AT his apartment. It was the last place I wanted to be, but I didn't have a choice. Kincade was making all the decision for me now. He had it with my shenanigans and was ready to pummel me into submission. I understood. I was a pain in the ass on a good day.

What he didn't understand was my compelling need to find my adopted mother.

Well, I called her my adopted mother, but she'd never finalized the adoption because Edward showed up to take me away.

I flopped on the sofa while Decker disappeared into one of the back bedrooms. Kincade took the seat opposite me. He leaned his elbows on his knees and laced his fingers ready for this in-depth discussion. I didn't wanna. We stared each other down for a long, silent moment.

"Why is Azriel after—" he began.

"Grace. Her name is Grace Clark." Saying her name aloud made it more real Azriel was after her.

"Okay," he said with a nod. "Why is Azriel after Grace?"

I swallowed hard. To answer that question, I was going to have to tell him how Azriel discovered her in the first place. I bit my lower lip.

"You don't want to tell me, do you?" he asked.

"Not really."

"But you are going to tell me, aren't you, Miss Walker?"

"You're exhausting," I snapped.

"As are you."

There was no getting out of this. I took a deep breath.

"That nightmare I had..." I paused, gathering my courage to find the right words.

His lips peeled back from his teeth in a snarl. "Azriel was in that nightmare, wasn't he?"

"I forgot to put up my mental walls." It hurt to admit the truth. "He dream walked me, took control before I knew what was happening. Then he rifled through my memories as easily as if he were paging through a book."

His fist clenched into a tight ball, the knuckles leaching of color reminding me of the time he did it in the hospital in Hong Kong when he vowed to "fucking kill" Azriel if he ever put another hand on me. At some point, he was going to make good on that vow.

I hoped I was there to help.

"How much does he know?"

"Everything." God, my stomach churned acid at the thought of the fallen angel picking through my memories like they meant nothing.

His gaze never left my face. "Which is?"

"I told you before when my biological mother died, I was left as an orphan. Right here in Dallas. Grace Clark was my foster mother. She started the process of trying to adopt me when my uncle arrived to take me away," I said.

"You were thirteen."

I nodded, impressed he remembered that tidbit of information. "We corresponded for several years but then her letters stopped coming. Eventually my letters were returned, no forwarding address."

"Any idea where she went? Or why she would disappear?"

Oh, I had a good idea why she would disappear, but no idea where she would go. All the internet searches I did turned up nothing.

"Her sister was trouble. Her name was Ruby. Grace bailed her out of jail a couple of times, even tried to give her a place to stay. But Ruby was messed up on drugs and had a boyfriend who wasn't exactly the best influence on her life."

He sat back in the chair and swiped his hand over his chin, the skin swishing against the rough whiskers. I noticed, then, he had a few days growth of beard, something I never saw before even when he was in captivity with Azriel.

"Azriel plans to use her to get to me," I said. Then added, "Like Ben."

Compassion flickered through his eyes. "I know what he plans to do. This isn't my first run-in with him."

Something Kincade once said to me popped back into my mind. "Yeah. You said you've been hunting him longer than I've been alive."

He didn't respond. In fact, he decided that was the moment we were done. He stood. "I have enough to go on. I'll find Grace."

"What does longer than I've been alive mean, Kincade?" I wasn't going to let it go.

"You're a smart girl, Miss Walker. I'm sure you can figure it out."

He headed off toward the kitchen. I followed. "I've been alive twenty-eight, almost twenty-nine, years. That doesn't seem that long. What's the real story?"

He wasn't having any of it. He turned, peered at me with those eyes that were intimidating at times and approachable at other times. "Do you want me to find Grace or not?"

Ah, so Kincade was a master of evasion much like my uncle. Fine. I played along. "Yes, I do."

"Sit your ass down somewhere in this apartment. If you leave again, I will hunt you down and tie you to the nearest chair."

And with that, he stalked off down the hallway. I had no doubt in my mind he would make good on that threat.

He disappeared into one of the bedrooms. I huffed out a breath. How was he able to find her and I wasn't?

And then it occurred to me.

He wasn't going to search databases.

He was going to dream walk her.

I was certain he had that ability but had never shared the knowledge with me verbally. But I knew. Hell, maybe he didn't even know he did it.

Why didn't I think of that? In my panic, I forgot my own superpowers.

I hurried back to the living room, kicked off my pink combat boots and settled into the cushions. I crossed my legs under me, placed my hands on my knees, closed my eyes and cleared my mind.

The last time I dream walked someone without sleeping was in Antarctica. It worked then, but I wasn't sure if it would work now. I had no way to know if she was awake or asleep or even if I could get into her mind. I had to try.

I conjured memories of the woman I called Mama. I remembered her face as clear as if I saw her yesterday. Clear blue eyes, blonde hair and a youthful face belying her true age.

It took several agonizing moments to finally force my mind to focus. My body relaxed as I found the place to tap into the dream walking ability. Moments later I was thrown into the dream.

I was at my childhood home. The red brick house with white shutters. Inside was how I remembered. The modest décor had seen better days. It was beyond shabby chic. Grace worked hard to provide everything she could. She'd always wanted a child but had never been able to conceive. Her marriage crumbled because of it.

I walked through the foyer, the hardwood floors creaking with every step.

Grace was in the kitchen chopping onions. I paused in the doorway. She looked exactly how I remembered her. My gut twisted with relief she was safe, at least, in the dream. She stopped chopping to look at me. Her eyes were wide and bright with recognition.

"Mama," I said by way of greeting.

She went back to chopping as though I hadn't spoken.

I tried again, this time with more urgency. "Mama, where are you? I need to find you."

"I left this place." She spoke with a slight Texas accent I remembered well.

She meant the red brick house. I nodded. "I looked for you here. Where are you now?"

"I can't tell you."

"Why not?" I asked.

"Because Ruby will find me."

Her sister was always trouble. I guess she still was. "Ruby won't find you. I promise."

"She won't, but I did," Azriel said from behind me.

While Grace continued chopping onions, I spun to face him. He stood there in the dining room wearing his normal attire. His enormous black wings were spread out behind him giving him that lethal appearance.

I reached for my dagger, but it wasn't in my waistband. Where the hell had I left it? "You stay away from her."

"I can't do that, *chérie*. She will make a nice addition to my collection, don't you think?"

"Your demented collection of souls, you mean?" My hands fisted. There was no way I would allow him to take her life and add her soul to his dark army. "I'm not going to let you turn her into one of your demons. I will kill you if you harm her or her guardian angel."

His brows rose. "Are you certain she has one? Perhaps she, like you, no longer has a guardian. Oh, but that's not true now, is it?" He tapped his chin in thought with that wolf grin.

"That's right. She has me."

Kincade stepped out of the shadows that pressed in from nowhere. My heart skipped. Seeing him here in this dream verified my thoughts he had dream walker capabilities. He was a dream walker like me.

Azriel's wolf grin faded as his eyes narrowed into a glare. He stared daggers at Kincade.

"I grow tired of seeing you, *gardien*."

"Get used to it," he replied.

I glanced between the two of them as they faced off. Like two roosters about to fight. Each one had their chests puffed up. I wanted no part of that cock fight. I backed into the kitchen toward Grace, my footsteps light on the tile floor. Meanwhile, Kincade planted himself between me, Grace and Azriel, his feet shoulder-width apart.

"Move aside, *gardien*."

"No." His response was succinct at least.

"I thought you learned before you cannot win against me. Or have you forgotten who gave you that pretty scar on your chest?"

I blinked, remembering the silvery scar that went down the left side of his chest. I saw it after Azriel returned his soul. When he wore nothing but blue pajama pants and a blanket wrapped around his shoulders. When he stood in the hallway with me as we both gazed at the portrait of my biological mother.

The image was still powerful and vivid in my mind. Even in the dream state.

"That was quite a long time ago, wasn't it?" Azriel continued. "Centuries, even. Perhaps you would like to finish the battle we started?"

I sucked in a sharp breath. *Centuries*? What the actual fuck?

I stared a hole in the back of Kincade's head, willing him to look at me but he remained with his back to me. Not even a muscle ticked or flinched in his back. Not even his hands flexed into fists.

"Here's what's going to happen," he said, ignoring Azriel's taunt. "You're going to leave this woman's dream. You'll leave her unharmed in the real world, too."

Azriel laughed. "Or what?"

"Or I will hunt you down and we will finish that battle in person."

I focused on Azriel's face to gauge his reaction. A muscle ticked in his cheek right under his left eye. He bared his teeth and charged Kincade. I spun to Grace, grabbed her arm and started to drag her out of the kitchen in the opposite direction. I didn't dare look back to see what was happening between those two.

"Anna, honey, is that you?" Her eyes cleared, as though a fog had lifted.

"It's me, Mama. We need to leave this place. It's not safe here."

I tugged her along through the kitchen into the tiny mudroom off the garage. I flung open the door and led her down the two steps into the garage, frantically looking for the button to open the door. In the kitchen, sounds of a skirmish between Kincade and Azriel.

"Why isn't it safe? I don't understand," Grace said. "Where have you been? I haven't seen you in years."

"I've been…" I halted, unsure what to tell her. "I'll answer that later. Where is the damn button to get out of this godforsaken garage?"

Grace reached behind me and punched the opener. The door lifted, a bright shaft of light slicing in through the darkness. I grabbed her hand and dragged her toward it.

"I will find her, *chérie*," Azriel called from somewhere behind me.

Then he grunted as though punched in the gut. I hoped Kincade punched the crap out of him.

We stepped into the blinding light. I shaded my watering eyes trying to adjust to the sudden brightness. Dreams were strange like that. Sometimes, the places were vivid detailed memories that had been translated into a dream-world the sleeper wanted to revisit. Sometimes, they were nothing more than images, feelings, shapes.

In the distance, a loud banging sounded throughout the dream. I did a three-sixty trying to discern where it came from.

Grace flinched then, put a hand to her head as though she heard it, too. I gripped her by the arms.

"You hear it, too, don't you? What is it?" I asked.

"Something…I'm not sure."

"Tell me where to find you. In the real world, Grace. I need to find you." I tried to hide the panic in my voice, but it still came out.

She shook her head as the banging happened again. Her brows drew together as if in pain. I placed my hands on her cheeks, held her face steady.

"Focus, Grace. Tell me where to find you so I can help you."

"In the country," she said.

"Where?" I pressed.

"I grew up there. My daddy used to say a broken clock is right twice a day."

That didn't make sense. I opened my mouth to ask another question when the dream faded.

My eyes snapped open. I sucked in a sharp breath, trying to calm my erratic heart.

A broken clock is right twice a day.

I heard her say that before when I was small. She often talked about her childhood home where she had fond memories of her parents and even Ruby before she was sucked into the seedy underworld of drugs and biker gangs.

Someday we'll go back there, Anna. You and me. And I'll show you the house I grew up in.

Her words, once deep in the back of my mind, surged forward. I sat rock still, my hands still on my knees as I stared into space trying desperately to grasp that thread of memory. I almost had it. It was so close.

Is it a house like ours, Mama?

No, honey, it's much bigger.

Where is it? I asked.

Where there are pine trees and you can breathe in the fresh, clean air. In a little town called Jefferson.

I woke with a gasp.

Footsteps thundered down the hall. A second later, Kincade burst into the room—hair disheveled, breath hard, eyes sharp and focused.

Before he said a word, I blurted, "I know where to find Grace."

CHAPTER 12

I LEVELED MY GAZE at him as the truth clicked into place. Not suspicion. Not theory. Certainty.

What I didn't understand was how he, a Watcher, had the ability to dream walk.

But then Azriel did, too, so maybe it wasn't a stretch.

"You're a dream walker." I said it calmly. Like a fact. Like something already decided.

His face went impassive. Damn, he was good at hiding his emotions. I wish I had that ability but no. Everyone knew exactly what I was thinking and feeling because I had no control over my facial expressions.

He didn't respond. I pressed on.

"You were there, in the dream, too. And it's not the first time you've been in my dreams." I kept my eyes pinned on his, determined not to blink or look away first. And then I added, "Guardian."

If I hadn't been staring so hard at him, I would have missed the little twitch of the muscle under his eye.

"Are you my guardian? Is that what you've become?"

"Where do we find Grace, Miss Walker?"

"Oh, hell, no." I stood and tried to ignore the tingling sensation coursing up and down my legs from sitting with them folded too long. "You're going to answer me."

"Don't threaten me."

"That was not a threat, Kincade. It was a demand."

Amusement glinted briefly in his eyes. "You demand nothing from me."

"I'll demand whatever the hell I please. Especially since you won't let me out of your sight. Now are you my guardian or not?"

His lips twisted in a cynical smile. "You think because that's what Azriel calls me it makes it so?"

"Does it?"

"I think you're drawing conclusions that suit you." He turned away.

I reached for him, grabbed his upper arm and forced him to turn back toward me. It didn't escape me I damn well wouldn't have been able to do that if he hadn't allowed it.

"You want answers from me? Well, I want answers from you, too."

His eyes darkened. "Yet you've told me nothing about how Azriel marked you," he said. "Or why the destroyer angel can still track you. Or what that darkness in your blood actually is."

I swallowed hard. I did *not* want to tell him. Because the second I did, I would never hear the bloody end of it.

"There's nothing to tell."

"Lie."

Curse him and his internal lie detector. I hated that so much.

"Tell me the truth once and for all," he demanded, hearing my thoughts.

I realized I still held his arm. The warmth of his skin radiated through my fingers. I dropped my hand and turned away. Eventually, I was going to have to tell him the truth.

But not today.

"Grace went home to Jefferson. That's where she is. It's in East Texas," I said, deftly changing the subject.

"I know where Jefferson is, Miss Walker."

"I'm going. You can't stop me. If you're going with me, then I suggest you pack a bag." I looked at him over my shoulder and punctuated my statement with an emphatic, "Partner."

He snarled and walked away.

I wouldn't be able to avoid the subject of my dark magic with him much longer. But I was going to delay as long as possible.

It occurred to me I told him to pack a bag, yet I didn't have one. I was in the same clothes as when I tried to leave the manor with the painting. I probably needed a shower and a toothbrush, too.

A knock sounded on the front door, startling me. I stared at it, wondering if I should answer. Who would want to visit a grouch like Kincade?

Another knock. This time more persistent. I went to the door and peered through the peephole.

"You have *got* to be kidding me." I flung open the door to my uncle standing on the other side. "What are you doing here?"

"I thought that was readily apparent," he said. He pushed by me and stepped into the apartment. He held two duffels—one I recognized as mine.

An eerie sensation went through me. "Are you joining the party, too?"

"My private plane is waiting at Dallas Executive."

"Oh, you've come to take me back to England, then."

"At first, yes. But not now," he said.

"He came because I asked him." Kincade appeared in the doorway looking larger than life and angrier than ever. He held his own bag in one hand.

My brows drew together in question. "Why?"

"Kincade shared your plan to find Grace Clark," Edward said.

Oh, I hated that. My first thought was when and how. But then I had the answer to these questions, didn't I? They both had superpowers like me. "Are you two besties now gossiping behind my back?"

"Your true purpose lies in Acre," Kincade said, his tone hard. "Edward is here to expedite the trip to find Grace and get it over with."

"Get it over with?"

Edward cleared his throat. "I think what Kincade means is your real purpose lies in Acre—"

"Yeah, yeah, yeah. The Holy Relics, I get it. Let's just fucking go."

I hadn't forgotten about my real purpose any more than I'd forgotten about Darius and the poison coursing through him. I still intended to save him with the Staff of Moses as I intended to find Grace.

I snatched the bag out of my uncle's hand and stomped through the door.

"I'm surprised Darius isn't tagging along, too," I grumbled as I stalked down the hallway.

"Darius is quite ill," Edward said from behind me.

I halted and spun around. "What do you mean by that?"

"He came to me after he dropped you off at the cemetery. The demon poison in his veins has weakened him considerably."

"Where is he now?" I asked.

"He remains at Walker Manor."

Darius was sick and getting sicker because of me. I hated to admit Kincade was right in that my true purpose was in Acre searching for the staff. But Grace...she was in danger from Azriel. I couldn't bear the thought of something horrible happening to her. If I didn't get to her before Azriel, I would never forgive myself.

But Darius...he had been there for me. He came when I blew the Horn of Gabriel and saved me off that rooftop when Lexi betrayed me and left me for dead. He saved me from the depths of Hell not once, but twice. He gave me his name on my tongue.

Torn, I stood there unmoving trying to decide my next move.

"There's nothing you can do for him at this moment, Anna," Edward said as though reading my thoughts. Or maybe he read the indecision on my face. "We will fly into East Texas Regional. I have a car waiting for us there."

Of course, he did.

I nodded and, without another word, headed for the elevator.

⊹━━━⊹

THE CAR RIDE TO the small airport was silent. We parked, got out and boarded the private jet. Kincade went to the back, took a seat and settled in for a nap. He crossed his arms over his chest, closed his eyes and immediately started snoring. I envied that. I stowed my duffel and took the second row. Edward planted himself across from me.

A quick pre-flight check and then we were off. Once we were airborne, Edward pulled a folder from his bag. He held it in his lap and flipped it open. I spied the postcard of Acre. He handed it to me.

"You left this behind."

"Why are you giving it to me now?" I took it from his hand, refusing to look at it.

"Do you know what that structure is in the picture?"

I glanced down at the picture of the fortress. A high wall surrounded it as the Mediterranean surf lashed the rock face. Anyone familiar with Templar history knew this was where they had their last stand in Acre before their defeat. What secrets did it hold? Were there still holy artifacts hidden there? Would I find the staff there?

"Yes," I said.

When I lived with my uncle as a teen, his tutors were determined to teach me history, theology and ancient languages. Not to mention all the other subjects I found boring and annoying. I spent a whole month on the rise and fall of the Templars with one tutor who was an author and expert on the subject. Now I questioned if we dream walkers had some sort of connection to them.

Something Decker said resurfaced. He said when the Templars were attacked at Acre in 1291 and fled the city, they—meaning the Brotherhood of Watchers—could no longer protect them from their human enemy. Did the Brotherhood flee as well?

Azriel asked Kincade if he wanted to finish the fight they began hundreds of years ago.

A tingling sensation crept up my spine.

I met my uncle's unwavering blue gaze.

"It's like a puzzle, isn't it?" I asked.

"Are you assembling the pieces?" Edward countered.

"You said the Brotherhood were divine, but of a higher order. Decker said they couldn't protect the Templars when they fled Acre in 1291." I paused and waited for confirmation.

It didn't come. Edward granted me a rare small smile. "You are clever, Anna."

But I was still at a loss. I chewed on my lower lip.

"Think it through," he urged.

I had to be right. The Brotherhood was there at Acre. I stole a glance back at a sleeping Kincade.

"The Brotherhood was at Acre in 1291. Kincade and Decker were there."

And so was Azriel. For fuck's sake.

"They were." He nodded.

"How did you figure it out?"

Again, that small smile. "I read a lot."

"And know everything."

He snickered. "At any rate, Kincade may be able to help you track down the staff by retracing both his steps and that of the Templars. There may be clues in the underground passages at the Acre fortress."

"That was over seven hundred years ago, uncle. How is he going—"

I snapped my mouth shut and looked at Kincade again. If that was over seven hundred years ago, and he was there fighting Azriel...how bloody old was Kincade? Was he immortal or just freaking old?

"Stop fighting him and let him help you," Edward urged.

That rebellious part of me wanted to sneer at him and say stop telling me what to do but I didn't. As much as I hated to admit it, he was right. I was in too deep in this thing. Kincade had my back and that gave me comfort.

So why was I so resistant?

I also knew the answer to this, and it was because my uncle insisted on pushing us together. Even Ophelia was trying to get us to stand under the mistletoe before all hell broke loose at the manor.

I also didn't forget how furious I was with my uncle. I dropped my voice on the off chance Kincade was still awake and eavesdropping on our conversation.

"Why did you tell Kincade that Azriel marked me?"

"Because he'll give you a fighting chance against him and the darkness inside you."

I frowned. "Did you tell him about that, too?" I referred to the tattoo without saying it aloud.

"I did not." He leveled his gaze at me. "That's for you to do. I suggest you share that information with him sooner rather than later. But he already knew about the darkness—just not the whole story."

"Why?" I didn't bother to hide the suspicion in my voice.

He sighed annoyance and gave me a look of bemused resignation. "I thought I was clear he can help you."

"With that?" I shook my head. "No way I'm telling him."

"It's your choice, of course."

The plane began its descent.

"We'll be landing soon." He turned his attention back to the folder. "I did some digging on Grace Clark and found her address on the outskirts of Jefferson. She's also owner of a clock shop in downtown."

My daddy used to say a broken clock is right twice a day.

"It's her family's clock shop, isn't it?" I asked.

"I believe so. Her father ran it until he passed away a few years ago."

When I was growing up, Grace never talked about her parents. I didn't even know her father was still alive. The only family I was aware of was Ruby. That girl was a total disaster.

"The car will take us directly to her home."

"Good."

Even though I sounded confident, my stomach erupted in butterflies.

He flipped the folder closed and handed it to me. "Maybe you'd like to see this."

I hesitated. Edward's talent was to find anything on anyone anywhere in the world. I didn't deny I thought of Grace often. More so these last few months when my life started falling apart and I was tasked with finding the Holy Relics.

I slipped the folder from his hand and tucked it into the side of my duffel for future reference.

We landed and, true to his word, a car waited at the tiny municipal airport. I grabbed my bag and followed Edward off the jet.

Kincade's steps were heavy behind me. Silence descended as we all got in the car. Kincade took the front passenger seat while I slid in the back. Edward spoke to the driver, handed him a piece of paper I assumed was the address, and then got in next to me.

Childishly, I was glad I didn't have to sit by Kincade.

We remained silent during the car ride. I was too busy trying to decide what to stay to her when I saw her for the first time in fifteen years. Everything I came up with sounded lame.

It was nearing dusk when the car turned up a long dirt driveway and headed up to a house on a hill shrouded in trees. My stomach clenched and my nerves were on edge. The driver stopped the car, a cloud of dust in our wake.

Edward got out first. I followed. Kincade popped open his passenger door and stood, standing in the open door of the car leaning on the hood. As if he intended to wait right there for the duration. His keen eyes took in everything as he glanced around the area.

Edward leaned down to the driver. "If you don't mind waiting?"

"No problem, sir," the driver said.

Edward nodded and stood straight. "Come, Anna." He started for the front door.

"You're coming with me?" I blurted.

He halted, gave me a quizzical look. "I thought I might."

"I think it's better if I go alone." I glanced toward the house. Yellow light played in the front windows. "At first."

Edward had the nerve to glance at Kincade who gave him the go-ahead nod.

"He's not here," Kincade said.

And I realized then he referred to Azriel. Ah, ok. He was going to stay out here and play guard dog. But I wondered if he had an internal Azriel detector kinda like his internal lie detector.

"Very well then," Edward said. "Go ahead, Anna."

I swallowed the thick lump rising in my throat as I turned toward the front door. The red-brick house wore white shutters like it was trying to look cheerful on purpose. A small porch held potted plants, hanging baskets of flowers, and an old rocking chair that had seen a thousand quiet evenings. The screen door sagged in its frame, weathered and tired.

I drew a cleansing breath, crossed the porch, and hit the doorbell before I could talk myself out of it.

Footsteps approached.

The door opened—and there was Grace.

She was a little older than I remembered, but it was still her. The same bright blue eyes. The same face I'd clung to in memory for fifteen years. Her hair had gone gray at the temples, and fine lines crinkled at the corners of her eyes, but the delicate gold cross at her throat was unchanged—like time had passed around it instead of through it.

She stared at me like her mind couldn't make the image settle.

All the words I'd rehearsed vanished. I stood there with my heart hammering a wicked tattoo against my ribs.

Tears filled her eyes.

That did it.

I stepped over the threshold and wrapped my arms around her.

For a second she went rigid—shock, breath held—then she hugged me back so hard it stole the air from my lungs.

"Anna..." Her voice broke on my name. "Oh, honey..."

Her hand patted my back like she was trying to convince both of us this was real. Then she pulled away, holding me at arm's length, looking me over as if she expected me to disappear if she blinked too long.

"When your uncle took you..." she whispered, swallowing. "Lord, I never thought I'd lay eyes on you again."

She hooked an arm around me and guided me inside toward the kitchen, like her body remembered what to do even if her brain still hadn't caught up.

The house was modest and warm, decorated in a country style that felt like a different universe from the English manor I'd grown up in. Worn furniture. A crocheted afghan folded over the couch. The kind of lived-in comfort that made my shoulders want to drop and my eyes want to close.

But I wasn't here for comfort.

"Sit down a minute," Grace said, already moving like she had a script. "I'll get you a glass of iced tea."

"No," I said too quickly. "I came for a specific reason."

I stopped in the kitchen. Pale-yellow cabinets. Worn Formica counters. A tea pitcher sweating on the table like it belonged there.

Grace barely heard me.

"I had a dream about you," she said, turning toward the refrigerator as if dreams were an everyday topic. "You and…" She paused, lips pursing as she searched for it. "There was a man. And someone else, too, though I can't quite remember."

Kincade and Azriel.

She remembered the dream walk, but only in fragments—impressions and feelings, blurred at the edges.

"I was in danger," she continued, picking up the tea pitcher. "But I didn't know why. You were there to save me. You and that man." She shook her head with a small, breathy laugh like she didn't want to give it power. "I was scared at first, but then I wasn't."

She set two glasses on the counter, scooped in ice, and poured the tea like normalcy was something you could build with your hands.

"Just a silly dream," she added, waving it off.

"It wasn't," I said before I could stop myself.

Grace glanced at me, eyebrows lifting. "What wasn't?"

"A silly dream."

"Oh, it was," she said gently, like she was soothing a skittish animal. "Honey, it was just a dream."

She pressed a glass into my hand. The cold shocked my fingers. I welcomed it.

"How long's it been," she asked softly, "since Edward took you away?"

"Fifteen years." The number tasted strange. Too big. Too heavy.

Grace's gaze went distant, the past pulling her under.

"That day is still clear as crystal to me." She shook her head once. "I was determined to keep you. But Edward refused to leave without you. Said you were destined for a higher purpose."

She sipped her tea, eyes bright with memory and grief.

I remembered that day, too—not as cleanly. For me it had been anger and despair. A bag packed with my favorite things. Edward telling Grace he'd send for the rest. Boxes showing up later like the pieces of my childhood were freight.

I hadn't spoken to Edward for days.

"Why did you stop writing to me?" The question came out sharper than I intended.

Guilt flickered across her face.

She turned away and set her glass on the counter, then leaned a hand on the edge of the sink like she needed something solid.

"I wanted to," she admitted quietly. "Lord knows I wanted to." She swallowed. "But I thought maybe... it might be best if we stopped."

She didn't look at me when she added, "You have to understand, Anna. It was hard. Hard in a way I didn't know how to fix."

She left it there.

I filled in the rest.

That lump returned to my throat, thick and aching. It had never occurred to me—not really—how she must've felt when Edward barged into her life and demanded he take me back to England. For my own good. For a higher purpose.

"I understand," I said at last, because I did. Because the adult part of me did, even if the thirteen-year-old inside me still wanted to slam doors.

Grace nodded once, blinking fast.

"Ruby was becoming more and more unreasonable," she said, voice warbling. "Unstable." She sniffed, then shook her head like she hated the word. "So I left the city and moved back here, knowing she'd never follow me. She hated it out here."

I stared at her. "I never knew."

"And my daddy…" Grace's voice softened. "He was suffering from dementia. I needed to be here for him."

She turned back toward me, eyes damp. "We didn't speak for years after I left. He expected me to stay and take over the clock shop." A sad smile touched her mouth. "It hurt him that I never wanted it."

Even though I already knew the answer, I asked it anyway.

"Does he still live here?"

Grace shook her head. "No, honey. He passed a few years ago. I inherited the house and the shop." Her gaze dropped to the counter. "I'm just grateful we were able to reconcile before he died."

No mention of Ruby, but she didn't have to say her sister's name for me to understand. Dead, incarcerated, or simply gone in the way some people chose to be gone. Either way, Grace wasn't offering that door, and I wasn't going to kick it open.

"Grace, I'm here because—"

The doorbell rang, sharp and jarring, cutting the sentence clean in half.

I snapped my mouth shut and glared at the sound like I could intimidate it.

Grace gave me a faint, apologetic smile and started toward the front door.

"I'll be right back," she said. "Seems strange to have another visitor. I don't get many out here these days."

It wasn't strange.

The person on the other side of that door had followed me like a shadow my whole life.

Grace opened it—and Edward stood there.

My stomach sank.

Her whole body went still, like a switch flipped inside her.

Edward gave a nod of greeting, polite as a blade. "Hello, Grace. I hate to interrupt the reunion, but..." His gaze slid past her to me. "Anna, we've lingered here long enough."

Grace spun around, eyes wide and full of accusation and hurt.

"Why are you here, Anna?" she demanded. "And why didn't you tell me you were coming?"

I shifted, suddenly thirteen again and too old for it at the same time. I didn't even know where to start. How did you tell someone the world was bigger and darker than they'd ever imagined—without sounding insane?

I opened my mouth—

And Kincade shoved past Edward and into the house, gun in hand.

"Anna. Now."

Grace went pale. Her gaze locked on him like recognition punched through fear.

"You," she whispered. "You were in my dream."

"What did you tell her?" Edward snapped.

"Nothing yet!" I shot back. "I didn't have time."

Kincade didn't touch me. He didn't grab. He stepped in close enough to block my line of sight to the door—close enough to make it clear the argument was over.

"We're leaving."

"I'm not leaving without Grace."

Grace's voice sharpened, fear turning into offense. "What in the world is going on?"

"No time," Kincade said, eyes flicking to the windows. "Grace—if you're coming, move. Now."

Edward was already moving, heading out the door like he'd been waiting for permission all his life.

Kincade shifted again, angling his body between me and the front of the house, and caught my elbow—firm, brief—trying to pull me with him.

I tore free.

"I'm not leaving without her." I planted myself beside Grace and refused to budge.

Kincade's jaw clenched. His eyes went flat.

"Anna," he said, voice low. Warning. "He's coming."

"Who's coming?" Grace demanded.

Before I could answer, the explosion rocked the house.

The front windows flashed white-hot. The air punched inward. Somewhere outside, metal screamed and shattered. The car became a fireball.

Edward stumbled back inside, slamming the door hard enough to rattle the windows.

My blood turned to ice.

Azriel was here.

CHAPTER 13

I SHOULD HAVE LISTENED to both Edward and Kincade. But did I? No.

"We're about to be overrun," Edward said.

"By what?" Grace demanded.

"Minions?" Kincade asked Edward, ignoring her.

Edward nodded. "And more."

"Fuck all." Kincade went to the front window. He pushed aside the sheer curtains and peered out. "He's out there all right."

"I would appreciate it you didn't use that kind of language in my house." Grace propped her hands on her hips sounding every bit like the southern belle I remembered. "And who is out there?"

I turned to her, took her by the shoulders. She dropped her hands to her side. "This is going to be difficult to explain and even more difficult for you to understand."

"Demons," Kincade barked, interrupting me.

I shot him a glare. Edward pulled his flaming sword from thin air. Grace gasped as her eyes went wide and round as she stared at Edward.

"What the devil is that? How did you do that?" She started pull away. I held her in place and gave her a little shake.

"Listen to me, Grace. I...see things. Supernatural things."

She focused on my face, her gaze meeting mine. Her brows drew together in question and suspicion, as though she didn't believe me. "What kind of supernatural things?"

I cleared my throat.

"Bloody hell just tell her the truth, Anna," Edward said, holding his sword aloft. He didn't even turn around when he spoke. He stood there, ready to do battle.

"I see angels and demons. Specifically, I see fallen angels and right now there's one out there trying to take you from me."

Grace jerked away and stepped back. Disbelief lined her face as she peered at me. Her hand flew to her neck as she fingered the small cross resting there. She shook her head. "Those things don't exist."

"Yes, they do." I pointed at the car on fire outside the house. "He blew up the car to send me a message. To send us a message. He's coming for you."

She cut a glance at the window where Kincade stood. "I don't see anything, Anna."

Kincade swore under his breath. "He's using his dark magic to hide it."

Which meant if we hadn't been there, she'd never see them coming. It occurred to me then she didn't have a guardian angel hanging around. Normally, in these types of situations, her guardian would be ready to protect her.

One conclusion came to mind.

"He's already killed her guardian angel," I blurted.

"Likely," Edward said with a nod.

"What do we do now?" I asked.

"We fight." Kincade continued to peer out the window, his gun held aloft.

I whipped out my jade-handled dagger. But apprehension swept through me. I didn't want to do battle here in Grace's house. Not in the house she inherited from her father.

Her face turned ashen as her hands started to shake. Fear creased her face as she backed away, shaking her head.

"This is all a bunch of malarkey." Even as she said it, she pressed her fingertips to her lips as she backed away from me ready to bolt.

"No, Grace, it isn't," I said, trying again. "Edward, please help."

He hid his flaming sword and then turned toward her. Her gaze flew to him. She moved to stand next to me.

"Grace, do you remember what I told you when I came for Anna fifteen years ago?"

"You said she was destined for a higher purpose." Her voice shook when she spoke. "And then you told me I wasn't good enough to provide for her."

I snapped my head in his direction, but he didn't even flinch at her words.

"I said she was destined for a divine higher purpose. Remember that?"

"I suppose that's what you said, though I will never forget those hurtful words. I provided as best as I could for Anna."

"I know you did," he said with a nod. "But her best chance was with me. I thought you understood that."

"You took her from me." Bitterness and resentment laced her words.

My heart kicked into high gear. Edward had never shared this with me. Neither had Grace. It was clear she harbored resentment against Edward for taking me away from her.

But Edward didn't miss a beat as he continued.

"Anna is telling you the truth. She sees angels, demons and everything in between. And if you don't do exactly as we tell you, then you will die. Lucifer will have your soul and add you to his army of demons." His urgent tone was cold and unemotional, though I understood he merely stated facts. "Do you understand?"

To Grace, he must sound like an unemotional automaton. She glanced between the two of us and swallowed hard. "I understand."

"Good. Anna, take her to the bedroom. Barricade yourself—"

"No," I said. "I'm staying to fight."

Annoyance flickered over his face. "Barricade yourself in there. If they get past us, you're her only defense."

"Do it now, Anna," Kincade added. Then said, "I hope you're ready for this, Ed."

If the situation wasn't dire, I might have laughed at Kincade calling my uncle Ed.

I took Grace by the hand and led her from the living room down the hallway to the last bedroom on the right. It was the master. I shut the door and then looked for a piece of furniture to move in front of it.

Not that it would keep Azriel out. He had the ability to appear wherever he wanted at will. I, however, refused to share that information with Grace. No need to freak her out any more than she already was. The dresser was too heavy to move. I abandoned that idea.

White lacy curtains at the window billowed with the tell-tale sign it was open. I dashed across the room to close it. I sheathed my dagger to have the use of both hands. The second I reached for the window to push it down, Grace's shriek halted me.

I didn't have to turn around to know who was behind me and what was happening.

"You lost, *chérie*."

I slipped the dagger from the sheath, turned my head, and glared at him over my shoulder. He held Grace to him, a silver blade at her throat. His black wings were spread wide behind him ruffling in sheer delight with triumph. Flashbacks of Ben surged forward, but I kept them at bay. I couldn't afford to let emotions get in the way. Not this time. I had to stay focused.

"Your demons and minions are keeping Kincade and Edward busy. They were merely a distraction," I said.

He gave me that awful wolf grin. "I'm glad you figured that out on your own." He tightened his grip on her, the blade pressing deeper into her skin. A drop of blood appeared on the edge. "I did warn you."

I nodded. "You did."

In my head, I called out to Kincade. *He's here. In this room with us.*

And Kincade's reply. *For fuck's sake.*

That was one of the things I liked about Kincade. He never minced words.

"But you're not going to take her like you did Ben," I said aloud.

A dark brow lifted in amusement. "I'm not? Would you care to tell me how you plan to stop me?"

As if on cue, the door to the bedroom blew open and Kincade barged into the room. It was enough to startle Azriel into releasing Grace enough for her to react. She stomped on his instep, then used her fist to swing her hand backward and punch him in the balls.

Azriel was not prepared for that. He grunted, the blade slipping from her throat enough for her to wiggle out of his grasp. She spun around to face him and used the heel of her hand to pop him in the face. His nose spurted blood.

Kincade and I both stood frozen in place staring in utter disbelief at the beating Azriel took at the hands of a petite woman in her late fifties.

Behind me, glass shattered as demons poured inside the room through the window.

"Kincade!"

He high kicked Azriel in the chest and grabbed Grace by the arm in one slick move. He shoved her behind him. The man was amazing at that kind of stuff. No wonder he wanted to train me. Azriel fell backward into the dresser, the items on top bobbling and toppling over. His head cracked against the edge with a sickening smack. He fell to the floor, unconscious.

As demons poured into the room, I faced them. Stabbing as many as fast as possible watching them turn to ash. One particularly large angry demon charged me. I tried to stab him, but his red clawed hands were around my throat in a matter of seconds.

Behind me, I heard the high pitch whine of the demon gun and cringed.

I squeezed my eyes shut as the demon's head exploded all over me. The thing tumbled to the ground in a stinking heap. Gross.

"That is so my favorite thing," I groaned.

"Let's go. Now, Anna."

Grace dry heaved at the sight of the dead demon and probably the brain guts all over me. Kincade snagged her by the arm and dragged her out of the room. I, however, took a second to step into the master bathroom to grab a towel.

"Anna, now!" Kincade barked from the other end of the hall.

"Sheesh," I muttered, wiping my face.

But I paused a second to look at Azriel. I saw no blood behind his head, so I assumed he was still alive. With him unconscious, I had a chance to kill him. To remove him from my life once and for all. I gripped the dagger in my hand and took a step toward him.

This was it. This was finally going to be over. The darkness inside me swirled into a maelstrom urging me to take another step and another. It clouded my senses, leaving me with thoughts of violence and revenge. I lifted the dagger, ready to plunge it into his heart.

And that's when I was hit with the paralysis with which I had become all too familiar. My hand froze midair as I stood over Azriel's lifeless body.

Oh, balls.

"Oh, my dear, you are a brave one." Abaddon chuckled with delight.

I sensed him behind me. He leaned over my shoulder, his heated breath trickling over my neck.

"And now you are mine."

He wrapped his arms around me. The last thing I remember was my dagger clattering to the floor.

And then there was nothing more.

* * *

I AWOKE TO A stabbing pain in the back of my head. With my eyes still closed, I rolled to my side, the ground cold and hard beneath me. Fear lanced through me. Fear at the thought of where Abaddon brought me. My guess was somewhere in the pit of Hell.

Not my idea of a swell time.

I opened my eyes to a cell that was like the one Azriel held Kincade when he'd taken him to the Second Circle. This did not bode well. I managed to push to a sitting position, my head still pounding away with such pain, my eyes hurt. I propped up my knees and rested my forehead there, waiting for the pain to pass.

It didn't.

What did that bloody dark angel do to me?

I glanced around the cell. It was empty save for a marble slab that looked like it could be a bed. No shackles, though, so I suppose that was something to note.

I still smelled like demon guts. My clothes were stained with them thanks to Kincade and his killer gun. One of these days he and I were going to discuss his penchant for killing demons next to me.

Thinking of him made me think of Grace and Edward. I hoped the three of them got out of there without anything else happening. But they had to wonder where I was and what happened to me.

I reached for my dagger, then remembered I dropped it when Abaddon paralyzed me. Kincade or Edward would find it and suspect someone took me. They were smart, so I didn't doubt for a second they'd figure out who it was.

I didn't have much hope they would find me and get me out of here, though.

Faint footsteps approached. I got to my feet and peered out the cell bars, waiting for Abaddon to appear. I didn't have to wait long. He arrived in a flourish dressed all in black and looking well pleased.

"Hello, my pet." He practically purred the words.

I said nothing. My mind raced to come up with something—anything—to get me out of this. I had no dagger. All I had were my wits.

"Are you wondering where you are?" he asked.

"No," I replied, my voice deadpan.

He clicked his tongue. "Pity."

He waved his hand. The bars disappeared giving him access to my cell. He halted a breath away from me. Still smiling. His long-nailed hand ran down my arm. He traced each finger with the tip of his nail. Bile rose to the back of my throat.

"Take your filthy hands off me." I sounded a lot braver than I felt.

He paused, one tip still on my index finger. He chuckled. "You are so feisty. I love that about you. Did you know that?"

"I don't care," I said.

He stiffened, the irritation emanating off him in waves. He didn't like when I talked back to him. He removed his hand.

"Do you know why you're here?"

"No doubt so you can torture me," I replied.

In the other situations when Abaddon was around, the dark magic inside me flared to life. Not this time. I took a second to quickly analyze that. Before, when it blazed bright and hot inside me, I experienced darker emotions—rage, hate, vengeance.

That must be the key to controlling the dark magic swirling inside me.

Somehow, I needed to keep those darker emotions in check. And suddenly Obi-Wan Kenobi's voice flickered through my mind. *Don't give into hate. That leads to the dark side of the Force.*

Yeah, no kidding.

He leaned forward so his lips were a breath from my ear. "There's no one to hear you scream. I look forward to hearing you scream."

Bastard.

"You won't hear me scream."

A brow lifted in amusement. "And why is that?"

"Because you're not going to soil your Lord Master's prize."

It was the best I managed to come up with. I recalled Kincade mentioning it was possible I was one of the relics. I also recalled Lucifer telling Azriel he was determined to have me because the Holy Relics were useless without me.

I peered at Abaddon's face, looking for clues of a reaction. His expression remained impassive. But then I saw it. He clenched his jaw tight.

I was right. He knew it. I knew it.

"He will be finished with you one day and when he does, it will be my turn."

I almost laughed. Azriel said something similar once. "Get in line, bucko."

He didn't like that one bit.

But I decided I wasn't afraid of him. I was not going to allow the dark magic to surge forward again and control me. I didn't have my dagger, but that was okay.

"Take me to Lucifer," I demanded. When Abaddon didn't respond, I ventured a guess. "That is why you captured me, isn't it? For Lucifer?"

His eyes narrowed. "One day, your cavalier attitude will get you killed."

"Maybe so, but not today."

I truly didn't know what Abaddon's plans were for me, but judging by his reaction, I hit it close to home. Perhaps he intended to use me and discard me and then tell Lucifer I was already dead when he found me. Perhaps he intended to use me and turn me into one of his little minions.

None of that sounded fun to me.

Abaddon said nothing more. He retreated to the hallway, waved his hand, and the cell doors returned. He left me there.

Super.

Now what?

I perched on the edge of the marble and waited.

I had no idea how much time passed but at last there were more footsteps. This time, it sounded like more than one person. I glanced toward the cell, my breath pooling in my chest. A man appeared at the cell door. A strikingly good-looking man. Tall with a head full of wavy black hair, the length of it brushing his broad shoulders. His brutally handsome face peered at me with a faint smile curling up oh-so-kissable lips. Stubble shadowed his cheeks and chin. And his eyes...I had never seen eyes that blue before. They struck me right to the core and made my girl parts stand up and take notice.

I didn't want my girl parts to stand up and take notice. But, alas, I had no control over them.

He wore a black three-piece suit, black dress shirt, black tie, black shoes. He was sin and temptation all rolled into one tall, dark and sexy package.

"Hello, Annabelle."

The sound of my full name lingered on his lips, sending a little zing of delight through me.

I was no fool. I knew exactly who this was. This was not the leather-winged beast I saw speaking to Azriel in my dream-vision. No. Though that was his true visage, he appeared to me as a man because he understood that appearance would be most appealing to me.

I gave him a little hello nod. "Lucifer."

He chuckled, a deep rumble in that broad chest of his. My senses thrilled at the sound. I mentally chastised myself for being tempted.

Words from the family history book drifted through my mind. *She will be tempted beyond all temptations.*

Lucifer was just that—temptation. A temptation I did not need.

"Thank you, Abaddon, for doing what Azriel could not." Though he spoke to the dark angel behind him, he never broke eye contact with me. "I appreciate you bringing her to me."

"It was my pleasure, Lord Master."

Funny he didn't mention it took him several tries to nab me. My gaze flickered to Abaddon, but he kept his head bowed in reverence.

"You are dismissed," Lucifer said.

Abaddon disappeared into the shadows, melting away to nothing. Lucifer regarded me with those piercing, cold eyes for a long silent moment.

"You wished to see me?" he asked.

"I did." But now that he stood in front of me, I had no idea what my next move was. I improvised. "I believe you were looking for me."

"I was. No longer. Such a lovely prize."

"I'm no man's prize," I retorted.

"I'm no man," he replied.

"Forgive me. You're the Prince of Darkness."

"I am the King of Hell." He flashed a wicked grin, as if he enjoyed our verbal volley. "And you are soon to be my queen."

I snorted. "Yeah, right."

"Even now the darkness grows inside you," he said, ignoring my outburst. "Give yourself to it and you will know all the pleasures you've denied yourself. All the pleasures you desire."

As he spoke, that familiar tingling sensation erupted inside me. As though he called to that darkness and used it to his advantage.

"I sense it as you do," he continued with a nod. "The lust. The wrath. It lingers inside you, calling to me. Beckoning me."

He waved his hand and the cell bars disappeared. He stepped in front of me as Abaddon had. I remained still, holding my breath, as he reached for me. He pressed his cold hands against my cheeks. His eyes never left mine.

"Embrace it, Anna. Embrace me. Together, we will find the remaining relics. I will crown you my queen. Together, we will rule over all mankind."

My breath caught in my throat as I peered deep into his soul and saw the vision he wanted for himself, for me, for the world. He wanted to use the relics and me to conquer all of mankind. He wanted to sit higher than all, on a golden throne, while the world fell into debauchery and evil and sin. And he wanted me at his side while he did it. In his vision, he reached for my hand, took it and kissed it with his black lips. Our bodies entwined in sordid lovemaking.

No. No. It cannot be that way.

My heart rammed hard against my chest as I squeezed my eyes shut. I shoved him away and stumbled backward. My breath see-sawed in and out, in and out. I pressed a hand against my pounding heart.

"That will never happen." The words exploded out of me, as though I were out of breath. His vision would never come to pass. Not so long as I lived despite the dark magic inside me. I had faith in that.

He peered at me with those damned disturbing eyes for a long moment, his gaze narrowing, his dark brows furrowed.

"You will come to understand your role in this war, Annabelle. You will be my queen. It is foretold and it is your destiny."

With that, he left the cell. The bars re-materialized as he retreated, leaving me alone.

I was so screwed.

CHAPTER 14

I PACED THE LENGTH of the small cell biting my thumbnail trying to figure a way out of this. It was about four steps one way, four steps the other way.

At least now I understood what Lucifer wanted with me—to hunt down the rest of the relics, be his queen and rule the world.

If I thought my life sucked before, it truly did now.

I stopped pacing and perched on the edge of the marble, staring at the black bars of my prison, thinking about all the ways I managed to fuck everything up. I was a walking disaster. Everyone was right about me. I was a selfish brat who spent more time trying to get out of being Keeper of the Holy Relics than embracing who I truly was. My birthright.

Lucifer was wrong. Being his queen wasn't my destiny. Being Keeper of the Holy Relics was. It was time to start believing in myself. It was time to start trusting my faith and having the courage to trust it. To give hope back to mankind, to all those who supported me. To control my bloody impulses.

Faith. Hope. Courage. These were the virtues I needed to embrace.

Coming to that decision wasn't easy. In some ways, it felt as though I gave up part of myself and maybe I did. Embracing change was also acceptance. I accepted the past for what it was. Now it was time to accept the future.

That future did not include Lucifer.

A sense of peace cascaded through me. As though I released a deep breath I hadn't realized I was holding. As though a weight was removed from my soul.

More footsteps echoed through the chamber. I stood, anticipating seeing Abaddon return.

Much to my surprise, Azriel paused outside my cell. His face had bruises. One eye was black. It seemed like moments ago I left him on the floor of Grace's bedroom with murderous intent. He looked at me with those dark, devastating eyes and an expression that read he was not in a good mood.

"What are you doing here?" I asked.

He produced a key in his left hand, holding it for me to see it. He said nothing as he placed it on the ground outside the cell then started to walk away.

"Azriel, wait."

I moved to the cell bars and peered out, trying to see him amidst the shadows. He paused, his large black wings ruffled as he turned his head to side eye me over his shoulder and waited.

"Why?" I asked.

"Vengeance," was all he said. "Best hurry, *chérie*."

And then he was gone.

I didn't need an explanation, but I surmised this was Azriel getting back at Abaddon for stealing me out from under him. Leaving the key for me to escape was a giant fuck you to Abaddon. Lucifer, in turn, was unhappy with Azriel's performance and would likely face consequences from the Prince of Darkness—sorry—the King of Hell. Perhaps he already had faced those consequences judging by the bruises on his face.

The black key glistened in the half-light. Odd the bars had a key when before Abaddon and Lucifer merely magicked them away. But who was I to complain?

I kneeled and reached through the bars for the key. When I had it in my hand, I stood and fumbled to get it into the lock. It wasn't easy but I managed. I swung open the door.

And hesitated.

What if this was some elaborate trap Azriel set for me and I was walking right into it? What if he was working with Abaddon and Lucifer to get me out of the cell for a nefarious reason I was too dense to realize? I didn't have much of a choice, though. I had to find my way out of here—wherever here was.

I dropped the key into my pocket, not knowing what else to do with it, and stepped into the shadowy hallway.

I waited for alarms to go off, but nothing happened. With my heart in my throat, I took a tentative step in the direction Azriel had gone. It would have been nice if he'd given me an exit strategy. The farther I ventured into the shadows, the more my nerves were on high alert. But I kept going in the hopes I would find my way out.

I doubt I would get lucky, though. Luck was rarely on my side.

Up ahead was a cacophony of noise. It sounded like a lot of cheering and nonsense. I rounded a corner. Light flooded the chamber. I squinted, my eyes adjusting to the sudden bright light.

Lucifer, still in human form, was surrounded by his minions and dark angels. I scanned the crowd but didn't see Azriel or Abaddon. He stood in the center, higher up than the others looking well pleased.

"My friends, I found our future queen."

An eruption of cheers. He waved them down to silence and continued.

"She is here with us now. She will help us find the remaining relics. When she possesses them all, our armies will be ready. You, my dark angels, will march upon all the lands and seize control. We will take the souls of those who resist. They will fight for us. And a new age will begin."

More cheers from the demonic masses.

Holy shit. He was going to destroy mankind and rule on high.

"But humans will resist you." I stepped into the light, making my presence known.

Silenced descended in the cavern. Lucifer's brilliant blue eyes pierced me as they narrowed. No doubt he wondered how I managed to escape the prison.

"No one can resist me," Lucifer said. "Not even you."

My back stiffened. Something deep inside me tingled and snapped. It wasn't anger that erupted, but a deep-seated desire to prove him wrong. A need to make sure he understood he did not control me.

"Especially me," I corrected.

Anger creased his face. "Seize her and bring her to me."

He made a hand motion toward his minions and dark angels. They all turned to me with their beady little eyes boring into me. I realized then the mistake I made. Another one in a long line of mistakes. Why didn't I just keep my mouth shut, keep walking, and find my way out of here?

No, I had to open my big mouth.

The group of his miscreants charged me. I inhaled a deep breath and stood my ground, unwilling to be intimidated by any of them. My hands clenched into tight fists. That thing that snapped inside me moments ago erupted with a fierceness I had never experienced before.

Brilliant white light exploded all around me. It was different than the light that erupted from me when I attacked Kincade and Decker. This was not born out of anger and revenge, but something else—faith and hope. It shot toward the minions and the dark angels determined to take me down. The first few the light blasted through turned to ash.

And everything and everyone halted.

Surprise flickered through me as I peered down at the pile of ashes. I did that? How? I didn't even have my dagger. Lucifer, meanwhile, had shielded his eyes but his skin had turned a charred black.

"You bitch! You have the Godlight!"

Wait. What? I had the what?

"Go back to whence you came!" He flung his hand toward me as if to shoo me away.

Darkness slammed into me like a fist in the middle of my chest. The breath pushed from my lungs. I felt myself falling, falling, falling into an abyss.

And then darkness shrouded me.

⊸———⊷

A WONDERFUL SENSE OF peace filled me. At first, I wasn't sure if I was awake or dead. Then I realized everything ached. The pain in my head was still there and had never abated. Now, a bone chilling cold seeped into my bones. I was aware my body was sprawled out on the cold, hard ground. I had no idea where I was. I inhaled and smelled damp bracken.

All indications I was not dead.

I opened my eyes to a canopy of leaves overhead. As I sat up, I realized I was in a forest not unlike the one from where I entered Dante's Cave, a passage to Hell. I took it to retrieve the Horn of Gabriel.

Huh.

I surmised Lucifer threw me out of Hell to the first available place. Hence, here I was shivering and alone, smelling like demon guts and wondering how the crap I was going to get back home. I had no cell phone—I never carried one. I imagined Edward worried about me while Kincade was furious I gave him the slip once again.

I rolled to my feet and managed to stand. My head screamed with the agony of movement.

The sun slanted through the trees from the west indicating late afternoon. Standing there staring at the trees was not getting me any closer to home. I started walking.

And thinking about my recent stint in Hell. Moments before Lucifer kicked me out, he shouted I had the Godlight. I had no idea what that meant. I hoped Edward would be able to give me more information.

I walked and walked as the sun dipped closer and closer to the horizon and the shadows deepened in the forest. An eeriness crept up the back of my neck, making my spine tingle. I paused to scan the shadows, looking for...what? I had no idea what I was looking for, but I was certain I sensed someone. I sniffed the air but didn't scent any demons. Small victories.

I continued walking as night descended, giving the leaves and trees an ominous appearance. It was the absolute last place I wanted to be, but seeing as how I didn't have any transportation, I didn't have much of a choice. I was going to have to bed down for the night.

Good times.

As I trudged through the darkening forest, I sensed a presence again. I halted again but saw nothing and no one. Even so, my hair stood on end and that spine-tingling sensation was back. Someone was out there in the shadows. Stalking me. My heart pounded double-time.

I wished I had my dagger.

Glancing around, I found a stick the size of a baseball bat. I snatched it up, holding it as a weapon, ready to strike.

"Show yourself," I demanded. At least my voice was strong and sure.

"I didn't mean to scare you," the familiar female voice replied.

I scanned the area but still saw nothing. "Where are you?"

Astrid stepped out of the shadows, as if materializing out of thin air. Her gray and black wings spread open behind her, giving her a majestic appearance as the first slivers of moonlight slanted through the trees over her. Her long black hair cascaded over her shoulders in soft waves. Her bright blue eyes were guarded.

Killian stood behind her with his strange kaleidoscope eyes glowing in the dark. Without the hoodie, his pointed ears were apparent. He had an ethereal look about him. That vision of him wearing the crown wielding a sword struck me again. Who was this guy?

I took a deep breath to calm my racing heart.

"You scared the shit out of me." I lowered the stick but still gripped it. "How did you find me?"

"Killian told me what happened after you blew up the crypt," she said, though she didn't elaborate. It didn't escape me she didn't answer my question either.

"That I was almost captured by the destroyer angel?" I asked.

She nodded but said nothing else. I started walking again.

"Anna, wait."

"I want nothing to do with you," I barked. "I killed innocent people because of you."

"Those people you killed were part of the seedy underground Azriel was cultivating to become part of Lucifer's dark army. I wouldn't lose sleep over their deaths." She sounded so bitter and angry it took me aback.

"Great, but I still have guilt."

"Anna, I can help you—"

I spun to face her, pointing the stick at her. She halted mid-step, eyeing the makeshift weapon. "No. I don't want your help. You helped me enough."

Deep down, I blamed Astrid for nearly succumbing to the destroyer angel that night at the crypt. She'd given me the explosives and nurtured that deep-seated wrath within me for Azriel. And I fell for it. If it hadn't been for Kincade, Abaddon would have captured me then.

I started walking again, this time faster.

"I owe you a debt." She hurried after me with Killian trailing behind. Their footsteps shuffled on the forest floor.

"You owe me nothing."

"You don't understand." She huffed out a breath. "Will you stop a minute and let me explain? Please, Anna."

I sighed. It was the please that got me. I stopped and turned to face her. "Fine but make it quick. I want out of this forest."

"You aren't going to get out of here without help," she said and cut a glance at Killian.

Suspicion lanced through me as I peered at him. "And why is that?"

"You're in the forest of the Fae. My people guard this place from demons. We will let you leave when we're ready."

"Of course." I rolled my eyes and turned my attention back to Astrid. "Spill your guts."

"I admit blowing up the crypt was self-serving." At least she had the nerve to look ashamed.

"You don't say?"

"I was Azriel's prisoner. He had me tethered to the place."

I regarded her with speculation. "Tethered how?"

"He wanted to make sure she couldn't use her power against him," Killian said. "When you blew up the crypt, his dark magic released his hold on her."

"That's why she convulsed in your arms?" I asked.

He nodded.

"And this power of yours…" I paused, trying to decide how to put the question.

"I will show you," she said.

She cupped her hands, holding one on top of the other. A faint blue light appeared between them, circulating and spinning like a mini vortex. She expanded the distance between her hands and then a lantern materialized glowing with bright yellow light.

"I can create anything I want from nothing."

She extended the lantern to me. I took it, holding it up to light her face.

"Is that all?" I asked.

"No." She cut a glance at Killian who gave her a nod. "I can also do this."

She waved her hands again and this time the world spun on its axis. Suddenly the sun rose in the east and light filtered through the trees, illuminating the dew on the forest floor. I stared at her, hard, as I realized what she did. Kincade said she was a time warper, but I didn't buy that.

Now I did.

"You can alter time."

"And space," she added with a nod.

"And this debt you owe me?" I asked.

"You saved me from Azriel. For that, I owe you my life. A debt to be repaid, Keeper."

I shifted from one foot to the other, wondering if I was supposed to continue to hold the lantern.

"How will I know your debt is paid?"

"You'll know."

"I suppose you want to tag along, then."

She nodded. "Where I go, Killian goes."

"All right then, both of you. Can we start by getting the hell out of this forest? I have to get back to my uncle. Also, you never answered how you found me."

"I am half-demon," she said. "I can track you as Azriel can."

Super. I made a mental note to find out if there was some way to get rid of this godforsaken tattoo.

"You are tired, Keeper," Killian said. "Come with me. My people will allow you to rest and…" He paused as he looked me up and down. "Refresh."

"Yeah, I stink. I get it," I snapped. Thanks to Kincade and his demon gun. "Lead the way, your majesty."

Astrid sucked in a sharp breath as Killian's eyes widened in shock.

"How did you know that?" Astrid asked.

Ah, so the image that burst into my mind was correct. I played dumb hoping to get the truth out of her. "Know what?"

"It doesn't matter, Astrid." He waved her off.

"But—"

"It doesn't matter." He shushed her with a slash of his hand. Then turned to me. "Come."

He started back through the forest, weaving his way deeper and deeper through the trees. Astrid gave me a sheepish glance as though she'd been chastised. She fell in step behind the Fae.

As did I, with the hope I wasn't going to regret this decision.

CHAPTER 15

I DON'T KNOW WHAT I expected to see walking through the forest, but it wasn't a live working village built among the trees. As we walked through it with its wooden bridges, rope and pulley systems, and houses built at the top—real live treehouses!—we garnered quite a few stares from the villagers.

Or rather I did.

The Fae tree village appeared to be well-established. I wondered how long they had lived here in this hidden forest.

I smoothed my hand over my still demon-encrusted hair and cringed. I must have looked like a fright walking behind Killian and Astrid. I wished I didn't stink like demons and remnants of Hell to make a better first impression.

All work stopped as we made our way through the village. Past a man chopping wood. Past a woman weaving a basket. And little girls making wreaths of flowers for their hair. All Fae. All with pointed ears. All with curious and suspicious stares.

I was out of place here.

But I wasn't going to let that bother me. I never fit in anywhere.

A tall, silver haired Fae man stepped in front of Killian. Suspicion creased his face. We all halted. The man had pale blue eyes and a delicate face with high cheekbones and a thin nose. His long hair was plaited into small braids behind both pointed ears, while the rest hung down his back. Despite the ethereal look to his face, his body was all muscle with broad shoulders, thick forearms and thighs. Like he could bench press two hundred pounds.

His regal gaze was firmly planted on me. I shifted from one foot to the other.

"You bring another stranger here, Killian?" His voice was stern and hard. It was clear he was unhappy I was there.

"Anna is no threat to us, Merric."

Merric, however, frowned in displeasure. His disdain was all I needed to make me want to turn around and leave.

"Maybe this was a bad idea—" I began.

"She needs rest," Killian interrupted. "And you have my word she will do us no harm, nor will she reveal our hidden location." He turned to me, pinpointing me with those eyes of his that were so disturbing. "Will you?"

"You have my word." Mostly because I had no idea where it was.

Merric shoved Killian aside, ignored Astrid and moved to stand right in front of me. "And what good is your word to me, human?"

"Merric, please—" Astrid said.

"Quiet, demon girl. I do not ask for your opinion." He practically spit the words before he turned his deadly attention back to me.

But I'd faced scarier foes than a silver-haired, elegant-faced Fae. I lifted my chin a little higher. "I don't go back on my word."

He regarded me coolly. "We will see, won't we? You will have to earn my trust, human." Then he stepped aside. "Take her to your home, then, Killian, if you must."

I didn't miss the sniff of derision he projected at Astrid. She shrank against Killian's back.

Merric stalked away, disappearing into one of the houses carved at the base of a tree. The rest of the Fae who witnessed the exchange went back to work while keeping a side eye on both me and Astrid. Killian gave me an apologetic smile.

"Don't worry about him. Merric doesn't trust strangers."

"I guess."

He waved for us to follow him. Astrid fell in step beside me, her head low and her shoulders slumped. Merric's sharp words affected her.

"Don't let him get to you," I said, low enough for her to hear. "He's nothing but a bully. I can handle bullies."

"He doesn't like me."

"I gathered."

"Because of what I am."

"But Killian seems to like you a whole lot," I pointed out.

She glanced at him leading us to one of the rope ladders. "He does."

And that was the end of our conversation as we climbed the ladder to the house high in the trees. Killian's home was built around one of the giant redwood trees and sprawled between several thick branches. It was small, yet cozy. Inside, the furniture was also made of wood. A thick plushy carpet covered the floors. A tiny living room gave way to an even tinier kitchenette. Beyond that, a bedroom where the four-poster bed dominated the entire room.

Killian disappeared into the room and returned a few minutes later with clean clothes and a thick towel.

"You can clean up in there." He pointed toward the bedroom.

"Are you sure about this?" I asked, eyeing the stack of clothes and dreaming of a hot bath.

He gave a nod. "It is my pleasure."

I took the clothes and the towel and headed through to the bedroom, wondering why the would-be Fae king and his half-demon girlfriend wanted to help me. It seemed odd.

The bedroom had a small bathroom en-suite. I stood in the center of it, marveling at the tub and shower, the toilet, the sink. How was all this possible? Fae magic?

I was delighted even more when I turned on the shower and hot water came out. I would no longer smell like death and rot.

⎯⎯⎯✦⎯⎯⎯

Twenty minutes later after a hot shower, I was clean again. I toweled off and dressed in the soft brown suede pants, the tunic and the matching suede vest Killian gave me. I pulled on my pink combat boots. All I needed now was my dagger at my side.

Alas, that was currently lost to me.

In the next room, Killian and Astrid had a small feast spread out on the table. My stomach rumbled loudly at the thought of food. I couldn't remember the last time I ate. A ceramic teapot sat in the middle of the table along with a wheel of cheese, a loaf of crusty bread, a pile of fresh fruit, and a log of summer sausage.

When Killian saw me enter, he poured a cup of steaming tea and waved me to the seat across from Astrid. I sat, took the cup of tea, and inhaled the wonderful herbal scent.

"So," I began, "why are you being so hospitable to me?"

Astrid and Killian exchanged a look of contemplation. He took the seat next to her and grasped her hand. It was Astrid who spoke.

"You saved me from Azriel. It's the least we can do to repay you."

I almost snorted. "No, that's not all. There's more, isn't there?"

Astrid started to respond but Killian squeezed her hand and said, "Nothing more than that."

"Sure, okay." I plunked the teacup down on the table. The dark liquid sloshed over the rim and splashed onto the wood. But I ignored it as I got to my feet and headed toward the door even though I had no clue how to get out of here.

"Where are you going?" Panic edged Astrid's voice as though she watched her last hope walk out the door.

"You're wasting my time and I need to get back to my uncle before he sends everyone he knows looking for me."

"Wait, please, Anna." The scrape of Astrid's chair on the floor punctuated her words.

I halted, less than a foot from the door, and waited.

"Killian, you have to tell her," she implored.

"There is nothing to tell."

He sounded so bitter, I spun to face him. "Sure sounds like there is."

He swallowed hard, his throat working. Finally, he took a deep breath, exhaled it. "Perhaps you should sit, Anna." He motioned to the chair I vacated.

Against my better judgment, I trudged back to the table and sat. "Spill your guts, then."

Astrid rested her hand on his arm in a sign of encouragement.

"You called me your majesty," he said. "What made you say that?"

I shrugged. "Hard to explain. I had a vision when I met you. You in a golden crown wielding a glowing sword."

Astrid's fingers squeezed his arm, her nailbeds turning white.

He clenched his jaw, the muscles working there. "I was a king once."

So, my vision was right. I'd had a similar experience when I met Chen in Hong Kong. I saw the Horn of Gabriel when we shook hands. This was a little different. Was this some new power that manifested within me? I sensed something about Killian when I met him and now, I had the beginnings of truth.

"What happened?" I asked.

He lifted his chin a notch, his gaze never leaving mine. "Have you heard of the Tuatha dé Danann?"

"In Celtic myths and legends." I wondered where he was going with this. "They don't exist."

"They do. We do. Because they—we—are also known as the Fae." He thumbed at his chest.

He paused for effect, no doubt allowing that to sink into my muddled brain. It wasn't that I disbelieved him. I had my fair share of run-ins with supernatural beings, after all. It was just that...well, the Fae were nothing more than children's fairy tales.

"I assure you we are real, Anna," he added, as though reading my thoughts.

"Tell her what happened, Killian," Astrid urged.

"The Fae were gifted by the fairy gods with the Four Treasures. Have you heard of these?"

I shook my head. This was nothing my uncle made me study when he had his tutors hammering me day and night.

"The Stone of Fál, the Spear of Lugh, the Sword of Light and the Cauldron of Dagda. They each held their own power and were sacred to us," he said.

"Were?" I lifted an eyebrow with my question, fearful of the answer.

"They were stolen," Astrid put in. "By Lucifer."

I cut a glance from Killian to Astrid, who pressed her lips together. Then looked back at him. "How is that possible?"

"Evil knows no bounds. He went after each of the Four Kings, the keepers of these Four Treasures. One for each," Killian said. "He killed them all except one, stole their lands and destroyed all that remained of our Fae realm."

I understood then. "You're the last living King of the Fae, aren't you?"

"The last of the Four Kings," he said with a nod. "Once the Keeper of the Sword of Light."

My gut clenched. "How did you escape with your life?"

He cut a glance to Astrid. She dragged her lower lip through her teeth.

"I helped him escape," she said. "I was one of Lucifer's favorite dark angels. One of the Fallen along with Azriel. I used my gifts to free Killian and allow him to escape. When Azriel learned of my betrayal, I was tethered to him, to the crypt, as punishment for my crimes. It was a way for him to control me."

I stared at the two of them. What was their story? Why would Astrid free Killian? Other than their certain attraction to each other, that is.

Instead of asking the obvious questions, I asked, "But he was wrong?"

She nodded. "I still had some power left in me. Some I stored for the right moment to break free."

And that moment was when I entered the crypt looking for blood. How fortunate for us both. Now, Astrid was free of Azriel and Azriel was pissed as hell at me for letting her go. Good times all around.

"Lucifer destroyed the realm of vampires as well," Killian said.

"As well as the realms of shapeshifters," Astrid added.

"Shapeshifters?" I asked

"Dragons, wolves, bears, etcetera," she answered.

I recalled seeing vampires in Azriel's underground crypt but I'd yet to see a shapeshifter. Lucifer was finding ways to get into these other realms, destroy them, and take the souls of these supernatural creatures to build his army. Which made me wonder how big was his army? Maybe I didn't want the answer to that question. It might terrify me.

"And now he's looking for the five Holy Relics. Isn't that right?" Killian said.

Prickling fear went through me. "Yes," I said, the word ice as it escaped my lips.

"Like your Holy Relics, our treasures hold power and can be wielded against us. And you are the Keeper of the Holy Relics," he added, though it wasn't a question.

I nodded, not liking where this was going.

"You're all that stands between him and total domination," Killian said.

My heart pounded in my throat as my stomach twisted into a sickly knot. If Killian was right—and I suspected he was—then I had allowed myself to be captured by Lucifer and almost turned against the Light. Did Kincade and Edward know this? And if they did, why hadn't they shared it with me?

And if they did know, it was no wonder Kincade was determined to keep me at his side and out of the hands of evil.

Fuck all.

"He doesn't have all the Holy Relics," I said at last. "At least not yet. I have the Horn of Gabriel."

But I handed Azriel the Spear of Destiny to save Kincade. Which meant, by way of scoring, Lucifer-1; Anna-1. I had to find the remaining relics before Lucifer and his band of merry dark angels got their grubby hands on them.

I didn't want to mention the Spear of Destiny to Killian and Astrid.

"You're telling me this as, what, a cautionary tale?" I asked.

"This forest is hidden by Fae magic and the last remaining sacred place on Earth for my people," Killian said. "If Lucifer wins this fight against you, against mankind, there will be no more places for us to hide from the human realm."

"What about the other supernaturals?" I asked.

"Most of them can blend in with humans undetected," he said.

Astrid nodded agreement.

I tried to wrap my head around the thought of what he was suggesting. What would the world look like then? I shuddered.

Astrid reached for me, placing her hand on top of mine, "Anna, I am sorry I used you the way I did. But it was an opportunity."

"And one you seized," I said with a nod.

She flushed, her cheeks turning pink. "Can you forgive me?"

"Yes." I waved away the thought.

Because dwelling on that was no use. I had to let that go and trust Astrid was correct in that those in the club were being groomed by Azriel for Lucifer's army.

"Your fight with Lucifer is far from over," Killian said. "All that remains of my people are here in this forest. But we are willing to fight."

I blinked as shock rolled through me. "Fight?"

"Don't be dense, Anna. He's offering you an army."

Did I need an army? I didn't even know at this point, but I didn't want to insult him. "Is that why you brought me here?"

"Yes, and…to let you know you are not alone in this."

"What about Merric? He seemed less than friendly."

"I'll handle Merric. I'm still his king, after all," he said. "We have lost much in the wars. He's protective of the Fae people."

"I'll consider the offer."

I intended to keep that information to myself for the time being. I wasn't sure how Edward or even Kincade would react to the idea of having a Fae army. I didn't have a human army at the moment.

I rose from the table. "Now, I have to find my uncle. I need to return to England."

They both stood.

"We understand, of course," Astrid said. "I can take you back there."

"And Keeper," Killian said, "please know my offer stands."

I nodded thanks. "And know, should I need you, I will find a way to call you."

He laughed, which took me aback. "She doesn't understand, Astrid. Tell her."

"Tell me what?"
A smile creased her face. "We're coming with you."
Super.

CHAPTER 16

ASTRID HAD SOME AMAZING powers, that was for certain. I admitted I was rather glad she was on my side and not Azriel's anymore. Otherwise, things would get ugly fast. I described Walker Manor to her in as much detail as possible. She did her magical thing and altered time and space and the next thing I knew we stood on the lawn of my uncle's estate in Somerset.

As soon as we arrived, she collapsed against Killian, her face drained of color.

Alarmed, I asked, "Is she all right?"

"I'll be fine." She waved away my concern.

"Manipulating space and time takes a toll on her," Killian said. He wrapped an arm around her waist to help her walk.

The house loomed in the distance with boarded up windows from the earlier attack. It hurt me to see the manor that way. But, knowing my uncle, he would already have the repairs under construction. A cold wind shifted through us with the reminder it was December. Late afternoon gray clouds threatened rain.

"Welcome to England," I muttered.

"This is where you live?" Astrid peered at the construction zone with a skeptical eye.

"Yes. The manor was attacked by minions and Abaddon."

I motioned for them to follow me. We walked across the pristine lawn dampened by the already fallen rain up to the main house. When I tried the front door, it was locked.

"I thought you said you lived here?" Killian asked.

I flushed hot as I cut him a heated glance. "I do."

I rang the bell and waited. A few minutes later, Piers opened the door. His pinched expression gave way to one of surprise as he looked at me and then the two behind me.

"Miss Walker." He stepped aside to let us enter. "Your uncle will want to see you posthaste. Come with me."

He started for the stairs to the library before I managed a reply. He didn't even question who the two were with me.

"Should we wait here?" Astrid asked.

"No, come on." I waved them an invitation to follow.

We trudged up the stairs and, as we approached the library, my stomach erupted in a swarm of butterflies. My nerves were shot by the time the door opened and I got a peek inside. There was Kincade, Decker, Grace, Edward and Ophelia. Edward sat at his desk talking to someone on his cell phone. Kincade paced the length of the room. Decker perched in one of the chairs, his legs stretched out in front of him, his ankles crossed, head back and eyes closed. Ophelia and Grace were on the sofa. Ophelia had her arm around her in comfort as worry lines creased Grace's face. They both jumped to their feet the second they saw me. Kincade stopped pacing. Edward hung up on whoever he was talking to and charged me.

Piers had the good sense to immediately step out of the way.

"Anna, where the bloody hell have you been? We've been looking for you for days."

"Days?" I repeated. How long was I gone?

He grabbed me in a giant bear hug, squeezing me tight. Very uncharacteristic of him. I was so shocked by the outward display of emotion, I stood lifeless like a ragdoll. When he stepped back, he held me at arm's length and gave me a good once over.

"Are you all right?" he asked.

"I'm fine."

"What happened to you, Anna?" Grace clenched her hands together as she moved to stand behind Edward. "You disappeared that day into thin air."

"What the hell are you wearing?" Kincade stood where he halted, his arms crossed over his massive chest. I glanced down, forgetting I was dressed in Fae attire. "And what is she doing here?" His heated glare landed on Astrid.

"She's a friend—" I began.

"No, she isn't," he interrupted. "She doesn't belong here."

"If Anna says she's a friend then—" Edward started.

"She's half demon," Kincade butted in.

That seemed to get Decker's attention as his eyes opened and he came to his feet and sauntered over, mild curiosity on his face. He paused next to his brother giving us all a good once-over.

"I thought she was dead," Decker said. "I'm amazed she's still alive."

Astrid's cheeks turned bright pink. Killian growled but that was far from intimidating to Kincade. Decker wasn't fazed either.

"Clearly, I am not dead." Astrid didn't bother to hide her irritation.

"And who is he?" Kincade turned his glare on Killian.

"Everyone calm the fuck down. I'll happily explain if you'll let me." My heart raced and my hands shook as I took a deep breath and looked to my uncle. "Can we all take a moment and sit?"

"I'll ring for tea," Edward said.

I sighed. I didn't want tea but that was Edward. If the world was falling down around our ears, he'd ring for bloody tea.

"In the meantime, please do enlighten us on your where-abouts these last four days," he said.

"Four days?"

My stint in Hell and then the Fae forest seemed like a moment in time.

"Yes, Anna. I've been doing everything I can to find you." Edward took his usual wingback chair.

Kincade remained where he stood, glaring at me the entire time I moved to the chair opposite Edward. It was the one Decker vacated. The seat cushion was still warm from his body heat. He kept his position next to his brother while Grace and Ophelia moved back to the sofa. Killian and Astrid remained near the door of the library, appearing as though they were seconds away from making an escape.

"First, this is Astrid." I motioned to her. "She is, in fact, half-demon and Azriel's sister."

"Half-sister," she corrected.

Edward jumped to his feet and drew his flaming sword in one smooth move. He held it aloft, ready to defend me against Astrid.

"Relax, uncle. She doesn't mean us any harm."

"Put away your sword, human," Killian snarled.

Edward gave me a questioning glance. When I nodded, he put away the sword and took his seat again. Piers arrived then with the tea tray. Some of the tension eased from the room. Thankfully, there were tiny lemon cakes and finger sandwiches on the tray as well as a silver teapot, sugar and creamer.

"Thank you, Piers," Edward said by way of dismissal.

The old butler high-tailed it out of there and closed the door behind him. I didn't blame him one bit. I longed to do the same.

"And this is Killian. He is Fae, uncle." I left out he was the last remaining Fae king.

Edward narrowed his eyes at the man as he looked him up and down. His gaze paused on the Fae king's pointed ears before he glanced back to me.

I made the rest of the introductions to Astrid and Killian.

"Now that we're all well acquainted," Kincade said, his tone laced with unabashed annoyance, "perhaps you tell us where you've been."

I took my time as I poured a cup of steaming Earl Grey, added light cream, stirred. It made me happy to watch him fume. I picked up a lemon cake and popped it in my mouth.

"Yes, Anna, do enlighten us." Edward clenched his fist, clearly annoyed by my delay.

I chewed the lemon cake and smiled. "I've been in Hell."

"Told you," Decker said.

Kincade granted him a death look.

"We suspected Abaddon took you when we found nothing but your dagger," Edward said. "How did you get away?"

"Oh, that story is the best." I grabbed another lemon cake and shoved it in my mouth.

Edward sighed, exasperated. Kincade continued to glare. Grace peered at me with wide, unbelieving eyes.

"And are you going to tell us?" Edward finally asked.

"I am." I nodded and sipped my tea.

I told them everything from the time I woke up in Hell to seeing Abaddon and Lucifer. When I shared with them Azriel was the one who let me escape, Kincade appeared as though he was going to vibrate out of his skin.

"Why would he do that?" Edward wanted to know.

"My best guess is he was pissed Abaddon one-upped him with Lucifer," I said.

"He will want something in return at some point, Anna," Astrid warned.

"That wasn't part of the deal," I said.

"It doesn't matter." She shook her head. "He will come back to you and demand payment for your release."

"None of that matters right now," Kincade growled. "You left the cell. Then what happened?"

"Then I found Lucifer."

I told them, too, of the minions coming for me. And the power within me turning them all to ash. And Lucifer shouting I had the Godlight and kicking me out of Hell.

"I woke up in a forest. That's when Astrid and Killian found me and brought me back here."

"Wait a moment, Anna." Edward scooted to the edge of his seat. His face drained of color. "What did Lucifer say to you?"

"He called me a bitch and said I had the Godlight."

Silence descended in the room. Nobody moved a muscle. I wasn't even sure if any of them continued to breathe. I looked around the room, glancing at each of their faces. Kincade still looked pissed as hell. Decker was back to his bored and annoyed face—pretty sure that was his resting face. Astrid moved closer to Killian. And Grace and Ophelia huddled together on the sofa.

"What does it mean, uncle?" I asked.

But it was Kincade who answered. "It means, Anna, you are divine."

I almost laughed. But one look at his face told me he was dead serious.

I had a difficult time believing I was divine because, well, I was walking disaster. I made bad choices and wrong decisions. I allowed my emotions to overrun my common sense. Kincade standing there was proof of that.

Edward, however, managed to regain his stoic façade. He stood and turned to Killian and Astrid. "Forgive me for being a terrible host. I'll show you both to a guest room."

He opened the door to the library and paused in the threshold waiting for them to join him. Astrid shot me a questioning glance.

I gave her the go-ahead nod. She and the Fae king followed him out.

Ophelia hopped to her feet. "It's time for my workout."

"I'll come with you," Grace said.

They were gone next. Decker shuffled out without a lame excuse which left Kincade behind.

He was the only one with balls who remained. He moved to the door, shut it, then stood there looking at me with those green-gold eyes that made me want to crawl under the rug and hide.

The lemon cakes in my stomach turned into a ball of dough and soured.

"Is that what happened?" he asked.

I wanted to throw my teacup at him. "You of all people, Kincade, know if I'm lying. Am I?"

He was silent a long moment, his jaw clenched tight. "No."

He walked over to the bar my uncle kept stocked with the best and most expensive whiskey and poured a glass. He downed it in one gulp, then poured another and a second one for me. He walked it to me, holding it down to me.

I cast aside the tea and took it, grateful for the drink. Instead of downing it, I sipped it, letting the alcohol burn my tongue and the back of my throat.

"Explain to me how I'm divine," I said.

"You don't get it, do you? Even still." He shook his head in frustration.

I huffed out a heated breath. "For me to be divine, I would have to be—" I bit off my own words.

"Angelic," he offered. He lifted one brow as if to challenge me.

I stared at him, hard, gripping the glass in my hand so tight my fingers cramped. "No."

"Yes."

"I don't believe that."

"You should."

"Why?"

"Because you have the Godlight. Lucifer said so himself."

"And you're going to believe that dark angel?" I snapped.

"You destroyed his minions by turning them to ash with a thought. What do you think?"

I didn't know what to think. I didn't want to think anything. I peered down into the amber liquid looking for answers.

"My mother wasn't an angel. She was like me."

Kincade said, "You have a father."

Hearing that sparked a memory. When I first came back to England searching for answers, Edward showed me the family history book. I asked him once what "born of the Light" meant. He thought it was a clue to my father's identity. His words came back to me full force.

I believe he is an angel.

Was it true? Did Edward know it and not want to tell me?

"Why did Edward leave?" I asked.

"Probably because he doesn't want to tell you the truth."

I guess I had my answer. "Why?"

"He's afraid. Like you."

I swallowed hard. He was right. I hated when he was right. I was afraid of everything happening to me. I didn't know how to mentally process it all. But if Edward knew my father was an angel, why not tell me? Why all the secrecy?

"Stop dodging, Anna, and accept it for what it is." Kincade's voice broke into my thoughts.

"Lucifer said being his queen was my destiny." I kept my eyes firmly planted on the whiskey.

"Lucifer's poison. He wanted in your head."

Finally, I lifted my eyes and met his. "Are you sure?"

Kincade gave me one of those looks that told me not to be stupid. "He wants you for your abilities to find and use the Holy Relics."

One of the things I liked best about Kincade was he never minced words. He always said what he was thinking.

Killian's story of the Four Treasures flickered through my mind. Who had Lucifer used to get them? How did he destroy the Fae realm with them? I hadn't shared that information with the group, nor did I want to. That was for Killian to do, not me.

"I had no idea I was gone four days," I said.

"Time moves at a different pace in other realms. Even Hell."

He sounded like he knew what he was talking about, so I didn't disagree with him. I downed the whiskey then and placed the glass on the table in front of me.

"Well, good talk. I'm going to my room," I said.

I headed for the door. As I reached the knob, his voice stopped me.

"I'm glad you're back."

I didn't want to turn around and look at him for fear it would cause a flurry of feelings I wasn't prepared to deal with. "Me, too."

And with that, I left him sitting alone in the library.

The door clicked shut behind me. I paused a moment, closing my eyes and taking a deep breath. Fatigue hit me hard, slamming into me with the force of a freight train. All I wanted to do was get back to my room, shower and sleep in my own bed.

As I rounded the corner, I spied Ophelia pacing the length of the hall. When she saw me, she halted and gave me an expectant look. I suppressed an inward groan. Now what? She headed straight for me with a determined stride, her face pinched with concern. I mentally steeled myself for the barrage of questions to come.

"I'm glad you're back. I need you to come with me."

She grabbed my hand and dragged me down the corridor, away from my room toward hers.

"Ophelia, I'm exhausted and—"

"You need to see this." Her tone was hard, which was very unlike her.

The first hints of worry flickered through me. "What is it?"

She didn't answer as she pushed open the door to her room and led me inside. She closed it with a snap, her back against it. When I saw Darius, I sucked in a sharp breath.

He sat in a chair, his shoulders hunched and his head hanging between them. Most of his feathers were black and gray now. I approached him, dropping to my knees in front of him. I reached for his face, pressing my hand against his cheek and whispering his name.

He lifted his head a little. His ashen skin was a stark contrast to his darker feathers. Those once bright blue eyes were a lifeless dull sheen that held no spark. His cheeks were sunken. His face looked hollow, reminding me much of those catatonic patients I saw back in my hospital days.

All of this was because of the demon poison pulsing through him. And it was my fault. If he hadn't come after me in Hell, if he hadn't saved me not once but twice, he wouldn't be sick.

"You have to help him, Anna." Ophelia's voice cracked in the silence of the room.

"To do that I need the Staff of Moses," I said. "And even then, I'm not sure it will work."

Darius lifted his hand and wrapped his cold fingers around my wrist. He gave me a small smile. "There is no helping me, Keeper."

"Don't say that," I said. "There has to be a way."

"Do not worry for me. My time is coming."

He dropped his hand and closed his eyes, a little sigh escaping through his pale lips. Ophelia emitted a gurgled gasp. She shoved past me and reached for him. She shouldered his weight as best she could. Realizing what she was trying to do, I took his other side. We walked him to the bed and lowered him down. He curled on his side, his wings folded against his back, and was out.

"How long?" I asked, watching him and trying to ignore the pang of guilt.

"His illness accelerated rapidly after you left," she said. "I can't bear to leave him alone. He doesn't eat or drink. All he wants to do is sleep. I'm afraid he won't wake up."

She moved to the other side of the bed where I stood. She gripped my arms, holding them tight.

"You have to find that staff, Anna."

The sense of urgency did not escape me. But as I looked at her, at the worry lines creasing her face, I realized she was in love with Darius.

Or in serious like. Either way, now was not the time to bring it up. I glanced back at Darius. She was right. I had to find that staff. Not just for Darius, but for all of us. All of humanity.

"You're staying with him, I take it?" I asked.

"Yes," she whispered.

I swallowed the nervous ball of fright that developed in my throat. Kincade would never let me go after the staff without him. That meant we would be traveling alone together. Unless Edward or Decker decided to tag along. Or Killian and Astrid.

Honestly, I didn't want any of them to come with me but that wasn't an option.

I had was to find that staff no matter who decided to tag along.

Time to pack my bags for Acre.

CHAPTER 17

NO REST FOR THE exhausted. That was the way of things in my life. I made it back to my room and paused as the door closed behind me. There, lying on the bed, was my jade-handled dagger. I almost wept with joy seeing it. I snatched it up, grateful to have it back in my hand. I resisted the urge to hug it. Next to the dagger was the postcard of Acre, Israel.

I shed the Fae clothes and showered. The hot spray felt good on my tired body. I dressed in my favorite clothes—cargo pants, undershirt, long-sleeved Henley and pink combat boots. I stuck the dagger in the sheath at my waist.

In the bottom of the closet, I found a discarded duffel. My wardrobe was sad and boring, dark and depressing. The one color I wore was the pink combat boots. There was no sense in wearing anything other than black, though. Odds were, I'd end up with demon guts on me again.

I threw clothes in the duffel, not bothering to fold them neatly. All I had to do now was get myself to Acre.

A knock sounded at my door. I grabbed my bag and opened it.

Kincade stood there. His gaze dropped immediately to the bag, then lifted back to my face.

"Going somewhere?"

"I have a date with Acre." I held up the postcard.

He took it from me in one smooth motion and studied it. I caught the flicker of recognition in his eyes before he masked it.

"So this is your mysterious postcard," he said.

"Yes."

He flipped it over, scanning the block handwriting. "Whose is this?"

"No idea."

His gaze lifted to mine, assessing. Deciding whether I'd lied.

"Do you know what this place is?" He held the card out.

I studied the image more carefully this time. Not a photograph—a rendering. Stone walls. Watchtowers. A fortress built to withstand siege.

"It's the Templar fortress in Acre," I said. "Modern-day Akko."

He nodded. "The Mamluks got through in 1291. After that, nothing stayed buried."

"And supposedly hid their treasure there," I added.

His jaw tightened. He had more to say. He wasn't saying it.

"Say it," I said.

"Say what?"

"Whatever you're holding back because you think I can't handle it."

He considered me for a long moment. Then, "The relics were there."

Not *might have been. Were.*

My pulse ticked up. "Which relics?"

"I doubt any remain," he said. "Not after all this time."

"Then why send me there?" I asked. "Why Acre at all?"

He didn't answer immediately. When he did, his tone was neutral. "Perhaps there's something left behind. A trail. A reference."

A clue.

Antarctica hadn't led me to a relic. It led me to my mother.

I nodded slowly. "Or someone."

His gaze sharpened but he didn't disagree.

We stood there, both aware we were circling the same truth without touching it. He knew more than he was saying. I knew he knew.

"Why are you still standing here?" Edward barked from down the hall. "If you're going, then go."

Kincade stepped aside. I moved past him into the corridor.

Another quest. Another breadcrumb trail someone expected me to follow.

And another place where his past and mine overlapped in ways neither of us were ready to name.

<hr>

OUR TRAVELING PARTY WAS bigger than I expected. Me, Edward, Kincade, Killian and Astrid. Kincade was less than thrilled the Fae king and the half-demon girl tagged along. He gave them both a sour look. I didn't mind—we might need her talents. Decker had, apparently, opted out. Probably just as well. He was likely still mad at me for handing over the Spear of Destiny to Azriel.

Ophelia remained behind to tend Darius.

Grace bid me farewell with worry lines creasing her face as she implored me to be careful. She didn't know I'd already been halfway around the world looking for these relics. There wasn't time for an in-depth catch-up with her, something I vowed to do when I returned. At least I had the comfort to know she was safe. Edward assured me he had replaced all the wards around the manor house. No demons or fallen angels would get in while we were gone. Plus, I knew Ophelia would guard her with her life.

The car ride to the airport was silent. Well, except for Edward who was constantly on the phone speaking Hebrew to whomever as he made our travel arrangements. The plan was to land at Haifa International, then check into a small boutique hotel located in the city center. From there, Kincade and I made plans to visit the Hospitaller Fortress in the Old City that once housed the Order.

Thinking about walking through all that history made a tingling sensation erupt on the back of my neck. I thought of the picture on the postcard and wondered how much of it would resemble today's world.

We boarded the plane. Kincade headed to the back to take up his normal spot. Killian and Astrid sat together in the middle. He was back to wearing his hoodie to hide his Fae ears, while Astrid used a glamour to conceal her wings.

I took the second row. Edward sat across the aisle from me. As I settled in, he reached into his bag and brought out something to hand to me.

"This is for you." He held a smartphone in his hand.

I peered at it with suspicion. Even when I lived in Dallas, I never had one. I didn't want that feeling of being tethered to something all the time.

"Why?" I asked.

"Because it's time you had one. I should have given you one much sooner."

Begrudgingly, I took it and stared down at the blank screen. I didn't even know how to turn on the thing. "Thanks, I think."

"Things are unsettled in the Middle East, as I'm sure you know. Despite Israel being the Holy Land, it is not exactly friendly to Westerners."

"I'm aware," I said with a nod. "Is that why you want me to have it?"

He nodded.

Okay, I respected that. I didn't have to like it, though. "Why the plane, uncle?"

"What do you mean?" His brows knit with the question.

"Why not have Astrid time warp us there?"

"We do not need to garner any more attention than necessary."

He had a point. I hadn't a clue how her time warping worked and if it alerted the demons of the deep to our presence. Aside from that, every time she used her powers, it weakened her.

"And," he added and paused as contemplation creased his features. He leaned toward me and lowered his voice. "I had an opportunity to speak with her and Killian. Anna, are you sure you can trust her?"

I shook my head. "No."

"Then, why—"

"She says she owes me a debt." I paused, spinning the smart-phone around in my hand. "She coerced me into blowing up Azriel's crypt. I'm not proud of that but it did send him a message and I freed her from him in the process. I believe she's an asset."

"Until she betrays you." He cut a glance behind him to where she sat with Killian. "She will have to earn my trust."

"And mine," I agreed. "There's something else we need to discuss."

He shifted in his seat, as though uncomfortable. "You have questions."

"And you know what those questions are, don't you?"

"Not here, Anna," he said, his voice still low.

I tried hard not to feel slighted at his response. "Kincade said you were scared to tell me. Are you?"

"When I do, it will reveal truths you must be prepared for."

That sounded ominous. "What sort of truths?"

"When we arrive in Akko, I'll tell you all I know. For now, rest. We have a long journey ahead."

I nodded and heaved a sigh as I leaned my head back, the smartphone heavy in my hand and his words heavy on my mind.

It wasn't long before we were airborne and headed to Israel.

***

MY UNCLE HAD CONNECTIONS across the entire world, it seemed. As soon as we landed in Haifa, he had a car waiting to take us to the small boutique hotel, which had about fifteen rooms. Edward, who also had a bottomless bank account, booked all the rooms on the west side of the hotel with a view of the Mediterranean.

After nearly two days of traveling, we were all exhausted and headed to our own rooms. Killian and Astrid shared, but Edward, Kincade and I had our own. Thank goodness, because I wasn't interested in sharing with anyone, even my uncle. I relished the thought of being alone.

I never enjoyed my uncle's money more than I did at that hotel. The outside of the hotel was rustic, built with natural stone bricks the color of earth. But inside was modern with all the contemporary features and comforts of this century. My room hosted a wrought-iron queen size bed with a white bedspread and the biggest, fluffiest pillows I'd ever seen. The bathroom had a white granite shower, a large mirror over the black granite vanity, and luxurious bathrobes and towels. A built-in desk and bookshelves were on the wall opposite the bed. Instead of floor to ceiling windows, a French door with a balcony.

I dumped my duffel on the bed and headed for the balcony, the serenity of the sea calling to me. Listening to the waves and smelling the sea breeze relaxed me, something I hadn't done in a long time. I closed my eyes, enjoying the play of the wind along my face and the warmth of the sun.

I'd almost managed to empty my head—almost—when the balcony door next to mine slid open.

I opened my eyes to see Kincade step out onto the adjoining balcony.

I exhaled slowly, gripping the railing.

I waited for him to say something. He didn't. He stood there instead, staring out at the water, posture rigid, expression unreadable.

I turned to go.

"I thought I would never return to this place."

I stopped.

The words weren't emotional. They were factual. Final.

I glanced at him. Surprise flickered through me before I could stop it. This was the closest he'd ever come to acknowledging the past without being forced.

"How long has it been?"

"Years."

Centuries, more like.

I took that to mean 1291 was the last time he'd stepped on Israeli soil. I shifted from one foot to the other. Unable to see his face, his expression was shrouded.

"I don't have fond memories of this place," he said then.

That was all.

Not a story. Not an explanation. A boundary.

I remained rooted in place, hoping he would spill his guts, but knowing he wouldn't. He wasn't the kind of guy who confided in others, but he expected me to confide in him.

I related to what he said, though. Growing up with Grace, she scraped money together to keep me fed and Ruby appeased. She did what she could. It wasn't much, and it cost her everything.

I was never the popular, trendy girl in grade school. I never wore what was fashionable. I wore what was available from the local

Goodwill. Perhaps that was why I chose my black cargo pants and Henley shirts. I never needed fancy. I still didn't.

Except for the pink combat boots. They were my signature, the thing that made me who I was, and I loved them.

I nodded once. "I'm sorry."

"There's nothing to be sorry about." He turned then, fixing me with a steady look. "Tomorrow we begin. Be ready."

And just like that, the moment ended.

He stepped back inside and shut the door.

I trudged back inside as the weight of another quest weighed on me. Exhaustion was a constant state, both mental and physical. I perched on the edge of the bed, eyeing the fluffy pillows.

"You will not find the staff here."

Sariel's voice behind me made me jump and kicked my heart into overdrive. I pressed a hand against my chest as I looked at him standing on the other side of the room, his hands clasped in front of him. I took a deep breath to calm my ragged nerves.

"Just once it'd be great if you angels would knock on the freaking door."

"Apologies."

A small smile tipped the corner of his mouth as he moved deeper into the room. He paused at the door to the balcony and looked out, as if enjoying the view. I waited for him to elaborate on his statement, but he didn't.

"So, what does that mean? That I won't find the staff here?"

"Just that." He turned to face me, this time clasping his hands behind his back.

"Where is it?"

"That I do not know."

I huffed exasperation. "Then why was I sent here? Is this a waste of time?"

"No."

But again, he didn't elaborate even though I sensed he had all the answers.

I tried a different question. "What will I find here then?"

"Understanding," was all he said.

My brows drew together at the cryptic response. I leaned back into the pillows and blew out a breath. "All righty then. Is that all you came to tell me?"

"That and to proceed with caution, Anna. This is a dangerous place."

And with that, he was gone.

It was hard to shake the feeling there was more to Sariel's brief visit than a plea to be careful. Like there was more he wanted to say but wouldn't. My suspicion sending me to Acre for a different purpose may have been right. And, I believed, it had something to do with Kincade.

Perhaps I would learn more about him after all in this city.

It was the last thought I had before drifting off to sleep.

CHAPTER 18

MOMENTS AFTER CLOSING MY eyes, my arch nemesis, Azriel, made an appearance. In my fatigue, I failed to put those mental walls. He didn't taunt me as he usually did, though. He was merely there in my dream state. Something was off about him. Why did he appear to me now? What did he want?

"Are you waiting for me to thank you for letting me go?" I asked.

A small smile cracked his hardened features. "You and I both understand that isn't going to happen, *chérie*."

As he moved closer in the dream, I saw his left cheek had deep bruising. Purple and dark blue tinged his skin, marring his wickedly beautiful face worse than when I saw him before. Lucifer must have discovered his insurrection and punished him for it. What else had the dark one done to him?

"No, it's not," I agreed, ignoring his beat-up face. "Why are you here? Trying to seduce me again?"

"No, those days are over. It is clear you and the *gardien* are devoted."

I wanted to snort derision. Azriel wrongly assumed Kincade and I were a thing from the beginning.

"Then what do you want?" I demanded.

"Has your lover told you what happened in Acre all those long years ago?"

"Why don't you tell me yourself?"

His face broke into that familiar wolf grin. "I would not want to steal the pleasure from him. Our destinies have always been intertwined, *chérie*. Yours, mine, his. Everything that's happened since that fateful day has brought us to this point. I hope you are both prepared."

"For what?"

But he was gone in a blink. I startled awake, bolting upright on the bed, still fully clothed, my heart racing. Was he sending us a message? A warning? I had to tell Kincade. I had to find out what Azriel meant by our destinies being intertwined.

I flung open the door to my hotel room and stalked next door to Kincade's. I pounded on it, ready to demand answers—ready to burn the whole night down if I had to.

No answer.

I knocked again and leaned close to the seam of the door like proximity would make him cooperate.

"Kincade. Open up. I need to talk to you."

Nothing.

"It's important!"

The door yanked open.

And there he stood in nothing but a towel, hair dripping, water still beading on his chest and rolling down the hard lines of his stomach like the universe had decided I didn't have enough problems tonight.

My brain stalled. Full stop.

Heat flashed through me—fast, stupid, traitorous—and I hated myself for it.

His expression was carved out of irritation, sharp and lethal, until his eyes landed on me. The anger eased, not into softness, but into alert attention. Like he'd been braced for an attack and realized the threat was... me.

"Something you need?" His tone was flat. Controlled. Already prepared for bad news.

I swallowed, forcing air into my lungs.

"No." The word came out too quick. Too high. I hated that, too. "Sorry to bother you."

I turned like I could retreat with dignity.

His hand closed around my wrist—firm, not rough—and he pulled me back inside before I could decide whether leaving was cowardice or survival.

The door shut behind me with a hard click.

He didn't shove me. He didn't pin me. He stepped in close enough that my body understood exactly who had the advantage, and my back found the door without my permission.

I lifted my hands automatically, palms up.

A mistake.

They landed on his chest—warm, damp skin under my fingertips, muscle and heat and the faint, clean bite of soap. For one humiliating second my body reacted before my brain could throw a knife at it.

Get it together, Anna.

His gaze dropped to my hands. Then back to my face.

"Lie," he said.

One word. Quiet. Controlled. Worse than shouting.

My stomach flipped.

"Now tell me the truth."

Unwanted heat jolted through me again, chased by anger—at him, at myself, at the fact that my pulse had no shame. The scent of soap, clean and unfamiliar, steadied me when everything else threatened to tilt sideways.

For god's sake, get a grip.

His mouth curved faintly, like he could hear the fight happening inside my head. That strange connection between us—ever since Azriel took him—had only grown sharper. I didn't like it. I didn't like anything that let someone get too close without permission.

"Well?" he prompted.

"I had a dream about Azriel."

Fuck.

The words landed wrong, like I'd thrown the blade and it spun in the air.

Everything in him changed.

He jerked back like I'd struck him, not physically—something deeper. His jaw flexed, eyes going flat and furious.

"So he's in your head again."

His voice was steady. Deadly. And the jealousy wasn't about me—it was about contamination. About possession. About something that didn't belong to Azriel touching what Azriel had no right to reach.

Before I could correct myself, he turned and stalked to the bathroom. The door closed hard enough to rattle the frame.

I dragged a hand through my hair, frustration tightening my throat.

"No, Kincade," I called after him, "that's not what I meant."

Silence.

Then the bathroom door opened again and he stood in the doorway, still in that towel like he'd chosen the most inconvenient form of existence possible. I kept my eyes locked on his face on sheer principle.

"Then what did you mean?"

"He asked me if you told me what happened in Acre," I said, forcing the words out clean. "Years ago."

His expression shifted—rage draining, replaced by something like shock. Like I'd named a ghost.

"Why would you assume that?" he demanded.

"Because I'm not stupid." My voice came out sharper than intended. I drew a breath and tried again. "I followed the clues. Things you've said. Things Decker said. I put them together."

"You're guessing." His tone went colder. A boundary, not a tantrum. "Stop."

The bathroom door shut again—not a slam. Just... final.

I exhaled hard through my nose, irritation lighting my blood.

I marched to the hotel door and wrapped my fingers around the knob.

"And my guess is right, isn't it?"

Nothing.

"Aren't I, Kincade?"

"Go away, Anna."

I laughed once, humorless. "You don't want to talk about it. Fine. I'll find Azriel and ask him myself."

I turned the knob.

Behind me, the bathroom door opened.

"Do you know what he said about you?"

My hand froze mid-turn. My stomach clenched. My mouth went dry—ash, instant and bitter.

His voice was low when he spoke again. Controlled, but threaded with something that made my skin prickle.

"Every day I was chained in his prison, he told me exactly what he'd do to you." His jaw flexed like the words tasted like poison. "And I had to stand there and listen."

Slowly, I turned to face him.

The fury on his face wasn't aimed at me. It was aimed outward—at Azriel, at the world, at the memory of helplessness he refused to name.

And it dragged something up in me, sharp and unwanted.

That day in the prison. When Azriel invaded my mind. When everything in me had gone cold and powerless and—

"When he used his dark magic on you and invaded your mind…" Kincade started.

Then he stopped himself. Mouth clamping shut. Teeth grinding. Like saying it aloud would make it real in a way he couldn't survive.

He didn't want to admit what he'd done. What he could do. That he'd dream-walked—attacked Azriel—saved me.

I still didn't understand why he wouldn't tell me. Why he kept that part of himself locked behind iron.

But maybe… maybe because it tied us together in a place neither of us could armor.

A breath shuddered out of me.

I remembered him saying he'd kill Azriel if he ever put another hand on me. I'd believed it then, but I understood now it wasn't a threat.

It was a vow.

"I understand," I said. And it came out rougher than I wanted, because I meant it. Because I understood far too much.

His gaze held mine—burning, contained.

Something in my chest tightened, and I hated that it felt like relief. Like being seen. Like having someone choose to stand between me and the dark.

It was becoming harder not to think about kissing him.

Harder not to think about what Azriel meant when he said our destinies were intertwined.

But I wasn't going to get answers tonight. Not with Kincade standing there half-naked and furious and wounded in ways he refused to name.

And I'd already botched enough.

I backed toward the door, reaching behind me for the knob without taking my eyes off him.

"We can talk more later," I said.

This time he didn't stop me.

The door closed behind me with a snap.

I leaned against it, drawing in a slow breath until my lungs stopped stuttering. My fingers still tingled where I'd touched him—still warm, still damp from the shower. His scent clung to my skin like a lingering mistake.

Whatever was happening between us was getting harder to ignore.

Harder to survive.

I kept telling myself Kincade was not the man for me, yet I kept finding myself in precarious situations with him. The workout room back home. The hotel room here. This connection between us had somehow deepened. It made me want to hide.

What had happened between him and Azriel over seven hundred years ago? Why did Kincade hunt him with the intent to kill him and why was he so protective of me?

I wanted to know the truth, to know their history. I doubted I would ever get it.

My shattered nerves would never allow me to sleep again. I made my way to the lobby where I found Edward perched on one of the dark green velvet sofas reading the afternoon paper—in Hebrew—and sipping a cup of tea. My Hebrew was rusty. I understood a few scattered words across the printed page.

I was always impressed and amazed by his ability to read the local news and sip tea as though he belonged there.

"Ah, Anna. Care for some tea?"

"Does that tea come with answers?" A subtle way to remind him of the promise he made me on the plane.

He gave me a look that said he didn't want to talk about it. I pointed an accusatory finger at him. "You gave me your word."

He flushed. "Indeed, I did. Please sit."

He waved to the chair nearest him. As I sat, he placed the newspaper on the coffee table, then poured a second cup of tea and slid it my direction. He had acquired a tray of hummus and pita bread.

"How do you do it?" I asked, marveling at his ability to make himself at home wherever we went.

"Do what, dearie?"

"This." I waved at the food and tea tray.

"Ah." He nodded and gave me a smile. "Ephrem, the proprietor, is a good friend."

Which confirmed what I thought about Edward. I wondered, then, if Ephrem was in the contact book shoved to the back of the drawer in his desk. I picked up the cup and sipped the steaming herbal tea.

"Tell me, Edward, about the Godlight." When he didn't answer, I placed the cup onto the saucer with a gentle hand and tried again. This time getting right to the point. "Uncle, you told me when I first came to England you believed my father was an angel. Was he?"

"Yes."

He offered the truth without having to dig it out of him. Stymied, I stared at him trying to make my mind work, trying to make sense of his answer, wondering if he was fucking with me.

"Kincade was correct. You have the Godlight, Anna, because you are divine."

A cold tingling sensation crept up my spine. Words escaped my brain. First Kincade, now this. My mind was hard-pressed to process all this information.

"Is that what you wanted to know?" he asked.

"Why didn't you tell me before?" My voice was a roughened whisper.

"You weren't ready for the truth. I'm not sure you are ready now, but here we are. You have discovered the greatest gift within you and used it. I'm surprised it does not war with the dark magic inside you."

I thought about that, remembering how each differed when I used them. Both inadvertently. "They don't, oddly enough. It's as though they are separate entities."

"You can tell the difference?"

I nodded.

Fear flickered over his face before he contained it.

"Does that scare you, uncle?" I reached for a piece of flatbread and swiped it through the hummus.

"Yes, quite frankly." He placed his cup on the table and leaned toward me, his elbows on his knees. "You do not yet know all the power you possess, dearie. You have begun to discover it."

"And the Godlight and dark magic could clash?"

He nodded. "It's possible, though it's hard for me to know."

I understood how they both felt but it was difficult to explain.

My mouth went bone dry, the hummus turning sour on my tongue. His tone was the most serious I'd heard. It startled me.

"When you dream walked your friend in the hospital back in Dallas, it was the catalyst that set everything into motion," he continued. "You somehow managed to break through all the barriers we set to keep you from dream walking."

The 'we' was Sariel and Edward. When I was a girl, they discovered Azriel was trying to seduce me into helping him and Lucifer. They used angel magic to remove some of my memories as well as block me from dream walking—which turned out to be an Azriel homing beacon.

"But I didn't realize then what it would do," I said, sounding more defensive than I intended.

"No," he agreed. "And that is partially my fault. I should have equipped you better instead of trying to control you, to bend you to my will. To make you forget who and what you are."

It was hard to deny the guilt I heard in his voice. He somehow felt responsible for everything that happened to me with Marcus/Azriel. We lapsed into silence. He picked up his cup and sipped again. Consternation crept along the lines of his face.

"Tell me about my father, uncle." I leaned back into the cushion of the velvet chair, no longer interested in the tea or hummus.

He heaved a sigh as he held the cup in his hands, peering at me over the rim. "Where should I begin?"

"How about start with how he met my mother?" I suggested. My stomach was in knots at the very idea of finally learning something about them.

"That I don't know," he said. "You mother was quite secretive when it came to him. And I was rather overprotective of her. I thought what she was doing was a mistake. She left England because of me."

He sounded so sad a pang of sorrow went through me. "I'm sure that's not true."

"Oh, but it is." He pressed his lips together in a thin line as he considered his next words. "I disapproved of her choice and so they fled together to America. Our last words to each other in this world were far from kind."

I sank deeper into the cushions understanding how deeply hurt he was over the loss of my mother. Even though I'd found her in Antarctica, I understood why he didn't want to accept the super dream walker was her. I had a hard time with it, too, but I still believed deep down Natasha was my biological mother.

"I'm sorry, uncle." And I truly was. It must have been hard for him, seeing her leave England, putting her life behind her and shunning her gifts. I recalled something he'd told me before about her. He'd dream walked her and discovered her whereabouts. "You said you followed her to the States."

"I did and tried to convince her to return with me, to no avail. She told me to leave her alone and never look for her again. I did as she asked."

"How did you know she died?"

"Sariel came to tell me."

Hearing the archangel's name made me blink surprise. "Sariel? Why?"

"You should understand by now we dream walkers are connected to archangels and other heavenly creatures," he said.

I nodded. "I think I do." Thought I wasn't sure why or how. That was still an enigma.

"Sariel told me she was gone, but there was a child." He gave me a pointed looked. "A child, he said, that I was to never search for because Annabelle wanted it that way."

My gut clenched. "Why would she send me into the foster system? What happened to my father?"

"I assumed he, too, was dead," he said. "For a few years, I abided by Annabelle's wishes but after a while I could not, in good conscious, abandon you knowing what you were destined for."

"That's why you started searching for me?" I asked.

"Indeed. You know the rest."

From that point forward, I did. Strange how my path and my mother's were somewhat similar. We'd both left England for America. But unlike her, I made it back alive. I still had questions about how she survived and ended up as Natasha.

"All I know about your father was he was an archangel. One of the most powerful. He helped make you what you are." He took another sip of tea, then placed the cup aside on the table with a finality that indicated he was through talking.

I had the distinct feeling our discussion was over. I stood and yawned. "Thank you for telling me. I think I'll go nap."

"I wish I had more for you, Anna. Truly."

I nodded but something told me there was more to my parents' story even Edward didn't know.

I trudged back to my room. As I opened the door, I noticed the scrap of paper just beyond the threshold. As if someone had slipped it under the door. I bent to pick it up. It was a map of the Old City in Jerusalem. *The First Temple* was written in that familiar block lettering.

I clutched the paper and dug my smartphone out of my pocket. I hadn't used it much since Edward gave it to me. I wasn't excited about using it, but since it was like carrying around a mini computer, I figured it would come in handy. I did a quick internet search for the First Temple.

The First Temple was also known as Solomon's Temple.

One of the last known resting places for the Staff of Moses.

I flipped the paper over. On the back was a rendering of what the temple looked like in 957 BC.

But according to this internet source, it had been destroyed in 587 BC.

Why, then, would I go there?

And why was I led to Acre in the first place?

I tapped the edge of the paper against my chin, thinking of what Azriel had said about our destinies being intertwined. And Kincade saying he never expected to be back here.

There was something more to the story. Something more Kincade wasn't telling me or didn't want to tell me. But what was it?

I placed the map of Jerusalem on the nightstand and perched on the edge of the bed. Weariness edged through me from head to toe. As I leaned back into the pillows once again, I put up my mental wards and at last drifted off to sleep.

CHAPTER 19

A POUNDING ON MY door dragged me out of a dead sleep.

I fumbled off the bed and opened it to find Kincade standing there, already dressed, expression set.

"Good," he said. "You're up. Let's go."

"What?" My brain lagged several beats behind my body.

"I told you we were doing this today." Irritation creased his brow.

"I need a shower. And a toothbrush."

"Then do it and meet me in the lobby."

He turned and walked off.

I shut the door and exhaled. Coffee first. Then I could pretend I was human.

I moved through the routine on autopilot—shower, coffee, clothes. Cargo pants. Henley. Pink combat boots. Same uniform I always wore. I tied my hair back, strapped on my dagger, and headed downstairs.

Kincade was pacing the lobby when I arrived. He stopped long enough to look me over.

"What took you so long?"

"Basic hygiene," I said. "Highly recommended."

"Come on."

He turned and headed straight out the door.

"The others?" I asked.

"No."

That was all I got.

We moved through the streets without talking. He walked fast, purposeful, eyes forward, jaw tight. Not lost—locked in. Whatever we were heading toward had his full attention, and none of it was good.

We reached the citadel just inside the Old City walls.

He stopped.

For the first time since waking me, he didn't move.

I followed his gaze up the stone tower. Ancient. Unyielding. Waiting.

Something tightened in his posture. Subtle. Controlled. But it was there.

Something had happened here.

I stepped closer—not touching, just present. I opened my mouth to say something.

"Let's go."

The words were clipped. He strode forward. I hurried to keep up.

Inside, he bought tickets without looking at me and passed one over. We crossed into the fortress proper.

He paused again, just long enough to scan the space.

Nothing on his face. Nothing I could read.

Then he moved.

We threaded through tourists and audio guides and camera flashes, and none of it touched him. He wove through the vaulted halls with certainty, as if the layout was burned into him.

We reached the Refectory.

This time, he stopped for real.

He stood in the center of the room, eyes moving—not seeing what was there now, but what had been. Not imagining. Remembering.

I didn't speak.

Neither did he.

The weight of the place pressed in, heavy and old and unfinished.

And for the first time since arriving in Acre, I understood—

This wasn't another stop on the hunt.

This was a reckoning.

Tourists drifted through the space around us, voices echoing softly off the stone. None of them lingered. None of them seemed to feel it.

The air pressed in on me, thick with age and unfinished history.

I stepped closer to him—not touching, just near enough that he'd know I was there.

"How long has it been?" I asked quietly.

He looked at me then. Really looked. Blinked once, as if pulling himself out of something he hadn't meant to revisit.

For a moment, I expected deflection. Dismissal.

Instead, he inhaled through his nose and let it out slow.

"Over seven hundred years."

The words landed heavy between us.

I didn't react. Didn't comment. Didn't gloat. Whatever this was, it wasn't a victory.

It was a door opening.

He reached up, pulled a chair down from one of the tables, turned it backward, and straddled it. The movement was deliberate—grounding. He gestured for me to do the same.

I dragged a chair down and sat, spine straight, hands braced on my knees. Waiting.

"You were right," he said at last. His voice was even, but there was something worn underneath it. "I was here. In 1291."

I held his gaze. "What happened?"

He hesitated.

"I don't know if you're ready to hear it."

That struck harder than any refusal.

He wasn't protecting me from the story. He was protecting himself from saying it out loud.

"Don't decide that for me," I said. "I want the truth. Tell me."

A long silence followed.

Then he nodded once.

And began.

CHAPTER 20

London, England, Late March, 1291 A.D.

SEBASTIAN CRANE SUMMONED ME.

That alone meant something had cracked.

The commander of the Brotherhood of Watchers didn't call his generals into his chamber unless the Heavens demanded payment or the world had begun to tilt. Either way, there would be blood. There was always blood.

Decker walked beside me with that easy, careless arrogance he wore like armor. Marcus followed on my other flank—quiet, steady, the kind of man who could stand in hell and still look like he belonged there.

We reached Sebastian's door. No guards. He didn't need them. Not in this house. Not in this life.

Decker opened the door without knocking.

Sebastian's chamber was windowless—power never required light. A heavy oak desk anchored one wall. Books filled shelves behind him, spines worn from use, not decoration. A red-and-gold rug lay beneath our boots like a warning.

Sebastian didn't rise. He didn't waste time.

"There is news of a man marching across the world conquering all who oppose him," he said. "He carries with him several Holy Relics."

Decker's brow lifted, amused. Marcus stayed still. I felt the weight of the words settle into my bones.

"What relics?" Decker asked, bored like this was a tax dispute.

"The Spear of Destiny," Sebastian said. "The Staff of Moses."

The names hit like a blade drawn slow. Those weren't stories. Those were anchors. Weapons, if placed in the wrong hands.

"This Keeper was entrusted with them," Sebastian continued. "To keep them safe."

"And failed," I said.

Sebastian's gaze sharpened on me like I'd spoken out of turn.

"The archangels are not pleased with this dream walker."

"Dream walker?" Marcus asked, voice careful.

"That is what the archangels call him." Sebastian leaned forward, hands clasped. "He has the ability to see and enter dreams."

Something cold moved through my chest.

I didn't let it touch my face.

Around me, the Brotherhood was built on secrets and violence and obedience. Abilities were currency—used, bartered, punished. Decker could vanish and reappear like smoke. Marcus could step through shadow and return with answers.

And I... I could walk into another man's mind.

I'd never told anyone.

Not Decker. Not Marcus. Not Sebastian. Some gifts made you useful. Others made you dangerous in ways even the Brotherhood feared. Dream-walking wasn't a tool. It was invasion. It was violation.

It was the kind of power that got you watched.

"At any rate," Sebastian said, "Michael wants us to retrieve the relics from him. The dream walker is called Ezra."

Decker scoffed. "Why don't they smite him and be done with it?"

Sebastian's mouth tightened. "You should know why."

Decker's smirk deepened. "Because warriors do the dirty work."

"Watchers are bound by duty," Sebastian snapped. "We stand between good and evil."

"And bleed in the middle," Decker murmured, but Sebastian ignored him.

"How do we find him?" I asked. "We don't even know where he is."

"He and his army are headed for Acre," Sebastian said. "The Orders have been hiding relics in their fortress. The archangels believe Ezra is going to retrieve them."

Acre.

The word scraped something old inside me, like a scar remembering the blade.

Sebastian stood, finally. "I'm dispatching the three of you. Retrieve the relics by any means necessary. Once you have them, the archangels will deal with Ezra."

They, the archangels.

Always a clean hand. Always someone else's blood.

Sebastian's gaze moved over Marcus, Decker—then paused on me.

"Understood?"

I gave a single nod. "Understood."

"When you arrive," Sebastian said, "you will speak with the Grand Master. Guillaume de Beaujeu. You will forewarn him.

Before Ezra arrives, the relics must be taken from the fortress and secured elsewhere."

Decker's laugh was soft and sharp. "You want us to convince a Templar to abandon his own walls."

"Convince him," Sebastian said.

Marcus's voice was quiet. "If he refuses, we can't force an entire Order to flee."

Sebastian's jaw tightened. "Then I fear what the outcome will be. Too many lives have already been lost in the Holy Land. Do what you can to avoid more deaths."

He dismissed us with a gesture.

Marcus and Decker turned for the door.

"Kincade," Sebastian said. "A word."

I waited until the door shut behind them. The silence pressed in.

Sebastian came around the desk, stopping close enough that I could see the fatigue at the edges of his eyes. Not weakness. Calculation.

"You should know," he said, "the Grand Master blames the Brotherhood for the war between Venice and Genoa."

I didn't react. Politics were always a knife—wielded by cowards who couldn't win with steel.

"Why?" I asked anyway.

"It divided their Order. They believe we did not do enough to stop it. They blame us for the fracture."

"So we'll be treated as enemies," I said.

Sebastian nodded once. "And one more thing. Ezra poses a significant threat."

"I gathered that."

"The archangels want him alive." His gaze held mine. "I do not believe you can retrieve the relics while he still lives."

There it was.

Not said outright. Not necessary.

"You're authorizing an execution," I said.

"If that's what it takes," Sebastian replied. "Yes."

I didn't hesitate. Hesitation was how men died.

"Understood," I said. "By your command."

⬥————————⬥

Acre, Days Later

DECKER DIDN'T LIKE TO show mercy unless it cost him something. Still, he offered it to me without comment.

He vanished, reappeared, and the world shifted.

One moment London's air sat damp and cold in my lungs; the next, Acre's heat wrapped around my skin like a living thing. Salt, smoke, horse, sweat. The sound of gulls and shouting. The distant crash of waves against stone.

Marcus appeared a step away, already scanning the street, eyes tracking exits and threat. Decker looked mildly annoyed at the inconvenience of arriving.

I stayed still long enough to take in the walls.

Acre was old. Ancient in the way a blade was ancient—sharpened and used and waiting to be used again.

The fortress rose above the city like a promise.

Or a tomb.

We requested an audience with the Grand Master and were greeted like plague.

The Hospitallers and Templars had learned to distrust strangers. They distrusted us more.

Still, after threats and delays and muttered curses, we were escorted through stone corridors to a chamber that smelled of wax and sweat and iron.

Guillaume de Beaujeu stood at the center of his room like a man built to command. Tall. Broad-shouldered. Thick auburn hair and a beard to match. His eyes were hard and suspicious, the eyes of someone who slept with one hand on a sword.

He didn't offer a seat.

He didn't offer civility.

"I will not pretend to like this," he said, voice like gravel. "But the Brotherhood has long been an ally. To what do I owe the pleasure of this visit?"

Decker's mouth twitched. Marcus remained calm.

I took the lead.

"We believe a threat is headed here," I said. "A man marching with an army. He carries Holy Relics."

Guillaume stared at me like I'd insulted his mother.

"You expect me to believe this?" he said. "We possess relics. I have never seen them used as weapons."

"He uses them to bend men," I said. "And burn the rest."

The Grand Master's eyes narrowed.

"He is coming for what you have," I continued. "To turn it against you. He will descend within days."

"And what would you have me do?" Guillaume snapped. "Move the relics?"

"Yes."

His laugh was sharp, humorless. "Do you understand the enormity of that request? I cannot load sacred things onto carts like sacks of grain. It would take weeks."

Marcus stepped forward. "It is your best chance to keep them out of his hands."

Guillaume's glare cut to Marcus. Then back to me.

"Why should I do your bidding?" he said. "You have failed us before. There is no reason to listen to you now."

If I'd been a different man, I might have argued. I might have pleaded.

I didn't plead.

"If you don't," I said, voice cold, "Ezra comes with his army. He does not stop until he has what he wants."

Guillaume's nostrils flared.

"Take the treasure and leave," Marcus urged. "It is the only chance—"

"Abandon the fortress?" Guillaume scoffed. "I think not."

"Grand Master—" I started.

He cut me off with a lift of his hand.

"I thank you for the information," he said, like it tasted sour. "I cannot and will not leave. I will not abandon my men. You may stay the night, but you will leave on the morrow."

Dismissed.

Like we were merchants.

Fury rose in me—hot, immediate—then I locked it down. Anger was a luxury in war. Control was survival.

We left his chamber with Decker muttering curses under his breath and Marcus watching the corridors like he expected them to turn on us.

Once we were out of earshot, Decker turned to me.

"Now what?" he asked.

I looked toward the walls.

Ezra was coming.

And the man who commanded this fortress was too proud to run.

"Ezra is real," I said. "And the relics are real."

Marcus's voice was quieter. "Then we stay and fight."

"He doesn't want us here," I said.

"Then we do something he can't ignore," Marcus replied. He tapped his chin, thinking. "I'll go. Find Ezra's position. If we can tell the Grand Master exactly how close he is, it might force his hand."

Decker's eyes flicked to mine. *Is he serious?*

I nodded once. "It's worth a try."

Marcus clasped my shoulder, solid and familiar. "Before dawn."

Then he was gone—one blink and empty air.

❖

Before Dawn

MARCUS DIDN'T RETURN.

The first sign was the silence changing.

The second was the way the city began to move—fast, panicked.

Carts jammed streets. Citizens hauled children, sacks, anything they could carry. Doors barred from the inside. Prayers spoken too loud.

Then the horizon filled.

Catapults.

Lines of soldiers.

The Sultan's forces arranging siege engines outside the walls like men setting a table for slaughter.

The Grand Master ordered the outer gates cleared.

And—because pride was pride—he ordered us out.

We took rooms at a local inn and waited, because waiting was sometimes the only move left.

I sat at a scarred table with a tankard of ale that tasted like rot. I gripped it until my hand ached, because pain was simpler than thought.

Decker lounged across from me like this was a tavern tale.

"Something happened to him," I said.

Decker's eyes sharpened. "There's one way to find out."

"No." The word left my mouth hard. "I'm not sending you out there too."

He stared at me, suspicion flickering.

He didn't know.

He couldn't.

Because I had already found Marcus.

Not with feet. Not with eyes.

With the part of me I kept locked down so deep I almost believed it didn't exist.

That night, while Decker slept, I walked into Marcus's dreams.

I saw him on horseback.

I saw the black wings spread behind him like a crown.

I saw the way his smile had changed—wolfish, cruel, pleased with itself.

I saw the fall.

And I understood the worst truth of all:

Marcus had not been dragged into darkness.

He had chosen it.

I hadn't told Decker because Decker would kill him without hesitation.

And because if I admitted how I knew... I'd never be allowed to forget it.

Decker leaned forward, dropping his voice. "War is upon us, Kincade, and we sit here doing nothing."

He was right.

The loss of Marcus sat in my chest like a stone.

Decker's tone shifted, not teasing now—serious.

"Despite the Grand Master's refusal," he said, "it is our duty to return and fight."

And it was our duty to stop Ezra.

I drained the tankard and slammed it down.

"You're right," I said. "We go."

The Streets of Acre

THE SIEGE HAD BEGUN by the time we reached the fortress again.

Catapults hammered the outer walls with terrifying regularity. The Templars and Hospitallers answered with their own, but their stones looked like pebbles thrown at a storm.

We couldn't get inside.

Decker scanned the chaos. "What now?"

"We find another way," I said. "Harbor."

He grimaced. "Or I teleport us in."

"No." I shook my head once. "Save your strength."

We moved through the city, keeping to narrow streets and shadows, heading for the smell of salt and tar and ships.

Then I saw them.

Two riders leading a tide of men.

One held a spear like it belonged in his hand.

The other—

Black wings. Black hair. A grin I knew too well. My gut went cold.

"Ezra," I said. "He's here."

Decker's gaze narrowed. "And he's got a fallen angel with him."

No. Not a fallen angel. A fallen friend.

The two riders came closer, their army swelling behind them like a living wall. Men with weapons. Men with eyes too bright. Men who looked... convinced.

Decker's voice dropped. "Is that Marcus?"

"Yes," I said, tasting bitterness like blood.

Decker turned his head sharply to me. "You knew."

I didn't blink.

"How?" he demanded.

"I sensed it," I lied.

The lie slid out smooth because it had to.

Because the truth would get me caged. Because the truth would get me used. Because the truth would make me something the Brotherhood watched.

Decker stared at me, jaw tight, then looked back at Marcus—Azriel—and the anger in him sparked like a fuse.

I pulled my sword free.

"You intend to fight him?" Decker asked, incredulous.

"He betrayed the Brotherhood," I said. "He dies."

Decker didn't argue. He drew steel.

We stepped into the street like we could stop an ocean with our bodies. We both knew we couldn't. But duty didn't ask if it was possible. Duty asked if you would stand.

Ezra lifted a hand.

The army slowed.

He didn't order them to trample us. He watched us instead, calm as a priest.

"Stand aside," Ezra said.

Azriel's grin widened. "They won't," he said. His gaze found mine. "Will you, Kincade?"

Ezra's eyes flicked between us. "Friends of yours?"

"You betrayed us," I said to Azriel. "You know the punishment."

He laughed. "Marcus died when he fell from grace." He turned his head toward Ezra. "These two aren't worthy of your attention, excellency. I'll handle them."

"Very well," Ezra said. "We have business at the fortress."

"I don't think so," I said, voice flat.

Ezra's mouth curved. "You wish to fight me as well?"

He shut his eyes.

The air changed.

Men on horseback behind him shifted, turning, rerouting—like their minds were being rearranged on a table.

Ezra opened his eyes again.

"There are other ways to reach the Sultan," he said mildly. "We will still take the city. We will still win."

"You'll never find the relics," I said. "The Templars already moved them."

Decker's head snapped toward me, disbelief blazing.

He didn't need words. His look was enough.

What are you doing?

Ezra's gaze narrowed. "You're lying."

"Am I?" I said.

Azriel had enough.

He dismounted in one smooth motion and stepped forward, sword singing from its sheath.

"Stand aside," he said, voice low. "The Brotherhood has lost."

"I will never stand aside."

"Then you die."

He came at me.

Steel met steel with a crack that shuddered up my arms. Azriel was faster than he'd ever been. Stronger. Like the fall had fed him.

Like the darkness had rewarded him for betrayal.

He hammered me, driving me back, each strike heavy with intent.

Across the street, Ezra dismounted too—his spear glinting as he moved toward Decker.

Two fights.

Two deaths waiting.

Azriel thrust.

I misjudged.

His blade ripped up and across my abdomen, slicing through cloth and skin.

Pain bloomed hot. Blood soaked my tunic.

I staggered, breath sharp.

Azriel smiled. "You cannot defeat me, *mon ami*."

I pressed a hand to my wound, gripping my sword with the other, arm trembling.

I looked for Decker.

My brother was face down on the stones.

My gut turned to ice.

"Oh, he's not dead," Ezra said, watching my reaction with interest. "Not yet."

He turned his head toward Azriel. "Finish them, then meet me at the fortress. I want those relics."

Ezra started to walk away.

Azriel lifted his sword, ready to end me.

And then Decker moved.

He rolled onto his back like he'd been waiting for the moment. A jade-handled dagger flashed in his hand—green stone catching the light.

He threw.

The blade hit Azriel in the side.

Azriel gasped, the sound ugly and shocked. His sword clattered to the cobblestones as he staggered back, hand closing over the hilt.

He yanked the dagger free and dropped it like it offended him.

"You will pay for that," he hissed.

Then he was gone—vanished in a blink, swallowed by whatever darkness he now belonged to.

Ezra's face twisted. His calm broke. He charged Decker with the spear, fury turning his movements sloppy. Decker rolled, barely avoiding the point.

I dropped my sword, grabbed for my own dagger.

My vision narrowed.

Everything became a single line. Stop him. Before he kills my brother.

I drove forward on pure adrenaline and hate.

Ezra lifted the spear again—

And I buried my dagger into his kidney.

He made a sound like he hadn't expected pain to be real. The spear slipped from his hand as the life drained from his eyes.

He fell to his knees.

I yanked the dagger free.

Ezra collapsed on the stones.

The air went still.

Then the Heavens opened.

Light speared down, blinding and merciless. Decker and I raised our arms, shielding our eyes as pressure pressed us into the earth like we were insects beneath a boot.

When the light faded, three figures stood where none had been.

They weren't men.

They were judgment given form.

Michael stood in the center—gold threaded through his wings like fire caught in feathers, eyes blue and endless.

Sariel to his left—green-eyed stillness, quiet power, a blade that didn't need to move to cut.

Gabriel to the right—dark-eyed, broad-shouldered, presence like a locked door.

Michael reached down and plucked the Spear of Destiny from the ground as if it weighed nothing.

He turned his head slightly. "Check the saddlebags."

Sariel moved without sound, returning with a silver horn and a long staff.

Michael took them with a nod.

He looked at me and Decker.

"We preferred to take the dream walker alive," he said, voice calm as a grave, "but I understand why you killed him."

Decker shifted, pain etched across his face. I helped him stand, my hand steady even as blood soaked my tunic.

Michael's gaze didn't soften. It didn't need to.

"You have allowed us to recover these relics," he said. "For that, I thank you."

"What happens to them now?" I asked.

Michael's wings didn't move, but the air around him felt alive.

"Now they must be hidden," he said. "Scattered across the world. Kept out of the hands of tyrants who would use them to do harm."

"And if they could be used for good?" I asked, because the question burned.

Michael didn't blink. "There will come a time when another Keeper of the Holy Relics will rise. Chosen. Bound to them. Meant to keep them safe." His gaze cut through us both. "To save the world from the evil that will threaten to consume it."

"A new Keeper," Decker rasped, half disbelieving.

And then—without farewell, without softness—the archangels vanished.

The light went with them.

The relics were gone.

And the war around us continued like the Heavens had never opened at all.

I stood in the street with blood on my hands and a wound burning in my abdomen and the taste of something bitter in my mouth.

Duty.

Loss.

And the first faint shape of a truth I wasn't ready to name. Acre was going to haunt me for a very long time.

CHAPTER 21

KINCADE FINISHED HIS STORY and gave me a pointed look. I shifted in my seat, uncomfortable under his scrutiny. *To save the world from the evil that will threaten to consume it.* I understood that person was me. I also understood Sariel was there that day.

But one specific detail did not escape my notice—Decker once had the jade-handled dagger. My jade-handled dagger. What happened to it after the fight with Ezra? Did Decker recover it? How, then, did Li Mei get it to give it to me in Hong Kong?

"Decker and I managed to help get a few of the Templars out to Cyprus. We escaped through the Templar Tunnel to the harbor." He motioned toward the tunnel in the fortress. "I don't know what happened to the treasure. I never saw it. Nor did I see any of the other Holy Relics. I assumed they loaded it on the ships as the Mamelukes were setting up their catapults and preparing to attack," he said.

He lapsed into silence at last. It stretched between us. I stared at him, dumbfounded, unsure what to say or think. My mouth had gone dry. My nerves were shot. I wanted a drink.

Everything was so much clearer now. Azriel was once part of the Brotherhood of Watchers and named Marcus Davenport. That wasn't merely some alias he came up with on the fly. He used his Brotherhood persona to try to seduce me, turn me against all I was and use me for Lucifer's end game.

It was also difficult for me to process the very idea Kincade killed my ancestor, Ezra. Certainly, I knew the story of the first Keeper of the Holy Relics. Michael told me about him, that he used the Holy Relics as weapons to kill all those who defied him. But he didn't tell me the whole story. Perhaps wanting me to discover the truth myself.

Michael's words came back to me. He told me he sent his army to take back what was given to Ezra, that he was destroyed on the battlefield. I assumed it was a large army, not two men from the Brotherhood of Watchers.

I never imagined it was Kincade who put an end to him.

I looked at him in a different light now. Kincade wasn't only here to guard me. He was here to end me if I broke. If I turned—if I let Abaddon or Azriel claim me—Kincade wouldn't hesitate. He'd do what he did to Ezra. Take the relics back. Deliver them to the archangels. And I would be a body on stone.

He'd made sure the archangels received the ones Ezra possessed. A cold breath shuddered out of me. Azriel was right. All our destinies were intertwined. I was connected to all of them, whether I liked it or not. And it scared the hell out of me.

Before either of us could speak, we were interrupted

"You there. This section is restricted. You'll have to move along."

One of the caretakers of the fortress shooed us away from the Refectory. We both rose and put the chairs back where we found them. Satisfied we were leaving, the caretaker continued on his original path. I turned away from Kincade and made my way deeper into the fortress.

"What? No snarky comments?" He was hot on my heels.

"You'll forgive me if I have nothing creative to say over the fact you killed my ancestor."

He stepped into my path and caught my elbow—brief, controlled—long enough to stop me. Then he let go.

"I had no choice."

I nodded. "Just like you'll have no choice if that happens to me. I am not going to fall into darkness."

"You were close."

"Oh, you had to point that out, didn't you?"

I walked through the fortress again, past the artisan's hall. I didn't pay attention to anything or anyone. My mind was numb with all the information he'd shared.

"The staff isn't here, is it?" I asked, not looking at him.

"No," he said, his voice flat.

When I found myself at the entrance to the Templar Tunnel, I halted, trying to force my muddled mind to put the pieces together. If the staff wasn't here, then it had to be in Jerusalem. Why else would I have received the map in my hotel room?

I had suspected before someone was helping me on these quests, now I knew for sure. But why send me to Acre? To discover the truth about Kincade, Decker, and Azriel? To learn about the first dream walker who betrayed us all?

And who was the mystery person sending me all these messages written in blocky handwriting?

"It's in Jerusalem," I said out loud.

Kincade had halted next to me. "The staff?"

"Yes."

"How do you know?"

"Because whoever's guiding me wants me there next." I spun on my heel and headed back out the way we'd come.

He started following me again. "Where are you going?"

"I need to talk to my uncle."

But as I approached the exit of the fortress, the veil descended between me and Kincade and the other humans. I inhaled but scented no demons. My heart rammed into my throat. My blood went cold in one clean snap.

There was Mammon, the Prince of Greed, standing there as if he'd been waiting patiently for my appearance all day.

Realization palpitated through me.

He had come to collect his debt.

CHAPTER 22

I HALTED. KINCADE MOVED to stand between us. The Prince of Greed gave a disgusting thin-lipped smile, his black eyes pinned on mine. He pressed those long slender fingertips together, his sharp pointed nail tips touching.

"Hello, Anna," he said, not acknowledging Kincade.

I stood rigid next to the man who would both protect and kill me. "I'd ask what you want, but I think I have that answer."

His smile continued. "You do."

Kincade glanced down at me over his shoulder. "What does he want?"

"I've come to collect my debt," Mammon said before I could answer.

Kincade's brows drew together. "What did you do, Anna?"

Not anger. Calculation.

"She promised me a favor. And now it's time to pay up."

Mammon's words were like fingernails on a chalkboard. I shivered, gooseflesh skittering up and down my arms. Kincade still gazed at me with those disbelieving green-gold eyes. I wanted to shove him away, to bark at him to stop staring at me, but I didn't. I kept my gaze on the dark prince in front of us.

"It's not done yet," I said.

"Pity." He glanced over his cuticles as though we spoke of nothing more inconsequential than today's weather.

"What did you promise him?" Kincade demanded.

"Nothing." My voice was low and tight.

"Tell me." His lips peeled back from his teeth. His voice was full of warning.

"She made me a promise in Hell if I returned the Horn of Gabriel to her, she would grant me one favor."

"You are so delightfully helpful with your explanations," I sneered.

He spread his hands and shrugged. "I do what I can."

I clenched my hands into tight fists. Kincade growled low in his throat. He was aware I had the Horn of Gabriel. I had never shared with him exactly how I retrieved it. I gave him a surreptitious glance. His lips pressed together in a grimace.

"What was the favor?"

"One of my choosing at the time of my choosing," Mammon supplied. "She knows what I want."

Damn him. I shot him a heated glare that said *shut the fuck up*, but he seemed unflustered by the intensity of my stare.

Next to me, Kincade nearly vibrated out of his skin. Fury emanated off him in waves.

Do you know what you've done?

His voice boomed in my head. I winced, pinching the bridge of my nose between thumb and forefinger. I took a deep cleansing breath.

I did. And I would do it again.

What was the favor? he asked.

I didn't want to tell him. Kincade was the absolute last person on the planet I wanted involved in my giant fuck up. It was bad enough Edward already knew.

I dropped my hand and met his gaze, swallowing the fear as my gut twisted. *He wants me to kill Edward.*

He didn't react. Not even a little. He stared at me as if I were the dumbest person alive. I probably was.

If I don't, he wants my soul, I added.

His jaw clenched tight. Finally, he turned his gaze from me to the Prince of Greed.

"Ah, so she didn't tell you," the prince surmised, sounding triumphant. "You cannot protect her. Not from me."

"But I can."

Edward's voice boomed out from behind Mammon. A breath of relief and utter shock trembled out of me. Where the hell had he come from? The prince turned slowly to face him, a mixture of total disdain and disbelief on his pinched face.

"I don't think so," the prince said with a laugh.

My stomach clenched back into a tight knot. I didn't like this situation at all.

Edward produced his flaming sword. "You will leave this place, or I will kill you."

"I will do no such thing. She will fulfill her promise to me, or she will hand over her soul."

"I will do neither," I finally said, finding my voice.

I stepped around Kincade. I sensed he wanted to stop me from doing it, but I moved a few paces ahead of him out of reach. My nerves were definitely shot now. My knees threatened to turn to water as I faced my biggest and worst mistake since this whole Keeper thing began.

"There's no getting out of this, my pet," Mammon said. "I want what I've come for. Edward's death or your soul. It makes no difference to me, though I confess I prefer Edward's death."

"Then kill him yourself," I snarled.

Behind me, Kincade sucked in a sharp breath. It was something I had never heard him do. I met Edward's gaze, but his face registered no emotion. He understood I was bluffing. Mammon's face went still, a darkness coming over his features.

"He can't," Edward replied.

"Why not?" I demanded.

Mammon's fevered stare never left my face. A blue vein throbbed under the paper-thin skin in the side of his neck. I shifted from one foot to the other as I awaited an answer to my question.

"It matters not," Mammon said. "His death is imminent."

"This is not the place." Kincade moved to stand directly behind me. "There has been enough bloodshed in this fortress for all our lifetimes."

"I agree with Kincade," I said.

"As do I," Edward said. He hid his flaming sword. "Therefore, I challenge you to a duel at daybreak."

"What?" The word squeezed out of my lungs on a heated breath. My eyes flew wide as I gaped at my uncle.

A long, slow smile spread on Mammon's thin black lips. "A duel to the death?"

Edward nodded. "If I win, she keeps her soul and her promise to you is fulfilled."

"And if you lose?" One black brow rose in question.

"You take my soul instead of hers."

"Edward, you can't—" I began.

"Done," Mammon said, cutting me off. "On the morrow then, at daybreak. Outside the Old City walls in the port near the lighthouse."

And with that he was gone.

As soon as he disappeared, the veil vanished, and all was righted inside the fortress. Tourists still milled about as though nothing was amiss. My knees gave out as I collapsed on the hard, stone floor. My heart was in my throat.

"Edward, why?"

"You know why."

His reply was terse as he left the fortress. I suspected he headed back to the hotel. Kincade held a hand down to me.

"Come on. People are staring."

"I don't give a shit." My whole world had crumbled—again—and he thought I was worried about people staring?

He wiggled his fingers in urgency. "Let's go, Anna."

I clenched my jaw as I grabbed his hand. He pulled me to my feet, but immediately released me. He headed for the exit. Numb, I followed. Where else was I to go anyway?

We left the fortress behind. Tears welled in my eyes and burned the back of my throat. I had to find a way to talk sense into Edward. The last thing he needed was to fight Mammon for my dumbass mistakes. I had to stop this insane duel between the two of them.

My booted feet pounded the pavement, leaving Kincade behind, as I jogged back to the hotel. My one thought was getting to Edward to talk him out of this craziness. I practically ran to his hotel room, my heart ramming hard in my chest. I pounded on his door until he opened it.

He gave me a nod of greeting. "Anna." Then turned and walked back inside the room, leaving me on the threshold. As though I was there on a social visit.

My hands shook as I shoved closed the door and stood with my back against it trying to calm my erratic breathing and slow my rapid heartbeat.

"What the bloody hell, Edward?"

"Would you like some tea?"

He paused in the center of his palatial suite where a tea tray rested on the coffee table between two oversized sofas. Beyond, the windows were open to let in the early afternoon sea breeze, the gauzy curtains billowing on either side.

I blinked the hot tears away. "No, I don't want bloody tea. I want a bloody explanation."

He perched on the edge of one of the sofas and calmly poured a cup of tea from the delicate china teapot. He said nothing as he added a cube of sugar and stirred, tapping the spoon on the edge of the cup and then placing it aside. He blew across the steaming tawny liquid before taking a sip.

"How can you be so calm about this?" I demanded.

"Please do sit down, Anna." He waved to the sofa opposite him and gave me a pointed look.

In a huff, I went to the sofa and flopped down. "Well?"

"There is nothing to discuss. It's done."

"Like hell it's done. You can't mean to fight Mammon."

"I can and I will."

"Edward—"

"You wanted a way out of your promise to him. I gave it to you."

My stomach lurched. "Not like this, uncle."

"It is the only way."

"But you could die!" I wailed.

"That's a risk I'm willing to take to keep your soul safe."

I fought back hot tears again. "But then the Prince of Greed will control your soul."

He said nothing to that as he sipped his tea. The look on his face told me I was right to worry.

"How did you even know he was there?" I asked.

"There are certain things that are inherent knowledge."

My brows drew together. "What does that mean?"

"It means I sense things." He waved it away as if it was nothing. "Besides, he can't kill me."

"Why not?" I demanded.

He heaved a sigh. "It doesn't matter."

"It does. Tell me. If this is your last bloody day on earth, then I deserve all the answers to my questions."

"I suppose you're right." He regarded me with a cool expression as he contemplated his next words. "My soul is protected by the archangels. No demon can harm me."

I openly gaped at him. "I don't...how..."

"Anna, it was no coincidence I found you in Texas. I was sent to find you, to bring you back, to teach you who and what you are, to prepare you to become Keeper of the Holy Relics."

"The archangels sent you?" I asked.

"No." He paused, considering how to answer. "The Brotherhood of the Watchers sent me."

All the fight went out of me as I stared at him. "Was it Kincade?"

"Sebastian Crane, commander of the Brotherhood, came to me with a message and a blessing from the archangels. *Find the Keeper. Protect her with my life.* The blessing was to keep me safe from all the demons of Hell that would try to kill me before I found you."

A throbbing pain took up residence in the back of my head. I leaned forward, my elbows on my knees as I took a deep cleansing breath. I was, of course, familiar with Sebastian Crane. Kincade told me he was the one who sent him to kill Ezra. I had met Sebastian when Kincade went missing. He refused to assist me in finding him, telling me he was lost to the Brotherhood.

"Mammon knows this," Edward continued. "Therefore, he knows he cannot kill me."

"That's why you challenged him to a duel," I said, my voice muffled. And yet tears slipped down my cheeks.

He did it to protect me because he couldn't lose.

"Yes," Edward agreed. "At any rate, if I die, you'll inherit my title and estate."

He'd told me this before. Edward held the title of Baron and appeared to have amassed a bottomless wealth. My head snapped up. "I don't want your title. I want you to live."

"Nevertheless, should my death come to pass, we need to plan."

His nonchalant attitude infuriated me. I wanted to argue with him more, but there was nothing more to say. He'd made up his mind and there was no changing it, no matter how hard I tried.

"I don't want to plan for your death." I said it with as much petulance as possible.

He placed his cup on the table and got to his feet, ignoring my frown. "Let's get started."

I looked at him as though he'd grown a horn out of the center of his forehead. "On what?"

"Teaching you."

I remained where I was, gaping at him. "Did you get hit on the head?"

"No more questions, Anna. You must accept what will happen at dawn. Now come. We have much work to do."

He beckoned me to follow him deeper into the suite. Then he moved furniture out of the way as though we were about to have some type of hand-to-hand combat.

I would never accept what would happen at dawn. I conceded to asking no more questions. To stop trying to change his mind. I pushed off the sofa and joined him in the center of the room. Perhaps someone else could convince him his plan was a death sentence.

And that someone was Kincade.

⊷─────⊶

IT WAS DEEP INTO the night when I stumbled out of Edward's suite, exhausted. All my mental and physical energy was drained to the point I sagged against the wall in the corridor. Faint light trickled over the gaudy patterned carpet. My tired addled brain had a hard time trying to comprehend the obnoxious pattern. Though why I was trying to read the carpet was unexplainable.

I chalked it up to fatigue.

I stumbled down the hallway to Kincade's door and paused, my hand midair ready to knock. Was this the best course of action?

I convinced myself it was. He was my last hope.

I knocked and waited.

Long seconds ticked by before he opened the door. He didn't look surprised to see me. His eyes were sharp and assessing as he waited for me to speak.

"I need your help," I said.

He swung open the door and stepped aside to allow me to enter. When I was inside, he shut the door with a soft snick. I faced him, taking a deep breath.

"I need you to talk Edward out of this duel with Mammon."

But he was shaking his head before I even finished. "I can't."

"Why not?"

"Because he made a deal with one of the Princes of Sin. Nothing and no one can break that."

I bit my lower lip to keep from crying. "There has to be some way."

"There isn't." Remorse laced his quiet tone.

I spun away from him. His balcony door was open, allowing the cool night air to spill into his room. A lamp was on next to the oversized club chair, spilling yellow light over an indentation in the leather seat indicating he had been there. I wondered if the leather was still warm from his body heat.

"I don't want him to fight Mammon."

"I know," he said softly.

"I can't watch him die."

"You don't know that's what will happen," Kincade said.

"He is the Prince of Greed, Kincade."

"And Edward is strong-willed and highly skilled."

I agreed Edward was a skilled fighter. We'd fought side by side a few times. Edward could hold his own but that was against demons and minions. Against a Prince of Sin? I wasn't too sure. No matter what he said about this blessing that protected him.

"Did you know Sebastian sent him to find me?"

There was a long pause before he finally answered. "Yes."

My heart skipped. "Did you also know Edward was blessed?"

Another long pause. "I did."

My eyes shuttered closed. "Did you know who I was when you found me in Dallas at the hospital?"

"Not at first, no. But when I saw you staring at the demons on the street, I began to suspect."

It was unusual I got a bit of truth from him. Since I saved his life by trading away the spear for his soul, things had changed between us. As though we formed a silent, uneasy alliance. I wasn't sure if that was for the better or not. Most of the time I infuriated him.

I wanted to ask him more questions about why he never told me, but what was the point? It would make no difference now or later and it certainly didn't change the past.

"It's almost time now," he continued. "There's no turning back."

I'd heard that before and I still hated it. I brushed by him and flung open his door. "I'll see you at the port."

He didn't try to stop me.

There was nothing left for me to do but shower and change clothes.

Alone, in my room, a numbness took up residence. I felt nothing. I raked a hand over my hair and yanked out the hair tie holding up my ponytail. My scalp tingled at the sensation. I tossed the hair tie on the nearby table, then ran my fingers over my scalp.

Edward taught me things tonight that left me reeling. My body hurt. A fog rolled into my mind. I couldn't think straight.

I lifted a hand in the air, holding it aloft, and envisioned my jade-handled dagger. I closed my fingertips together and drew down my hand, like Edward showed me. The dagger appeared in my hand, the weight of it resting against my palm and my fingers curled around the hilt.

It was the one trick I had longed to learn. He'd taught it to me tonight. He even let me wield his flaming sword.

He called it drawing down. The flaming sword was his weapon of choice, just as the jade-handled dagger was mine.

Satisfied I was able to still do it, I returned the dagger to its hidden place somewhere in the ether. That he hadn't explained, and I was too tired to press him for answers.

What mattered was I would never again be without my weapon of choice.

I headed to the shower to prepare for the duel at dawn.

CHAPTER 23

I DRESSED IN MY normal black cargo pants and Henley. I stared at my frightful face in the mirror. The dark circles under my eyes were nothing more than slashes of black. My mouth drew down in a grimace. I needed about a week's worth of sleep to stave off the permanent feeling of exhaustion. That was never going to happen.

I pulled on my pink combat boots and left the room, mentally preparing for what was to come. As I entered the lobby, Kincade, Edward, Killian and Astrid waited for me. I was, as usual, late to the party. They all gave me expectant looks.

"For the record," I said, "I am not a fan of this situation."

"Noted," my uncle said. "Shall we?"

He started for the door. Astrid and Killian fell in step behind him. Kincade gestured for me to go next. With reluctance, I followed while he brought up the rear.

Somehow, it felt very much like dead man walking.

The lighthouse was in the southwestern corner of the Old City atop the foundation of the Crusader fortress. The white concrete tower was painted with black horizontal stripes and stood as a beacon to sailors in the bay. But now it was our beacon for the battle at dawn. I hated everything about this.

As we arrived, dawn smudged the horizon in colors of pale pink and blue. The thick veil hiding us from human prying eyes surrounded us. Mammon was there already, standing with his feet shoulder-width apart. Two lesser demons flanked him. Perhaps his lackeys. I didn't like that one bit. He grinned as we approached.

"Quite the entourage you have, Edward," he said. "Did you wish to have an audience for your death?"

"Did you?" Edward retorted. He nodded to the two demons at Mammon's side.

His response was one of haughty derision. "There is no need to delay this. How shall we do it? Weapons? Hand to hand combat? The choice is yours."

Edward produced his flaming sword. Mammon smiled.

"Ah, so weapons it is."

He produced his own weapon of choice—a black-bladed sword which I assumed was his personal version of a demon blade. He held it aloft in one hand as though it weighed nothing. His long sender fingers ending in pointed nails wrapped around the black hilt as he readied his stance.

Kincade cursed under his breath when he saw it. Never a good sign.

"Recognize this, Edward?" Mammon asked. "That blessing will not save you from this, Lord Edward."

Edward didn't react whatsoever. His face was unreadable.

My head snapped toward Kincade as I looked at him, questions swimming in my mind.

It's a black demon blade, he said in my mind. *It's the most powerful weapon there is.*

My gut clenched into a tight knot. Part of me wanted to turn away and not watch but the other part of me had to stay and see it through. How was I going to stand by and watch the Prince of

Greed try to kill my uncle without interfering? My hands clenched into fists so tight, my muscles ached and my fingernails, albeit short, dug into my palms.

Kincade stood to my right. Killian and Astrid to my left.

We cannot interfere, Kincade said in my head.

I swear, sometimes he read my mind. It was unnerving.

I cut him a glance that I hoped said, *try to stop me.*

Mammon and Edward wasted no more time as they charged each other, the first clang of their crossing swords echoing throughout the port. My breath hitched. If I was this edgy on the first hit, how was I going to survive the remaining?

Edward pulled back and swung again. Mammon blocked. He pushed the prince backward toward the edge of the port, looking confident and as though he had the upper hand. I held my breath and clenched my jaw as the prince blocked swing after swing. Edward gave him hell. I refrained from cheering out loud.

Edward pushed him against the stone wall, the flaming sword lighting up the prince's ghastly face as he held it to his throat. It had to be the shortest battle in the history of battles. He was going to win.

But not so fast. Mammon head butted him, their skulls cracking together. Edward staggered away from the prince, shaking his head to clear it. Mammon seemed unaffected as he charged, his sword pointing at my uncle.

I sucked in a sharp breath as I watched Edward swat his attacker's blade away with his own. He hit him so hard, the black blade flew out of Mammon's hand and landed on the ground spinning out of reach. Edward took that opportunity to attack, slicing his flaming sword in a wide sweep at the prince. He jerked back, but Edward's sword hissed through his upper arm, burning him and leaving behind a cauterized wound.

That did nothing but anger the Prince of Greed even more. One of the demons snatched up his weapon and handed it to him, re-arming him. Mammon fought back. Edward miscalculated the prince's attack and turned to the side. The black blade sliced through his arm. Edward clenched his jaw and spun back around to block his next attack. But it wasn't enough. Mammon was faster and used the blade to slice across Edward's abdomen.

Edward stumbled backward, somehow managing to hold onto his flaming sword with both hands.

Then the unthinkable happened. One of Mammon's demons pulled out a blade and lunged. The scream lodged in my throat as the demon stabbed Edward in his exposed side. He cried out, the sword limp in his hand.

Next to me, Astrid gasped.

"You son of a bitch!" The words ripped from me as I charged. Kincade wrapped his massive arms around me from behind and held me in place. "Let me go, Kincade."

"No one said he'd fight fair." His voice was low and hot in my ear. "Edward knew this going in."

I whimpered and struggled against him, trying to wiggle free, but Kincade held fast.

The demon's blade dripped red as Edward swayed to regain his balance. The side of his shirt was soaked through with blood. My breath hitched in my throat as I fought back tears because I was aware the blade that stabbed him would infect him with demon poison.

Edward clutched his flaming sword in his right hand and pressed his left against the wound. His fingers came away stained red. He gave it a passing glance before two-handing the sword again and taking his fighting stance, though he swayed on his feet.

Edward had been hurt before and come out of the battle still standing. My hope was he'd do that again.

Mammon charged him, wielding his black blade. He swung, narrowly missing Edward. The Prince of Greed had a determined, feral look creasing his face as he swung again. This time, Edward put up his sword to stop his blade before it came close.

Every muscle in my body tensed. Kincade tightened his grip. His body was rigid against mine, an indication he was as on edge as me.

Edward shoved Mammon backward with his flaming sword. They proceeded to dance around each other, their blades clanging, as though their fight had been meticulously choreographed.

Mammon lifted his black blade, ready to strike again, when Edward seized the opportunity to even the odds. He swung his sword in a wide, blazing arc. The tip sliced through the prince's exposed side. His lips peeled away from his teeth in a snarl as black blood dampened his shirt.

I nearly cheered, but kept it contained.

The blow, though, infuriated the Prince of Greed. With one snap of his head, the second demon charged Edward. I shouted his name as a warning which gave Edward enough time to defend himself from the attack. He shoved his flaming sword into the heart of the demon, killing him instantly.

The other demon, who had initially stabbed Edward, took offense to that. He charged my uncle, but he took evasive action. Almost as though he expected the second attacker. He swung his flaming sword and cleanly sliced off the demon's hand holding the knife. The demon shrieked, grasping his wrist as blood spurted. Then Edward finished the job by killing him.

Mammon growled low in his throat as he clutched his black blade. Edward turned to face him, his stance wavering. Sweat beaded his forehead and trickled down the side of his ashen face. He wasn't doing well, but he was making a valiant effort to stay on his feet and fight.

He didn't have to do this for me. Guilt swarmed through me. This was all my fault because I made a deal with the prince.

"Now it comes down to you and me," Edward said, his voice strong and steady, belying his outer weakened state. He was in pain, but he did his best to mask it.

Mammon lifted a brow. "It does, human. However, you are mortally wounded. Even if you kill me here, now, you will still die."

I stifled the cry that wanted to erupt. I stared hard at Edward's bloody shirt, trying to see how deep the wounds were but it was useless. I suspected demon poison coursed through his body, polluting his blood stream, but he was too stubborn and too strong-willed to surrender.

Edward clutched his flaming sword in both hands. Mammon twirled his one-handed sword with a flourish. He barreled toward Edward and instead of slamming him with his sword, he crouched low enough to kick Edward in the knee. We all heard the sickening snap as Edward cried out and crumbled to the ground. The sword fell from his hand, the fire snuffing out. Mammon stood over him, triumphant.

I elbowed Kincade in the gut. He grunted, his arms loosened enough for me to wiggle free. In a quick move, I drew down my jade-handle dagger and leapt over my uncle's writhing form. I positioned myself between my uncle and the prince.

Clutching the dagger in my right hand, I prepared to do battle.

"Now you fight me, you sorry sack of shit."

"Anna, no," Edward groaned.

I ignored him.

Mammon merely gave a gleeful grin. "I would be delighted."

He tossed his black blade to his other hand with his showmanship. I didn't wait for his attack. I spun on the toe of my boot and kicked out with my other leg, landing my foot where my uncle slashed him. He cried out in shock as his shirt damped more with his black blood. He lurched backward.

"Guess what? I don't fight fair either, you fuck," I said.

I took advantage of his momentary weakness to do another kick. But this time I aimed for his hand holding the blade. My boot connected with his hand, knocking the blade away. It clattered to the ground, out of reach and no demon left to retrieve it. I barreled into him like I had Kincade once and shoved him back toward the stone wall. When our bodies collided, I realized he was not much more than a sack of bones and scary teeth.

But powerful and strong.

So was I.

I was once afraid of him. I was no longer.

He grunted with an oof when he smacked the stone wall. I put my blade to his throat, pressing the edge against his ashy skin. He grinned, showing off all those wicked teeth and looking well pleased.

"Go ahead," he taunted. "Kill me."

I peered into those black, evil eyes and for a moment, I glimpsed his soul. It was nothing more than an oozing miasma of scum, villainy and the purest evil. And in that vision, I saw myself, what I would turn into should I kill him for the sake of killing him.

He hissed at me.

I hissed right back.

But this wasn't killing for fun. This was vengeance.

"Killing you makes me no better than you," I whispered. "Killing you will turn my soul a little darker."

"You saw that, did you?" Delight creased his ugly features.

"Yes, if I were to kill you for the sheer pleasure of it," I said. "I'm not. I'm killing you because you deserve it. For justice. For Edward. To rid this world of you. You will die and my debt to you is paid."

He opened his mouth to form a tart reply, but I didn't give him the chance. I slashed his throat. Warm black blood spurted, hitting me across the chest and neck. I jerked my chin upward to avoid it hitting me in the face. He gasped as it gurgled in his throat. I released him, letting him slide down the stone wall and land on the ground, leaving a black smear behind. I stood there a long moment, watching him bleed out. Watching him take his last breath.

He dematerialized into a wisp of black smog and was gone.

It was so silent behind me, I spun around to see if they were all still there. Astrid and Killian stared at me with wide eyes. Kincade knelt at my uncle's side, helping him sit up. Still clutching my dagger, I dashed to his side and fell to my knees. His eyes were closed. He looked pale. His shirt was soaked in blood.

"Uncle." I gave Kincade a questioning glance, assuming he had inspected the wound.

"It's deep," he said.

"I'm dying, Anna." Edward gasped the words as his eyes fluttered open. He reached for me, fisted my shirt in his hand and pulled me close to his face. "I was stabbed with a demon blade."

"But we can get you help. We can remove the poison."

He shook his head before I finished. "Not...this time. The blade..." His words trailed off.

"The blade that sliced him mortally wounded him," Kincade said.

"But that was just a slice," I said.

"With the black blade," Edward gasped.

I glanced back at Kincade, trying to form another question.

"It's a weapon wielded by a Prince of Sin," he explained. "The most powerful weapon that can defeat anyone, even someone whose soul is blessed."

"Anna." Edward's warm breath trickled over my cheek. "Listen to me carefully. The poison from his blade is meant to turn me..." He paused, sucked in a breath and closed his eyes, as though speaking was an effort.

"Turn you to what?"

"A demon prince," Kincade supplied.

"You said he couldn't kill you." My voice warbled with sheer fright.

"The demon blade...changed things...My soul is at risk."

"But—" I began, trying to find some reasonable explanation, some way to save him.

"You have to finish me off," he said.

"No!"

"Yes."

"I can't!"

"You must. With your dagger." His fist tightened on my shirt. "The demon poison..." He winced, clearly in pain.

I looked at Kincade, tears clouding my vision. Terror coursed through me. He shook his head, his face a crease of regret.

Edward wrapped his fingers around my wrist, pulling up my hand still holding the jade-handle dagger. He pressed the tip against his heart.

"Do it," he begged.

Hot tears blinded me. "No, uncle. You cannot ask me to do this!"

"You have to," he said. "It is the only way to...save me. To save my soul."

He pressed the tip deeper into his chest. The blade pricked through the cloth to his skin. His other hand released my shirt and wrapped around mine on the hilt.

"Anna, be the light in the darkness. Be the light of the world."

With all the force he had left, he shoved the dagger deep into his heart. A scream ripped from my lungs as it plunged to the hilt. He took one more gasp of breath and then he was gone.

Dead.

And I dealt him the final blow.

A blinding light exploded from him, hovered over the two of us for a moment and then punched into me with such force I flew backward. The last thing I remembered was smacking the hard ground and then blackness.

CHAPTER 24

WHEN I REGAINED CONSCIOUSNESS, my entire body ached from head to toe. Movement was an effort. Pain shot through me. I remained where I was, my eyes closed as I used my other senses to figure out where I was and remember what had happened.

Oh, yes. I killed the Prince of Greed.

And my uncle.

Hot tears burned my closed eyes and trickled out through my lashes, spilling down my face. My throat clotted with the anger, the sadness, the all-consuming grief as I remembered his last words.

Be the light of the world.

I didn't want to be the light of the world. Or the Keeper of the Holy Relics. Or anything special. I wanted my life back. I wanted to be normal. Hell, I wanted my uncle back.

But he was gone. Dead by my hand.

No, that wasn't entirely true. His body was riddled with demon poison from his battle with Mammon. He likely would have died anyway because Darius wasn't around to help him. I understood that deep down. But I didn't have to like it.

My hand pressed against what felt like a thick coverlet. I opened my eyes. I was in my hotel room in Acre. Late afternoon sun slashed through the windows and balcony door.

When I sat up, my head pounded with a fierce throb that made me wince. I scrubbed my hands over my tear-dampened face.

On the desk was a covered silver tray. I slid off the edge of the bed and picked up the lid, looking down at the food. I wasn't interested. Good thing, too, since the food looked as though it'd been sitting there for hours. I dropped the lid back on the tray.

Next to the tray was my jade handle dagger. Someone had cleaned the black blood from the blade. I picked it up and stuck it in the sheath at my waist, needing to feel the weight of it on my belt.

I staggered to the bathroom, pausing to lean heavily against the door jamb. The face that stared back at me in the mirror was hardly recognizable. Dark circles were under both my eyes. My nose was red. My eyes puffy and bloodshot. My skin was pasty. I looked like fucking hell.

Someone had thought to clean the black blood off me. I guessed that someone was Kincade. Maybe Astrid. But I was still in the same clothes as when I was knocked out. I also guessed Kincade brought me to my room and left me on the bed.

Turning, I put my back against the jamb. The clock on the bedside table indicated it was early evening. What did I care?

I'd lost everything dear to me.

My uncle was gone.

A soft rap sounded on the door. "Anna?"

Kincade's voice floated through the thick wood. I stood rooted in place, not moving. He was the last person I wanted to see. I said nothing as I gave the door the hairy eyeball.

"Anna, open the door."

No. I don't want to see you. I mind-spoke the words, hoping he heard me.

"Yes, I heard that," he said. "Anna, it's been two days."

Two days? Had I been unconscious for two days?

"Yes, two days," he repeated.

Curse him and his mind-reading powers. I hated that.

"Go away." My voice was scratchy from nonuse.

I wanted to be alone in my grief. To climb under the covers and never come out. What was the point? The one person I trusted—my true family—was gone. How was I supposed to go on from that? How was I supposed to accept the fact I was the one who pierced his heart and let him die? I should have done more to save him. To rid the poison from him.

"There wasn't anything you could have done, and you know it." His muffled voice came through the door.

I closed my eyes, putting up my mental walls to keep him out. It was bad enough he was a walking lie detector, but I drew the line at him reading my every thought. Besides, I didn't need him or Astrid or Killian because I resolved to stop hunting for these relics. I wanted no more part of it.

"Fine, then, don't open the door. I'll be back later," he said.

I hoped he walked away. I went to the balcony, my hand reaching for the door when I halted. If I went out there, there was a chance Kincade would eventually be on his and then he'd want to chat again. I did not want to chat.

I dropped my hand, my mind blank. What now? What would I do now?

"You go on."

Sariel's soft voice was behind me. I closed my eyes again and shook my head.

"I don't want to."

"I know." He was closer now, his voice right behind me. He placed a warm comforting hand on my shoulder. "But your uncle would not want you to curl up into a ball of grief. Would he?"

"I can't go on without him."

Funny how admitting that cut me to the bone. We recently mended our relationship. He was the one who knew everything, the one I relied on, trusted with my life.

"It will be hard, but you can. He'd want you to."

But I didn't want me to.

"If you give up now, more souls will be lost to Lucifer's dark army and he will win."

It was a truth I didn't want to face. I realized Sariel was right, but I lacked the energy to continue this quest for the Holy Relics.

"Edward lives on in you, Anna," he whispered. "Remember that."

I no longer felt the warmth of his hand on my shoulder. When I looked behind me, he was gone.

***

HOURS LATER, DARKNESS SETTLED into the room. I didn't bother to turn on a light. The night gave me an odd sense of comfort.

I wandered out of my room, pausing in the hallway to stare down the length of it to the closed door of my uncle's suite. I forced my feet to move, taking one step after another. I wasn't sure what I expected to accomplish standing outside his door. He wasn't going to answer when I knocked. I didn't have a key to get inside.

Instead, I turned around and walked to the lobby, mindless of where I was going. Numb. No clue what time it was other than it was dark.

When I arrived, Kincade sat on the sofa reading the day's paper.

It struck me as odd. I had never seen Kincade read anything. This was something more like what my uncle would do. For a moment, I paused there, staring at him in disbelief as my mind tried to process what I was seeing.

He put aside the paper. In front of him on the table was a decanter of amber liquid and two glasses. Perhaps he was expecting me and biding his time until I made an appearance. He poured two glasses and motioned me to the nearby chair.

I hesitated.

"Whiskey," he said.

"So, this is what we do now? Guzzle whiskey when Anna has a life tragedy?"

His face remained expressionless as he picked up a glass and extended it to me.

My feet moved before my brain said go. I took the glass and downed it in one gulp, not bothering to sit. The wonderful liquid burned all the way down, sizzling in my empty gut and shooting warmth through me. Even my ears tingled. I held it down for a refill. He obliged.

I sat, holding the glass in between my hands.

And suddenly the flood of tears welled in my eyes. There was no stopping them. I put the glass on the table and bent in half, my forehead on my knees as I cried my eyes out. Kincade let me. He said nothing. Merely scooted a box of tissue my direction on the table. A gesture I appreciated more than I wanted to admit.

The wracking sobs stopped. The tears finally halted but I remained where I was. Bent over staring at my kneecaps.

"Where is my uncle's body?" I asked, my voice faint and muffled.

"I had Astrid and Killian return him to Walker Manor. They're waiting there for our return."

I nodded. They couldn't leave him there in the port or bring him back to the hotel. And no calling the authorities, either. There was no other choice. I wished I wasn't the one to make it.

"I need to make arrangements."

"I assumed."

I lifted my head and grabbed a tissue, blowing my nose. This wasn't the first time Kincade had seen me at my worst. I reached for the whiskey and downed it.

"And yeah, this is what we do. Drink whiskey when you have a tragedy," he said.

"Good to know."

Sarcasm. I appreciated that from him more than sympathy. I didn't want his pity. Or his comfort. I wanted to get drunk. I held out my empty glass. He poured. I drank. And so, it went.

We put away more than half the decanter, though I suspected I was doing most of the drinking. And I was even more numb than when I arrived.

He didn't pressure me about moving on or tell me it was time to get to Jerusalem to search for the staff or urge me to get over my grief. He allowed me to drink without a lot of chatter.

I had a sense of loss I struggled to put into words. Edward was the one constant in my life, despite our differences and the fact we hadn't spoken to each other for a few years before I returned to England.

"I don't know what to do now." I hadn't intended to blurt the words.

"What you always do."

I cut him a glance. "What's that?"

"Kill demons and hunt relics." He reached down and picked up something off the floor. The long object was wrapped in a piece of cloth. "I thought you might want this."

As soon as I took it, I knew what it was. I unwrapped it and stared down at the shiny silver blade. My uncle's sword, now flameless. Dammit, more tears formed in my eyes.

"Thanks," I choked. I cleared my throat, regaining composure as I ran a finger down the blade. "I can't do this alone."

"You aren't alone. You never have been."

My gaze met his green-gold one. He gave me a point-blank look that said he meant it. He didn't beg to help me. He merely gave me that look that said he was all business, that he didn't need or want my permission to tag along. That he was going to tag along whether I wanted him to or not.

Strangely, I wanted him to.

I clenched my jaw, trying to keep my emotions in check.

"You'll also want this." He reached into the pocket of his cargo pants and pulled out a key, handing it to me.

It was the key to Edward's room.

"His belongings are still in there."

I nodded. "I want to return to Walker Manor and bury him properly."

"The private jet is waiting when you're ready."

He emptied the remaining whiskey into my glass. He stood and walked away without another word. I watched him leave, scrutinizing his square shoulders and how he walked with purpose. Like he was pissed off at everyone and everything in the world.

He didn't talk about his feelings. I wondered if Edward's death affected him. Even when he told me what happened here in Acre centuries ago, he showed no emotions. I had a deeper understanding, though, of why he wanted Azriel dead. His betrayal cut him deep.

I downed the rest of the whiskey. It was time to clear Edward's things from his room, return to England, and put him to rest. Clutching the sword in my arms, I made my way back to the hallway of rooms.

I took a deep breath as I unlocked his door and shoved it open.

The suite was silent and dark.

I moved deeper into the room, fumbling for the light switch. My fingers grazed across it and I flipped it on. His room was tidy and neat. The bed made. The towels fresh in the bathroom. His toiletries were nowhere to be found. His duffel sat on the edge of the bed. Next to it his soft-sided leather briefcase.

Almost as though he expected not to come back to this room.

On the desk, an envelope with my name written on it in his perfect penmanship.

My heart rammed in my throat.

I put aside the sword to pick up the note.

My hand shook as I pulled out the paper.

Anna –

Everything you need to continue your journey is in my briefcase—a list of trusted contacts across the world, access to all my bank accounts, and more. Piers will be able to assist you in any way you need.

I did not intend to die in Acre, but I also could not allow you to give up your soul to Mammon. I could not allow the darkness to win. It was the only way to ensure your survival and your continued search for the Holy Relics. It was a sacrifice I was willing and ready to make.

My one regret is I will not be there to see you succeed. And I know you will. You have so much power and light within you, so much life ahead of you, so much raw potential. You are more than special, Anna. You are divine. I should have told you the truth long before. It's why you have the Godlight, why you are more powerful than us all, and why Lucifer wants you for his own.

Your Godlight will defeat the darkness. Trust in that.

You were right about Natasha. I believe there is a good chance she is your mother. My dearest sister. Find her. Help her.

I always thought of you as my own daughter. That is why you are named my heir. I am so deeply proud of who you are becoming and who you will become. You have restored the Walker name with the Most High and the archangels. Remember that as you continue down this path of valor.

Always,
Edward

I refolded the letter and clutched it against my chest. Closing my eyes, I let the tears fall once more.

CHAPTER 25

KINCADE AND I RETURNED to England on the private jet. I hadn't spoken much, nor did I care to. He gave me space to let me process my grief in my own way, in my own time. On the plane, he took his usual seat in the back and prepared to nap.

The truth was, I was never going to get over Edward's death. Not for the rest of my life.

I understood why he wrote the letter. He wanted me to know those things—things he couldn't say to me, but he wanted to share them before he was gone.

My wish was the lost feeling would eventually subside.

When we landed, a car waited for us. I recognized the chauffeur who greeted me with a nod as he opened the back door. He'd been Edward's driver before on our many trips abroad. I slid in behind the driver. Kincade took the other side. A cold, dismal rain fell as we drove from the airport to Walker Manor. At least the weather matched my mood.

Piers must have been watching for us because he opened the front door as the car pulled up and parked. He came to the car as the trunk popped and unloaded the luggage before I even got out. Kincade unfolded his long frame and exited the car, heading inside, leaving me alone with the driver.

He opened the door for me. I stepped out and paused, shifting from one foot to the other. Did I tip him? Tell him thanks? What now?

"If you need a driver again, Miss Walker, call me," he said, sensing my awkwardness.

"Do you work for my uncle?"

"Did, yes. Now I work for you. The name is Clive." He gave me a brief smile, then got back into the car and drove away.

I guess I never realized my uncle had a personal driver.

When I entered the house, Kincade was nowhere to be found, but Piers, Ophelia, Grace, Astrid and Killian waited for me. My welcoming party. I suppressed an inward groan. The last thing I wanted was to be showered with condolences. All I wanted was to go to my room, shut the door and never come out.

Unrealistic, of course, but that's what I wanted to do.

Ophelia immediately gave me a hug, nearly squeezing the life out of me. She was broken up about Edward's death, but trying hard to contain her emotions.

"How's Darius?" I asked.

She shook her head. "The same."

That was better than I expected. I worried he was sicker than when I left.

Grace hugged me next. "I'm so sorry, Anna," she whispered in my ear.

"Thanks."

Astrid and Killian also offered their condolences. She clutched my hands in hers. "If there's anything I can do..."

"I wish there was."

And Piers. Even he had a distraught look on his pinched features. He gave me a half bow. "My lady."

I put up a hand. "You don't have to call me that."

"As you wish." He gave one nod. "I have prepared the master's chamber for you."

My heart palpitated at the thought. I had never stepped foot in Edward's bedroom. I wasn't about to start now. "Thanks, but I'll stay in my own room."

I expected him to bristle at that, but he didn't. He merely nodded. "We should discuss the arrangements, if you have a moment?"

I dreaded discussing the arrangements, but it was necessary. It was the sole reason I was back in England. I nodded and followed him to Edward's office. It didn't matter I was now the one in charge, the office would always belong to him in my mind.

I refused to sit at the desk. We discussed the funeral at length—it would be a small, simple affair. I wasn't obliged to invite any of the other family members because why? They all hated me anyway. Edward had two other sisters—Matilda and Josephina. I hadn't spoken to either in years. My grandmother, Elinor, had been dead for quite some time. I had a handful of cousins, too, but I hadn't seen them since my childhood and, well, why start now?

Grace was my family now.

Edward's final wishes were that he be buried on the estate in the small cemetery I never even knew existed until today. According to Piers, no one was buried there yet. I wondered if my uncle had prepared it hoping he would one day bring home my mother's body.

It was a morbid thought I didn't want to dwell on.

As we finalized the plans, I said, "Piers, one more thing."

"Yes, my lady?"

I suppressed an inward groan. As much as I didn't want him calling me that, I sensed I was never going to get him to stop. "I need...something to wear."

I flushed, hot, embarrassed I had to even ask. My wardrobe was simple. I no longer owned a dress or heels and since the funeral was tomorrow, I didn't have time to shop in town.

"Already taken care of, my lady. I had a suitable dress and shoes brought in from town earlier today. You'll find what you need hanging in your wardrobe."

I didn't ask how he knew my size. "Thanks."

I headed up to my room, clutching Edward's briefcase. Once inside, I leaned against the door and blew out a breath. This room had always been my sanctuary.

Throbbing pain took up residence behind my eyes and at the base of my skull. Fatigue pulsed through me. I dropped the briefcase on the floor and sat on the edge of the bed, staring down at it.

Everything I needed to continue my journey was in that briefcase, or so the letter said. May as well take a peek now. I unzipped the top and reached in, pulling out a notebook I immediately recognized.

CONTACTS was embossed in gold on the leather cover.

It was the same notebook I found in the back of his desk drawer not too long ago. In my frenzy, I didn't have time to look through it thoroughly then. But now I did.

The pilot, Harry Humphrey, was listed first. Then the driver, Clive. Rafiq Al-Ashab, the merchant from Marrakesh we'd met to get more information about the Knights of the Holy Lance. Luiz Santos whose apartment we used in Rio.

Beyond that, more names I didn't recognize. Who were they? Other dream walkers? Allies? Enemies? A few had a line drawn through them and the word DECEASED next to it. One was Rodrigo Marques. The next, Isabel Marques, my cousin who died when Azriel attacked us in route to the airport and kidnapped Kincade.

One name caught my eye. Tamar Mizrahi, Jerusalem. Next to that a string of numbers. A phone number?

I stared at that a long time, my heart clawing its way to my throat. Who was she? How did Edward know her?

My eyes grew heavy as I pondered the woman's name. I leaned back into the pillows, the book landing on my chest as I drifted off to sleep.

It wasn't long before Azriel paid me a visit, that wolf grin on his face. I realized too late I'd forgotten to put up my mental walls.

"Ah, *chérie*, it's good to see you."

"What do you want?" I was in no mood for his lascivious behavior.

"To offer my deepest sympathies on your loss."

"Fuck off," I said. "I don't want your condolences."

He snickered, well pleased with my retort. "I admit it does make things easier with Edward out of the way."

My eyes narrowed. "Easier for what?"

"Easier to get to you, of course."

He infuriated me. "As I said before, fuck off."

His expression turned serious then. "You have something of mine. I want it back."

I shook my head. "I have nothing of yours. In fact, you have something of mine. I want it back."

"Astrid and I have unfinished business. I want her returned to me immediately."

"You'll have to take that up with Astrid," I said.

"I propose a trade. You return my sister to me and I return the spear to you."

He was out of his mind. "No way."

"Pity. You leave me no choice, then."

"And what choice is that?"

"I will have to retrieve her myself. Au revoir, *chérie*."

My eyes snapped open and I bolted upright. I had to warn Astrid. I left my room and hurried down the hall to the room she shared with Killian and knocked. She opened it a moment later.

"Anna?"

"I had a visit from Azriel," I said without pleasantries.

Her eyes clouded with something akin to fear. Killian appeared behind her.

"What did he want?" he demanded.

"He wanted me to trade her for the Spear of Destiny," I said.

Her brows knit in question. "He has the spear?"

"Yeah, long story. I'll tell you later."

"You didn't agree to that, did you?" Killian's chest puffed up, ready to attack.

"Uh, no, I didn't. I'm not heartless." I returned my gaze back to Astrid. "But he said he'd have to retrieve you himself."

Astrid stiffened at my words, her back straight and her shoulders squared. Defiance creased her features.

Killian pushed in closer to her. "Over my dead body."

"I'm sure that's what he's hoping for, dearest," she said, her gaze never leaving mine. "He can no longer control me, Anna. And he will have a fight on his hands should he try."

"I was hoping you'd say that." I made a mental note to check the wards around the perimeter of the manor house, though I hadn't a clue how to do that. It was something Edward did. "He'll have a lot of people to go through to get to you."

A smile lifted the corner of her mouth. "I thank you for the warning."

As she shut the door, I headed down the stairs, my booted feet pounded down the steps. I paused at the front door, which had been replaced since Abaddon's attack. It occurred to me then as I stood there staring at it. In the parlor, the windows had also been replaced as well as Ophelia's Christmas decorations.

The girl must have Christmas magic in her veins.

"Where do you think you're going?" Kincade's voice sounded from the landing behind me.

I glanced behind me to see him descending the stairs. "To, ah, check the perimeter. I had a dream visit from Azriel."

"I'll do it." He brushed by me as he reached for the door. "Go rest, Anna. You need it. And tomorrow is a long day."

"Tomorrow?"

"The funeral," he said and was out the door before I managed to reply.

How did he find out about that already? I huffed and headed back up the stairs. He was right. Tomorrow was going to be the hardest, worst day of my life.

CHAPTER 26

THE MORNING CAME BEFORE I was ready. Who was I kidding? I would never be ready. I watched the sun rise over the estate from my balcony. My gut churned acid. As the sun rose higher, I forced my feet to move. I showered and, for the first time in a very long time, I took my time getting ready. I wasn't much of a make-up girl but every now and then I liked to put on lip gloss and mascara. I'd forgotten how long my lashes were.

True to his word, Piers left a black dress and heels in the wardrobe. I shouldn't have been surprised at the perfect fit, but I was. Once I was dressed and ready, I headed down the stairs.

We planned a short graveside service. Naturally, the weather wasn't going to cooperate, and it was cold and rainy again. As I headed down the stairs, Piers waited at the bottom with a coat and a large umbrella in his hand.

"The car is waiting for you, my lady."

"Where are the others?" I asked.

"Already at the graveside."

I nodded, chewing on my lower lip. "Are you coming?"

"My place is here," he said.

"But Edward was your—"

"Employer, my lady. As you are now." He motioned to the door as if to usher me out. "Shall we?"

He handed me the coat. I slipped it on, grateful for the warmth.

I didn't argue, though it didn't seem right Piers wasn't going to be there, too. He handed me the umbrella. I stepped outside, my heels crunching on the gravel drive. Clive opened the door and waited as I slid in the backseat. He shut the door and got behind the wheel.

The small cemetery was on the back of the property. It was the furthest point from the manor house as possible. A wrought iron fence and gate surrounded the plot. I saw the freshly dug grave ready for the cherrywood casket to be lowered into it. A dark blue tent covered the grave as well as the few household inhabitants waiting for my arrival.

Everything about today sucked.

When we arrived at the gate, Clive got out and opened my door. As I stepped out, my heels sinking into the soft ground, I popped open the umbrella. Clive escorted me through the gate and to the front row.

My gaze landed on each face under that tent. Decker, his face impassive yet somber. Ophelia, her eyes red rimmed and her nose puffy. Grace, her grief written across her features. Astrid and Killian standing together off to the side both with sorrow carving their faces.

And Kincade. Standing rigid at the front with his hands clasped in front of him. His face was clean shaven. He wore a black button-down shirt, open at the collar, and black dress pants. And for a moment, I stared at him trying to comprehend this was the same man.

His eyes met mine, never leaving them. As I approached, I took the spot next to him in the front row. He gave me a nod of greeting and faced forward.

And so, it began.

◆————————◆

THE PRIEST GAVE A short eulogy. He read Psalm 23 and ended with 1 Thessalonians 4. We prayed. And the mist continued through it all. As everyone drifted away, I stayed, watching the casket lower into the ground. Kincade remained at my side.

I thought back to that day in Acre, when my uncle fell. When I stabbed him in the heart. He wrapped his hand around mine on the hilt and shoved it deep. The blade went through skin and bone with a crunch, sending a sickening feeling through me.

Something peculiar happened after that. A flash of light? Did I remember that correctly? Then I was knocked unconscious.

"When my uncle died," I began, my voice weak. "What happened?"

"A flash of light," Kincade said. "It hovered over you before punching into you. You flew back and smacked hard into the ground. The dagger remained where it was. I removed it."

But what was the flash of light?

"We thought, at first, you were dead. You weren't breathing. Your pulse was weak. The veil around us fell. That's when I had Killian and Astrid remove your uncle's body."

He paused. I glanced at him. He kept his eyes forward, his face all hard angles.

"And me?"

"I picked you up and carried you back to the hotel. To your room."

And waited for me to wake up. He didn't have a lot of answers as to what the mysterious light was that punched into me. I didn't either. I certainly didn't feel any different.

Silent moments passed as I stared down at the casket.

"He was the only family I had," I said.

"What about Grace?"

"Edward was blood."

He nodded understanding.

"He believed in me when I didn't. I trusted him with my life. I trusted him with everything. And now he's gone. Because of me."

"No."

"Yes, Kincade. Because I made a deal with the Prince of Greed. Because I was stupid and desperate to regain the Horn of Gabriel." I licked my lips and instantly regretted it as I tasted the pale pink lip gloss I swiped across them. "I killed him."

"No," he said again. "Edward did what he had to. You did what you had to. It's the way it had to be."

"I don't have to like it."

"You don't," he agreed. "But you do have to go on."

He was right. I had to go on to find the Staff of Moses and the remaining two relics. I had to find a way to defeat Lucifer and his dark army. I had to find a way to save myself, my friends, and mankind.

The weight of the world was on my shoulders and I no longer had anyone to share the burden. I was alone.

"You're wrong about that," he said.

Reading my thoughts again. I frowned but didn't let him see.

"You have me."

And then he stood and walked away.

A tingling sensation went up my spine to the nape of my neck. My hands shook a little as I thought about that. As much as I didn't want to accept his help, it was time to stop resisting. I was just going to have to guard my thoughts even more.

And it was time to pack our bags for Jerusalem.

———◆———

CLIVE WAITED FOR ME with the car outside the cemetery. The others were nowhere in sight. I assumed they all trekked back to the house on foot. It was still raining. My heels sunk even more into the damp earth. I sighed, wishing I had the sense to wear a good pair of wellies. By the time we made it back to the manor house, I was soaked to the bone, cold, tired, and emotionally drained.

I was too exhausted to go up to my room. I paused in the parlor and took one of the wing-backed chairs in front of the fireplace to thaw out. Shrugging out of the coat, I tossed it on one of the empty chairs, then kicked off my muddy heels, leaving them on the expensive rug and wishing Edward was there to chastise me for it.

Grace entered the parlor with a tea tray and placed it on the table. She granted me a smile as she poured a cup. I wished it was whiskey.

"Piers thought you could use this," she said.

There were tiny iced lemon cakes on a small dish. She handed that to me along with the cup of tea. I took it from her, wrapping my cold hand around the warm porcelain. She took the seat opposite me.

"Thanks," I muttered and took a sip. "I'm surprised he didn't bring it himself."

"I wanted to. Anna, I—" She clamped her lips closed, cutting off whatever she wanted to say. She peered into the fire, the light reflecting on her face making it glow.

I reached for one of the lemon cakes and popped it into my mouth. "Go on," I said around the mouthful.

She tried again. "*The Lord is close to the brokenhearted and saves those whose sprits are crushed.*" She paused, fingering her small golden cross.

"Psalms 34:18," I said.

She gave me a faint smile, nodding. She understood me sometimes even more than I, myself, understood me. And something about hearing that bit of scripture gave me peace.

"I am truly sorry about your uncle. We didn't see eye to eye when it came to you, but he cared for you a great deal." She wrung her hands, as though something weighed heavily on her mind.

"What is it?" I asked.

"I've been thinking I should return to Texas—"

"No." I cut her off, but she continued.

"I don't belong here."

"Grace, no. Not no, but hell no. You're safe here. You belong here as much as I do. Where did you get this idea?"

Worry lines creased her forehead. "Ophelia told me...things."

Great. She'd been talking to Ophelia. Likely the girl filled Grace in on everything from Azriel hunting me to our little soirée in the Second Circle trying to rescue Kincade.

"Darius is a warrior angel?" she asked.

"He is and he's very sick."

"Ophelia told me what happened to him." She wouldn't look at me. Just continued to stare into the fire. "She also said you killed demons and high lords together. All of this is...real, isn't it? These demons and...dark things?"

Ah, so that's what worried her. I wasn't going to sugar coat it. "Yes. It's all real."

She again reached up and fingered the dainty gold cross at her neck. We didn't go to church much when I was a kid, but I understood her. She was a southern, god-fearing woman. Likely all of this was difficult for her to process. And the cross gave her comfort.

"You can see them?"

"I can. And smell demons when they approach."

Her eyes widened. "What do they smell like?"

"Death. Decay. Rot. Like something that crawled out of the depths of Hell into our world to wreak havoc."

She chewed the inside of her cheek and shifted in her chair as she considered. "And this...Azriel. He's a fallen angel?"

"A high lord, yes." I nodded.

Her face paled. She continued to brush her fingers over the cross. I understood then. She was afraid. Of me. Of being here, in this house. She thought returning to Texas was the answer, that she would be away from all this dark, dangerous stuff. Nothing was farther from the truth. I put down the cup and reached for her free hand. I wrapped my cold fingers around her warm ones and gave them a quick squeeze. Her gaze finally left the fire and met mine.

"Listen, Grace. You're safest here. Azriel knows who you are to me. If I let you return, and something happened to you..." I shook my head. "I'll never forgive myself."

"You think he'd do me harm?" Worry and fear and doubt lingered in her gaze.

"I know he would." I took a deep breath, exhaled it. "Maybe it's time I tell you everything. Starting with Ben."

✦

WE TALKED LATE INTO the day. I filled my stomach on lemon cakes and tea. At one point, Piers brought us lunch allowing us to continue.

Grace listened to my story from the day I dream walked Emma in that hospital to meeting Kincade to Edward's death in the port of Acre and everything in between. I told her about the Knights of the Holy Lance and possibly finding my real mother. I told her about the Brotherhood of Watchers and how they were connected to the Knights Templars. I told her everything, as if unloading it to someone was a weight lifted off my shoulders.

She stopped me to ask a question here and there, but overall, she seemed to understand everything. Accepting it was another thing. I didn't expect her to right away. It was a lot to take in. It was still a lot for me to take in considering what I'd been through the last few months.

"You think the Staff of Moses will help cure Darius?" she asked.

"I hope it will," I said. "I have to find it first. I got another note in Acre. It was a map of the Old City in Jerusalem with the words The First Temple."

"Solomon's Temple. It was destroyed by the Babylonians and then the Romans. There are two Muslim shrines there now. I doubt there's anything left of the First Temple. However..." She paused, tapping her chin with her forefinger. "I recall reading something about the construction of an underground mosque near the site. Yes, that was it."

Her eyes lit with excitement as she hopped to her feet and paced the small area in front of the fireplace. A tingling sensation of anticipation trickled through me as I waited for her to remember the details.

"Something about the Jewish archaeologists sifting through the soil. They found numerous objects from the time of the First Temple including a two-thousand-year-old chisel." She stopped pacing and turned to look at me. "In the First Temple there was an elaborate chamber. The Holy of Holies. What if it's still there?"

"This chamber?" I asked. "Would it be underground?"

"Today it would be. In the time of the First Temple, no. There were also relics kept there. Specifically, the Ark of the Convent, but no one knows what happened to it after Nebuchadnezzar's army destroyed the temple. The story was it was taken to Babylon."

She gave me two ideas—one the Staff of Moses may be in this Holy of Holies, and two, the Ark may be hidden somewhere in ancient Babylon.

"I don't know if that helps you," she said.

"It does. It all does. At least it gives me a place to start." I got to my feet and kissed her on the cheek. "Thanks."

"You're leaving soon, aren't you?"

I nodded. "I have to find the staff before Azriel does."

She took a deep breath. "Then I promise to stay here. But I need a task. I feel useless hanging about all day doing nothing."

I grinned. "Maybe Piers can help with that." I hooked my arm in hers. "Let's give him a shout."

PIERS AND GRACE HIT it off in a way I hadn't expected. They had something in common—they both loved to bake. I hadn't spent much time with Piers, so it was news to me. I left them to discuss the finer points of baking macaroons and headed back to my room carrying my destroyed shoes in one hand.

As I approached the stairs, Kincade leaned against the banister. He'd changed from his funeral attire to something more familiar—cargo pants, long-sleeve Henley and boots. I didn't miss the way he looked me up and down as I approached.

"I know what you're going to say," I said.

"And what's that?"

"It's time to go."

He smirked. "Is that what I was going to say? Maybe I was just checking on you."

I snorted. "I doubt it." I paused at the foot of the stairs and looked up at him. "I'm ready."

"You sure?"

For a moment, I was taken aback at the genuine concern on his face. "I'm sure. I admit I was ready to give up on everything after Edward died, but I can't."

"Why not?" He tilted his head to one side, inquisitive.

"I don't like letting people down and there's a whole lot of people depending on me. Whether they know it or not."

Like, the whole world.

He nodded. "Good. Shall we begin?"

CHAPTER 27

Arrangements were made. The strange thing was I was the one who made them. I wondered if this was how it felt to be Edward...

While in the parlor, I called Harry to get the plane ready. I called Clive to have him pick us up for the airport. I expected them to give me trouble or at least act begrudgingly about it, but they didn't. They were ready to go whenever I was.

I wondered if this is what it felt like to be Edward. He had all this knowledge and rapport with people. I wanted to keep that going in his name. I didn't want to tarnish it.

Then I called Tamar Mizrahi of Jerusalem.

I assumed the number in the contact book was a phone number and I was right. Except it wasn't Tamar Mizrahi who answered. It was a man who answered with the salutation of a hotel name.

In Hebrew.

Which I understood as though he spoke English.

"King David Hotel."

And I replied in Hebrew. As if some recessed part of my brain fully understood and spoke this language all my life. I asked for hotel accommodations for me, Kincade, Astrid and Killian. Decker decided not to make this trip. In fact, he performed his disappearing act shortly after the funeral. I booked three suites with views of the Old City. No way was I sharing a room with Kincade, even if it was a two-bedroom suite.

When I disconnected the call, I tucked the cell phone in my pocket unsure how I managed to get all the way back to England with it fully intact. It was the last thing my uncle had given to me, which meant I would now have to keep it forever until the blasted thing no longer worked.

There was a strange sense of...something residing inside me. As if a shift had occurred and I was no longer afraid of what was yet to come. As if there was some form of power deep down that had been awakened.

I wondered if that dark demon magic was still there, poisoning my system. It hadn't reared its ugly head in a few days, and I hadn't thought about it much. I'd been distracted by everything that happened in Acre from Kincade telling me about his past to my uncle's death. Now more than ever I was certain the postcard sending me to Acre was a way for me to learn about what happened to Kincade in his past, to show me that he was not only my guardian but my assassin.

Kincade, Astrid and Killian hustled down the stairs, all carrying some type of baggage. Astrid didn't bother to hide her wings. Killian didn't bother to hide his Fae ears. Kincade didn't bother to hide his hardened look of impatience. Seeing Astrid's wings and Killian's Fae ears verified they were both comfortable here in Walker Manor.

"The car is waiting outside," I said, nodding to the door.

"Are you sure this is the best method of travel?" Killian asked. "I can simply sift us there."

"I think we should stick to the plan," Kincade said before I could answer.

Ophelia bounded down the stairs then, her sword strapped to her back. Her blonde hair bounced in waves over her shoulders.

"Where do you think you're going?" I demanded. Because the last conversation we had was about her staying behind to protect Darius and Grace.

"I came to see you off," she said. I eyed the sword on her back. She grinned and thumbed at it. "The sword is for just in case."

I understood. In case the manor was attacked again. She wanted to be ready. She hugged me tight.

"Be careful," she whispered in my ear.

She didn't have to tell me to hurry back with the staff. That was understood. She wanted to heal Darius as much as I did.

Piers appeared seemingly out of nowhere. It always astounded me he did that. I never heard him coming. The man was always in stealth mode. He opened the front door for us to a frigid English morning.

"Safe travels, Miss Walker," he said by way of farewell.

"See you on the other side, Piers." I gave him a jaunty salute. He was not amused.

I was out the door, the others on my heels. Ophelia followed, pausing on the stoop to see us off. As I approached the car, every muscle in my body seized. I went rigid and lost my balance, falling toward the ground. Since I was paralyzed, I was unable to break my fall and landed on the hard ground, jarring every bone in my body and smashing my face on the gravel. Pain exploded everywhere. Blood spurted from my nose.

"Anna!" Ophelia's shriek was all I needed to hear to know who and what was in the nearby vicinity.

Abaddon made another appearance.

Since I was unable to move, I assumed the others were in the same predicament. Abaddon kneeled in front of me, that sickly grin on his pallid face.

"Oh, my dear, we meet again. And this time your uncle is not here to save you."

He brushed hair from my face. I wanted to swat his hand away but was still unable to move. He scooped me up and put me on my feet, turning me so I got a good look at Azriel standing on the other side of the car. The Spear of Destiny was in his hand, no longer wrapped in the cloth of Ophelia's scarf.

Well, shit.

The two of them must have been waiting to ambush us since they were unable to get inside the manor due to the wards.

He lifted the spear and pointed it directly at me. "You and I have a score to settle, *chérie*." His gaze flickered from me to someone else—that someone else had to be Astrid. "And you, my dear sister...oh, how I've missed you."

"Stay away from her." Killian gritted the words out, but his voice sounded muffled.

"I wish I could," Azriel said. Then he turned his attention back to me. "Anna, go to Astrid. Bring her to me."

The spear whispered to me. *Take the girl to Azriel. You know you want to. She is nothing. She will destroy you if you don't do it. She is evil incarnate.*

Abaddon leaned down and pressed his lips close to my ear. "Yes, my dear. Do as he orders."

As he said it, the paralysis released its hold on me.

With his words, the dark magic churned deep inside me, the wrath and fear coming to life once again. Bubbling up through my veins and overcoming all the good sense I had left. I recognized it pulsing through me as my feet obeyed and moved toward Astrid. Her eyes were wide with fear as I stepped closer, unable to disobey.

"Don't listen to him, Anna," Kincade said. "Fight him."

But everything within me was telling me to do as he command-ed. Even as the darkness surged forth, the rational side of my mind told me Kincade would kill me to put an end to it.

And yet, I grasped Astrid by the wrist and pulled her along. As though she were nothing more than a helium balloon on a string. She stumbled after me, following me as I took step after step toward Azriel. And then my brain understood why—the dark demon magic Abaddon projected did not affect her in the least.

"Anna, don't do this," she begged. "He's controlling you with the spear. Don't you see that?"

"Shh." I placed a finger on her lips. "It will all be over soon."

"Anna." Kincade practically growled my name. "Listen to her. She's telling you the truth."

I ignored him and pulled her along. She fought me every step of the way, struggling to get out of my iron grasp but I refused to release her. In fact, I tightened my fingers, the anger surging forward over the thought she wanted to flee.

"That's right," Azriel cooed. "Bring that traitorous bitch to me."

Astrid jerked backward, trying to break my grip on her wrist but failed. "Anna, please don't do this."

"Let her go," Killian barked. Panic laced his tone.

"Your Fae magic does not work here," Azriel growled. "And once Astrid is back where she belongs, you will die. As you should have died before."

"You stay away from him!" she shouted.

Something that sounded like a war cry ripped from Astrid. She yanked her wrist free from my grasp with a strength I hadn't expected. The jolt knocked me off my feet and I tumbled once again to the ground. My elbow took the brunt of the hit, sending shooting pain up to my shoulder.

The hold of the spear released me. I shook my head to clear it enough to look up and see Astrid had Azriel pinned to the ground, her hands around his throat as she choked him. He clawed her face.

The spear had tumbled from Azriel's grasp and rested nearby in the damp grass. I climbed to my hands and knees just as Abaddon reached down and plucked it from the ground as though he picked up a prized possession. He turned it on me.

"You and I will make a powerful pair," he said. "You will come to me, Anna, and together we will do what's necessary to complete the dark army."

Go to him. Do as he says. Embrace the darkness, Anna. Change your destiny as you so desire. You no longer must be this Keeper of the Holy Relics. You are something more powerful than anyone knows. You have that within you, and you will wield it.

"Yes." I climbed to my feet, my palms red and covered in gravel.

"She will not!" Ophelia wielded her shimmering sword as she charged out of the house.

Abaddon hit her with his paralyzing demon magic. She froze in place, holding aloft her sword.

Kincade got to Abaddon first. He tackled him, like he'd tackled me on so many occasions. His head smashed into the destroyer angel's gut, shoving him backward. They landed in the grass with an audible thud. Kincade had a hand wrapped around his wrist. He pounded the back of the destroyer angel's hand against the ground once, twice, three times. Abaddon refused to release it. Kincade elbowed him in the face, then when the destroyer angel relaxed his grip, Kincade pounded his hand against the ground again until he released the spear. Abaddon grunted.

The anger flared bright in a powerful burst that sent me to my knees. I groaned as I fisted the gravel and took a deep breath, trying to calm my ravaged mind. I closed my eyes, trying to push it back and out. Abaddon chuckled.

"Embrace the darkness, my pet."

The darkness was there, pushing into me and controlling me. Telling me to get to my feet, my hands and arms throbbing from the impact. Shadows pressed around the edges of my eyes. It was nothing more than the black magic pulsing through me. My rational mind understood this. My irrational mind—the one controlled by the black magic—didn't care. It balked at the sight of Kincade keeping Abaddon to the ground.

"Kincade, release him." My voice was quiet and calm.

He hauled Abaddon to his feet by the collar, still holding him. The forgotten Spear of Destiny nestled in the grass near their feet. "I will not."

"Yes, you will." I pinned him with my most lethal gaze.

His eyes narrowed at me before he opened his hand and shoved the destroyer angel off. Meanwhile, Azriel and Astrid were still locked in a brutal battle. But I ignored that. Killian and Ophelia were still paralyzed.

Abaddon looked well pleased. "You have embraced the darkness within you. Good. Now come." He held his hand out to me.

I looked at those long, slender fingers that beckoned me and promised evil. An inner battle began. A light edged out the darkness, smudging it as I stood warring with my inner demons. Trying to make them understand I was not an agent of evil. The darkness planted inside me was not who I was, deep down. I pressed two fingers against my forehead, wincing.

"What's wrong with you? Do something, Anna!" Ophelia said.

Yes, I needed to do something. But what?

Be the light of the world.

Edward's words came pushing back through me. My head snapped up as I looked at Abaddon's outstretched hand. I'd lost count of how many times he tried to beckon me into service for the Dark One.

I thought of Edward and all that he was—his faith, his courage, his temperance. That's when the Godlight burned bright and hot deep inside me. Pushing back the darkness.

"No," I said.

He looked taken aback. "No?"

"You have not defeated me, Abaddon. You can never defeat me." I lifted my head a little higher, looking down my nose at the destroyer angel.

He faltered a little as he dropped his hand. "Why is that?" he snarled.

"Because I have the Godlight and I am no longer afraid."

I closed my eyes, opened my arms and allowed it to burst forth. The bright light flared to life and streamed from me, smashing into Abaddon with a sizzling fervor. He screamed an unholy scream and then all was silent. When I opened my eyes, he was nothing but a pile of ash at Kincade's feet.

The destroyer angel was no more.

Even Azriel and Astrid had stopped fighting long enough to watch. Azriel held her by the hair, keeping her still. Kincade stared at me, his face expressionless. Ophelia gaped at me with her shimmering sword still held aloft ready to attack.

"Anna...?" My name was a question on her lips.

I took a deep breath, poking around inside my innards for the dark demon magic. I no longer felt the stir of it as I did before when I was in danger, when fear took hold of me. What I said was true—I was no longer afraid.

"You may have won this battle, but not the war, *chérie*," Azriel said. He wrapped an arm around Astrid and suddenly they were gone.

"NO!" Killian emitted a gurgling shriek as he fell to his knees.

Azriel had taken Astrid.

Killian looked as though he'd been kicked in the gut. I stood rooted in place, staring at the empty spot where Astrid and Azriel were. The Fae king surged to his feet then and charged me, murder on his face.

"You bloody bitch! This is your fault!"

He reached for me when Kincade intervened. Kincade moved instantly—stepping between us and shoving Killian back with enough force to make him stumble.

"This is not Anna's fault," he said.

Killian's face crumpled. He didn't bother hiding the anguish.

"Do you realize what he will do to her? He believes she betrayed him. He'll torture her and then kill her."

"He won't," I said, sounding sure of myself. Kincade gave me a questioning glance but I ignored him. I shoved him aside and reached for the Fae king. I took him by the shoulders. "Listen to me! I will get her back. You have my word."

"He took her to Hell. A place I cannot follow. Do you realize that?" His breath hitched.

"Yes," I said. "I've been there before. I'll go there again. For Astrid. I will save her."

His strange, kaleidoscope eyes met mine. "Swear it."

"Anna—" Kincade began.

"I swear it," I said, keeping my gaze fixed on Killian.

We stared at each other a long, quiet moment. Then he finally nodded, taking a step away from me. "I believe you will find her and bring her back."

"I will."

"But first the staff," Kincade said, stepping next to me.

"Azriel will torture her and keep her alive for as long as possible," Killian said. "As punishment for her traitorous acts."

"And I will get to her as soon as I come back with the Staff of Moses," I said.

"I understand your warrior angel's life depends upon it," Killian said, "but Astrid—"

"If Anna says she'll get to her, she will," Kincade said.

I looked up at him, surprised despite myself. He didn't offer reassurances lightly.

"I have to find the staff before Azriel or any of his minions do," I said. "I need you to come with me and help us find it."

He shook his head. "I cannot. Not without her."

"Then stay here." Ophelia sheathed her sword. "It's a big house and Grace and I could use the company."

I understood what she was doing. It almost made me smile.

"I should return to the sacred Fae forest and remain there until Astrid returns."

"If that's your wish."

He gave me a nod. "It is. I appreciate your hospitality, Anna, but this is not my home."

I opened my mouth to try to talk him out of it, but he used his Fae magic and sifted away. I puffed out a breath.

"So that's that, I guess," I said.

"Maybe it's for the best," Kincade said. "It's just you and me, then."

My stomach churned acid as I thought of the two of us on this journey. Alone. No Edward. No Astrid. No Killian. Just me and Kincade. I swallowed the lump that formed in my throat and tried to keep my tone even.

"Yep."

Clive popped out of the car then. "Now that all that's settled, are we ready?"

I'd forgotten he was in the driver's seat of the car. I guessed he had been frozen by the demon magic, too, and was unable to leave the car. I doubt he wanted to do that anyway. He acted as though what just occurred was situation normal. I flushed, my cheeks turning hot.

"We're ready."

He popped the trunk. Kincade and I put our bags inside. I gave one final glance at the manor house with Grace and Darius inside. Ophelia gave me a thumbs up.

"I'll take good care of them," she said, as though reading my mind.

I nodded and stepped around the back of the car and then halted. I'd forgotten about the spear still lying in the grass. I kneeled next to it. The last time I touched the thing, it tried to control me. Because that's what I wanted. I wanted to change my destiny and the spear somehow sensed that. It pierced through my mind and beckoned me to make different choices.

Feet crunched on the gravel and then Kincade paused next to me.

"Take it, Anna."

"I can't. It will try to control me."

"Not if you don't let it."

My heart pounded hard in my throat as I reached for the spear, hesitated, and then wrapped my hand around it. I picked it up, held it a long moment...and felt nothing.

Azriel was more interested in retrieving Astrid than hanging on to the spear and for that I was grateful. After giving it up to save Kincade's life, it was back where it belonged. Safely in my hands.

"Thank you," I said.

"For what?"

"If it hadn't been for you, I wouldn't have the spear now." I got to my feet and turned toward the house, thinking of the velvet lined box in the vault. "Give me a moment to put it away."

I didn't wait for a response as I headed back into the house. I bounded up the stairs to the library, closing the door behind me. Edward showed me the vault when I recovered the spear the first time. Now, it would go in its rightful place. I pushed aside the shelf to reveal the steel door with the massive lock, then punched in the combination. I turned the dial, spun the wheel and pulled open the door.

The vault was home to numerous first edition books, paintings, sculptures, and the Horn of Gabriel in a specially made box. I placed the spear next to the horn on the shelf, thankful it was back in my possession.

As I left the vault, closing it up I thought of Edward and how relieved he would be. Hell, I was relieved myself. And now I had to go after the Staff of Moses.

Onward to Jerusalem.

CHAPTER 28

WHEN WE BOARDED THE plane, I expected Kincade to take his normal seat in the back and immediately fall asleep. This time, he took the seat across the aisle from me. I suppressed an inward groan. I wasn't in the mood to chat.

But he was.

"Mind telling me how the Fae is involved in all this?"

"You know how," was my cagey response.

"Not the whole story."

I remained silent as I decided how to answer. The plane lurched as it rolled down the runway to take off. Moments later, my silence was punctuated by the plane climbing to thirty-thousand feet.

"The Fae are an ancient race that do not live in this realm, Miss Walker."

Back to the Miss Walker thing which, I discovered, he used when he wanted to pry information out of me. Or he was super annoyed with me.

"I'm aware," I said.

"He mentioned he was returning to the Fae forest. Is this the one he found you in?"

"Yes." And that was my final answer.

He clutched his hand into a fist, his knuckles leaching of color. Annoyance at its finest.

"Care to elaborate?" he asked.

"Not really."

I was aware of his anger flooding through him. It radiated across the aisle to me. "Keeping secrets will do no one any good. Especially you."

Well, hell. "Killian told me Lucifer stole the Fae's Four Treasures and destroyed his realm. The forest he mentioned is the last place remaining where Fae are safe." I glanced at him to gauge his response.

He stared at me as though I should be checked into a loony bin. "How is that possible?"

I shrugged, because I honestly didn't know.

"Someone is helping him, then. Lucifer should not have access to any other realm." The leather seat squeaked as he leaned back, his mind working. "It would have to be someone powerful."

"Someone who has access to multiple realms?" I asked.

"Yes. Someone who knows how to bend time and space." He gave me a pointed look.

Astrid was the one person who had that ability. I gaped at him. "No."

"She has to be the one."

"I refuse to believe that. Astrid and Killian—"

"Are an odd pair, don't you think?"

My mouth went dry as I thought back to meeting the unlikely pair. I agreed with Kincade in that they were odd, but I accepted it without question. Killian adored her. That much was clear. When Azriel took her, it deeply affected him.

"He doesn't suspect she had anything to do with it," I said.

"No, but you've seen how powerful she is. What she can do. And how do we know that little escape wasn't orchestrated by the two of them?"

"Azriel kept Astrid as a prisoner. She told me so herself. She's the one who helped me blow up the crypt. I can't believe they were in cahoots." Because I refused to believe it.

Kincade was less than convinced. "I think Astrid helped Lucifer gain access to the Fae realm so he could steal those Four Treasures. He used them against the Fae, didn't he?"

"He did. Killian told me he managed to escape with his life." With Astrid's help. I clenched my jaw until it ached. "I made a promise to Killian. I will find her and get her back." No one was going to change my mind about that. Not even Kincade.

"Why would Azriel show up with Abaddon when he did?" Suspicion laced his tone.

"He was trying to capture me again," I said with a duh tone. "With Edward gone, they figured they had a shot."

I shifted in my seat. Was this a ploy to get me to tell him about the dark magic inside me and how Azriel tracked me? The butterfly tattoo on my shoulder tingled, letting me know it was still very much there.

And then there was the matter of the Godlight. No one had so much as mentioned it when I used it to eradicate the destroyer angel.

"I can't help you if you won't tell me what I need to know."

My head snapped in his direction. "And what is that? Every minute detail of my life?"

"No, Miss Walker, just pertinent details."

I crossed my arms and leaned back in the leather seat. "I don't have any details to share."

He let it go and settled in for his airplane nap. Thankfully, he didn't ask any more questions. I was aware he wasn't going to let it go for too much longer. Eventually, I was going to have to tell him about the tattoo. I was not looking forward to that day.

WE LANDED AT THE airport and took the hired car to King David Hotel. It was a five-star hotel offering opulence and luxury built with quarried pink limestone in the heart of Jerusalem overlooking the Old City.

Kincade didn't blink an eye at the hotel as we entered the lobby and I headed to the registration desk. The female clerk greeted me with a smile which quickly faded when she saw my disheveled, exhausted look. My nose was bruised. The side of my face was scraped where I smacked into the gravel driveway. I tried to make myself presentable, but I was still a mess.

Or maybe she didn't like I wore cargo pants, pink combat boots, and a Henley with the sleeves shoved to the elbows. There was nothing feminine in my luggage, but a quick glance around the lobby told me I was not appropriately dressed. I held my head high and walked up to the desk like I owned the joint.

"Checking in?"

"Yes. Under the name Walker."

She tapped away on the computer with her long red nails, her face twisted into one of concern. She glanced up at me, giving me a sheepish grin.

"I'm afraid we're sold out."

"What? How? I made a reservation."

"I do understand that, however, we've had to cancel several reservations due to special dignitaries visiting the city."

I frowned as I shifted from one foot to the other trying to decide if I wanted to make a scene. I was annoyed my reservation was canceled. I was tired, hungry and wanted a hot shower and a long uninterrupted sleep.

"And you didn't think to let me know?"

"My apologies, Miss Walker, but—"

"No. No buts. You're going to find us a room right now or I'm going to make a scene that rivals the mom in *Terms of Endearment*."

Her face paled. I wasn't sure if she grasped the movie reference and I didn't care. She tapped away on her computer, her fingers furiously going over the keys. No doubt she didn't want me to throw a fit in the middle of their posh lobby with these secret dignitaries walking around.

"There is one possibility, Miss Walker."

"And what is that?" I asked in my best haughty tone.

"We have one deluxe suite available. A two bedroom. I understand your reservation was for four?"

I cleared my throat. If I told her Killian and Astrid didn't make the trip, would she try to shove me and Kincade in a regular room together? I didn't need that happening. I smiled sweetly and nodded. "That's right."

"Will this change in accommodation work for you?"

"It will," I said, though I didn't bother to hide my annoyance at the situation.

She apologized profusely as she got our room keys ready and then handed them over. When I got the keys, I waved Kincade toward the elevator. I handed him one.

"Fourth floor."

"Both rooms?"

"One room." I punched the button harder than necessary.

His eyebrows lifted. "We're sharing?"

"Don't get excited. It's a two-bedroom suite."

"Don't worry. You're safe from my enthusiasm," he said.

It made me want to punch him. But I heard the humor in his voice.

"That's the first comforting thing you've said all day."

My stomach was in knots as we rode the elevator and then walked down the hall to the room.

When we arrived in the room, I was relieved to see a small seating area separating the two bedrooms. It was decorated in lush décor. A sofa was against one wall, a dark oak coffee table in front of it and two end tables on either side topped with gold and white porcelain lamps. Opposite the sofa were two leather club chairs with a short round table between them. A stubby white vase hosting one long red daisy was on the table.

The room reminded me of the one I shared with Edward when we were in Istanbul.

Each bedroom had its own fainting couch along with a king size bed covered in rich, luxurious fabrics and its own enclosed bathroom, which gave me some relief. At least we wouldn't be sharing a bathroom.

"Nice place," Kincaid said as he headed off to the bedroom on the left.

He promptly shut the door leaving me standing in the middle of the living area holding my luggage.

"Good talk," I muttered and skulked off to my room.

I didn't want to spend any more time with him than I had to, so that was a good thing. Besides, I had a hot shower beckoning.

I closed the door to my smallish bedroom, then dropped the bag on the floor next to the bed. The room had one window. I pushed aside the curtain. In the distance was the Old City and, I hoped, Temple Mount with the hidden Staff of Moses.

And here I was with Kincade instead of Uncle Edward. It seemed both right and wrong. Right that I was here with Kincade. Wrong that I was here without Edward. I was missing him on this little venture and wondering if I would misstep like I had in Istanbul. He'd saved my ass then. He wasn't around to save my ass anymore.

But Kincade was.

Maybe that's the way it was supposed to be now.

With a sigh, I toed off my boots and headed to the shower. I examined my beat-up face. I looked like shit. Taking a cloth, I ran it under cool water and did my best to clean it. After a long hot shower, I prepped for a good long nap and wondered what Kincade had in mind as far as finding the staff. We hadn't discussed it. All he managed to do was plant the seed of doubt about Astrid. What if he was right and I was making another horrible mistake rescuing her from Hell?

I fell into the bed, exhaustion setting in from everything that had happened over the last few days. I put up my mental walls to keep out any unsavory fallen angels and quickly fell asleep. It wasn't long before my rest was disturbed.

I sensed the evil presence. Something or someone lurking in the deepest, darkest shadows of my mind. I took control of the dream and pressed through the shadows, unsure what I was looking for but determined to find it. I stood in the middle of a light on an obsidian floor with sparkles glittering in the faint glow. It was not unlike dreams I had in the past.

"Show yourself."

"You sense me. Good."

Humor laced the familiar voice. I glanced around, trying to pinpoint who it was.

"Who are you?"

"My future queen." The oily voice slid across my skin, making the hair on my arms stand at attention.

Instantly my blood ran cold. How had Lucifer managed to invade my dreams? I took the proper precautions and put up my mental walls prior to falling asleep. I took a step back and reached for the dagger at my waist only to realize it wasn't there. I'd hidden it and didn't have the ability to access it in my dream state.

My last interaction with Lucifer wasn't exactly fun. I burned several of his minions with my Godlight before he kicked me out of Hell. I poked around deep in my psyche for it, but I couldn't access it. Perhaps here, in this space, he realized I was unable to use my powers.

"What do you want?" I asked.

"You defeated my destroyer angel. You killed my Prince of Greed. There will be consequences for these actions. And yet I find I'm impressed with your skills. It makes me want you even more."

"That will never happen." I clenched my fists tight. Consequences was a veiled threat. I understood that. At the time when I killed Mammon and Abaddon, it had never occurred to me those actions would not go unnoticed. I was foolish to think they would be.

"Oh, but I will. At some point, you will let your guard down."

He sounded so sure of himself. I did a three-sixty in the small illuminated space but still he did not make an appearance. He was nothing but a disembodied voice in the shadows, which was very disconcerting.

"I thought you didn't want me. Because of the Godlight."

"Even that can be controlled."

I didn't like the way that sounded. "I have powerful friends protecting me."

He chuckled. "You think to intimidate me with that?"

Well, I did. But clearly that backfired.

"The Brotherhood of Watchers have fallen before. More will fall again. Perhaps your friend, Kincade, would be a worthy addition to my legion of dark lords. After all, he and Azriel have a long history."

Fury ignited deep in my gut. I clenched my hands so hard, my fingernails dug into my palms. "You stay away from him."

He laughed again. "I'm coming for you, my queen. I look forward to that day. Until then, enjoy this gift."

He was gone. I tried to wake up, but something still had hold of the dream. I heard the scrabbling of feet nearby. That was a sound

I hated. A sound I never wanted to hear again. That was the sound of Hell's mindless minions.

Shit.

And I had no weapon on me at all.

I backed up. To where, I had no idea. There was no place to go and nothing but darkness and shadows surrounding me. I needed help but I didn't know how to call anyone in a dream. Edward was always there when he thought I might be in trouble. My heart pounded at the base of my throat. My breathing increased as I gasped for breath.

They came out of the shadows. I had nowhere to run and nowhere to hide but I'd be dammed if I stood there and took it.

I sprinted through the gloom, the light following me all the way as though I stood under some demonic spotlight. Sweat rolled down the side of my face and down my back. My breath see-sawed in and out of my chest as I searched for someplace to hide. But there was nothing. I was screwed.

Yelping resounded, covering up the little feet scratching to get to me. I halted, holding my breath as I scanned for movement. The whoosh of a blade sliced through the area. A thump and roll and a minion's head landed at my feet.

I almost puked.

Whoever it was moved closer as I saw the flash of the steely blade now through the faint light in the shadows. This person had mad skills. A black figure held two blades killing minions left and right. Spinning, turning, slashing, cutting. Black blood spurting. A high-pitched squeal and the rest of them scurried away, back into the darkness like the cockroaches they were.

Everything went still.

The figure stepped into the circle of light. Her gloved hands held two short swords stained with black blood. She was dressed all in black, her long dark hair hanging over her shoulders. She peered at me with those purple eyes so much like mine.

"Natasha."

I breathed her name as though it were a sigh of relief. Natasha, AKA my mother. I found her in Antarctica when she tried to kill me with her mind powers. Then again in Istanbul. At the time, she was working with the Knights of the Holy Lance, but she'd disappeared.

At least this time she didn't appear to try to kill me with her mind. No, she was in my mind. Which was so much worse.

"Do you comprehend the danger you face?" Her soft voice floated to me.

"I'm aware," I said with a nod. "Why—how are you here?"

"It matters not."

I probably had the answer to my question anyway. She was a super dream walker. Likely, she dream walked whenever she wanted with whoever she wanted. She had mind powers I didn't understand. What I wanted to ask was how she found me and how she knew to find me. But those questions edged away for more important ones.

"Where are you? How do I find you?" I asked.

She said nothing as she peered at me a long moment. "Step carefully, dream walker."

And then I woke up.

I bolted straight up, my heart racing with the punch of adrenaline through my veins. I was drenched in sweat. My mother was in my dreams. And what did she mean by step carefully?

She'd basically saved my ass and yet there was no explanation from her. How did she know to find me that way? Furthermore, how did she know I was in danger? So many questions. No answers. It was literally the story of my life.

Whenever I had those types of dreams, it was impossible to go back to sleep. My clothes were drenched in sweat and there was no use trying anyway. I slid out of the bed, went back to the bathroom, and took another shower.

Dressed in fresh clothes, I opened the bedroom door.

And stopped short.

Kincade perched on the edge of the sofa peering at what appeared to be a map. A tray of bread and fruit sat on the table along with a silver teapot and two delicate porcelain cups. It all looked very out of place with the very manly Kincade sitting there.

For a split second, something in my chest loosened—relief, maybe. Or the dangerous knowledge that I hadn't been alone while I slept. I shoved the feeling aside before it could take root.

"I ordered room service. Hope that's all right."

The simple normalcy of it hit me harder than it should have. I swallowed and nodded, forcing my voice to cooperate.

"Yes."

I cleared my throat and approached, trying to act as natural as possible. The last thing I wanted to do was tell him about the dream.

"Tell me about the dream."

Irritation clawed through me. "How do you know about that?"

"Your mind is loud, Miss Walker." He gave me a brief glance before turning his attention back to the map. "I suggest you tell me without me having to drag it out of you."

"Or what?" I propped a hand on my hip.

He lifted his gaze, fire flashing in those green-gold eyes of his. "Tell me."

Exhaling a sigh, I plopped down in one of the club chairs, stretching my legs out in front of me and crossing my ankles. I wasn't keen on telling him about it, but if I didn't, he'd pester me until I did. And since he now had this mind-reading ability, it seemed easier to spill my guts.

"It was Lucifer." I paused, trying hard not to gag on the name of the evil creature.

"And?" he prompted.

"I think it was a warning. He's pissed I killed Abaddon and Mammon."

He didn't move and continued to stare at me with unblinking eyes.

"I don't know how he got into my dream. I put up my mental wards."

"He's the Dark One, Anna. He can do whatever the fuck he wants."

"He threatened you," I added.

The fear sharpened then, slicing past my irritation. This wasn't just about me anymore—and that terrified me far more than Lucifer ever could.

"How?" he asked.

"He said the Brotherhood had fallen before and you'd make a nice addition to his dark lords."

He clenched his jaw. The muscles ticked along the edge. "That's not going to happen."

I wanted to believe him.

"I hope, for both our sakes, it doesn't." The last thing I wanted to see was Kincade turned into a fallen angel like Azriel.

His expression seemed to relax some. "It won't."

He sounded so determined, so sure that I believed him. "He said he was coming for me. What does that mean?"

"Likely he's getting ready to unleash Hell against you. Nice going."

"Well, he already tried. He sent minions after me in the dream."

His brows creased in question. Before he asked, I pressed on. "My...mother killed them all."

"Your mother?"

"My biological mother," I clarified.

"The one you said was alive but told me nothing about." He lifted a brow.

I shifted in my seat. "Yeah, that one."

"Now is good, Miss Walker."

Somehow, I always managed to get baited into these confessionals. "I found her in Antarctica. I believe the Knights of the Holy Lance somehow captured her and…"

Thinking of the things they did to her and the vial of blood I found turned my stomach. I paused to swallow hard and choose my words.

"They did experiments on her mind. Used her to find out what made her tick. They managed to reproduce her abilities in others by using her DNA. They made her into a super dream walker."

He didn't respond—and I realized he was doing it on purpose. Giving me space. Letting me decide how much I could say without breaking.

His silence wasn't impatience. It was restraint—and somehow that made it worse.

"She tried to kill me with her mind."

There was so much more to that statement, so much more I wanted to say and explain but I didn't have the words. I pressed my lips together.

"And you want to find her?"

"I need to find her."

"She didn't try to kill you in the dream?"

"No, this time she saved me. She's…different somehow, I think. She told me to step carefully."

He looked thoughtful. "I think searching for these Holy Relics is about to get even more dangerous."

But he didn't say *for you*. I took it as that was implied. Super.

He dropped the map on the table next to the tray. "Eat and get some rest. You look like shit. Later, we'll talk about that." He pointed toward the map. "I'll be back."

"Where are you going?" I asked.

He didn't answer as he walked out the door of the hotel room. Okay, then.

I guess that was none of my business.

I peered down at the map. He'd circled the area marked Temple Mount. I took that as a sign he had a plan.

I sure as hell hoped so.

CHAPTER 29

I WASN'T INTERESTED IN resting. I was running out of time to save Darius and needed to get on with finding the staff.

I munched on bread and reached for the map. Kincade had made notations in faint pencil along the streets in a tiny, perfect penmanship. No matter how hard I tried, writing that small was beyond my abilities. One notation had an arrow pointing to the west side of Temple Mount and the words *possible underground entrance.*

Grace mentioned Jewish archaeologists found relics from the First Temple when sifting through the soil. I believed there was a possibility that underground entrance was still there. If it was still there, then it possibly led to the chamber she mentioned called the Holy of Holies. I jumped to my feet and paced the length of the living area.

If Kincade thought it was there, then that's where we needed to start. I halted, my gut churning the bread into a ball of dough in my stomach. I wished Edward was there to ask. He would know. He always knew everything.

I glanced at the room door wondering where Kincade went. Maybe to get supplies? And if so, what kind of supplies?

Then I remembered Tamar Mizrahi. I pulled out my cell phone and punched in her number. The person who answered was someone at the hotel.

In Hebrew, I said, "I'd like to speak with Tamar Mizrahi, please."

There was a long pause. Then the reply in Hebrew, "Who's calling, please?"

It was time to use my uncle's name. "Tell her I'm a close friend of Edward Walker."

Another long pause. "One moment."

I was put on hold. I paced the length of the room again for the indeterminable amount of time I was listening to the Arabic music. Finally, the person who answered came back on the line.

"I'm afraid Ms. Mizrahi is unavailable. Would you care to leave your name and phone?"

"No, I need to speak to her. Tell her Edward Walker is dead."

It was so silent on the other end I wasn't sure if the call was still connected. I looked at the phone to see that it was.

"One moment."

On hold again. More music. Finally, someone picked up.

"Who is this?" It was a woman on the other end. I assumed Tamar.

"My name is Anna Walker. I'm Edward's niece."

A long pause. And then, "Meet me in the Wine Bar in twenty minutes."

And then she hung up.

Well, that was progress at least. I stuck the phone in my pocket, reached for the room key and headed out the door. I made my way downstairs to the Wine Bar where several patrons were seated in the garnet velvet chairs at dark cherrywood tables. None of them gave me a second glance as I made my way to the bar and perched on one of the chairs, my back to the bar to keep an eye on the entrance.

I didn't have to wait long. A tall woman dressed in a black pencil skirt, stilettos and a crisp white button-down shirt eyeballed me the second she entered the bar. Her hair was pulled back away from her beautiful face in a tight bun. Her chandelier earrings sparkled, reflecting the light of the room as she walked with a confident gait toward me. She had wide, black eyes, high cheekbones, and lips painted red.

"You must be Anna Walker." She paused at the chair next to me and gave me a once-over.

I wished then I'd at least brushed my hair and maybe even my teeth. "I am."

"Shall we?" She motioned to the other side of the room.

I followed her through the bar, her heels clicking along the wood floor as she made her way to a small private alcove off the main bar area. Here, there was a bench seat against the wall in the same garnet velvet as the chairs, a table, and two more chairs across from the bench. She motioned for me to sit.

A votive flickered light, casting elongated shadows across the dark lacquered table. Four wine glasses were already set. I took the bench seat. She took the chair opposite me. A waiter appeared seemingly out of nowhere. She ordered a bottle of red. When the waiter was gone, she turned to me. Her red lips were not smiling.

"How did he die?" she asked.

Crap. How was I supposed to answer that one? "He was stabbed in the heart."

"By whom?"

I swallowed hard. "I don't think that matters."

"It does to me. What happened?"

Why did she care? "With all due respect, Ms. Mizrahi, I have questions."

"Answer mine and I will answer yours," she said, her voice firm.

I dragged my lower lip through my teeth. "It's complicated."

The waiter returned, poured wine into the glass in front of her. She picked it up, holding the bowl in her elegant hand with fingernails the same color as her lips. She sniffed, sipped, nodded and put the glass down. He topped her off, then filled the glass in front of me. He left the bottle and disappeared once again.

"Try me," she said.

I huffed out a breath. "I don't—"

"I knew Edward for many, many years," she said, cutting me off. Her gaze pierced mine, never leaving my face. "I understand what sort of business he was in."

"And what was that?" I asked, genuinely curious.

One corner tipped in a smile. "The business of collecting antiquities."

I thought of the numerous paintings and first edition books in the vault and nodded.

"I also understand how dangerous this business is and the types of people he dealt with," she continued. "So, you'll forgive me if I'm a little leery of you, Miss Walker, especially since he never mentioned he had a niece."

That didn't surprise me. We weren't exactly on speaking terms for several years. "My uncle and I had a complicated relationship. It wasn't always the best family dynamic."

Some of the tension seemed to ease from her shoulders. She took a sip of wine. "I understand that, too. I'd like to know how he died."

"It was a knife fight," I said. "He lost. That's all I can tell you." Because if I told her more, she might not believe me.

A breath shuddered out between her lips. "I see. How did you find me?"

"Your number was in his contact book," I said. "I'm looking for something."

A dark brow rose. "Which is?"

"A holy relic."

She took a sip of her wine, holding the bowl of the glass in the palm of her hand. "What sort of holy relic?"

I took a deep breath. "The Staff of Moses."

She stared at me a long silent moment, not moving. Not even blinking. It was even hard to tell if she was still breathing. Finally, she downed the rest of the wine and poured another glass.

"There is nothing like that here in the city."

"I believe there is."

"And what do you want from me, Miss Walker? I cannot help you."

What did I want? I had no idea who Tamar Mizrahi was, honestly, and meeting with her was a long shot. "I assumed you were someone of importance since you were listed in my uncle's contact book. Perhaps I was mistaken."

I slid toward the edge of the booth intending to get the hell out of there.

"Wait, please."

I halted, gave her a pointed look. Her eyes were downcast as she ran her forefinger around the rim of the wine glass.

"I have information."

"About the location of the staff?"

She lifted her gaze to mine. "Yes."

I scooted back into the seat and waited.

"Edward asked me once, not so long ago, to listen for information regarding the archaeological site at Temple Mount. They have been digging there for some time in preparation for building a new underground mosque. But they halted progress when they discovered several artifacts dating back to the time of the First Temple. Or so it's believed," she said.

She paused and took another sip of her wine. "A few days ago, there was a raid on the site. No one knew why or what they were looking for. But there were strange...observations about the men."

"What do you mean, strange observations?"

She took a deep breath, exhaled. "There were reports several of the men...had wings."

I stared hard at her as a tingling sensation went up my spine and tickled the base of my neck.

"It sounds ridiculous, doesn't it?" she asked with half a smile, wanting me to confirm it was nothing.

I shook my head. "No, it doesn't."

She gripped the stem of her wine glass, her fingers leeching of color. "Are you telling me these...creatures exist?"

"I am."

"What do they want?" she demanded.

"The same thing I want. The Staff of Moses. The difference between me and them is they'll kill for it. I won't."

"These men...they raided the site because there was talk of a chamber deep underground that contained several holy relics," she said.

"One of them was the staff?"

"I'm not sure. I promised Edward I would give him this information when he came to see me. He was supposed to have already arrived."

"He was killed in Acre on our way here," I said, throwing her a bone.

I didn't want to tell her much more than that and I certainly didn't want to tell her Mammon was the one who poisoned his soul with the black blade. She would never understand that. She already didn't believe winged men existed.

"I am sorry for your loss," she said.

"And yours. You and Edward were clearly friends."

"We were. I will miss him." A flicker of sadness came over her face. "If the staff is there, it will be in this underground chamber. They call it the Holy of Holies. It's on the west side of the Temple." She reached for my hand then, her fingers wrapping around mine in a gentle squeeze. "But know this, Miss Walker. The men were unable to enter the chamber."

My brows drew together. "Why not?"

She shook her head. "It is said only the most divine can enter."

That tingling sensation at the base of my skull returned. "Thank you for the information. I appreciate it."

She released my hand as I slid toward the edge of the seat.

"What do you plan to do with it?" she asked. I gave her a questioning look. "The staff, I mean."

"To keep it safe and out of the hands of those winged men," I said.

She seemed satisfied with that response. "God speed, Miss Walker."

I gave her a nod and left her sipping wine to find Kincade and get the staff before Azriel managed to get to it first. I headed back to the room. When I arrived, Kincade was there pacing and looking furious. He halted when I entered the room.

"Where have you been?"

"Where have *you* been?" I countered.

He pressed his lips together in a thin line. "It was a recon mission."

"Of Temple Mount?"

"Yes."

"I have information about that," I said. I relayed the conversation I had with Tamar.

"And you trust her?"

"She was in my uncle's contact book. He only has contacts he trusts," I said. "I trust her."

He gave me a nod. "Not a lie. Very good, Miss Walker."

I scowled at him. "When are we going?"

"I scoped out the Temple," he said. "The information you got from Tamar is accurate. There is an excavation that was going on but looks like it was halted. There is fencing around the site to keep people out."

"But that won't keep us out," I said.

"Exactly."

I cracked a smile. "What's the plan?"

⁎

WE WAITED UNTIL IT was dark to make our move. Kincade wouldn't let me leave the hotel room, despite all my nervous energy. I paced a lot and refused to eat. Pretty sure I was driving him bat shit crazy. But I didn't have Edward to keep me calm and centered. I was also busy trying not to think about the fact Edward wasn't with us on this trip.

When dusk settled and night was in full swing, we left the hotel. He strapped his gun to his waist while I kept my weapons in the cloud—what else was I going to call it? Both Edward's sword and my jade-handled dagger.

I thought for sure he'd want to walk it, but it was longer than we wanted. We grabbed a cab. I used my new language skills to tell the driver to drop us off on the western side of the Temple. I didn't miss the sideways look Kincade gave me as we settled in the backseat.

"Since when do you speak Hebrew?" he asked.

"Since always."

He looked unconvinced.

The truth was, I did learn it when I was younger but since I didn't use it, I'd forgotten it. Until recently. I couldn't quite recall when it started clicking inside my brain. Not that it mattered.

Ten minutes later, we arrived. I gave the driver his fare and he sped away. Kincade wasted no time. He headed toward the Western Wall with a destination in mind. I fell into step behind him without argument. For once, it was easier not to lead.

We arrived at the fenced off section where the excavation had been ongoing. A sign in Hebrew warning to KEEP OUT was on the fence. The gate was padlocked.

"How do you propose we get inside?" I asked.

"Oh, ye of little faith," he said.

He motioned for me to follow. We walked down the fence line to a place shrouded in darkness. I noticed then the overhead street-lamp was out. Convenient. But I suspected he had something to do with it. He kneeled at the edge of the fence and pulled up the bottom of the chain link that had clearly been cut into a neat little opening.

"After you." He motioned with his head for me to slip inside.

I didn't waste time. I hurried to the other side. He followed, letting the flap of fencing close behind us.

"I almost don't want to ask how you knew that was there," I said.

"Trade secret. This way."

He kept to the shadows and something told me this was not the first mission he'd been on where stealth was of the utmost necessity. I stepped where he did, keeping up with his long stride with more exertion than I wanted.

Near the edge of the Temple, the cavern was obvious. Cold air breathed out of the opening, raising goosebumps along my arms. My body reacted before my mind could talk it down.

It had been sectioned off with caution tape, but that wasn't much of a barrier.

"This is the opening," he said, his voice low. "This is where those 'winged men' tried to enter." He put air quotes around winged men, referring to the description Tamar gave me.

I peered at the yawning darkness, my heart suddenly in my throat. "You're coming, too, right?"

"I'll stand guard," he said. "You go ahead."

Alone? I didn't want to go down there alone. I stood, hesitating.

"Anna, I got your back."

The steadiness in his voice settled something frantic inside me. If I was walking into Hell, at least he'd be standing at the gate.

I glanced up at him.

He gave me a nod encouragement and said, "Go get it."

Then he shoved a flashlight into my hand.

Taking a deep breath, I clicked on the light and stepped into darkness.

CHAPTER 30

I WASN'T FOND OF this at all.

The beam of light flickered off the dusty ground and walls as I stepped into the shadows. It sloped downward as I made my way, one hand trailing across the textured wall. There was no way to be certain the Staff of Moses was down here, but I had to at least try to find it.

One step, then another. The only sound was that of my erratic breathing as it shuddered in and out of my chest. Down, down, down I went until there was another opening deep inside. I paused outside the dark doorway, peering into it looking for...what? Some sign the staff was there?

I took a deep breath, expelled it. I waited for some divine influence to appear and show me the way. But the only person there was me.

Swallowing my fear, I stepped into the chamber.

A breath of cold air trickled over my naked arms, raising the hair and making it stand at attention. The hair on the back of my neck also stood up as this same breath rolled through me.

I was in the presence of something divine. Holy. I wasn't sure how I knew that, but I did. I expelled a shuddered breath. It plumed in the air.

Above me, there was a muffled commotion. I spun around ready to bolt back up the long tunnel, back to Kincade when I heard gunshots and the high-pitched whine of his gun. He was shooting which meant there were demons which also meant Azriel found us.

Son of a bitch and curse this stupid tracking tattoo. I hated it even more now.

Kincade shouted something incoherent down the tunnel. I heard it then—the crashing of rock against rock. Kincade shouting and the next thing I saw was him running as though his feet were on fire through the tunnel right for me. A plume of dust followed him in.

He crashed into me at full force, grabbing on to me to halt his momentum, which did nothing but make me stumble back into the chamber. We crashed on the hard surface. The flashlight smashed against the ground, flickered, and went out.

Great.

The darkness pressed in instantly, thick and absolute. For a heartbeat, panic clawed up my throat—then anger slammed down over it, hot and familiar.

"What the bloody hell, Kincade?"

I shoved him off me to reach for the dead flashlight. My hand fumbled over it as I grasped it and realized the bezel was busted. Super great.

"Maybe you tell me how Azriel manages to turn up everywhere you are, eh?"

He sounded mad. In the darkness, I was unable to make out his facial expression, but there was no mistaking he was pissed off at me. I sighed.

"How should I know?"

"Lie. Now tell me the truth, Miss Walker."

"Stop with the Miss Walker bullshit. My name is Anna." Irritation clawed through every vein in my body. I wanted to hit something. Namely Kincade. "The flashlight is broken, thanks to you. Now we can't see shit."

"And thanks to Azriel the entrance to the tunnel caved in. We're stuck in here."

"Well, isn't that the best news I've heard all damn day?" I snapped.

I plopped down on the floor, my back resting against the wall. To my surprise, he did the same. He slid down the wall next to me. In the shadowy darkness, he put up one knee and rested his forearm on it. As though we were doing nothing more than having a picnic.

"You ever going to tell me how Azriel keeps tracking you?"

I suppressed an inward groan. This again. He was like a dog with a bone. I remembered something my uncle told me, though. That I should tell him because he may be able to help me. I sighed.

"Ten years ago, when I was living with my uncle, there was a stable boy who caught my eye. He flirted relentlessly with me and I was unable to resist his charms."

"I trust there is a point to this?" he interrupted.

"Shh. There is. We planned to run away together. We were in the stable making plans to leave when my uncle barged in and caught us. That stable boy's name was Marcus."

Kincade went still. I didn't even hear him breathe for a long moment. The silence was deliberate. Held. Like he was locking down something dangerous.

His features were shrouded in darkness. I was unable to see his expression, but I guessed it was one of fury. He hated Azriel more than I did and with good reason.

"He marked you," he said.

"Yes. With a butterfly tattoo on my left shoulder. He uses it to track me. That's how he finds me wherever I go. He can't get inside Walker Manor because of the wards my uncle placed there."

"Why didn't you tell me before?" It was hard to ignore how he sounded wounded. Like I didn't trust him.

"It's not like it's something I'm proud of."

"And the dark magic inside you?"

"Azriel put it there, too."

Silence stretched between us, then he said, "You do realize I have to kill him now, don't you?"

The way he said that gave me the heart squeeze. "We'll kill him together."

He chuckled. "If you wish. Where is the staff?"

"It's not in here," I said. "Not that I saw anyway."

"Too bad. I promised Ophelia we would be home before Christmas."

What an odd thing. Why in the world would he make her a promise like that? I twirled the broken flashlight in my hand, dreading Christmas without Edward and missing him when today's date occurred to me. I almost laughed out loud but managed to stifle it.

"What?" he asked.

"Nothing."

"Nothing you want to talk about you mean. But there is something going on in that head of yours."

"There is always something going on in my head," I retorted. "Do you know what today's date is?"

"December 21," he said.

"Right. The Winter Solstice." I paused, my heart thumping hard in my chest. "And my twenty-ninth birthday."

He said nothing for a long quiet moment, then, "Happy birthday, Anna." I didn't miss the emphasis he put on my name.

I snorted. "Yeah, sure. Happy birthday to me. I'm stuck in an underground tunnel in the dark with you."

"Gee, thanks. I feel so honored." Sarcasm laced his every word.

"How the hell are we going to get out of here?"

"I'm thinking," he said.

"Maybe you think faster before we suffocate."

"Maybe you shut your face and let me figure it out," he said.

"Rude," I muttered.

He got to his feet. I heard him walk the area of the room, the brush of his hands on the walls as he looked for some secret door or something to spring us from this place.

"I thought it would be in here." I was unable to hide the disappointment in my voice.

"Are you giving up already?" he asked. "That's not like you."

"I'm not giving up. I'm being realistic."

"Sure, you are," he said, deadpan. "Stop being realistic and help me find a way out of here."

I stood, still hoping the dead flashlight would work but it was a no go. I tossed it away and headed to the opposite side of the room from Kincade. I ran my hands over the wall, the texture smooth as glass. But the palm of my hand bumped across something. I moved it back, feeling with the tips of my fingers.

"I think I found something," I said.

He was at my side in a second. His hand bumped against mine as he felt along the wall. "It's a crevice."

He nudged me out of the way and went to work. I backed up, watching the dark hulking outline of his body move to and fro trying to figure out what he was doing. His hands went up in a long rectangle and then I heard a click.

Everything went quiet for a breathless second—like the chamber itself was holding its breath with me.

Something hissed and a door slid away with a grinding sound. On the other side of the threshold was a faint light coming from some unknown source. Like a beacon of hope. In the center of the barren room was a stone altar and on top of it, in a wooden holder, was the Staff of Moses.

I gasped.

We both stood there staring in disbelief.

"This must be the Holy of Holies chamber," I whispered. Though why I whispered it, I wasn't sure. Maybe it was because it was a place of reverence. Holy ground.

"Only the divine can enter," he reminded me. He gave me a pointed look.

The truth of it settled heavy in my chest. Not just that I could go in—but that I had to.

I swallowed hard, a lump suddenly in my throat. "I…"

"Hey." He took me by the shoulders and turned me to face him. "You can do this. You were born for this. Remember?"

I nodded. "Right."

He gave me an encouraging pat on the shoulder before dropping his hands. I turned back to the chamber, steeling my nerves, ready to enter.

"And when you get it," he said, his voice soft, "birthday cupcakes and whiskey on me."

Genuine humor laced his voice but somehow, I understood he was serious. "Chocolate with white icing."

I stepped into the chamber and paused. I turned back to look at Kincade. He shook his head.

"I can't enter even if I wanted to."

"Why?" I asked.

"There seems to be a barrier. As though I'm not permitted."

A puzzle, to be sure. Especially since Kincade was one of the Brotherhood of Watchers. Didn't that make him divine, too?

I approached the small altar. My shaking hand hovered over the staff.

I knew, with sudden certainty, that once I touched it, there would be no pretending my life was ever meant to be ordinary.

Who enters this Holy of Holies?

I snatched my hand back. The deep baritone voice trickled through my mind. I blinked, glancing around but there was nothing and no one.

"Anna," I whispered. "My name is Anna."

Are you the Keeper of the Holy Relics?

"Yes."

Proceed, Keeper.

The title settled over me like a mantle—heavy, inescapable.

With a shaking hand, I reached for the staff. As soon as I wrapped my fingers around it, the vision struck me. From the moment Moses took up the staff as a shepherd to the days of the ten plagues, to when he walked up Mount Sinai to receive the Ten Commandments, followed by parting the Red Sea leading his people out of Egypt. All of it flashed through my mind like a movie playing out. Then the vision turned fuzzy.

I understood the truth of it without knowing the names—as though the staff decided what I was allowed to see.

It appeared to belong to a king, passed down from him to his son and so on. I was unable to see what happened next to the staff until it ended up in Ezra's hands. When he died, it passed to the archangel, Michael, in Acre. The vision turned blurry again. It appeared to be on display in a museum until it was stolen and then, finally, landed here. Resting at last in the Holy of Holies under Temple Mount. Though how it got here was unclear. It had been waiting here a very long time.

I removed my hand, reeling from the vision pulsing in my mind. My knees felt weak, my breath unsteady, as though I'd run a great distance without moving at all.

Now that I touched it and the vision played out, I picked it up, holding it between my hands as though it were delicate.

And the voice in my head said, *Go in peace, Keeper.*

Peace felt like a foreign concept—but I nodded anyway.

I turned to Kincade, holding it in my hands, my heart in my throat.

"This is it," I said. "The real Staff of Moses."

A rare smile broke on his face. "Nice work."

I could hear the pride in his voice—and that mattered more than I expected.

I stood there holding it, unsure what to do next. In some ways, I was afraid to hold it, carry it, use it. How was I going to use it to save Darius? I hadn't a clue but the sense of urgency to return to England and try to save him pressed against me.

"Any idea how to get out of here?" I asked.

I exited the chamber and stood next to Kincade. He was already glancing around looking for a way out.

"No," he said.

"That's not very reassuring."

"At least it was honest," he said.

"I'd like to not die down here," I mentioned.

"You're not going to die." Annoyance laced his tone as he continued to search every nook and cranny of the small space.

"What about the entrance?"

"It's completely sealed off," he said. "Azriel made sure of that."

"Super." I pressed my lips together, disgruntled.

A rumble sounded at the mouth of the tunnel where the cave-in happened. We both exchanged a glance of surprise. He pulled his gun, ready to shoot. I gripped the staff in one hand and drew down my dagger with the other.

Another rumble that sounded much like rocks tumbling to the ground. Kincade took off at a run. It took several seconds for my brain to catch up. I bolted after him.

As we approached the mouth of the entrance, moonlight slashed into the underground tunnel. Distant voices were on the other side of the rubble and then a splash of light moving back and forth as though it were a flashlight.

"Hello?" a female voice called.

I caught up with Kincade who aimed, ready to fire. "Stand down, Kincade. It's Tamar."

He holstered his gun.

"We're in here," I called.

"Anna?"

"Yes!"

"Stand back," she called back.

We moved deeper back the way we'd come. A moment later, more rumbling and the remaining rubble was cleared. The tunnel opened to the night sky and the figure of a woman stood at the mouth holding a flashlight beaming light toward us.

Squinting, I headed out first. Kincade was on my heels.

Tamar stood at the entrance holding the light. She exchanged her pencil skirt for dark pants, boots, and long sleeve shirt. Four men holding shovels stood behind her. They'd dug their way through the caved in tunnel opening. Both Kincade and I paused next to her. She eyed first the staff then the dagger. Then gave Kincade a cursory glance.

"You don't know how glad we are to see you," I said.

"After our talk this afternoon, I assumed you were planning something. I had you followed. I'm sorry it took so long to blast you out. I see your time in the underground chamber was productive," she said. "You found it."

"I did," I nodded.

"We saw the winged men attack," she said.

"Those winged men are Fallen," Kincade said.

She cut him a glance, worry creasing her brow. Great. I hadn't told her the whole story and now she was going to have more questions.

"What are Fallen?"

He started to answer but I cut him off. "It's not important. Just know they are a group determined to get their hands on the Holy Relics."

She eyed the staff and held out a hand. "May I?"

Trusting her with it felt like stepping onto a narrow bridge—but something told me it wouldn't collapse.

I handed it to her. Next to me, Kincade nearly vibrated out of his skin.

What are you doing? he demanded.

It'll be fine, I replied.

Tamar turned the staff over in her hands, dragged a finger down the smoothed wood that had survived throughout the ages. I saw the reverence in her eyes, the look of wonder. She was as in awe of the staff as I was. She handed it back to me a moment later.

"Peace be with you, Anna Walker."

"And with you."

She and the men she had with her left us there at the mouth of the tunnel. No other questions asked.

"That was Tamar?" Kincade asked.

"It was," I said. "And it's time for us to return to England."

"We will. But first, I have a promise to keep."

I glanced up at him. He granted me yet another rare smile. "Cupcakes and whiskey?"

"You know it."

Chapter 31

I HAD THE STAFF. Now all I had to do was get back to England with it, save Darius and stash it in the vault. Easy.

Except nothing was ever that easy for me.

"Can't you hide that thing with that magic trick of yours?" Kincade asked as we walked down the street. I didn't miss his tone of annoyance. Or the way he constantly scanned the street crowd for threats.

I used the staff as a walking stick, pretending it was nothing more than something I purchased from a vendor in the street. I halted. Why hadn't I thought of that before? When we retrieved the Spear of Destiny, it was so small it was easy to conceal. I tried to put the staff in the cloud like my weapons, but it was no go. I shook my head.

"It doesn't work."

He gave me a nudge. "Keep walking then."

"Can't we just take a cab?" I whined. It was at least a thirty-minute walk back to the hotel.

"That thing won't fit in a cab."

I realized, of course, he was right, but I still wanted to whine about the long walk.

As we went a few more steps, the demon veil dropped down to surround us. Kincade pulled out his gun. I clutched the staff in one hand and drew down the dagger in the other. We were surrounded by demons moments later. And leading the pack was Azriel.

Why was I not surprised?

He halted in front of us, that wolf grin I despised etched on his face. "Thank you for retrieving the staff for us, *chérie.*"

"Because you weren't allowed in the chamber," I snarled.

"That is true," he said with a nod. "And now you will hand it over or pay with your life."

I turned my head and looked at Kincade. "Will you shoot this bastard already?"

He blinked surprise as if he hadn't thought of the idea himself. He pointed the gun. The high-pitched whine gave two demon lords enough time to dive in front of Azriel before his gun discharged. Demon guts exploded everywhere. For the first time, I got a good look at what that gun of his did to those demons and minions unfortunate enough to be in the line of fire.

Then things moved into a quick blur of motion. Demons and minions swarmed us, pushing us apart. The high-pitched whine of Kincade's gun went off several times as he defended himself. I used the dagger on ones attacking me, turning them to ash. Their stench invaded my nose, making me gag. The fuckers surrounded me, clawing at me, reminding me much of the rooftop attack in Hong Kong. Except then I had help from Darius.

Somewhere nearby was a scuffle. Kincade and Azriel maybe.

But then there were too many coming for me. I flung my hand out with the dagger to stab one, but he was bigger and faster. He knocked my dagger away. It flew out of my hand, landing somewhere in the milieu. I clutched the staff in both hands as they clawed me, determined to get it away from me leaving blood red trails behind with their demon-poison claws.

Where was that Godlight when I needed it?

I clutched the staff in my hands and closed my eyes to find that power within me as the demons were all over me, pulling hair and ripping clothing. Where was all this raw potential my uncle said I had?

A spark ignited behind my closed eyes. A bright white light pulsed there. Then a pop and a high-pitched screech and suddenly all the weight of the attacking demons was gone. I opened my eyes to see nothing but piles of ash around me and a glow fading from the staff.

Kincade was face down on the ground. Azriel was nowhere in sight.

Still clutching the staff, I hurried to his side as he groaned and rolled over. He had a bloody nose and a few scratches on his face but otherwise he appeared to be fine. He shook his head and sat up, giving me a once over.

"What happened?" I asked.

"You don't know?"

"I saw a light behind my eyes and then there was nothing."

"You glowed," he said. "Then there was a punch of air. It knocked me down and turned all of Azriel's minions to ash."

I glanced around. Sure enough piles of ash were all over the sidewalk. I spotted my dagger on the ground near his feet and bent to pick it up. I quickly hid it in the secret cloud.

The veil had disappeared, too, leaving us exposed to the human eye. He got to his feet.

"Are you all right?" he asked.

"A little banged up but ok." In truth, I had bloody trails on my hands from the demon claws.

He reached for one of my hands, eyeing it. Already, black puss oozed out of the wound. "You've been poisoned."

"I'll be fine."

"No." He clutched my hand and made me look him in the eye. "You'll die. We have to take care of this."

The one person who could remove demon poison was currently dying of it himself. "Any suggestions?"

"Come on." Still clutching my hand, he dragged me down the street.

I stumbled after him since he had hold of me. "What happened to Azriel?"

"He disappeared before you did your magic act," Kincade said.

"So, he's not dead." I didn't bother to hide my disappointment.

"Not yet," he said through clenched teeth.

It irked him Azriel kept getting away. I understood his frustration.

We arrived back at the hotel. We skirted through the lobby as quickly as possible trying not to garner too much attention. But it was hard since we both looked like we'd been in a fist fight and I was carrying the ancient relic.

We rode the elevator in silence. As we walked to the hotel room—with Kincade still clutching my hand—I started to feel the first effects of the poison coursing through my veins. It mingled with the dark magic that suddenly made an appearance. A wave a nausea pulsed through me, churning my stomach. I dragged him to a halt and bent in half, trying not to barf all over the carpet.

"What is it?"

I groaned in response. My knees wobbled and gave out. I crashed to the floor. Without saying a word, he scooped me up and put me over his shoulder. I heard the click of the hotel room door as he put the key in the lock, then kicked it open, then closed.

He dumped me on the nearby sofa and barked something about not moving. I couldn't even if I wanted to. The staff dropped from my hand and thudded on the thick carpet as I groaned again. I rolled to my side, clutching my gut. Sweat popped out on my face and rolled down my back. The back of my neck was hot and damp. My hands shook. A pain burned in the pit of my stomach. I fought the urge to vomit.

I heard Kincade cursing and making some noise in his bedroom. A moment later, he came out and kneeled on the floor by the sofa. I tried to focus on what he was doing but my vision blurred. He clutched my hand in his.

For a moment, I was touched.

"This is going to hurt."

He said it seconds before a stinging sensation exploded through the scratches on my hand. I cried out, tried to sit up and punch him in the face but was too weak. His grip tightened on my hand as he continued cleaning the demon poison out of the wound.

But it was already in my bloodstream with the dark magic.

"Move aside, Watcher."

A new voice. One I vaguely recognized but my brain was too muddled to comprehend it. Kincade released my hand, his presence gone from my side. There was a slight pressure on my shoulders as whoever it was pressed me against the cushions. I blinked and I looked up into the face, but my vision was fuzzy.

Sariel, maybe?

It was the last thought I had as I passed out.

⊷———⊶

I AWOKE IN THE bed, the blankets tucked neatly under my arms. Intense fatigue pressed me into the mattress. God, I was so tired.

"Hello, Anna."

I turned my head on the pillow to see Sariel standing in the doorway of my bedroom in the hotel suite. He looked relieved to see me awake.

"How do you feel?" he asked.

"Like someone kicked my ass and a Mack truck ran me over." My voice was scratchy from dry mouth.

Sariel moved to the side of the bed. He poured a glass of water and handed it to me. I struggled into a sitting position and took it, grateful for the cold, wet drink.

"What happened to me?" I said when I had my fill.

Sariel perched on the edge of the bed. He slipped the glass from my hand and placed it on the nightstand, then reached for my hand. He held it in his. "The dark magic inside you...converged with the demon poison. If I hadn't shown up..."

His words lingered in the air with the unspoken outcome of what would have happened to me had he not arrived. Which made me wonder...why did he? Was he watching over me and picked that moment to make an appearance and save me?

"What did you do?" I asked.

"I removed it. The dark magic, the demon poison. All of it."

My heart skipped a beat. When Darius did this before, he took it inside him. Now, that demon poison was killing him.

"I don't understand. How?"

A small smile creased his face. He brushed a lock of hair from my face. "Not for you to worry about."

"Are you...did you take in the demon poison?"

"No."

Something told me Sariel was way more powerful than he was letting on. My gaze narrowed. "Then how did you do it?"

His grin remained. "The Godlight inside you almost eradicated it, but when the demon poison entered your system, it reignited what remnants were left. I merely used the Godlight within you to eliminate it for good."

He still didn't answer my question but maybe Kincade would be able to tell me more.

"Thank you again."

He patted the top of my hand, then rose from the edge of the bed. "You did well, Anna. You found the Staff of Moses." He turned toward the door.

I sat up. "Sariel, wait." He paused, gave me a questioning look. "You were there in Acre. With Ezra."

A shadow crossed his face. "Kincade told you, did he?"

"Yes."

"Ezra allowed the power of the Holy Relics to consume him, Anna. He allowed them to corrupt his soul. That is why he used them the way he did. Why he was determined to take over the world with them. Kincade did what was necessary to save the world from his evil."

"But what if I—"

"You will not allow the power to consume as it did your ancestor. Do not fear the past, Anna. Embrace the future."

And then he was gone.

A knock on the door sounded. Kincade.

"Come in."

He pushed open the door and stood there, waiting.

"Sariel said the demon poison converged with what was left of the dark magic," I said.

"I know." He paused, then said, "Azriel did that to you, didn't he?"

"Yes."

He clenched his jaw tight as anger flickered over his face. He balled his fists and then released them. Kincade already hated the fallen angel. Now he had more fuel to add to that fire.

"When Sariel removed it...I've never seen anything like that before." He shook his head as though it were a mystery. "I stood there and watched as he pulled that dark, oily substance from your body. Somehow, he managed to ignite the Godlight within you to destroy it. There was this...light so bright and powerful and...beautiful. And then the oil blackness was gone."

There was no mistaking the wonder and awe in his voice. It unsettled me more than his anger ever had.

His gaze pinpointed mine then. "Now about that tattoo…"

I flushed again. Something that kept happening. "Yeah, I should have told you about that sooner."

He reached for something in his back pocket and brought out a small black pouch. "I have a solution."

"And what is that?" I eyed the black pouch with suspicion.

As he moved toward the bed, he flipped open the flap and held it down to show me the array of tiny needles and a bottle of black ink. I glanced back up at him.

"Yeah, and?" I asked.

"I can mask Azriel's tracking tattoo with one of my own."

I waited for him to give a lopsided grin or a bazinga or something but he didn't.

"You can do that?"

"I can." He gave one nod of his head. "Let me see it."

A warm tingling sensation took up residence in my gut. Not fear. Anticipation. "That's a little personal…"

"Cut the crap, Anna. Show me the damn tattoo."

Well, then. I didn't have much of a choice, did I? I pushed the blankets down and sat up, tugging my tattered shirt off over my head. I wore a black tank underneath the Henley. I scooted around in the bed until my back faced him.

He moved closer and sat on the edge. The mattress dipped beneath his weight, steady and unavoidable, anchoring me in place. With a gentle fingertip, he traced the outline of the butterfly. It sent a shiver down my spine. Gooseflesh erupted all over my exposed skin. He noticed. His hand stilled for a heartbeat before continuing.

"I can work with this," he said. There was no judgment in his voice. Only certainty. "Get comfortable."

"What are you going to do?"

"I'm going to make it so that fucker can't track you anymore. Now lay down."

I hesitated—just long enough to understand what I was giving him—then nodded and lay down, exposing the mark to him.

"Breathe," he murmured once, low and close.

I did. For him.

A few hours later, I examined his handiwork in the bathroom mirror. I had my back to the vanity, peering over my shoulder to see the blue butterfly had turned into black angel wings. There was something therapeutic—almost erotic—about letting Kincade tattoo me. The way his large hands grazed my skin. It made being stuck with needles one-hundred-percent worth it. He promised his divine ink would drown out the demon magic Azriel had burned into me.

Time would tell if he was right.

"Does it meet with your approval?" Kincade called from the bedroom.

I smiled at the girl in the mirror, pleased with these new results. I was finally free from Azriel's tracking.

"Yes." I walked to the bathroom door and paused. "Now, let's go save Darius."

CHAPTER 32

WE PACKED UP WHICH wasn't as dramatic as it sounded since we both traveled light. The biggest question was how to transport the staff. I wasn't able to hide it in the cloud with the weapons for safekeeping, so now what? I walked into the hotel with it. Maybe I walk out?

I booked a private driver to get us from the hotel to the airport. It was handy having a private jet to get us from one place to the other. I didn't have to worry about the staff on the airplane.

"You're stalling." Kincade stood at the door, his hand on the knob, as he waited for me to make up my mind about walking through the hotel lobby with the staff.

"What about the staff?" I asked.

"What about it?"

"Do I walk out of here with it?"

"You walked in here with it. I don't see what the big deal is."

But still I hesitated. Something in my gut was telling me to find some way to hide it.

"Let's go, Anna. I got your back."

It didn't reassure me much. I nodded, grabbed up my bag in the other hand, and followed him out the door. The need to get back to England and help Darius overwhelmed my sense of fear about walking through the lobby with the staff.

And, anyway, Azriel couldn't track me anymore thanks to Kincade's handiwork.

But as we made our way out of the elevator and through the lobby, my gut twisted. Something inside me was telling me to run. I glanced around the area and noticed we garnered quite a few looks. It was unwanted attention. Kincade put his hand on his holstered gun. I suddenly wished I had my dagger in the holster at my belt.

"Stay close," he said over his shoulder, his voice low.

He sensed it, too, then. Not sure that gave me comfort.

I clutched the staff tighter in my hand until it cramped. The men moved in from the edges of the lobby. There were three of them. I inhaled but didn't smell demon. Kincade unholstered his gun and turned to me.

"Run."

His calm tone made me halt. I blinked at him, confused.

"Run," he repeated through clenched teeth. "I'll meet you at the plane."

The absolute last thing I wanted was to separate. I shook my head, started to object. He grabbed my arm, spun me around and shoved me toward the door.

"Get out of here now."

I stumbled several steps toward the door before glancing over my left shoulder. Kincade fired off several shots and then dove behind a large porcelain pot that held a Fichus tree. The men returned fire. One of them shot at me. The bullet shattered the window to my left as I dove out the exit onto the sidewalk. Thankfully, the hired car waited for me.

I yanked open the back door, tossed the staff on the floorboard and collapsed inside. The driver gave me a startled look.

"Go, go, go!" I shouted.

Just as he floored it, Kincade barreled out of the hotel with the three men on his tail. He ran hard toward the fleeing car. I kicked open the back door while the driver sped through traffic.

Kincade's form was suddenly a blur. Then he plunged head first into the backseat with me. The car door slammed shut. Seconds later, the peal of a police siren sounded. He cursed under his breath. I shouted at the driver to hurry.

"Who were those men?"

"My best guess is someone thinks you stole an archeological find and they're pissed."

Tamar was the one person who could have tipped off the authorities. That didn't make sense since she rescued us from the underground pit. Then again, I didn't know her all that well and she could easily betray me.

"What are we going to do?" I asked, trying to remain calm.

We were leading them right to the airport, to the private jet.

My cell phone buzzed in my pocket. I fumbled and finally pulled it out. It was Tamar.

"Did you betray me?" I answered.

"Anna, no. Someone got to my men. They turned you in as a grave robber. They think you stole the Staff of Moses."

Well, shit.

"I trusted them." Her voice wobbled with emotion. "Now I can't."

I gripped the phone and glanced at Kincade who was busy peering out the back window watching the flashing lights approach. He readied his gun.

She continued. "I will do what I can for you. Get out of the country as soon as you can."

The line went dead.

"Who was that?" Kincade demanded.

"Tamar. She—"

Before I finished, an explosion rocked the street behind us. Our initial reaction was to duck as flames and debris flew into the sky. The flashing lights were no more. Someone blew them up. I sat straight and told the driver I'd pay him extra if he got us to the airport undetected.

"I'm not even going to question what just happened," he said.

"Me, either."

Because I was pretty sure Tamar was responsible for that explosion.

We made it to the airport in record time and boarded the plane. I collapsed in the nearest seat, sweat running down my face while clutching the staff in one hand. My whole body shook with the adrenaline punch. Kincade, though, seemed calm and cool.

I was on high alert until the plane took off. And even then, I wasn't comfortable.

Kincade did his normal kick back and nap thing.

How he remained so calm unnerved me. I was intelligent enough to grasp the situation. I was now a thief wanted for the removal of priceless archaeological artifacts. The hotel had my real name. My face was likely plastered across all the security cameras, while carrying the staff through the lobby. I swiped a hand down my face. What next? Interpol?

There was nothing to be done about it now. Likely there would be some type of fallout but for now, I had to focus. Focus on getting back to England and saving Darius.

And then, I'd worry about everything else.

◆——◆

It was nighttime and raining in England which felt just like home. It was good to be home.

When we landed, Clive was there with the car. What a relief to see there were no authorities waiting to arrest me. No longer did I have to look over my shoulder for Azriel. Now I had to look over my shoulder for someone willing to turn me in.

"Stop worrying," Kincade said as we got in the car.

He clearly sensed the gnawing anguish.

"I have to worry," I said. "What if I get arrested?"

"You won't."

I wanted his certainty. I just didn't have it yet. I gave him a surreptitious glance.

"How do you know? Are you a fortune teller now?"

"Would you relax?"

I blew out a breath, trying to relax. I told myself to focus on the other stuff I had to think about. Like Darius and how to use the Staff of Moses to save him. Now, I hadn't a clue.

Clive drove us up to the house and pulled up the long drive. All the Christmas lights were on, outlining the manor house in white lights. I snatched up the staff, ignored my bag and hurried inside. I bounded up the stairs, taking them two at a time, to the room Ophelia shared with Darius and barged in, startling her. She jumped to her feet.

"Anna, you found it." There was relief in her voice.

Darius lay in the fetal position on his side on the bed, his wings snapped closed and curled against his massive form. He looked thinner than I remembered. His face was paler, for sure. And those feathers were nearly all black now. I noticed a few of them littering the floor. He'd started molting.

The sight punched harder than any wound I'd seen on a battle-field.

Ophelia stood next to the bed, her eyes wide and her face drained of color. Behind me, Kincade stepped inside the room, pausing in the doorway and waiting to see what I was going to do next.

Hell, I didn't know what I was going to do next. I held the staff in one hand, my palm sweating, as I perched on the edge of the bed next to Darius. I pushed a lock of hair out of his face and was startled to see the harsh line of his cheekbone. He was skin and bones and not much else.

"I'm here," I whispered, though I wasn't sure he heard me. "Can you hear me?"

He didn't move. He made no sound.

I placed one hand on his shoulder and almost recoiled from the bone jutting out there. Even if I saved him, would he recover? Would he become the warrior angel he once was? I remembered the day he appeared to me in Hong Kong when I blew the Horn and Gabriel and summoned him. He'd come for me in the pit of Hell when I needed him the most. He even came for me, Ophelia and Kincade in the Second Circle.

My eyes drifted closed as I thought of all of this, of the way he looked, the way he fought off those minions on the rooftop in Hong Kong. He took me to his home in the clouds and let me heal. He understood my mission and held onto the Horn of Gabriel for a time until he realized he was dying.

It was because of me he was dying of demon poison. Because of me he was in this horrible state. And I could not bear to see him waste away into nothing.

I slipped into his mind. A dream walk, but not. He was the strong angel I recalled standing tall with his brilliant blue eyes and his blond hair shining like a halo, wielding his glowing sword ready to fight.

"Keeper." He gave me a nod of greeting. "What are you doing here?"

"I'm going to help you."

He shook his head. "You cannot."

"I can and I will."

For once, doubt didn't get a vote. And then the dream slipped away and was gone.

A brilliant light pressed against my closed eyelids. I opened them to see the staff in my hand glowing. My other hand on his shoulder hadn't moved. A dark, oily substance rose from his body. He jerked once, flipped to his back and sucked in a sharp breath. I placed my hand on his chest, felt the sure beat of his heart, and the rise and fall of his chest as he breathed. That dark oily substance continued to rise from him, hovering over him and then a flash of light from the staff snuffed it out like snuffing out a candle.

The light from the staff dimmed and went out.

Darius's eyes fluttered open and met mine. Sweat beaded his forehead. Confusion flickered through his gaze as he peered at me, then looked at the staff, then back at me. He placed his hand on top of mine still on his chest. His touch was strong and sure. Color returned to his face, though he was still thin.

"Keeper," he said, his voice a roughened whisper.

"Hello, Darius." I smiled.

"I...dreamed. It was you."

I nodded. "Told you I'd help you."

Nearby was a choking sob. Ophelia covered her face with her hands as she cried in relief. She moved to the other side of the bed and sat. Tears glistened her cheeks and filled her eyes. Tears of joy. Darius reached for her and pressed his hand against her cheek. She nuzzled his palm.

"I know your face," he said, his voice still quiet.

"Ophelia kept a vigil at your side," I said.

"I remember."

"Anna did it. Like she promised. It's a Christmas miracle," Ophelia said and beamed.

She pressed her hand against his still on her cheek. I noticed then some of his feathers faded from black to gray. I suspected they would return to white in due time.

"I'll leave you two alone now."

I slipped my hand free of his and rose from the bed, turning toward the door. I took two steps when Darius spoke again.

"Thank you, Keeper."

I glanced at him over my shoulder, gave him a nod. "I owed you one. It's the least I could do."

It didn't feel like enough—but it would have to be.

Kincade moved aside as I slipped into the hall, then he followed me out and closed the door leaving Darius and Ophelia alone. I wasn't sure how much the warrior angel remembered from his sickness stupor. One thing was never in doubt—Ophelia cared a great deal for him.

"That was impressive," he said.

Praise made it feel too real—and I wasn't ready for that yet.

I walked to the library, intending to store away the staff in the vault. He followed. I wasn't interested in rehashing what happened in there because I wasn't sure myself. And I needed time to process it, understand it.

"How did you do it?"

"I have no idea." I didn't want to elaborate. That was the truth. My best guess was somehow I managed to ignite the power within the staff. "I'm glad it worked. He'll be on the mend, now."

I was acutely aware of Kincade's jealousy of Darius. The last thing I wanted to do was exacerbate it. I had no romantic feelings for the warrior angel, but sometimes a thoughtful caring action was misconstrued as something else. I wasn't interested in talking to Kincade about Darius.

"You did a good thing, Anna."

His words stopped me as I paused inside the library and gave him a quick glance. It did not escape my notice Ophelia had decorated the library with Christmas décor. Her touches were everywhere.

"I mean it. You did."

"Thanks."

I moved deeper into the library to behind the desk and opened the vault. He followed me inside, leaning against the open doorway surveying the items inside.

"Your uncle's collection?" he asked.

I nodded. "And where I keep the relics." I motioned to the horn and the spear. "He has all sorts of stuff in here. Knowing my uncle, he must have catalogued it somewhere. I just haven't found it yet."

I chewed on my lower lip, thinking about our narrow escape in Jerusalem and wondering what happened to Tamar. Did she buy our escape with her life?

"I suppose now I'm a criminal," I said, mostly to myself.

"You have more important things to worry about than that, Anna."

I cut him a glance and nodded agreement, but that niggling sensation of our last moments in the city would haunt me.

"We never did get whiskey and cupcakes for your birthday." There was a hint of a grin on his face.

He walked to the cart with the decanters and poured two glasses. Two fingers neat. Just how I liked it. He handed one to me. I took it, grateful for the strong brew.

"Sorry I don't have those cupcakes."

"It's all right."

"Happy belated birthday." He lifted the glass in a mock toast before downing the amber liquid in one gulp.

I followed his lead. "Thanks."

And then my brows knit together as I recalled the date. We were traveling so much I almost lost track of time. I watched the white lights twinkling on the tree in the corner. A lit star was on the top.

"Do you know what today is?"

"Christmas Eve," he said.

He returned to the cart and poured another glass. Then he carried the decanter to me and refilled mine. In an uncharacteristic move, he clinked his glass against mine. "Happy Christmas, Anna."

It was a strange thing. Drinking whiskey with Kincade in my uncle's library and thinking about Christmas. The holiday hadn't even crossed my mind. But then, I was preoccupied with finding the Staff of Moses and saving Darius. Regret swept through me. Instead of shopping and caroling, I galivanted across the Middle East.

I reminded myself it was for a higher cause. Watching the tree lights blink and dance gave me a sense of serenity.

"It's so peaceful," I muttered.

"It is."

"I'm tired, Kincade."

"I know."

"So now what?" I asked, peering down into the drink looking for the answer.

"Now we enjoy some peace on earth for the time being." He replaced the decanter on the cart and then sauntered out of the room.

I knew better than to believe peace ever lasted—but I'd take it while it was here.

I downed the glass of whiskey and left it on the desk, thinking to return later for it. Exhaustion punched me in the gut hard. My pillow—my own bed—was calling. I was ready for it, too.

I closed the vault and left the library, closing the door behind me. I stifled a yawn as I headed for my room. Grace popped up at the top of the stairs, relief evident on her face.

"I heard you returned." She grabbed me in a hug, squeezing me tight.

"Yes. I had to—"

"Darius. Yes, I know." She held me at arm's length and looked me over. "Did it work?"

I nodded.

"Good. You look tired. You should get some rest. Tomorrow is a busy day."

"Tomorrow is Christmas," I said with a yawn.

"Yes." She broke into a bright smile and left me there on the landing.

I stumbled the rest of the way to my room, too tired to figure out what, besides Christmas, was happening tomorrow.

CHAPTER 33

I AWOKE WITH THE morning sunlight streaming through the windows. I thought it was strange since the night before had been nothing but drizzling rain.

It felt like the world had decided to move on without asking my permission.

I stumbled out of bed, stretching my weary limbs. The last few weeks had taken a toll on me and, despite a full night's sleep, I was still tired. I sat on the edge of the bed, dreading facing the rest of the people downstairs. Grace had an expectant look on her face the night before as though she'd planned something. I wasn't in the mood for a bunch of festivities.

Surviving had taken everything I had. Celebrating felt like too much to ask.

A knock on the door sounded. Odd.

"Come in."

The door pushed open and Kincade poked his head inside. Which surprised me. My pulse skipped, uninvited. I expected to see Grace or Ophelia.

"Everyone is downstairs waiting for you," he said without greeting.

"Great." I pulled my fingers through my tangled hair. "So much for peace on earth."

"Grace arranged a Christmas breakfast," he said. "She sent me up here to fetch you."

"Fetch?" It was funny coming from Kincade.

He shrugged. "That's the word she used."

That sounded like Grace. Nodding, I waved him away. "I'll be down in a minute. I need a shower."

But he didn't leave. He pushed open the door the rest of the way and stepped into the room, then closed it behind him. Surprise flickered through me. He stood there a moment, shifting from one foot to the other as though he were uncomfortable. That alone was enough to make me nervous.

"Before you go, I want to give you something." He reached into his pocket and brought out something. Something I couldn't see clutched in his hand.

"I don't have anything for you," I said, objecting to the thought of accepting a gift from Kincade.

"Call it a belated birthday present if you want, then." He extended a blue velvet box to me. "I didn't have time to give it you before we left Jerusalem."

I hesitated, staring at it as though it were a venomous snake. Gifts had a way of making things feel permanent. "What is it?"

"It's not a big deal. I saw it in a shop and thought of you. Just take it, will you?" He waved the box in annoyance.

It occurred to me then the day he disappeared and refused to tell me where he'd been must have been the day he bought it. I wondered if it was an intentional shopping trip or if he happened upon the gift.

Either way, the thought lodged somewhere warm and dangerous in my chest.

Swallowing hard, I took it and opened the lid. Inside was a pendant on a long silver chain nestled on white velvet. The pendant was of a guardian angel standing behind a girl kneeling in prayer. I stared at it a long time, unable to think of anything but the symbolism of the pendant. And the fact that Kincade thought of me when he saw it. It warmed me in a way I wasn't prepared for.

"It's lovely," I said, finally finding my voice. "Thank you."

"I'm glad you like it. Now, get dressed. I'll see you downstairs."

He shut the door with a snap, leaving me sitting there staring at the silver pendant with my heart in my throat. He wasn't exactly the mushy type. The fact he thought of me when he saw it touched me.

After I showered and dressed, I slipped the pendant around my neck. It had a long chain. I tucked it under my shirt. Somehow that gave me comfort knowing it was there and he had been the one to give it to me. For the first time in a long while, I felt protected.

I made my way downstairs to the dining room with the others for a breakfast feast. Everyone was in high spirits. Decker was still nowhere to be found. Kincade seemed unconcerned by his disappearing act. Even Darius joined us and looked much better than the day before. Ophelia stayed close to him, hovering like a mother hen. More of his fathers had turned from black to gray and some even to white. It was a relief he was finally on the mend and the poison was out of his system.

After breakfast, everyone disbursed. Kincade announced he was heading for a workout. Ophelia insisted Darius return to their room for rest. Grace and I were left. We made our way to the parlor, our stomachs full. As I sat to watch the twinkling lights of the tree, a sense of contentment swept over me. Having those closest to me safely tucked away in the manor house made me happy.

But this was merely the calm before the storm.

A little bit of peace on earth, as Kincade put it.

I'd killed Mammon and Abaddon. I understood what that meant even if I didn't know what to expect. I figured Lucifer would double his efforts in his quest to capture me and make me his queen of the damned.

Before she sat, Grace picked up a small shiny package from under the tree and handed it to me. Reluctantly, I took it. For the second time that day, I was given a gift I couldn't reciprocate.

"I don't have anything for you." I held the package in between my hands gazing down at the perfect bow on top and the shiny silver and blue wrapping paper.

"Hush now. That doesn't matter. You gave me the best gift of all," she said.

I glanced up at her. "I did?"

"You." She smiled as she took the seat next to me. "Open it."

I pulled off the perfect ribbon and tore open the paper. Inside was a leather-bound journal with a Templar cross embossed on the cover. I ran my finger over the cross wondering if she knew the Walker family had a connection to the Templars.

"When you were a child, I remembered you used to write in a journal every night," she said. "I hope you like it."

I hadn't written in a journal in years. Not since I left my uncle's when I was eighteen. I still had a few of the books on a shelf in my room. Ramblings, mostly.

"I thought journaling might help you..." She paused, searching for the right words. "Well, cope with your abilities."

I gave her a questioning glance. I had never been comfortable with the idea of having these strange abilities. Even after being separated all this time, she still understood who and what I was. When I was little, I had never quite mastered the dream walking skills. I used them when I shouldn't and startled her in her dreams more than once. When I was a child, she told me to stop using them.

"Thank you, Grace."

I intended to fill the blank pages regularly.

CHRISTMAS DAY PASSED IN peace and serenity. Grace and I spent most of it in front of the fireplace in the parlor, talking and catching up and dozing. That evening, we all joined once again for another feast Piers and Grace had cooked together. I had no idea she was such a culinary whiz. There were even cupcakes for my birthday.

Kincade and I exchanged a glance over the top of our sugary sweets. I didn't miss the faint smile he gave me as he bit into his. It wasn't anything anyone else would have noticed—but it felt like ours.

As the day turned into night, I bid everyone goodnight and headed back to my room. It was the best day I'd had in a long while. My only wish was Edward was still with us.

I was almost to my room when the cell phone buzzed my pocket. It was Tamar.

"Tamar?"

"Are you safe?" Her voice was a roughened whisper on the other end.

"Yes."

"And the staff?"

"Yes. Tamar, are you—"

"I'm fine. Don't worry for me. I called to tell you I removed all trace of your stay in our hotel. I wanted you to know."

She hung up before I could thank her.

I stared at the blank screen for a long moment, processing what she said. It would have been easy for authorities to track me down from the hotel records. She knew that as I did. I blew out a relieved breath.

As I pushed open my bedroom door, I spotted the card on the floor. As though it had been slipped under it while I was away. I bent to pick it up. The blocky handwriting was unmistakable and familiar with the words *Holy Grail*. On the other side of the card was a picture of a cathedral. In fine print along the edge were the words *Valencia, Spain*.

My next quest was for the Holy Grail.

I was terrified of what was to come.

Next in the Series: Smoke and Ashes

The Holy Grail could save the world...or cost her the man she loves.

Anna Walker's search for the Grail Cup—the relic of eternal life—puts her in Lucifer's sights once again. To force her hand, he threatens the one person she cannot lose...her mother. As Anna races to claim the Grail, vampiric zealots rise to steal it, and every path is fraught with blood and betrayal.

Through it all, Kincade is her anchor—fighting by her side, determined to keep her from the dark lord's grasp. But when an unlikely ally with divine power joins their fight, even Kincade's strength may not be enough to protect her.

With enemies closing in and time running out, Anna must decide how much she's willing to sacrifice for the relics, for humanity, and for the man who's claimed her heart.

Perfect for fans of action-packed urban fantasy, forbidden relic quests, and love that stands against the darkness.

Sneak Peek of Smoke and Ashes

I have a crush on Kincade.

I stared at the words like they might crawl off the page.

My heart beat a wild, chaotic rhythm. Thinking it was one thing. Putting it down on paper was another entirely. Like writing it made it real.

I didn't want to have a crush on Kincade any more than I wanted to admit it. But there it was. Written in my own hand.

Being in the same house with him is a challenge. Avoiding him has become more and more difficult. Ophelia seems determined to push us together—almost as much as my uncle once did. It's not like we have a future. He's a Watcher and I'm—

I stopped writing.
He was a Watcher. Divine. Immortal.
I was a dream walker. Divine. With the Godlight.
Immortal?

My uncle once said dream walkers lived longer than most. Didn't age the same way. I never asked him what that really meant. I wasn't sure I wanted the answer.

I closed the leather-bound journal with unnecessary force, fighting the urge to tear the page out. Defacing the journal Grace gave me for Christmas felt wrong. Sacrilegious, somehow. I shoved it aside and flopped onto my back, staring at the ceiling.

There was nothing to do about Kincade. Thinking about him didn't help. Not his steady presence. Not the way he always knew when I lied. Not the impossible mix of restraint and intensity that made my chest ache for reasons I refused to examine too closely.

With a frustrated groan, I rolled off the bed and padded toward the balcony. The floor was cold beneath my bare feet. I tugged my sleeves down over my hands and pulled the door open.

Morning gray greeted me. Cold air rushed in, sharp and bracing. Maybe freezing myself half to death would help clear my head. It didn't.

I shut the door and turned—

—and found a winged man standing in my room.

I yelped, my heart slamming against my ribs. I pressed a hand to my chest, drawing a shaky breath.

"I wish you angels would learn to knock."

"Sorry, dearie."

I froze. My eyes flew open as I stared at the angel in my room. His silvery wings were threaded with gold and spread behind him in a brilliant display. He was simply dressed in dark pants and a matching button-down shirt. He peered at me with familiar dark blue eyes. My knees buckled as sudden tears clotted in my throat. I fell to the floor, my cold fingers pressing against my lips.

"Is it you?"

He reached for me, placing his hand on top of my head. "They call me Cashiel now. My Seraphim name."

A Seraphim. My uncle, Edward, died and became a Seraphim.

I suppose I wasn't surprised because Edward, after all, was connected to everything and everyone, angelic or otherwise.

"Rise and let me gaze upon your face."

I got to my feet and, without thinking, I hugged him hard, fighting back hot tears of joy. He barely hesitated before he reciprocated the embrace. After a long moment, he pulled back and held me at arm's length, looking me over with those familiar blue eyes, contemplation creasing his face. I shifted from one foot to the other, self-conscious.

"Well? Do I pass inspection?" I asked.

A smile tipped the corner of his mouth. "You look tired. Have you been sleeping?"

The truth was, I hadn't. Since the whole ordeal in Acre and Jerusalem, I had sleepless nights. For the last few weeks, I'd dreamed of my mother. My biological mother. I had no explanation for that other than Edward's final words in his letter still haunted me. I memorized them and thought of them often.

You were right about Natasha. I believe there is a good chance she is your mother. My dearest sister. Find her. Help her.

I spent most of my days avoiding Kincade like he carried a communicable disease. Aside from that, I had constant worry about the next relic and how I was going to find it. The last postcard I received was for Valencia, Spain and the Holy Grail.

The relics I'd already recovered—the Horn of Gabriel, the Spear of Destiny, the Staff of Moses—currently resided in the library vault. Hidden away from prying Fallen eyes. Kept safe from the outside world for when I needed them. Whenever that was.

"I'm great," I lied.

He pressed his lips together in that all too familiar expression. That one that said I was lying, and he didn't like it. It gave me an odd sense of comfort. At least that part of my uncle wasn't gone forever.

"I'm glad you're here," I said before he chastised me. "And that you're..." I paused, trying to choose my words.

"I'm Seraphim?" he asked.

I grinned. "Yes, actually."

I was getting used to angels showing up in my life—showing up to watch over me, apparently. Joachim had been the first. The one who set me on this whole impossible path to begin with. Others had followed since then, appearing when things went sideways, offering help I hadn't known how to ask for.

Some stayed longer than others.

Some complicated things.

"And you're...okay with that?" he asked, still sounding faintly stunned.

"I don't have much of a choice," I said lightly. "Angels seem to find me whether I invite them or not. Uncle—"

"I'm not. Not really. I'm something else entirely."

I pondered that a minute. "I suppose you're right, but you'll always be my uncle."

"Fair enough." He gave a nod of his head as though in agreement to my stubbornness.

"There's something I need to know. Something that happened to me when you..." My words drifted off. I bit my lower lip. Having him here was almost as though he hadn't died. Almost as though I got him back in my life, even though my rational mind understood I hadn't.

"Died?"

I blew out a breath. "Yes."

"It's still hard for you to accept."

It was not a question, but I nodded as though it were. Hot tears pricked my eyes. I blinked them back at a furious rate to keep them from falling. I pressed cold fingertips against my lips.

"I miss you."

It was an admission I never thought I'd have. His face softened as a small smile creased his lips. "I'm still a part of you."

Sariel said something similar to me the day Edward died. That he lived on in me. It brought me back to my question.

"When I...when you..." I had trouble saying it out loud. Almost as though putting words to it again would bring back that horrible day. That day I pierced his heart with my dagger.

"When I died," he said.

"Yes. There was...a light. I don't remember much after that because it knocked me unconscious."

He nodded. "My power transferred to you."

I blinked, staring at him as though he'd grown a second set of wings. "Huh?"

"When you pierced my heart with the dagger, it eradicated the demon poison. The power residing inside me was released. That was the punch of light you felt when you were knocked unconscious."

I continued to stare at him. I wasn't sure how to take that. Was that why I was able to understand and speak Hebrew? Because he could speak the language? All his knowledge and power came into me? And if I possessed his knowledge and power, then...what did that make me? I sank to the edge of the bed, clutching my elbows, shivering.

"This is a lot for you to take in," he said. "But please understand, Anna, there was no time to tell you. I didn't know myself until afterward."

Afterward...? When he went to the afterlife? When he was resurrected as the angel, Cashiel? How did that work? On second thought, maybe I didn't want to know. Less information was better.

"Why?"

I wasn't even sure what I was asking. Why what? Why did I get his power? Did he have to die for me to receive his power? Why me?

"Because you are extraordinary, Anna. I would have thought by now you understood that."

I scoffed. "There is nothing special about me."

"I think you understand, deep down, you are special," he insisted. "You've been denying it far too long. Accept you are the one to lead mankind out of darkness."

"Yeah, no pressure or anything." I pressed my lips together in a thin line. Despite everyone cheering me on from the sidelines, I still felt like a fraud.

"You can do this."

"That's what everyone keeps saying."

"And everyone is right. Kincade, too."

To my chagrin, I blushed to the roots of my hair upon hearing his name. "Still trying to push us together, uncle?"

He lifted an eyebrow at calling him uncle.

I sighed. "It will take some getting used to calling you Cashiel."

"I understand, of course." He nodded as though punctuating the thought. "Your next quest is the Holy Grail."

A tingling of fear skittered up my spine. "Yes."

"You have doubts."

"Yes," I said again and nodded.

"Only those who are worthy will find the Grail. Only the divine will retrieve it." His piercing gaze bored into me. As if to say I was both worthy and divine.

When I retrieved the Staff of Moses in the Holy of Holies, only the divine were allowed to enter the chamber. Even Kincade wasn't allowed in.

"No, you should not."

His last words echoed back to me yet again. Be the light of the world, Anna.

I frowned. And he wondered why I wasn't sleeping.

"You are afraid, but you have no reason to be. Remember that, dearie. Now, I must take my leave of you." He extended a hand to me. I took it. His fingers wrapped around mine and squeezed. "Be strong, Anna. You can defeat this evil spreading through the land. And you will."

I wish I had his confidence.

Before I formed a response, he was gone, leaving my empty hand hanging alone in the air.

ALSO BY MICHELLE MILES

Age of Wizards (Epic Fantasy)
In the Tower of the Wizard King
On the Hunt for the Wizard King

Dragon Protectors (Paranormal Shifter Romance)
Desiring the Dragon Lord
Seducing the Dragon Knight
Tempting Her Dragon Bodyguard

Dream Walker (Paranormal Romance)
Call of the Dark
Blood and Bone
Flame and Fury
Smoke and Ashes
Light of the World

Dream Walker Related Novels
Guardian of the Soul (Coming Soon)

War of the Brotherhood (Dark Paranormal Romance)
Set in the Dream Walker Universe
Dark Night of the Soul (Coming 2026)
Fall of the Forsaken (Coming 2026)
Immortal Everlasting (Coming 2026)

Enchanted Realms (YA Fantasy Romance)
Once Upon a Midnight Clear (Cinderella)
Once Upon True Love's Kiss (Snow White)
Once Upon an Enchanted Kiss (Sleeping Beauty)
Once Upon an Enchanted Castle (Beauty and the Beast)
Once Upon a Midnight Dreary (Poe's The Raven)

Enchanted Realms Related Novellas
Once Upon an Ancient Curse (Red Riding Hood)
Once Upon a Silver Strand (Rapunzel)
Once Upon a Woven Wish (Rumpelstiltskin)

Enchanted Realms: Crossroads (Cozy Fantasy)
A Spin-off Series of the Enchanted Realms
Petals and Portals (Coming 2026)

Five Towers (YA Fantasy Romance)
The Sorcerer's Daughter

Highland Destiny (Paranormal Romance)
Desiring the Highland Laird
Loving the Highland Warrior
Captivating the Highland Rogue

Legends of the Five Crowns (Romantasy)
with Misty Evans
The Lost Kingdom
The Flame and the Dragon
Tide of Stolen Thrones

Realm of Honor (Fantasy Romance)
One Knight Only
Only for a Knight
A Knight to Remember
A Knight Like No Other
Shadows of the Knight

Shorts and Anthologies (Fantasy/Paranormal)
Newsletter Subscribers Only
A Dance Among the Faeries, A Short Story
Eorwulf, A Short Story
Dragons of Emhain Short Story Collection

Watch for more at MichelleMiles.net

About the Author

Michelle Miles is an empress with a war map in one hand and a romance vow in the other—writing fantasy, paranormal, and young adult adventures where magic crackles, danger prowls, and love refuses to back down. From fairy-tale retellings to angels and demons to Fae, elves, and time travelers, she builds big-hearted worlds full of quests, curses, kisses, and chaos—often in that order. When she's not plotting her next emotional ambush, Michelle narrates audiobooks and hosts Miles Beyond the Page, a podcast spotlighting writers' real journeys. A proud Texan, she's usually reading, hiking, rewatching favorite movies, or savoring a glass of wine while sharpening the blade for the next adventure.

Quests, Curses, Kisses, and Chaos!

Read more at MichelleMiles.net

www.ingramcontent.com/pod-product-compliance
Lightning Source LLC
Chambersburg PA
CBHW060222100726
47907CB00003B/466